TRAPPED

The running BattleMech lofted a barrage of rockets her way.

Grace slammed Pirate's throttle forward, but she hadn't taken two steps before rockets smacked down around her. At least two hit Pirate, bouncing Grace's head off the side of the cockpit. Her vision grayed, and the ringing in her ears didn't cover the screaming of gyros as they struggled to keep her upright. She tried a step forward. No go. A plate of Mick's armor was off and wedged between Pirate's middle and the ground. Grace activated her drill and applied it to the dangling slab as she staggered left.

Rocks sizzled as a laser slashed through where she'd just been.

Below her, the ugly BattleMech disappeared in the smoke of another salvo.

At least the smoke hid Grace as she nursed Pirate to an outcropping. Half his instruments were dead. Two cylinders weren't firing, and the engine gauges were a horror. Her Gatling gun hadn't been much good, and now Pirate couldn't move quickly. "Dan, pull back," Grace shouted on circuit. "I'll cover you."

"Gracie, I can't leave you."

MechWarrior
DARK AGE

PATRIOT'S STAND

A BATTLETECH® NOVEL

Mike Moscoe

A ROC BOOK

ROC
Published by New American Library, a division of
Penguin Group (USA) Inc., 375 Hudson Street,
New York, New York 10014, U.S.A.
Penguin Books Ltd, 80 Strand,
London WC2R 0RL, England
Penguin Books Australia Ltd, 250 Camberwell Road,
Camberwell, Victoria 3124, Australia
Penguin Books Canada Ltd, 10 Alcorn Avenue,
Toronto, Ontario, Canada M4V 3B2
Penguin Books (N.Z.) Ltd, Cnr Rosedale and Airborne Roads,
Albany, Auckland 1310, New Zealand

Penguin Books Ltd, Registered Offices:
80 Strand, London WC2R 0RL, England

First published by Roc, an imprint of New American Library,
a division of Penguin Group (USA) Inc.

First Printing, April 2004
10 9 8 7 6 5 4 3 2 1

Cover design by Ray Lundgren

ROC REGISTERED TRADEMARK—MARCA REGISTRADA

Printed in the United States of America

PUBLISHER'S NOTE
This is a work of fiction. Names, characters, places, and incidents either are
the products of the author's imagination or are used fictitiously, and any
resemblance to actual persons, living or dead, business establishments,
events, or locales is entirely coincidental.

BOOKS ARE AVAILABLE AT QUANTITY DISCOUNTS WHEN USED TO PROMOTE PROD-
UCTS OR SERVICES. FOR INFORMATION PLEASE WRITE TO PREMIUM MARKETING DIVI-
SION, PENGUIN GROUP (USA) INC., 375 HUDSON STREET, NEW YORK, NEW YORK 10014.

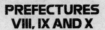

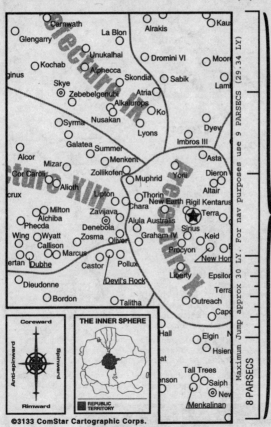

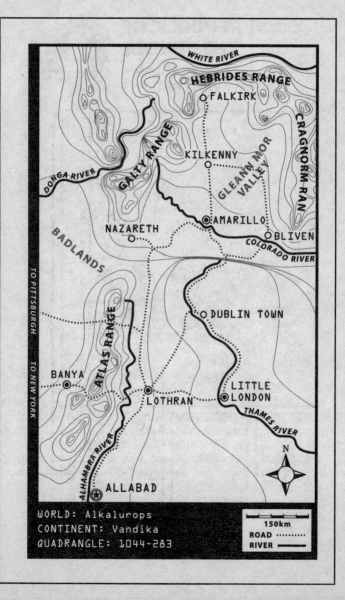

WHITE RIVER

HEBRIDES RANGE

○ FALKIRK

CRAGNORM RAN

GALTY RANGE

○ KILKENNY

GLEANN MOR VALLEY

DONGA RIVER

◎ AMARILLO

NAZARETH ○

○ BLIVEN

COLORADO RIVER

BADLANDS

ATLAS RANGE

○ DUBLIN TOWN

TO PITTSBURGH

TO NEW YORK

BANYA ◎

◎ LOTHRAN

LITTLE ◎ LONDON

THAMES RIVER

ALHAMBRA RIVER

N

✪ ALLABAD

WORLD: Alkalurops
CONTINENT: Vandika
QUADRANGLE: 1044-283

150km
ROAD ....
RIVER ———

$$\equiv\!\!\equiv \mathbf{1} \equiv\!\!\equiv$$

Near Falkirk, Alkalurops
Prefecture IX, The Republic of the Sphere
3 April 3134; local spring

Grace O'Malley loosened the straps on her harness, rested her elbows on the open cockpit of "Pirate," her MiningMech, and focused her binoculars. A quick sweep of the Gleann Mor Valley before her showed no sign of the raiders whose arrival she dreaded.

Lately the chatter on the Net had been scary. Usually, Grace ignored Net gossip, but Allabad, the capital of Alkalurops, had dropped off-Net a week ago with no explanation. Then hysterical postings and phone calls started pouring in about BattleMechs stomping through houses, tanks shooting up shops, and off-world troops hijacking 'Mechs—followed by that town dropping off the Net. Now the Net blackout was about to overwhelm Grace's hometown of Falkirk.

The evening before, her friend Gordon Frazier, mayor of Kilkenny, not two hours' drive south, slapped up a hasty e-note that BattleMechs and a whole lot of other armor were coming up the south road from Amarillo. Grace had called Gordon, but by then both voice and data links were dead. It looked as though Falkirk was on its own and raiders were coming to swipe Pirate.

Last night's town meeting in Falkirk had been the shortest since Grace had been elected mayor. Some citizens were for running, but most agreed: "Alkalurops takes care of itself." The vote was to fight. That didn't surprise Grace. For much of the week, Mick's 'Mech Maintenance Mavens had been adding armor to the six local 'Mechs and jury-rigging weapons like the Gatling gun made of six hunting rifles that was now strapped to Pirate's right arm. John Shepherd, the local gunsmith, had specially loaded them with high-powered, steel-jacketed shells.

Grace shook her head as if to clear it of a bad dream. Since she was a kid, her mom had told her how ancient Ireland once trembled at the name of Grace O'Malley, the pirate woman. Grace had even named her MiningMech Pirate "because he steals metal and hydrocarbons from the ground." But real pirates! She'd hoped never to face anything like this in The Republic of the Sphere.

She also hadn't expected the HPG interstellar com grid to go down two years ago. On an out-of-the-way planet like Alkalurops, that meant the news talkies spent more time on local chitchat. But even with trade disrupted and metals and coal fetching below-market prices, it seemed like a small price to pay for being left alone.

Once again Grace swept her binoculars over the Gleann Mor Valley, this time slowly, almost lovingly. This was her home. She'd grown up here, like her mother and grandmother before her, going back almost to the firstlanders. The valley hadn't changed much in all that time. It showed red and brown where native plants still held on, and green where Terran plants were slowly replacing them. In the spring air, the yellow of Scotch broom outlined the road from the south and sprang up in patches elsewhere. The mountains of the Cragnorm Range, only ten or fifteen klicks away, showed Scotch broom as well as the purple of heather. Behind Grace, the foothills of the Galty Range would show the same hues if she twisted in her cockpit to look. Instead she glanced north, up the valley to where the gray of Falkirk's stone buildings stood in the lee of Wilson Crag. Around the cliff were the large green circles of irrigated land, growing the Terran wheat, corn, barley, and oats that were sold outside the valley. Small gardens adjoining the houses provided all the vegetables the inhabitants needed. Falkirk was comfortably independent—or had been last week.

Now Falkirk needed help, so two days ago Grace sent out a call to all the small holdings in the mountains and towns beyond. She was more than grateful for the signs of digging beside the road in front of where she stood. Yesterday Chato Bluewater had led in two dozen Navajos from the White River Valley, on the other side of the still snow-capped Hebrides Range. Now they were working on a defense strategy that Chato had assured Grace would work, although she wasn't sure what it was.

Yesterday, while Pirate was in the shop having the Gatling rigged, the Navajo, aided by anyone willing to pitch in, had dug, strung line, and done other strange things. Grace watched and scratched her head. "How do you stop a 'Mech with a rope?" she called out.

Chato smiled softly at the question. "You fight the white man's way. We'll follow the warpath with the spirit of Coyote. Let's see whose path the MechWarriors wish they hadn't crossed."

Grace had never heard him use words like "white man" before. Then again, she'd never been on the "warpath" with him. A bit uncomfortable, she answered with "They're not warriors, just raiders. And I'm not a white man, I'm a Scotch-Irish woman."

"You are the mayor of Falkirk. That's enough to make you a white man to me," Chato said.

He laughed as Grace shot back, "Only on Thursday evenings during the town meetings."

But Chato quickly grew serious. "You are the one these hardheaded miners accept as their war leader. Put on war paint, Chief, and let's see how good your braves are."

Grace made grumbling noises at him—she'd never worn makeup in her life. With her creamy complexion set off by flaming red hair, she didn't really need it.

"Dust on the horizon." The voice of Dan McLeod snapped her back to attention. He was in his Agro-Mech, to her left, his machine listing a bit with the weight of the field burner now hanging from its left arm. Normally, the burner was used to clear native vegetation to prepare a field for Terran crops. Now the burner was equipped with a high-speed pump, and the hump of a two-kiloliter feed tank towered over Dan's open cockpit. Grace had heard that BattleMechs tended to heat up in combat. Dan's burner would help that along, big time.

Grace turned her binoculars south and leaned far forward. In the cockpit, Pirate's gyros protested her off-balance weight adding to the new front armor. Grace dropped her right hand back into the cockpit and used the joystick to edge the drill bit on Pirate's right arm out to balance her against the fifteen-meter-tall granite pinnacle she was hiding behind.

She returned her attention to the main road. Yep, she could see a dust cloud out there now. The road was straight, generally five klicks or more from the mountains, but below Grace a dry ravine forced it closer to the foothills. A spring gully-washer would have put the road under three meters of raging water, but there hadn't been a thunderstorm for more than a week. At least the dust gave warning even if the dry ground made it easier for the raiders to bounce around off-road.

Grace pulled a mirror from around her neck and aimed it at the valley to give Chato a warning flash. Someone emerged from among the brush and cheatgrass and waved a shirt back.

Now Grace cinched her harness. A quick check showed her neurohelmet was in place and none of her cooling lines were kinked. She brought Pirate's engine up from a fuel-saving idle to ready power. Working the pedals with care, she spun him around on his left heel to face the other 'Mechs and fifty men and women with rifles and the improvised rocket-firing tubes Mick called bazookas.

Projecting her voice as her father had taught her years ago, to carry to the crew two stories below and the 'Mech pilots with idling engines, Grace shouted, "What do you say we spread out some?" Even shouting, she made sure her words came across as a suggestion. Chato might call her Falkirk's war chief, but this bunch were not soldiers. That they followed her suggestions more often than not made her their leader. If she shot her mouth off too much, they'd pick a new mayor.

"Sounds like a plan," said Jim Wilson, owner of about half the irrigation circles around Falkirk. He closed up the newest AgroMech in town, its paint now marred from the additional armor welded to its front. As Wilson led the way to a pile of rocks a klick south, his son followed, piloting a similarly up-armored AgroMech that wasn't all that much older than Pirate. The Wilsons' rifle cabinet had been emptied to provide the barrels for the Gatling guns that both 'Mech MODs carried. A dozen tenant farmers with gopher guns and two rocket launchers trailed them.

Owen McCallester, who had never forgiven Grace

for beating him out of the mayor's job when his old man died, nodded to Dennis Brady, and the two troublemakers plodded a klick north with most of their own mine workers. Their 'Mechs' engines struggled even as they waddled; both men had insisted Mick weld armor to the front *and* back of their century-old machines.

That left Grace with Dan's AgroMech and its flamethrower, along with a score of town craftspeople and merchants, armed with whatever was handy. Most rifles had hardly been used except for plunking at rabbits and gophers during the annual sharpshooting competition at the Highland Games. The shooting was never much to brag about. The competition was always late in the day, after the racing and tossing the caber and way too much drinking. Grace didn't consider mixing drinks and loaded guns all that safe, but the schedule was sacred, unchanged for hundreds of years.

Everyone was sober today, even Greg McDougall, who'd never met a glass he didn't love more than his poor wife.

"Keep down!" Grace shouted. "They're coming up the road. We'll take them where it curves right into us."

"And won't that be a surprise for them," Dan said, grinning through the faceplate of his bulky helmet. The others laughed. Grace closed Pirate's cockpit and spun the 'Mech into position.

We'd better surprise 'em. Otherwise, we're toast, she thought.

The concrete road supported Captain Loren J. Hanson's *Koshi* comfortably. The advance had gone well this morning. He'd set an easy pace because after a week he didn't want to break anything on the last day. Word from his XO—his executive officer and second in command—was that the JumpShip had loaded the loot from Allabad and was ready to jump to the secondary pickup point. The mission here was snatch, grab and raise scatter-hell. The Colonel had made it clear he didn't think that should cost the Roughriders any major casualties. So far it hadn't.

L. J.'s targeting-acquisition screen flashed, letting him know it had found what he'd expected. He tightened his harness straps as he checked his cooling lines. No problem. Keying his mike, he announced, "Looks like the locals have got themselves an ambush up ahead where the road runs close to the foothills."

"Nice of them to come out to meet us." Sergeant Jack Godfrey chortled. "Think they baked a cake?"

L. J. frowned. Sergeant Godfrey had a big mouth, but he did know how to put his Condor Multipurpose Tank's pedal to the metal, and this *was* Hanson's Roughriders.

Not L. J.'s Roughriders. Great-grandpa Hanson had commanded when the Roughriders made their name. L. J. was just a distant great-grandkid by a daughter who'd chosen medicine over 'Mechs. Grandma was still a fine doc when it came to patching up the occasional casualty, but L. J. had earned his commission with sweat and hard work. This was his first independent command. No doubt the Roughrider HQ staff was wondering what he'd bring back.

So far he'd captured just one BattleMech to go with ninety or so late-model IndustrialMechs. Even with the client claiming half, Maintenance should be able to turn out some decent 'Mech MODs. After the long peace, they would be welcome additions.

L. J. eyed his screen. Six IndustrialMechs were scattered on the ridge above the bend in the road, along with enough metal for three or four dozen hunting rifles. The locals would probably run after the first volley. With half his ammo expended, was it worth a fight this far from the pickup point?

"Topkick."

"Sir," Sergeant Major Vincent Tanuso responded immediately.

"On my order, take the hoverbike team and investigate the town. There's nothing past it but mountains, so it's as far as we go. If you spot any decent-looking 'Mechs, acquire them. If not, raise scatter-hell and fall back on me."

"Yes, sir. Corporal Mavy, with me."

"Yes, Sergeant Major."

"The rest of you: This may be a hastily improvised ambush, but the only decent 'Mechs in town could be up there. Let's see if any are worth painting in Roughrider colors. Keep your eyes open and your fields of fire covered."

"Yee-haw!" Godfrey whooped. "Let's put the spurs to 'em." His hovertank surged ahead.

"Take it down, Roughrider," L. J. growled, and the hovertank on point slowed to keep pace with the measured tread of L. J.'s *Koshi*. "No need taking unnecessary heat into a 'Mech fight." L. J. wanted to get as close as he could, to see if the IndustrialMechs were worth a fight before he got into one.

L. J. studied the ground ahead. The road was lined with ditches on both sides. They were dry now, but the green along the verge showed there had been water. The landscape was rolling, giving plenty of dead ground. The bushes were low, mixed with clumped grass. Few places to hide there. Ahead rose foothills covered in purple and green, cut here and there by tree-lined creeks or sharply banked gullies. That might limit a pursuit. Then again, maybe the terrain would help him cut off a prize. Rocks and boulders jutted up to protect shooters. So far this planet had produced only slug-throwers fit for killing small furry things. They hardly scratched a BattleMech's paint.

Don't get cocky, kid, L. J. reminded himself. A cakewalk was nice, but cakes could hold surprises. Approaching the curve, L. J. spotted three fairly new 'Mechs and ordered his topkick off. "Sergeant, just tap the town if there's nothing worth taking. We may have some gear here for you."

"Yes, sir," came back fast.

That left L. J. with just his own *Koshi*, a *Spider*, and Godfrey's Condor tank, with two scout rigs to fill the intervals between the three. Time to get this battle going.

"I make our opposition as six IndustrialMechs and a few dozen infantry. Godfrey, bear to the right and see what you can do to those two. Webrunner, you have the left pair. I'll take the middle ones. Scouts, look for crunchies trying to cause trouble and stand by to take down any 'Mechs we disable. We've got them outnumbered two to six. Let's do it by the numbers, Roughriders," he ended.

"Roughriders!" came back in an enthusiastic shout. He pitied the poor dumb slobs up the hill, thinking that a 'Mech with a claw or drill gave them any chance against real BattleMechs piloted by MechWarriors.

"Advance on the enemy to the left, now," L. J. ordered, and throttled up his BattleMech. Beside him his team spread out, the *Spider*'s long strides eating up the distance to the target. Beneath his *Koshi*'s feet, brush crumbled. Footpads sank a good ten centimeters into the hard dirt under the light BattleMech's weight. It was good to be loose; L. J. echoed Godfrey's yell.

"Damn," Grace breathed softly. "So much for surprise," she said into her mike. "Here they come."

"How'd they spot us?" came over Falkirk's public channel.

"You clomping around raising dust would warn a blind Brit."

"I'm out of here."

Grace had to stop that. "Start running and they'll shoot you in the back. Stay down. Hold your fire," she ordered. Then she realized she was issuing orders and tasted the surprise. Well, this *is* a battle. Somebody had to give orders. Real orders, not polite suggestions. She glanced around. Surprise of surprises, people were doing what she'd told them, huddling in place. Maybe these eejits could tell a good idea when they heard it.

For a better view, she raised Pirate from his squat behind solid granite. The raiders were about three klicks out. A hovertank with a horrifyingly long gun cut through the tall grass, heading for her left, sending dirt and rocks flying as it made S-turns. A tall 'Mech with small wings trotted at the Wilsons. A shorter, ugly thing with scads of rocket launchers on its elbows was headed straight for her.

Someone with McCallester fired off one of Mick's bazookas. The tank in front of them vanished in a sheet of smoke and flame. A ragged cheer was cut short as they realized the tank had fired a salvo of its own rockets. The tank was already out of the smoke cloud and gunning for the foothills when the rockets started hitting. One smashed into the boulder Brady was hiding behind. The rock shattered, sending shards in all directions. The miner's 'Mech fell back on its ass. Count on Brady for slapstick. McCallester brought up the rocket thrower on the left arm of his Min-ingMech and fired. The rocket went wild, corkscrewing for parts unknown.

Grace held her breath, expecting the next salvo from the tank to shred both 'Mechs, but the tank suddenly lost interest.

A Navajo appeared as if from nowhere and tossed a satchel charge at the tank. The explosion blew the tank sideways but didn't seem to faze it. The tank's minigun cut a slash in the valley floor as it went for its attacker, but the Navajo had vanished back into the ground and another was up, shooting a rabbit rifle at the tank. Even at this distance, Grace heard the shot ricochet off the rocket launcher. Damn, even the missile boxes are armored. Don't those things have any weak spots?

Before the tank could draw a good bead on its tor-mentor, others were up, shooting, maybe running a few steps, shooting again, then vanishing. Other shots came from nowhere, like a rocket round that went straight but fell short a few meters.

The tank charged in a shower of dirt and dry grass just as Grace spotted a pattern. Had the tank driver realized what was being done to him? A Navajo would appear, attack, and disappear as another one, a bit farther to the left, jumped up, got a shot off, and drew the tank farther toward Falkirk. That was the last thing Grace wanted. The tank's miniguns couldn't be let loose among the homes of her friends. Some folks—old, sick or just too damn set in their ways—had refused to flee to the hills.

Grace tapped the throttle and edged Pirate around the boulder that hid her. The attack on the tank seemed to hold the ugly 'Mech's attention. Maybe she could do something the raiders would remember. MiningMechs often needed knee joints replaced, so maybe BattleMechs had the same weakness. She toggled her Gatling gun to full power. Mick said a light squeeze would send a few rounds out. "Good for ranging, me girl. When you got 'em where you want 'em, squeeze that trigger hard and that gun will cut them a new one, yes she will, a nice big new one."

Grace nudged the joystick until her crosshairs were right on the BattleMech's knee, squeezed off a few rounds, and watched as they cut the grass behind the BattleMech.

"Damn!" Grace grumbled as she walked the stream of high-powered 7.6-millimeter rounds into her target.

"Damn it, Godfrey," L. J. snapped, "don't play with them, boot them in the ass." How often had his uncle growled that at Loren as he learned the fighting trade? Now L. J. watched his sergeant's enthusiasm for the chase turn into a wild slalom. If he did any damage to the gnats that bit at him, no bodies were evident.

L. J. turned his 'Mech to face Godfrey, the better to give him a blistering dressing-down. At that moment the dirt and crud flying from the blowers that held the tank on a thin cushion of air took on more substance. For a second L. J. thought he was seeing rocks and chunks of earth flying out from under the tank.

Then he realized the truth.

The tank had charged into a section of the valley that wasn't there. What had looked like solid ground a second ago vanished as the hover turbines sent woven grass mats flying. The tank hung in thin air for a second, like some cartoon critter Loren might have laughed at when he was four.

But this was not a cartoon, and L. J. was a detachment commander, and a hovertank may hover a few centimeters above the ground but not over the middle of a deep gully. The tank's nose dropped. It smashed head-on into the dirt bank ahead of it, then flipped over, coming to rest with a screech of tearing metal and ripping armor. For a moment longer the blowers kept working, sending a cloud of dirt shooting into the sky as if to mark for all to see the resting place of this armored marvel.

"Damn," L. J. breathed. They'd never get that tank out without a retriever, and this detachment was budgeted on a shoestring. Maintenance truck, yes. Retriever, not on your life.

Then he felt the thud of bullets hammering into his 'Mech's knee.

"Damn!" he repeated, turning his attention back where it belonged. Slugs ricocheted wildly, but here and there a tiny bit of armor went with them. That 'Mech MOD on his front had some sort of multibarrel gun, and while its slugs might be tiny, it was enthusiastically sending them his way. Slightly off to the right of that tormentor, a second 'Mech MOD with an infrared signature stood up. Then things really got hot.

A river of fire curved toward L. J. It fell short, not even showing on his temp readout. He started to chuckle at these poor jokers' attempts, then swallowed it.

The fire might have landed short, but it hit a clump of those green shrubs with yellow flowers, and they caught fire like an open gas tank. The morning calm was gone, and the wind now drove the fire right at him. *Maybe it's time to be somewhere else.* L. J. turned away from Sergeant Godfrey's mess, snapped off four salvos of short-range missiles to encourage the locals to mind their own business, and aimed himself at a bit of good level ground well away from the yellow-and-green fire hazard.

The jump was good, right up until the landing.

His entire 'Mech groaned as the gyros struggled to balance him on just his left leg. He overrode the gyros and let his 'Mech settle, left leg bent almost double, right leg deep in a hole that woven mats had concealed a moment earlier.

L. J. tapped his mike. "All hands, watch your footing. This plain is pockmarked with traps."

"*Now* he tells me," came Godfrey's dry drawl.

L. J. ignored him and concentrated on his own problem. The enemy right was running; Godfrey's shots had put fear in them. Webrunner was herding the left up the hill. Still, the locals were making good use of folds in the land, and stopping to return fire with single-shot SRMs and two of those dinky miniguns.

L. J. snapped off another volley of SRMs in the general direction of the center of his opposition and got his leg out of the hole. Limping off to the right, he eyed his tormentors.

His first salvo made gravel out of the rock that the minigun was hiding behind. The fire-throwing 'Mech and the infantry were retreating but still firing as they backpedaled. The minigun slashed out at him from behind a new and larger outcropping. Without thinking, his hand worked the joystick to center the crosshairs where he wanted them. Fast as he could punch them out, he salvoed three of his four SRM quadpacks, reserving the fourth in case the first three blew a hole through to his target.

For a moment L. J. thought he might have gotten the joker, but as the dust begun to settle, his BattleMech's damaged left leg was taking fire again from another boulder. He sidestepped to the right. When that didn't throw the minigun off, he mashed out another full salvo at his attacker, turned in place, and throttled up to quickly cover the quarter-klick back to where a fold in the land hid his leg. *That guy sure is a leg man!*

L. J. snapped off another volley. *Damn, this is becoming a meat-grinding attrition fight. That's not why I'm here.*

"Captain, town is empty except for a gray-haired old lady who waved a Bible at me and lectured me on the evils of my life," Sergeant Tanuso reported.

"You shoot her?" Godfrey asked. The sergeant would have.

"I asked her for a date Friday night," Topkick shot back. "A woman with fire like that is worth more than the gilded cats you hang with any night. I see you need some help, Sergeant," the topkick finished, taking skin off Godfrey with that observation.

"I am in a bigger hole than usual," Godfrey admitted.

"I've warned you that fooling with married women could leave you walking home. Have a mind to leave you right here."

"Would make it hard to catch the JumpShip at recall."

"Would cost you some stripes," the topkick said as he brought his hoverbike to a stop at the rim of the gully that had eaten the hovertank.

L. J. cut off the banter. "Topkick, help our darling gift to femininity while Webrunner and I keep the locals busy."

"You do that, sir, and I'll see what we can do here."

L.J. turned back to the battle. His problems were now farther up the hills. Normally a stern chase was a long chase, and while his BattleMech could easily outrun IndustrialMechs, these folks did know the territory. Then again, they were tasting battle for the first time and the hills were cut with gullies. Maybe he could cannibalize this bunch if they weren't careful how they retreated. "Webrunner, you've got the left pretty much in reverse. I want you to edge over toward me. Let's see if there's a way to cut off that minigun."

"Will do, Captain."

Grace was in reverse. Reverse was all in a day's work for a miner, but for a fighter, it was hardly the road to success.

The rifle crews fled up the ridge, having learned to dash from one clump of cover to another. Even the slow learners caught on after they got shards of rocket in their backsides. Dan was being more careful now as his 'Mech picked its way from cover to cover. For a bloody disaster, it didn't look too bad. Winning hadn't been on Grace's mind for a couple of hours.

Grace put Pirate's engine in the red as she charged from a rock outcropping to a dry wash behind a knoll with a struggling evergreen perched on it. The engine screamed, but she got all the horsepower Pirate's builder had put in him, as well as the extra Mick had souped him up to. She fired a burst at the short ugly BattleMech—more to let it know someone was still fighting than to issue any kind of a challenge. She got a lot of rockets for her effort. One shredded the tree, showering her with burning splinters. Rich with turpentine, some stuck to Pirate as they burned, and Grace worked the edge of her drill bit to brush the bigger chips off. When the next salvo was aimed at Dan, she zigzag-jogged to a large boulder. She saved her ammo this run and hoped the damn cuss in the valley would ignore her.

Then it came to her. Except for the terror of possibly being blown to bits in the next second, fighting was just grunt work—harder than any day mining, even breaking ground for a new shaft. She offered a silent prayer: *Just let me get out of here and I'll leave this to the Knights of The Republic and all the other nuts who like it.*

"Uh, Gracie, I think we have a problem. Look at the Wilsons," Dan said, his voice straining over the radio. That team had also been retreating up the ridge. They were still running, but edging south as well. The taller BattleMech was now almost even with Grace. Maybe that meant nothing. Then again, only MacGilly's Gulch stood between Grace and the hunter. Of course, that gulch was plenty deep. Not the kind of thing you jumped. . . . Unless you could jump like that thing in the valley had.

And why else put wings on the taller BattleMech? *Oh, damn!* It gave the Wilsons a short laser burst. Another miss. Then it paused. "What's it doing?" Dan asked after he made a short move from one boulder to another higher up.

Grace studied the taller 'Mech, then glanced at the shorter one below her. It had been quiet for a while. Low on ammo? What else could make one of those killing machines slow down?

"Cooling?" she guessed.

"Cooling what? Speaking of cooling, I could sure use a cool one about now."

"Cooling themselves, maybe before they do something that will really heat them up," Grace said, not liking the sound of her words. "BattleMechs can overheat. You've seen it in the vids. Why do you think you're carrying that field burner?"

"Oh, right. I forgot."

"Get a move on. God only knows what they're gonna do next, and She ain't exactly talking to me these days." Grace slammed the throttle forward, broke cover, and headed for a fold in the ridge that would hide her from both 'Mechs. She fired off a burst at the tall 'Mech across from her, but it fell short.

Grace was back to cover before anything new came her way. It wasn't her imagination—both 'Mechs were facing her now. Grace broke cover, maxing out Pirate, galloping for a boulder. She checked; her rifles were well up the ridge. Not being attacked made them bolder runners. McCallester's and Brady's 'Mechs were way out ahead of their folks, but all were out of range of the two BattleMechs still herding Grace like sheepdogs.

Well, Falkirk wasn't burning, she had accomplished that much. Now, if she could just get out of this alive.

Halfway to another fold in the ridge, Grace spotted glare out of the corner of her eye. The taller 'Mech was up in the air, now falling to a landing on her side of MacGilly's Gulch. The other 'Mech was racing toward her, quickly cutting in half the distance Grace had managed to put between them. Grace paused, caught the descending 'Mech in the sights of her Gatling gun, and fired. A few rounds sparked fire as they ricocheted off, but they didn't even slow the Battle-Mech's flight.

The running BattleMech lofted a barrage of rockets her way.

Grace slammed Pirate's throttle forward, but she hadn't taken two steps before rockets smacked down around her. At least two hit Pirate, bouncing Grace's head off the side of the cockpit. Her vision grayed, and the ringing in her ears didn't cover the screaming of gyros as they struggled to keep her upright. She tried a step forward. No go. A plate of Mick's armor was off and wedged between Pirate's middle and the ground. Grace activated her drill and applied it to the dangling slab as she staggered left.

Rocks sizzled as a laser slashed through where she'd just been.

Below her the ugly BattleMech disappeared in the smoke of another salvo. Grace twisted in place, still working on the armor, then staggered back as another pair of rockets struck Pirate. One spent itself on the busted plate, the other smashed her drill, but also knocked the dangling plate free.

A stream of fire flew high over Grace's head. Dan had turned back and was taking on the taller 'Mech. The fire fell short, burning only some heather. A moment later Dan sent fire down the hill at the shorter, ugly BattleMech.

At least the smoke hid Grace as she nursed Pirate to an outcropping. Half his instruments were dead. Two cylinders weren't firing, and the engine gauges were a horror. Her Gatling gun hadn't been much good, and now Pirate couldn't move quickly. "Dan, pull back," Grace shouted on circuit. "I'll cover you."

"Gracie, I can't leave you."

"You stay here and they grab two 'Mechs. You go and they get maybe one. I'll cover you and then bust out of Pirate and run for it. They're after the 'Mech. They won't waste time on me."

"If you keep covering us, when will you bust out?"

"Soon, if you move it."

"I'm pulling back, Grace, but I don't like this." Dan shot off two more rivers of fire, one toward each BattleMech, then disappeared in a shallow draw only to reappear as his AgroMech hotfooted it from one bit of cover to another.

Grace kept Pirate upright, but one leg was grinding as he moved. She edged around the outcropping, keeping it between her and the taller 'Mech. It was the other one she wanted dead.

As she peeked around the rock, she found the short 'Mech right where it had been. It wasn't moving in for the kill! It stood tall, scanning the hills behind Grace. She worked the pedals, trying to turn Pirate, but the gyros screamed and nothing happened. She wanted that 'Mech. She jiggled the joystick until her sights were dead on it, then waited for it to come.

"Captain, you see them?"

"Roger, Webrunner, I see them," L. J. said.

Twelve 'Mechs were moving over the crest of the ridge ahead of them. The distance was too far for him to make out their types and equipment, but if they'd been modified like the ones he'd been fighting, they might be able to take him and Webrunner in their damaged state. Well, his damaged state. He looked at his ammo levels—not much left.

Pickup would be at the mouth of this valley. He had to expect that some fight might be left in the locals. For a moment longer, he considered continuing his pursuit of that troublesome MiningMech, but he had no way of knowing just how badly he'd damaged him. It was time to cut his losses.

"Task Team, fall back to the U in the road. Top-kick, can you do anything with the mess Godfrey made of his tank?"

"No, sir. It's wedged in there real fine."

"Render it unusable," L. J. ordered, keeping his voice even, disappointment out, exhaustion not present. *A commander leads,* Uncle said. *And a real leader never lets anyone know things are going bad. Because when things are really bad, that's when your men and women need leadership the most.*

L. J. would show the Roughriders he knew how to lead.

2

Near Falkirk, Alkalurops
Prefecture IX, The Republic of the Sphere
3 April 3134; local spring

Grace lay beside Pirate's battered hull. The clear sky above her had never seemed such a pure blue. A flowering sprig of Scotch broom smelled heavenly, almost overpowering the stink of burned carbon armor and the residue of exploded rockets.

She was alive! She hadn't been splattered all over the hill by rockets or lasers. She'd escaped and would live to see tomorrow. It was a heady feeling, especially if she didn't think too much about how she didn't deserve it. Luck. All luck.

She looked up to see Mick's flatbed truck bouncing from rock to rock, its engine struggling as he approached her. Mick backed up to Pirate, got out to take a good look, then gave a low whistle. "Well, that extra armor kept you alive."

"Just barely. He's all knocked around inside."

"Shock. Yeah," the short, wiry mechanic said. "We build MiningMechs to take the normal wear you jockeys put on them, not the crap a rocket does. Help me with the crane so we can lay your Pirate out. I want a look at that tank your Navajo friends caught."

Once they had Pirate loaded, gravity and the 'Mech's weight urged the truck to go wild, pick up momentum, and leave them all dead at the foot of the hill. Fortunately, Mick was a maestro on the brake and gears.

Chato's weathered and lined face had a big grin on it as they drove up to the hovertank. A dozen other Navajos, dressed like him in plaid shirts and work jeans, gathered around the tank, which they had managed to right.

"Looks to be in pretty good shape," Mick said as he and Grace joined Chato.

"They tried to burn it," Chato said, pointing, palm open, at a still-smoldering area of the canyon floor. "This contraption was upside down, and they couldn't get their charges to stay put. They tossed grenades into the underside. That's a mess."

A younger version of Chato, raven hair held back in four rather than the older man's two braids, popped his head out of the tank. "Uncle Chato, you have to look at this. They have sensors in here I never even dreamed of."

"And if Joseph hasn't dreamed of them, I didn't think a human could make them," the Navajo said.

Mick shook his head. "It's the engine I'll be wanting to tear apart. Never could understand electric stuff."

Grace and Chato squatted around the hatch as Joseph settled back into the belly of the monster. Gadgets were wrapped around the seat, leaving just enough room for one person to sit. "Will you look at this, Uncle," the young man chattered happily. "Their infrared scope. It's measured in kilometers, not meters. Coyote, grant me one wish: Let whatever sensor feeds that thing be working. I have to see it work."

"So they knew we were waiting for them," Grace said bitterly. "Knew just when to attack us."

"So it seems," Chato said. "We'll need to study this war pony a lot more."

"Lot of stuff to study," Mick said from where he'd pried open the engine compartment.

"I'd like to see how things are in Falkirk," Grace said.

Hours later she wondered why she'd hurried back. Her return became a town meeting right there on Main Avenue, but one she couldn't call to order. She learned that there were no deaths among the fighters in Falkirk, thanks to old Auntie Maydell. The old lady seemed to have single-handedly, well, single-sharp-tonguedly, talked a soldier into leaving the town alone.

But there were plenty of close calls to talk about—calls that got closer the more times they were discussed. As much as Grace hated the idea, she knew she'd better call a town meeting right away, while memories of the day's terror was still gut-puking fresh, and before the truth vanished beneath thick layers of varnish.

The meeting went long. Everybody wanted to talk, and Grace had to let them. The rules for town meetings had never included a way to shush anyone, but the yammering served to show the divide in town. There were those—few of whom had been on the hill with Grace—who figured the militia should have put up a better fight. A lot more were all for running for the hills in the event of another raid. That number now included about half the militia.

Grace took note of the quiet ones. Not surprisingly, Chato held his tongue, as did Jobe Kang. Jobe had led the dozen worker 'Mechs from the Donga River

Valley. Their arrival from the west appeared to be what had turned the raiders around. The Navajo with his long braids sat next to the bald African miner. They took in the goings-on but, like Grace, said nothing.

Jim Wilson sat in silence next to his son. The boy started to stand up a few times to demand the floor, but the elder farmer kept a restraining hand on his son's leg.

Hong Ho, owner of the town's sole hardware outlet, kept his eyes closed in meditation, which told Grace nothing about what he was thinking. Robert Laird, the town's grain operator and greengrocer, sat beside his Buddhist friend, keeping just as quiet, even if he did tend to fidget in his seat.

Grace mulled over the day as she let others' words wash over her, holding on to few of them. Still, some broke into her thoughts. "Damn, I don't want to do that again." "We should have been able to do better." And "What was it about those BattleMechs?"

"Where was the Legate's BattleMech?" came often, but no one knew the answer to that.

When Grace began to feel her patience growing thin, she rose and shouted into the racket of a five-sided argument. "I don't know about anyone else's bladder, but mine says it's time for a break."

There was a stampede for the facilities. Despite her claimed need, Grace stayed in her place. As Wilson, Ho, Laird, Chato, and Jobe gathered around her table, Mick joined them.

"You got that tank into your shop?" Grace asked.

"Yep. Chato's boy has juice flowing to its innards."

"Is it as dangerous as it looks?" she asked.

"Worse, if you ask me. That thing can damn near see you coming before you think of going. MagScan to beat the band. Infrared to tell your temperature. Real bad stuff."

"Not if it serves *you*," Chato said simply.

"But it served us up like fish on a platter," Wilson

said. "A bunch of optimists who never fought anything worse than a cranky engine or a bad headwind."

Folks around Grace looked at one another and nodded.

"Gracie," Wilson said, "I never want to go through that again. Leastwise not as dumb as I was today. I know how to raise cows. I'm damn good at farming this red dirt around here. I don't know crap about fighting 'Mechs."

"Me neither," echoed around the circle.

Grace took a deep breath and tried to pull from deep inside her what had been taking shape. "I'm not much in favor of running every time the Net says boo. Running for the hills and hoping there's something to come back to is no way for real people to live," she said, eyeing the group. Only frowns met that. "Now, if I don't know how to do something, I usually put out a call for someone who does. Pay them either to do it for me or teach me how. Seems to me that we need someone who can teach us a thing or two about fighting."

That brought a long pause, which Grace took to mean that the men were seriously considering her suggestion. She was glad of the help; the future of Falkirk hung on the handful around her.

"When I need something we don't make here," Ho said slowly, "I buy the best I can afford from where it is available."

"I don't like strangers showing up and pushing me around," Wilson said. "My family was here during the old wars. People from off-planet tried to take us on, and we bloodied their noses. If I have a vote, I say we do the same. And if we don't know how, I say hire folks to show us the way."

"That's the way I see it, too," Grace said. "The raiders came. We did what we could, and that was damn poor. I say we go to the Legate and demand that he train us to do what the people of Alkalurops have always done—defend ourselves. And if the Leg-

ate is as dead as I think he is, we find someone who
can," Grace said.

"That could cost money," Ho pointed out.

"Would you rather pay for a defense or try to bribe
the raiders, 'cause next time I wouldn't bet on Auntie
Maydell talking them down. The next raiders'll demand our money or our 'Mechs," Grace finished. Her
listeners frowned but nodded.

"Better to fight than give up, and if we fight, I mean
to fight a damn sight better next time," Wilson said.
"I'll put up ten percent of my profits from last year
to pay someone to teach me how to knock the next
raiders on their asses."

"Me, too," came from the rest in the circle. Grace
sighed. Now all she had to do was get the rest of
Falkirk to go along.

Outside Kilkenny, Alkalurops
13 April 3134

A nudge brought Grace awake. "You'll want to see
this," Chato said. Reluctantly, Grace opened her eyes.
Chato had volunteered to drive the jeep Jim Wilson
had donated to take the local reps to the capital, at
Allabad. Something to deal with the situation had to
be in the works at the capital, and Falkirk was damned
if those fancy pants in the big city would ignore the
working stiffs who paid the taxes. Or that the large
mining corporations would ignore the small mining
groups that made up the other half of the planet's
gross production. So Grace went straight from a gut-
wrenching town hall meeting that had adopted her
plan for defense to a night ride down gravel roads
that might end in a raider roadblock.

Blinking sleep away, her eyes met rosy dawn. The
morning sky was all that looked good. In the field
beside the road, three burned-out jeeps still sent up
smoke and made the morning stink. A half-burned

body manned a machine gun on one of them. At the side of the road, bodies were lined up in a careful row, a single blanket covering the faces. "I guess you were luckier than you realized," Jobe said from the backseat.

"Looks that way," Grace agreed.

"Should I stop?" Chato asked. Ahead, a young man was waving his arm slowly, struggling with the effort. A red bandage was wrapped around the light armor on his other arm.

"Stop," Grace ordered. She leaned out of the rig and asked, "What happened here? Who's in charge?"

"The raiders sidestepped the North Constabulary when they came through Kilkenny headed north, so we figured to catch 'em on their way back south, ma'am," the young man said, leaning heavily on the hood of their jeep. "I guess you'd say I'm in charge. Lieutenant Hicks, ma'am. I hate to do this, but I got wounded to transport. I have to commandeer your rig."

"Hicks, I'm the mayor of Falkirk, and these two men represent the Donga and White River Valleys. We're on our way to Allabad, but we'll be glad to carry as many of your wounded as we can."

The young man nodded his agreement. "We'll do it your way, ma'am. Sergeant," he said to a man standing nearby, "get the two stretchers laid across the back. You mind if my walking wounded ride your fender?"

"How many survivors do you have?" Grace asked.

"Too few," the weary officer answered. "I'll walk the rest back in. You take the six that are shot up into Kilkenny. There's a clinic this side of town." Grace counted four soldiers aside from the lieutenant and his sergeant.

"I know it," Grace said. "We'll take good care of your people. Chato, let's go."

"I'll get us there as fast as I can, War Chief," Chato said.

Grace eyed the wreckage as they pulled away. No one had stripped the dead or wounded of their body armor. What type of raid was this?

Dropping the wounded off at Kilkenny still allowed Grace and the others to reach Amarillo before noon. The largest town in the Gleann Mor Valley gave them the best of news. The raiders' JumpShip had blasted off from south of there that morning loaded with the last of them. Grace and her group saw how selective the raiders had been: Only 'Mechs ten years old or younger had been hijacked and walked aboard the JumpShip. Old 'Mechs still went about their business.

As the three hurried south, the land changed. Once they came off the caprock, fields were greener and broken with more streams. Only occasionally did they see a farmhouse shot up; rarely did a town show bullet holes. Dublin Town was a similar case. Like so many of the large towns on Alkalurops, it was sheltered in a deep canyon from the seasonal high winds. Grace was driving as they took the road down. No surprise, the IndustrialMech dealerships on the outskirts had old 'Mechs in for repairs but no new rigs. But the communication towers were still standing, as were the power lines.

The next morning, as they drove out of Dublin Town, Grace found the local Net had come back to life. The news was full of wild stories: Government House had been burned to the ground, and the Governor and Legate were dead. Grace made a quick call to her mother to tell her the trip was going fine, then turned the phone over to Jobe and Chato so they could call their wives.

As the men talked, Grace mused on what her pirate namesake would have taken in a raid. Her list included a lot of gear that was still up and working on Alkalurops. When Grace voiced her thoughts, Jobe offered, "Maybe their DropShip couldn't carry it all."

"Why go raiding with only a small boat for the loot?" she asked. Neither man had an answer.

Late that afternoon they drove off the plains and into the long canyon that protected Allabad from the high winds of the flat country above. The large transmission tower by the road was undisturbed. The largest city on Alkalurops didn't look that bad, either: Allabad now filled most of the canyon with wide rows of thick adobe homes and businesses. The long, shallow lake that had first drawn people to the city had been narrowed and deepened so that new buildings could be built on the old flood plain.

Except for that, nothing much had changed since Grace's parents had brought her here some twenty years back so Pop could get his first MiningMech—the first MiningMech in the Gleann Mor Valley. And Pop had pointed out buildings that had been pointed out to him by his own grandpa. Grace spotted the old market, its low walls stretching for several blocks north of the central plaza this side of the Alhambra River. There was the clock tower of the Guild Hall, though the hall had grown several new wings. This was what Grace loved about life on Alkalurops: It had been, was, and would be the same.

Except now raiders dropped in. They were a new experience—one she did not want to repeat.

Grace called the hostel she stayed at whenever business brought her to Allabad. She reserved a room for herself and one for Jobe and Chato to share. Then she called Angus Throckmorton, a family connection at the Miners' Guild who went back to her grandpa's time. She wondered if he'd remember her, but his voice was warm when he took her call. He was actually eager to meet her and her friends. "You know the inn I took your father to the last time he was here? Could you meet me there in half an hour?" Grace promised she would and he rang off.

"Where are we meeting him?" Chato asked.

"The Red Erin Inn," she said. "I've been there before."

"Sure you can find it again?" Jobe asked.

"It would be a shame if we got lost," Chato deadpanned.

"I remember the place," Grace shot back, then spotted the looks the two men were exchanging and realized they'd been teasing her. She settled back into the passenger seat. "We have half an hour before he can see us. We may as well take the scenic route."

After a couple of wrong turns, the three arrived at the inn to find that Angus was there before them. Grace had hardly given his name to the tall, pony-tailed barkeep before he led her across a wood-beamed great room to a dark corner where Angus waited. A big friendly bear of a man now gone to gray, he made to rise, but she quickly introduced Jobe and Chato, then settled beside him and gave him a hug.

"Lass, you're looking more beautiful every day."

She tried to return the compliment, but Angus had aged noticeably in the five years since she'd seen him. Up close she realized his plaid coat hung on him. His knuckles were red and swollen, his eyes sunken into dark bags. "Y-you're—" she stammered, then caught herself. "How bad was it here?"

"A good dark one for the lady, here," Angus called to the barkeep. Grace was happy to let Angus order for her—he knew the local brews. Jobe ordered a lighter ale, while Chato asked for coffee.

Only after the barkeep retreated did Grace repeat her question. "It's been bad?"

"Strange it's been, lass. Very strange."

"The raiders hit Falkirk," Grace told him. "Didn't take much. The militia got knocked around some."

"You lose anyone close to you?" Angus asked.

"A few wounded. None too bad to brag. How was it here?"

"Strange and then some," he said, then fell silent again as their drinks came. Grace wondered if she'd have to start the conversation all over again, but Angus went on as she took her first pull on her pint. A good brew.

"The raiders came in claiming to be a regular commercial DropShip. My friends at the port tell me that ships to Alkalurops never keep to a schedule. Anyway, they set down around midnight a week ago. They tore through the place, but not so fast that the alarm wasn't raised."

"Where was the Legate? And the Governor?" Jobe put in.

"You tell me and we'll both be knowing it," Angus said, shaking his head and taking another long pull on his drink. "I've heard that the raiders blew them away without so much as a by-your-leave. There's also a story that the two rushed out to the port in a car and got stomped flat. I also heard from the lass who's the Legate's housekeeper. She found him in bed, throat slit. I can tell you which one I'm believing—the maid, it is."

"The raiders got to him before the alarm?" Grace said, then shook her head. "That's not possible."

"The poor man's throat was slit before the raiders' ship ever touched down, I'm thinking," Angus said, looking around as if someone with a knife might be looking to slit his throat, too.

"What happened to the Central Constabulary?" Grace asked.

"They got smashed by the raiders as if they weren't even there. Not much of a fight at all, at all."

"We saw the North Cons on our way here. Not much left."

"That would be no surprise."

"So the raiders went through here pretty thoroughly," Chato said. "Strange, not much sign of looting."

" 'Cause there was none of that, or very little." Angus shook his head. "The raiders emptied the Legate's quarters of his *Ryoken II* and any spare gear that was handy. They hit the 'Mech dealerships and hijacked the new equipment and such that was nearly new. Gun dealers, too. They set up a base camp at the port and warned us not to come near it. Then those raiding parties took off like the thieves they were. We'd see 'Mechs stomping back under guard of a few gun bikes and stuff.

"Some of the men hereabouts tried a night raid, turnabout being only fair. It didn't work." That required another pull on the pint. "Ugly thing. Lad just wounded a mite said the raiders were on them before they were halfway to the port. Damn machines landed on them, scared them witless, and shot them up as they ran. 'Mechs that fly. My grandda told me what it was like during the old wars, but he didn't say anything about flying 'Mechs."

"We faced a pair of those. If Jobe here hadn't shown up, they might have jumped all over me," Grace said, trying to make sense of what she was hearing and what she'd seen. "So they left things pretty much as they are."

"Except for burning down Government House, you could say we got off lightly, now, couldn't you?" Angus said to his beer as if trying to persuade himself. "Yes, I guess we did."

"But what were the raiders trying to do?" Chato said, swirling his coffee slowly in its mug.

"Banshee take me if I can guess that," Angus exploded. "It's not knowing what's going on across The Republic that can drive a man to walk out thirsty on a hot dry day."

"Your Mick did a pretty good job of turning some of your MiningMechs into more heavily armored 'Mechs," Jobe pointed out to Grace.

"Right, so maybe someone else is turning worker 'Mechs into fighting 'Mechs?" Grace said, then took a long pull on her beer.

"Things have been peaceful for a long time. Not a lot of BattleMechs around," Chato said, as if he'd mined the sentences one word at a time.

"And if you wanted to grow an army in a hurry and cheap . . ." Grace let the words hang there.

"Steal 'Mechs from an out-of-the-way planet," Jobe said.

"But don't do too much damage. Let folks get back on their feet quickly, maybe even order new 'Mechs," Angus added, emptying his beer. "I need another drink on that thought. Liam, me boy, where are you hiding, and me with a throat all dusty."

The barkeep, no more a boy than Grace was a lass, hustled over. "You drinking your dinner again, Angus, or do you want something to put in that thin gut of yours?"

"Refills for all, and now that you remind me, some of that delicious lamb stew for us that you sometimes have hereabouts."

"Only every night," the barkeep muttered as he turned away.

"So you don't think this raid was a onetime thing?" Grace said, getting them back to the thoughts pounding in her brain.

"Even if this hard bunch doesn't come back, with us deaf and dumb as a post, other hard men will be looking around for things to grab," Angus said. "And even if we don't get back on our feet, if the whole Sphere goes to hell, what are leavings now will be a prince's ransom next year. The year after that, they may be stealing food out of our mouths. Ah, the bad old days are nothing to remember, lass. Not a life to live again, not at all, at all."

"And us with no Legate or Knights to call upon," Grace said, letting Angus' brogue slip off her own tongue.

"Aye, lassie, and us with only our own hands." A brimming pint clanked onto the table, so Angus naturally took a long swig to wash those thoughts away.

Grace noticed that Jobe was going slow on his first pint and settled for a sip of her own. "With Government House in ashes, and the Governor and Legate dead, what are we doing for a government?" she asked.

"The bureaucrats are back in business at a hotel down the street from the ruins. A bunch of big-town mayors are gathering tomorrow at the Guild Hall to see what they can make of matters," Angus said as the lamb stew arrived. "Mind you, small towns like Falkirk don't count with them, but no rule says who gets a say, either. Word is, they mean to elect a new Governor. Pro tem, or some such."

Grace put her beer down and attacked her stew. Angus could drown his troubles if he wanted. It looked as though tomorrow she and her friends would have work to do.

Allabad, Alkalurops
15 April 3134

The plaque on the Guild Hall's bell tower claimed that the thick adobe walls had stood for eight hundred years, keeping out tornadoes and torrential floods from upstream hurricanes. It did not say how often the roof tiles had been replaced. On this day roof and walls kept out the heat of the day. The latest attacks, unlike the old, had not shattered the stained-glass windows. The new louver system followed the sun, letting in enough light for business without overheating the hall. This morning's heat came from men and women talking, talking, and talking some more.

Grace, Chato, and Jobe arrived early, but not early enough to get seats around the tables that had been pushed together to make one long one. They scrounged up a table of their own and added it at one end, forcing other early arrivals to move. As more people filed in, more tables had to be added. Those already seated frowned as they had to keep making room, but they didn't muster a protest. In the end, the table was a big square, accommodating twice as many people as originally intended.

To Grace's left, the three mayors from Little London, Lothran and Banya—the three largest towns outside Allabad—looked none too happy. In the old days, before Devlin Stone required a planet to have one central seat of government headed by a Governor, Alkalurops had gotten along with a Council of Elders drawn from towns and major guilds. Now that the Governor was dead, it seemed that folks wanted to go back to the old ways, and even the mayors of the three largest cities did not dare go against them.

Garry McGuire, a short man with a confident air who was the mayor of Little London, applied a solid-looking gavel to a wooden plaque. This relic from the days of Elders and meetings had been momentarily removed from the display case that had held it for the last fifty years. The hall fell silent.

Dev Coughlin, dapper in Terran fashions six years out of date even before the HPG went down, and mayor of Lothran, rose to his feet from his seat between Grace and Garry. "I rise from among you to nominate Garry McGuire as Governor Pro Tem of our planet, until such time as The Republic appoints a replacement for the fondly remembered late Kristen LeSat."

The hall rumbled with talk. Garry McGuire gaveled them to order as the mayor of Banya half rose from the seat on his left to shout, "I second Garry McGuire's name and call for a vote."

"Guess we know what they were doing last night," Grace whispered to Chato, but Jobe was standing.

His deep bass voice carried easily through the babble. "I rise from among you to place in nomination the name of Grace O'Malley, mayor of Falkirk, for Governor."

Before Grace could react, Jobe was back in his seat, his face a wide grin of white teeth against ebony skin.

Chato shot to his feet. "I second Grace O'Malley's name."

"He can't do that," Dev Coughlin shouted.

"Yes, he can," Grace shouted back. She was none too sure she wanted to be nominated, but Chato and Jobe were recognized heads of their respective areas—as empowered as any mayor to sit and act in this council.

"And I stand to nominate Billy O'Leary," came from down the table. That started a nomination frenzy that lasted the better part of half an hour and ended only when most everyone had either nominated someone, seconded someone, or been placed in nomination.

When there was no one left to nominate and the entire hall was chattering among themselves, Grace stood up. She'd never thought much of her flaming red hair, but it often drew people's attention. It did today as the hall fell moderately quiet.

"We seem to have no lack of nominees. What we do lack are procedures for electing a Governor, or Prime Elder, or whatever it is we intend to do. I ask one question. Do we allow a simple plurality to decide the vote, or should we require a majority?"

It took a few seconds for the full impact of her words to sink in. With so many candidates, someone with only five or six votes might have more than the rest. Those pushing for a quick vote shut up, and the hall fell silent.

"Will the fine lady—from Falkirk, is it?—yield the floor she has so admirably brought to silence?" Dev Coughlin asked.

"For a question only." Grace had once found a book on the rules of order for official meetings. It had been helpful—as something to pound on the table to quiet Falkirk town meetings even if she couldn't follow its rules. Maybe today she could.

"I recognize that everyone is important to our planet's economy," Dev said, "but how can the vote of a mayor from a small town like Falkirk have the same weight as that of someone representing a city a hundred times larger? Shouldn't we apportion votes on a one man, one-vote basis?" Dev smiled at his two friends, who nodded their agreement.

"No," Grace snapped. "Not even if you modify your proposal to be one man or woman, one vote." Dev had the good humor to flinch at his gaffe. Grace went on. "We have not had a full census in fifty years, since Stone decided we'd have the Governor he appointed. Without a certified census, we can't tell who represents how many. Does that answer your question?"

Dev's smile faded under her temper. "No, it does not. We have to represent the people who sent us. We all know that I stand for two or three hundred times as many people as you do. We can't do a simple one mayor, one vote. It's not fair."

"That's not a question, Dev," someone shouted from halfway down the table. "Quit arguing with the woman or Gus and me'll throw you out." The murmur in the hall was going Grace's way—there were a lot more small towns than large ones. That had been one of the main problems of the old Council of Elders, according to what Grace's grandpa had told her. Stone resolved the problem before Alkalurops ever did.

"May I rise for a question, ma'am?"

This time the speaker was from down the table. A gray-haired man in a Terran business suit stood up. "Sir, I don't know how to recognize you," Grace said, intent on not yielding the floor quite so quickly this time.

"I am Theobald Chizhenzki, Local Manager for Kimberly-Somtog Minerals and Metallurgy. My associate here"—he indicated a thin, balding man beside him—"is Thomas Pennypage, General Manager for Howard-Kennicutt Extraction Operations. We were sent here by the Industrial Trade Group. The ITG employs over four percent of your planet's workforce, either full-time, contract or floating temps. A good estimate of people who live off the stones we pay in salary is twenty-five percent of everyone here. Even you independent miners benefit from the spare parts we warehouse here because we want them when we need them. How large do you think the selection would be at your local 'Mech or truck dealership if we didn't buy half of what they import each year?"

"I hear a speech coming on," came from someone at the foot of the table. "If I don't hear a real question soon, I'm going to show you what us independent miners can do on our own."

"Let the man ask a question," Grace said. Like every independent miner, Grace had her own opinion about how much the majors helped or hindered the little guy. Still, Alkalurops was in enough trouble without alienating a big chunk of its economy.

"My question is this," Chizhenzki said. "Things have changed a lot since the last time Alkalurops set up its own government. I'm not against trying anything. God knows when we'll hear from The Republic again. But shouldn't businesses that employ more men and women than any entity you represent also be included in this council?"

As he finished, the room broke into an uproar.

A short, round man in a waist-length jacket bearing the emblem of the Bakers' Guild was on his feet shouting along with half a dozen other Guild Masters, across the table from the mining reps. On the fifth try, Grace made out his words. "We represent Alkalurops businesspeople and workers, not—" Grace provided "someone off-planet." The new deposits opened up in the west had all ended up in the hands of conglomerates, which a lot of the old families attributed to having a Governor appointed from off-planet. Then again, maybe the new deposits did need the concentrated extraction techniques available only to the big companies. That was a good argument for several cold winter nights.

Garry McGuire leaned past Dev to say, "You'll

want to yield the floor just now, Gracie. Looks to me like we've got a long talk about who fits in this room and how we're going to do our business before we get back to voting."

Grace didn't want to establish any precedent, but at least on this one point, she was prepared to let Garry carry the fire. "You take it. But I want the floor back before we move to any boss-type votes around here."

"You'll get it," Garry said. Grace didn't like the look he gave Dev, but when Garry started hammering away with his gavel, the noise in the room did go down to a dull roar.

Garry stood, which brought the racket down a few more decibels. "The kind lady from up north has agreed to yield the floor while we get around to organizing ourselves. From the looks of things, we really don't know who should be included in our discussions and how we should operate. Kind of hard to put somebody in charge when we don't know what he's in charge of or supposed to do," he said, grinning at a couple of his associates. They dutifully laughed as if he was a vid comic and that got the room laughing with him.

Grace didn't hear anything to laugh about for the rest of the day. The only relief came from the front of the hall, where a couple of the sidewalk hawkers from the square brought their food carts inside and set up shop. Grace was the only one in her trio with stones, so she went for drinks and found a lot of other folks doing the same.

"You did a real fine job there. What's your name again, young lady?" an elderly woman asked. Grace told her, and found herself sharing her thoughts with the woman. Then a couple of men joined in. In whispers they reached a fairly quick conclusion on how they'd run things. Grace delivered drinks to Jobe and Chato, filled them in on her conversations, and left them at the table to keep an eye on that circus while she circulated around the hall, feeling people out, taking her own reading of what these people wanted. The gathering wasn't that different from a town meeting, just bigger, noisier and under someone else's control. An hour's lunch lasted three. Grace had no complaint; she was one of the last back, just ahead of Garry, Dev, and the two mining managers. As the sun fell below the rim of the canyon, Garry gaveled the meeting into an early recess, and Grace found herself juggling multiple dinner meetings.

Over suppers, consensus built among the small towns that everyone should vote, even the representatives of off-planet corporations. But every member of the council had to have the same single vote, and decisions should be by at least seventy-five percent of the vote.

It was well past midnight before Grace got to sleep, but she felt good. Alkalurops had some mighty fine inhabitants.

The next morning Grace, Jobe and Chato were approaching the Guild Hall when the roar of a DropShip coming in shook the quiet day. Grace wasn't the only one who did a frantic Net check. The ship docking was the regular one the raider had pretended to be. It was late but real. At her elbow, Jobe frowned. "You'd think the raiders would have stripped the port bare. Used landing radars and radios have to be easy to sell. Sloppy, if you ask me."

"Well, unless a lot of people rethought what we talked about last night, we ought to get a lot done today," Grace said, opening the Guild Hall door for the men.

But when enough people are gathered together, nothing comes quickly. Saying "everyone votes" didn't seem to cover all the possibilities. Hank Pintagras, mayor of Calgeron, was first on his feet that morning. "Do the Guild representatives in Allabad speak for *all* the Guilds?" he asked in a high, shrill voice. "Or

do we require the Guilds to establish an election process so each Guild can make sure the speaker represents them?"

Grace tried to suppress a groan. The master of Calgeron's 'Mech Sales and Service Guild was notorious
for disagreeing with anyone and everyone at the drop
of a welding torch. For the next hour the discussion
rambled, with Allabad's Master Baker unwilling to
grant anything at all to the "sticks." Grace leaned
back and studied the ceiling.

"We can't let this bunch stampede in circles," Chato
said. "I'll keep an eye on the table yammering. Could
you get me a cup of tea, Grace, and talk to folks?
Patch up what we did last night." Grace went, but
how often on the drive home from a meeting had she
thought of a good reason not to vote the way she had.

She was buying a mug of tea for Chato while Jobe
bought himself a cup of coffee, so they were in a good
position to see the man who walked into the Guild
Hall at ten sharp.

He was taller than most, and his expensive-looking
dark suit accentuated the lines of his thin frame. White
hair combed straight back gave him a regal bearing,
heightened by his aquiline nose. His feet didn't so
much walk as move him smoothly along. Grace saw
that she wasn't the only one whose eyes were drawn
to the stranger as his head moved slowly from side to
side, taking in everything, missing nothing, acknowl-
edging no one.

"I think our schedule for today just changed,"
Grace whispered to Jobe.

"I don't like the looks of that man," he answered.

"Neither do I, but he looks like a player."

"But for whom? Whatever he wants, we will not
be able to ignore him." Jobe followed Grace back to
their seats.

The stranger walked straight to the mining company
managers; they exchanged formal introductions. The
hall had been floating on a bubble of talk that almost

drowned out the person who had the floor. Now it settled slowly into silence as more and more heads turned toward the new arrival. The speaker who had been shouting to be heard suddenly realized he was bellowing into a silent hall. "That pretty much says it all," he muttered lamely, and sank into his chair.

Garry McGuire nodded, then turned to the standing man. "I don't think we know you."

"I suspected as much. However, I am prepared to correct that oversight." The stranger seemed to toy with words the way a cat might toy with a cornered mouse.

"Would you please introduce yourself?" Garry asked.

"It would be my pleasure. I would also like to present a solution to the problems that appear to plague you, if I may?" The words hardly sounded like a question, but Garry nodded and the man continued. "I am Alfred Santorini, at your service," he said with a tiny nod. "I see this planet also has been hit by raiders."

"Also?" Grace repeated, a comment echoed around the hall.

"Yes, you are not alone in these desperate times," Santorini went on. "Since The Republic of the Sphere has doubly failed in its duty to provide for common communications and the public defense, violent elements have risen up and moved against many planets. Some planets are lucky enough to have powerful patrons to protect them from these latter-day wolves. Others have been stripped down to the dirt by repeated bloody raids. From what I saw on my drive from the spaceport, you got off relatively lightly. Was this your first experience with the new vandals?"

"Yes, it was," Garry answered. "Would it be too much for me to ask what brought you to Alkalurops?"

"No, not at all," Santorini said. "May I take a seat?" A woman sitting near him yielded her chair. Santorini allowed her to position it before he settled on it with regal flair. Never having seen a king, Grace could only guess at the effect and note the goose bumps that went up her spine. There was a sense of power about this man. What she could not decide was whether it was for good or ill.

"I am in the employ of Lenzo Computing Industries of Nusakan. I expect we are familiar to you. No doubt many of you use our hardware and software in your homes and businesses. With the growing unpleasantness wracking The Republic, my corporation is looking for a new home for its central office. Such a move will impact several hundred thousand of our employees, and will provide jobs for millions more on the planet we choose for our headquarters." He smiled at Garry. Grace could almost hear the mayor of Little London calculating the incentives his town could offer Santorini and dreaming of a name change—Greater London!

Oh, crap.

It took Grace about five seconds to do the math. Alkalurops was at just about full employment. Of course, full employment usually allowed for either parent to concentrate on raising the kids or for both parents to alternate work time and volunteer projects. You needed a lot less government and a lot fewer taxes when folks pitched in without being told. Pirate had dug many a kilometer of roadside drainage ditch or cleaned them out after a bad flood. Wilson had a grader that divided its time between the roads on his farm and the public ones.

The only way Alkalurops could absorb millions more workers was to either let in immigrants or dig them out of their own population. That meant two workers from each family, which would probably be necessary for a family to survive. What with all the new mouths to feed and house and provide cars for, the price of everything was going to skyrocket.

"Isn't progress a wonderful thing to observe in action?" Jobe said, rolling his eyes. Around her, Grace could see people working it out for themselves. Some saw profits and smiled. Others, like her, counted the cost and scowled.

Santorini paused for a moment to sip from a cup of water at his elbow. A perfect pause for all concerned. As he put the cup down, he cleared his throat. When he continued, his voice was pitched to fill every corner of the hall. Even the food hawkers fell silent.

"At the moment, however, I believe the matter most urgent for your attention is the special relationship between me—or rather my corporation—and a group of freedom fighters."

He let the words hang in the air for a moment. "Those with business connections on Skye know that its transfer from the Lyran Commonwealth to The Republic left many unsatisfied." That was news to Grace, and she did have business connections on Skye. She glanced at Gordon Frazier from Kilkenny and a few other friends. Their faces were pretty well frozen in neutral. Maybe a slight furrow of the brow hinted that this was not going down well.

"Into the silence of the HPG links, Landgrave Jasek Kelswa-Steiner has raised his flag to correct that wrong by The Republic. People from Skye and all over The Republic have flocked to his standard, that of the ancient Stormhammer, and Nusakan has provided him a base for his operations. Not by chance, his presence has given us the kind of shield that other, less guarded worlds have come to envy. If I choose Alkalurops as the new base for LCI, be assured that the Landgrave will fully protect you from further depredations."

"Assuming we don't get hit by whoever is trying to hit the Landgrave," Grace said into the silence.

"The Stormhammers are most competent at protecting their interests," Santorini snapped.

"Where have we heard that before?" came from somewhere down the table.

Grace had no intention of letting this get away from her. She stood and spoke. "And what is the price of this protection? Is the Landgrave willing to do this out of the kindness of his heart? Is this company you work for"—Grace emphasized this point, one that she felt Santorini had skimmed over—"so important to the Landgrave that he protects it purely for the natural benefits, or is there more to the relationship?"

The off-worlder dismissed her concern with a wave of his hand. "I'm sure something can be worked out to everyone's convenience."

"What will it cost to have the Stormhammers protect us?" Grace demanded. "In plain language, please."

Now Santorini stood up, unwinding himself from his chair like a man bothered by a gnat. "What has your own poor protection just cost you? Is there a single good 'Mech left on any lot in town?" As he shot his glance around the table, Grace heard the Sales and Service Guild master mumble a quick negative.

"How many of you lost IndustrialMechs off your fields, out of your businesses, your mines?" Many nods around the table. "Are they easily replaced?" The head-shakes were near frantic.

"Defense against the raiders and scavengers roaming space is not cheap. The Stormhammers ask for a donation of thirty percent of your net off-world trade. For that, they give you the security that is essential if you are to have any trade at all."

"Thirty percent?!" came out in one breath around the table.

"You bought into the fairy tale that The Republic could keep you safe for a pittance: one Governor, one Legate, and a few trembling Constabulary jokes. What has it gotten you? Cleaned out, that's what. You want safety, but it is not free. Do you want to be alive and in business next year? The year after? Or do you want to be a pile of bones, picked clean by any roving band that happens by? The choice is yours. Now, if you don't mind, I have business with the Industrial Trade Group."

Santorini and the mining company managers stood, nodded curtly to the room, and left, the heels of their shoes beating a confident cadence on the tiles.

"You certainly queered that deal, woman," Dev snapped. "Now he'll probably jack the price up to forty percent."

Garry hammered the gavel, and the room stayed quiet. "Grace O'Malley, are you prepared to speak for the small-holders and small towns?" the mayor of Little London demanded.

Grace glanced around the table. Some nodded, while others seemed less willing to let her talk for them. No surprise there. "I'll start talking and see how long it is before someone sees the need to correct me." *At the top of their lungs, no doubt.*

"You have a counterproposal to Mr. Santorini's offer?"

Grace rested her hands on the table and leaned into the room as she might against the wind of a spring hurricane. "For eight hundred years we've walked this planet. There's aren't a lot of us," she said, standing tall. "You all know why. The air stinks, or so off-worlders tell us. It's too hot and dry, they tell us, except when a hurricane's blowing or a thunderstorm is dropping hail and maybe a tornado." That brought a familiar chuckle from around the table.

"But it's *our* land. The land *our* parents mined or farmed before us. This is the land we raise our kids on as *we* choose. Now this guy comes in here and offers to buy us out and load us up with a lot of strangers. He promises a wonderful business boom, but, oh, by the way, you'll have to pay for some goons to protect you from some other goons.

"Damn it, we've faced attackers before. Our great-great-greats stood up to them and drove them off— and people learned that attacking Alkalurops was not a good idea. Even the drunk-on-heaven Jihad freaks didn't come here."

She turned slowly, letting her eyes make contact

with the people scattered around the tables. "We may not have much, but we protect it. *We* protect it. Not some hireling. Not somebody with a bone to pick with someone else who just might come over here to pick that bone—and end up picking our bones.

"Alkalurops takes care of its own. We don't ask anyone to take care of us, and we sure don't take care of anyone else. I say take this off-world proposal and stuff it up his off-world ass." The room erupted in cheers, just as Grace had hoped it would. She stood there, enjoying for a moment the rush that came from knowing she was doing right and a slew of people agreed with her. It was a good five minutes before Garry even tried to hammer the room to silence. But as he did hammer, she waved down the ruckus, and the room went back to quiet.

"I guess that shows a pretty solid majority supporting you," Garry said. "Can I ask a few questions about your proposal?"

"Yes," Grace said.

"Make damn sure they're questions," came from down the table, "or we may just march up there and give her that gavel." That got the hall rumbling. Grace waved them to quiet, and most did.

"Thank you, Grace," Garry said, sounding as though he meant it. "My question is, how do we defend ourselves? Our Legate's dead. Most ranking Constabulary officers didn't survive the raid."

"We got our butts kicked," came from the foot of the table.

"Not to put too fine a point on it," Garry said, "but we did get our butts kicked. I haven't heard—how did the militia do around Falkirk? Did you call it out?"

"I led it," Grace said, "and we got our butts kicked."

"I'm sorry to hear that. I thought that with you saying we should defend ourselves, you might have been more successful."

"No, Garry," Grace admitted. "If there hadn't been

a hill to our rear, we'd have been massacred like everyone else. We were lucky."

"So, are you planning on all of us getting lucky like you next time?" Dev shot at her.

Garry shushed his friend, but then looked at Grace. "He does have a point. How are we supposed to defend ourselves?"

Grace took a moment to organize her thoughts, but the experience of talking Falkirk's town meeting through this had been solid preparation. "I don't know about the rest of you, but when I need something I don't have—equipment, skills, whatever—I hire it. We haven't needed fighting skills, so we don't have any. There are those who do. I say we hire them. Hire them to teach us how to take care of ourselves, and to fight side by side with us."

"You think you can do that?" asked Garry. A sincere question this time.

"I was on my way to the merc camps on Galatea when I stopped in here. Falkirk is for sending a team to Galatea. Have them look over the mercenary units there and hire a cadre to train us and fight alongside us."

"I don't know if that's the way the mercs work," Garry said.

"Maybe they didn't before, but then, we didn't used to have raiders dropping in. Times are changing. I'll find mercs who are ready to change with the times and train us to protect ourselves."

"Aren't BattleMechs different from our IndustrialMechs?" came from the Guild Master for 'Mech Sales and Service.

"Yes. We captured a hovertank at Falkirk," Grace began.

"You captured a hovertank," ran through the hall. At her side even Garry muttered it.

"Yes, the Navajo set traps," she said, indicating Chato beside her, "and caught a hovertank. The thing had armor tougher than anything we have, and it had sensors that go way beyond what any of us had ever seen. Nobody said taking care of ourselves was simple or easy. But we've been doing it for hundreds of years. Let's not stop now."

Garry nodded, then spoke into the quiet. "Not to sound unwilling, but I have to ask you the same question you asked Mr. Santorini. What will this cost us?"

"And to quote him, this doesn't come cheap. The major land owners around Falkirk promised to ante up ten percent of last year's profits."

And so began the hard part. Negotiations took the rest of the day and most of the night, but the next morning, when Grace, Chato and Jobe checked out of the hostel and drove out to the spaceport, she felt good. Not everyone had anted up, but a lot of money would be coming in.

As they turned toward the port after the long climb up West Canyon Road, Jim Wilson buzzed her on the Net. "Can you meet me at that hamburger joint along Spaceport Road?" he requested.

"You didn't think I was going to let one of my trucks sit in the parking lot for the months you were gone?" he said as Jobe parked the rig next to where Wilson stood with his son.

"I couldn't see you paying the bill for that," Grace shot back as she got out. "I figured I'd see you before I left."

"And you were going off-planet with just the change in your pocket?" Wilson said, raising an eyebrow. "How are you set for cash?"

Grace wasn't broke, but she had been wondering how her credit would hold up on a long trip, what with the HPG breakdown.

"I should be able to get by," she told him.

"Good, then maybe you won't have to use this," he said, producing a smart card. "This is paid in advance and issued by the First Bank of Galatea. My old man set up a couple of these on planets we did business with. I don't think he trusted the HPG. Me, I figured he was just old-fashioned. This ought to cover the personal bills for all three of you."

"I can't take that," Grace said.

"I hope you don't say that to everything I brought," Wilson said, " 'cause not all of it's mine. Here's a gift from the folks along the Donga River." He pulled out a small bag and tossed it to Jobe, who emptied it into his hand. A small fortune in cut diamonds poured out.

"Good lord," Grace said.

"Very good," Jobe said. "I will thank my senior wife for doing as she promised she would."

"Huh?" Grace got out.

"Ghome said she would get donations so we could pay soldiers to defend us, soldiers to protect us." Jobe smiled. "She told me that before I left. I told her it would not be necessary. We warriors could stand against mere raiders. You can see what she thinks of me."

"Sound more like she wants you home," Grace said.

"That would not be Ghome. Maybe Bhana, my second wife, but not Ghome."

"What do you have from White River?" Chato asked. A second sack spilled jade, turquoise and emeralds. "Good; very good. My sister did not let us be shamed among the others."

"Was I the only one who didn't plan on buying mercs until I got my butt kicked?" Grace asked the sky.

"Include me in that fine company," Wilson said.

"It's been a long time," Jobe said, "since you Irish, you Scots, went roaming on Terra, but still you walk as if nothing can defeat you. Some of us remember what it was like to be among your defeated. Now we fight side by side, but sometimes it is better to remember that you can lose. Is that not so, Chato?"

"We still sing the old songs around the winter campfires. You stay inside and watch your vids too much."

Wilson shook his head. "Well, as much as I hate to admit it, there's also Navajo and Donga River jewelry in the truck, enough to fill a strongbox. I've collected money from folks around Falkirk—enough to help with the first few months of the contract. I'm buying a major chunk of the hydrocarbons in the cargo of this DropShip. Even if the credit system is bonkers, you won't be without some serious cash once this cargo is sold on Galatea."

"Thanks for the help."

"I've been following the goings-on at the Guild Hall for the last two days. I'd say I had the easy job. Take care out there among all those off-worlders."

"Strange how that works, Jim," said Grace. "You go to some other planet and it's full of off-worlders."

"Chato, Jobe, Grace, you all take care," Wilson said, offering his hand. His son stood beside him, a newer copy of what life was like on Alkalurops.

This is worth fighting for, Grace told herself. *I will find a way to defend what is ours.*

3

The *Star of Dyev* was the kind of tramp DropShip that bothered to stop at planets like Alkalurops. Tramp ships had cargo holds, crew quarters and maybe some spare cabins for passengers. *Star of Dyev* had only one spare, so Grace would have to share tight quarters with Jobe and Chato.

"Too bad I did not bring my second wife," Jobe said. "This could have been a fun time."

"I thought your second wife was the one who talked too much and argued even more," Grace said.

"Yes, she does that. But she can be very nice when she chooses to be," he recalled with a sigh.

Chato handed him a reader. "I downloaded everything about 'Mechs, battles and the old wars on Alka-lurops. Most of it is political commentary, but there are a few schematics and tech readouts. Maybe if we put our heads together, we can make sense of what's been written."

"Warriors who survive battles have nothing but boasts," Jobe said.

"At least they survived," Chato pointed out.

"Gentlemen, we're stuck in this tin can for the next month," Grace reminded them. "Let's not kill one another too early. I understand the crew has set up a pool on who dies first and how soon."

"That is inconsiderate of them," Jobe said.

"I thought you would bet on anything," Chato said.

"Yes. That is what I mean. It is most inconsiderate of them not to offer us a chance to join the pool."

"Scan your reader," Grace said, ducking into her bunk.

Liftoff was noisy and heavy. The trip out was at a solid 1G acceleration. That was fine, but the company! What was it with men? They made the cabin unbearable! At first she joked about the betting pool, but after two weeks, she was ready to start her own by asking the crew to come up with creative new ways for her two companions to kill each other. Grace took to long walks in the cargo hold to read about war and avoid the warring men.

But the information in the reader left her more frustrated. Most of the histories were just glosses: Someone did this; someone else did that; someone won because of this other factor, which left Grace wondering if battle leaders really controlled what caused them to win. Other accounts about a great man's BattleMech were so technically detailed that Grace could not tell what was going on. She'd pushed a MiningMech most of her adult life, and Jobe had done the same for either an Agro or MiningMech as well, but neither of them could figure out how these

MechWarriors handled their machines. Was driving a BattleMech all that different from driving Pirate?

Grace felt as if she was trying to understand mining operations by reading one of the journals she subscribed to. Yes, she learned a lot from them, but if Pop hadn't spent years teaching her everything he knew and her mom hadn't insisted she sit her young butt down and learn all the basic stuff, most of it would have gone right over her head, the way this was.

"Who can teach me the basics?" she asked the huge gray hydrocarbon tank she was sitting under. It had no answer.

Spacesick, Grace watched on the mess deck screen as the *Star of Dyev* buried itself in a docking collar of the JumpShip *Brandon's Leviathan,* also known as "Big Lug." They were thirty-seven days out from Allabad: twenty-eight days climbing to this jump point at 1G, then twiddling their weightless thumbs for nine days waiting for a JumpShip to come by. JumpShips running between important points like Terra or Skye kept to schedules. Ships to out-of-the-way places like Alkalurops maintained a looser schedule. This one had been delayed four jumps back, waiting for a business deal to go down. The story around the *Dyev* was that the Big Lug would be back on schedule in another nine jumps. Until then DropShips could just drift and passengers puke. Maybe the reputed stink of Alkalurops' air wasn't the only reason big companies went elsewhere; the erratic JumpShip schedule was a real deterrent. If LCI moved its headquarters here, that might change. And that would probably lead to a whole lot of other changes.

Grace didn't much care for all that change.

Nine days later Big Lug's jump sail was recharged and Grace was up on all the news of the Sphere. She knew who had divorced whom on what thrilling vid. She knew what important people had been found sleeping in the wrong beds. Oh, and there seemed to have been a big fight on Terra. Specifics on that one would have required paying for some talking head's opinion. Grace saved her money. That even ancient Terra was the scene of fighting was all she needed to know. Things were bad all over. Sick of waiting, if not sick of weightlessness, Grace, Chato and Jobe were in their tiny cabin, waiting for the jump.

A knock at the door was followed a second later by a spacer sailing his weightless body in. "Cap'n wants you to take some sleeping pills. Jumpsickness can be a real mess. People who sleep through it are better off," he said, handing pills all around and a bulb of water.

Chato and Jobe dutifully took their meds, but Grace just smiled nicely, palmed the pill, and took a long swig of water. As a rule, she did not take any pill until she read the full list of possible side effects. But being a woman, she knew how to smile and let a man think he had won.

Besides, she'd heard that jumps gave the best hallucinations this side of banned drugs. Be nice to see them legally.

Grace kept her eyes closed as the countdown to jump reached zero. The men snored noisily as she'd discovered they always did. She felt a lurch, got a minor aurora show on the inside of her eyelids, and seemed to be pushed against the restraints holding her to the bunk. Nothing much else. She wondered who she could talk to about getting her money back.

There was a jiggle at the cabin's lock, and the door opened on its noisy hinges. Grace started to look, but something about the way the hairs were standing up on the back of her neck told her that lying still was the better option. Sneakers scraped on a wall as someone pushed off. She heard a thump as that same someone hit her locker. When a key started jiggling in its lock, she slit her eyes open. The spacer who had given them the pills was going through her underwear drawer. He lifted the sack of diamonds with a happy sigh.

"What the hell are you doing?" Grace demanded.

"Huh," was the only answer she got as the guy grabbed the other sack and pushed off for the door. Grace hit the quick-release on her bunk harness and lunged for him. He batted her away, and she bounced off the wall screaming, "Stop, thief!"

The guys slept through it all. "Sleeping pill in a pig's eye," Grace said as she steadied herself and discovered her inner ear really had taken a couple of rolls during the jump. Reeling, she pushed for the door and spotted the spacer headed aft. "Stop! Somebody get that spacer!" she shouted and took off after him, not nearly as quickly as she wanted to.

Her pursuit consisted of bouncing from one side of the hall—or as the spacers called it, passageway—to the other wall, or bulkhead. Damn—why did every Guild have to have its own set of words for the same stuff? "Stop, thief!" meant the same thing everywhere, so she kept shouting it as the guy went through the bulkhead at the end of the hall, closed the hatch, and dogged it.

A voice came from the speaker above the hatch. "What's all this ruckus?"

"That spacer just stole my diamond collection!" Grace yelled, stumbling up to the hatch and starting to work it.

"What spacer?"

"The one the captain sent to give us sleeping pills."

"I did no such thing," came a new voice. "What spacer did this?"

"I don't know. He didn't have a name on his shirt," Grace said, bracing herself and pulling the hatch open. A heavy wrench sailed through the hatch, missing her by only a centimeter. "He also just tried to kill me," she added.

"Ship's Sergeant at Arms, take anyone not essential

to moving ship and settle this. Where's all this happening?"

Grace glanced around—speaker but no camera. She read the numbers off the hatch to the captain.

"He's heading into the cargo holds," the captain said.

"And I'm following," Grace said, snatching the wrench out of the air.

"It's dangerous in there, young woman."

Lord, another old man. "I jogged around in there on the way up here. I probably know the *Dyev*'s cargo holds as well as anyone." And she was there and they weren't. She went.

Jogging in a vast space full of pipes, machinery and narrow walkways was one thing. Coasting from one handhold to another while searching for a man who'd tried to bash her brains out was something else entirely. Grace moved cautiously.

A computer voice began announcing the minutes until the ship would put on acceleration. "That's weight for you ground types," a man's voice added.

The thief was moving quickly, but he was noisy. Grace could hear him inside the space of huge tank ends, ice-caked compressors and pipe after pipe— some hot, some cold, most dangerous. She went as quickly as caution allowed, searching for the next handhold before launching from the last. The chase could kill her as dead as the hunted. Ahead of her, the man quit making noise. Grace paused at her handhold.

Behind her, some crew members—five, Grace estimated—were complaining about their assignment as they moved with the fast efficiency of those experienced in micro-G. A man with an impressive beer gut and two chevrons with crossed pistols on his collar caught up with Grace.

"You the woman what lost her jewels?"

The other men snickered at the joke.

"If your captain doesn't want to pay out a small fortune, you're the ones who are going to find them."

Grace smiled, showing teeth and the hard face she used when a new work crew wondered why they were taking orders from a woman.

"Yes, ma'am," the guy in charge answered, not looking her in the eye. "Abe, you and Bo cover the right. Den and Jess, take the left. This nice woman and I will cover the walkway."

"Okay," "Yeah" and a "Yes, sir" from the youngest followed as the men split up.

"He got quiet about the time you fellows started chattering along this metal sidewalk," Grace said, intentionally calling things what she wanted.

"How far ahead was he?" the Sergeant at Arms asked, pulling a sonic stunner from his back pocket.

"Hard to tell." Grace glanced around at the huge spheres that held liquid gas or chilled oil. "I'd say about two bays farther up. Don't you have a pistol?"

"Woman, no one in their right mind uses a slug thrower in here. Some of those tanks have liquid gas at a thousand psi. You ding one of them and this whole bay would be filled with gas slush in, what, ten seconds. You'd be an icicle before you could turn around."

"He know that?" Grace said, nodding toward the thief ahead.

"If it's the mess boy what I think it is, no, but I checked his bag when he came off leave and there weren't no pistol."

"Seen any sleeping pills?"

The man glanced away. "The *Star of Dyev*'s a drug-free ship. We don't keep crew who do drugs."

But for the right price, you'll look the other way, won't you, Grace thought.

"There he goes!" someone below them shouted as the thief broke from behind an ice-covered compressor, going hand over hand along the metal walkway. Now four men howled at his heels.

"That's Iav," the Master at Arms shouted. "Iav, give it up! We've got you!"

The boy kept going. Grace made a note of the number 38 that was written above the compressor the kid had hidden behind. He might have ditched the diamonds. She pushed off in chase right about the time the computer voice said, "Acceleration in zero minutes," and went crashing down as 1G was restored.

The spacers found her yelp of pain hilarious. Her only consolation was that Iav fared no better.

But for five minutes more the boy fled farther aft. "Boy, you ain't going into reactor country—not if you ever want kids, you ain't," the Sergeant at Arms taunted him. The thief hooked a right, and they found him huddled behind a compressor, trembling from exhaustion. Maybe from fear.

"Come on out, boy. You got no place else to run."

"You were supposed to be asleep," the young man whined at Grace. "The other guys were."

"I don't follow instructions very well," Grace said gently. "Toss the diamonds out, and I'll talk to the captain for you." Grace didn't really mind what happened to the kid once she got her trading stock back.

A shot rang out. More like a pop, but there was no missing the slug's wind as it shot past Grace's ear too damn close.

"What the hell—" the Sergeant at Arms yelled.

The young thief was looking down at the bag of jewels he'd been about to throw to Grace. His eyes grew wide as he took in the hole in his chest and fell back against a pressure vessel before collapsing on the walkway. The sacks of jewels fell from his hands, clattering as they fell to the machinery below. Grace could hear the small tinkling of jewels spilling free. She had a hunt ahead of her. Wonder how many of the diamonds will end up in other hands?

Turning, Grace faced the shooter. The Sergeant at Arms' face was purple, his mouth was open, but no words were coming out.

"Hello. Mr. Santee, is it?" Grace said, intentionally mangling the name.

"Alfred Santorini," the shooter corrected her. "At your service."

"You seem to have shot an unarmed man," Grace said.

"I thought he was about to throw explosives at us," Santorini said, with almost enough sincerity to convince a well-bribed judge.

"I'll get the boys hunting for what he dropped, ma'am," the Sergeant at Arms said, apparently more than happy to leave this conversation.

"I posted an inventory, complete with photos of each jewel, with the purser when I came aboard," Grace informed the Sergeant at Arms. "The diamonds are also numbered. You might mention that to your crew."

"Right about the diamonds," he said. Which said nothing about the jade, turquoise and emeralds. But with luck, she'd at least cut her losses.

"I didn't know you were aboard," Grace said, turning her attention to the man who'd destroyed her chance to find out who had come up with the idea of the theft and provided the drugs to pull it off.

"I came aboard at the last moment. Since my business proposal did not appear to meet your planet's needs, it seemed senseless to waste any more of my time there."

"And I never saw you in the mess?"

"I rented the captain's cabin," Santorini said lightly, "the better to get some work done on this enforced break. I take my meals in my cabin."

"That poor young man wouldn't happen to be the one who brought you your meals?" Grace said, nodding at the body being bagged by two of the crew.

"I really wouldn't know. A mess steward is hardly the type of person I bother myself with. Do you know the name of the last waitress who touched your life?"

Grace ignored the question as she leaned over the rail, watching as spacers used hand vacuums to scour the equipment for wayward jewels. Santorini didn't offer an explanation as to how he'd come to join in the chase for the thief. No doubt he would have just as empty an alibi. Grace wasn't sure she could stomach any more of his transparent lies.

"Are you going to Galatea?" she asked his retreating back.

"I have no business there." He paused for a moment to glance back. "I will transfer to another JumpShip immediately for transport to Nusakan. Your mad idea has cost me time and money. I have no more to waste on a backwater like Alkalurops. There are many other planets standing in line for an offer as fine as mine. I wish you luck finding mercs willing to help you."

"And I wish you the same luck," Grace said, keeping her face straight. For a moment the mask he wore wavered, and for a moment Grace thought she might get a look inside the man, but he turned away and quickly made his way out.

The Sergeant at Arms presented Grace with the two sacks the thief had dropped as he died. Both were about half the weight she remembered. "Keep hunting," she said, "there's a lot more down there."

An hour later the Sergeant at Arms stood by as each of the hand vacs was emptied in Grace's presence. The diamond sack now felt over three-quarters of its former weight. The other sack was a bit lighter than that. "We'll keep looking, ma'am. The kid could have dropped some as he ran."

"Possibly," Grace agreed, then opened the emerald sack. "Would you take your pick, sir? You've led a good hunt and deserve a reward."

"Why, thank you, ma'am. There's no call for this."

"Yes, but you have helped me, and I pay for what people give me. Take your pick, and I will register you as the owner with the captain." He didn't quibble with her twice but picked the largest emerald in the sack. Grace didn't bat an eyelash. He probably had no idea he'd passed up several more perfect stones for that less valuable one.

"And line up your work crew. Each one gets a stone from me." That didn't take very long, and Grace noticed two fellows who seemed a bit shamefaced at her largesse. She was not surprised when the Sergeant at Arms handed her a dozen more diamonds that seemed to have gotten "hung up in the hand vacs."

Two hours later Chato and Jobe came out of their enforced sleep, begging for water. "Land and Sky, I don't want to do another jump like that," Chato breathed.

"You won't. Next time you skip the drugs," Grace said, and then brought them up to date.

"Dead," Jobe said, "and that one walks among us."

"Or stays in the captain's cabin, busy with planning," Grace corrected.

"May his plans keep him far away from us," Chato said.

Nine days later the *Dyev* grounded at Galaport. Grace had hidden the loose jewels in the seams of her clothing. Her mom had always insisted that sewing would come in handy. Jobe converted the strongbox to a backpack, and the rest of their gear was packed in two duffels, which Grace and Chato could handle.

This port was large, busy, dirty and noisy. Grace led the way, Jobe beside her. Chato followed, keeping an eye on Jobe's backpack. As they rode an underground walkway toward the central terminal, Grace tried to get her bearings. She'd never seen so many people in so small a place. They were moving in every conceivable direction, but purposefully. Electric trucks and Loader-'Mechs shared the space, choreographing a dance in which one misstep could leave someone a puddle on the floor.

"This place smells bad," Jobe said. The blend of

ozone, oil, sweat and other odors Grace could not identify left her wondering how anyone could say Alkalurops' air smelled bad. They passed a men's room that was backed up and gushing water and noxious smells.

"Bad, and not just the smell," Grace said. The place needed paint. Tiles were off the walls. The driveway beside the slidewalk had potholes in it, and the slidewalk moved with enough fits and starts to make her stomach queasy.

"If I never leave White River again, it will be too soon," Chato muttered. "This headman business is not what my sister told me it would be."

"You should tell your women what to do, not let them tell you," Jobe shot back.

"And you think you are running the Donga River Valley, not your wives, huh?" the Navajo said, the slightest hint of a smile curling his lips. "Tell me again why you are here with us and not with one of your willing wives?"

Grace let the men retreat into their familiar banter as the slidewalk dropped them at the main terminal. She hefted her duffel and made herself a promise not to be run over by bigger traffic. There wasn't a risk. While the slidewalk ended in an immense room with a glass ceiling that made it hard to see where the dirty glass ended and a dusty sky began, heavy traffic was shunted to an underpass to the floors below.

Grace began the trek to the doors with overhead flashing EXIT signs. Around her were men and women, hard of muscle, hard of face, booted and dressed in shades of military tan and green. They talked in clipped sentences and the words "rally point" ended most of them.

"Light Horse, fall in here," came in a voice that carried through the babble. It wasn't so much volume but a hard edge to the words that let them cut through every other sound.

Around Grace, several people stopped, turned to

locate the order-giver, and marched in step for him. Not all.

"No, man, you don't what to be one of those horse's asses," someone near Grace said. "There's bound to be a Highlander recruiter around after that big fight on Terra."

"Oh, so I'm going to war in a skirt?" a young man responded. "No thanks."

"Ya like to live dangerously, don't ya, boy?"

"I like to ride where I'm going. There's the recruiting sergeant for the Twenty-first Centauri Lancers. That's the man for me."

Now the vast room began to make sense to Grace. Along the wall behind her were ticketing agents. In front of her were small groups of men and women eyeing a couple dozen others, some with banners— guidons, if she guessed right from her reading. Some she recognized. The plaid of the Highlanders, displayed in the kilts of their recruiters, was impossible to miss. Similarly, the ax of Bannson's Raiders was unmistakable. Other outfits were harder to place, or their emblem too stylized to recognize. What was clear was that they wanted fighters and they were none too picky.

One man caught Grace's eye. Standing alone and tall in flowing, if somewhat tattered robes, he scanned the crowd with his right hand resting lightly on the pommel of the long sword that hung from his left hip. Other than the slight turning of his head from side to side, he did not move for the entire time Grace studied him. Most gave him a wide berth. One man stomped up to him, bowed at the waist, then took station behind him without speaking a word. Now the two of them stood like statues, studying the crowd.

"That one looks like a hard case," Jobe muttered.

"Anyone have a plan for us?" Chato asked.

"I'm thinking," Grace said as they came to the end of the row of recruiters, where two men in tan uniforms stood in that kind of relaxed stance as only powerful men can. They were talking to each other, but the taller and older one's eyes missed nothing. He cracked a smile as he took in Grace and her companions.

"Only the best make it this far," he said, extending a hand.

"We haven't made up our minds," Grace said, taking it. The handshake was firm—maybe a bit of a test. She squeezed just a tad more than he did. Unlike some insecure men, he didn't turn the handshake into a contest to see if he had a tighter grip than a woman. She liked that.

"Well, you've come to the Roughriders—one of the best and longest-surviving merc units in the Sphere. We train hard, we fight rough, and we win every time."

"That sounds like a good unit," Jobe said.

"To join," Grace added quickly, smiling back at the men to keep them from saying more.

"I'm Sergeant Major Tanuso, this is Sergeant Godfrey, formerly of armor, now of our infantry," he said as if rubbing an extra dash of salt in a fresh wound. "He will take you to our van while I see if there are any more top-notch candidates among the DropShips today."

"Yes, sir, Sergeant Major, sir," the Staff Sergeant said as he led the three away. Out of Tanuso's earshot he added, "And I'll be grinding you crunchies into the dust just as soon as I earn a tank back."

"You prefer armor to infantry?" Jobe asked.

"I prefer riding to walking," Godfrey replied.

"It is also good to walk good earth," Chato said.

"Not when artillery is digging it up and throwing it in your face." The sergeant grinned. "And you?" he asked Grace.

" 'Mechs, I believe."

"Any experience?"

"Industrial," Grace said. "Me and Jobe both."

"It's a big jump from those low-powered Indi walkers to real BattleMechs, though we've got a few 'Mech MODs ourselves."

Grace said nothing. The van was in the middle of the parking lot, baking under the distant sun. Grace was sweating before she got there, and found the van a furnace. "I'll get the air-conditioning going," the sergeant said, starting the engines. "Nothing too good for a Roughrider recruit—I mean, candidate." Grace suspected that once they were away from the port, nothing was what a recruit would get.

The Sergeant Major showed up a half hour later with four more "candidates" whom Grace would not have taken on as mining apprentices. They looked tough, but they had that brittleness that she'd come to notice in "tough" men. They set up a chatter in the middle of the van that covered a low question from Jobe.

"What are we doing here?"

"We want to look at mercs. This ought to get us out where we can see some. You want to pay for the privilege?"

"Hope this doesn't cause any trouble."

"At ease back there," the Sergeant Major growled. "If I want to hear something from you, I'll tell you what to say. And Sergeant, turn off that damn air-conditioning. You trying to turn these candidates into weenies?"

"No, sir, Sergeant Major, sir."

The tough guys shut up, and everyone started to sweat. Grace glanced out the window. Yep, they were leaving the city and heading out into country still barren from the last war—maybe the last three wars. *Okay, tough guys, let's see if any of you want to get out and walk back,* she thought. Nope, the guys stayed quiet as pink-nosed bunnies hiding in tall grass.

The camp entrance was easy to spot; guards waved them through an arch announcing HANSON'S ROUGHRIDERS, THE TOUGHEST OF THE BEST. They parked at the recruit barracks, a whitewashed adobe building. The Staff Sergeant was quickly out of the van, yelling at the recruits—no candidates now—to get off their duffs and start moving like they wanted to be Roughriders. The boys tumbled over themselves trying to get out fastest. Chato waited until the door wasn't blocked, then moved with smooth speed to exit, with Jobe right behind him and Grace on Jobe's tail.

"What took you so long?" the Staff Sergeant bellowed. "Give me fifty." The boys dropped.

Jobe stepped forward. "I'll give you fifty more than you can do," he challenged the Staff Sergeant.

The Sergeant Major stood like a statue, his arms behind his back, only his eyes moving. Grace joined him.

"You want to be a MechWarrior," he said through tight lips.

"I've fought my 'Mech, Sergeant Major. May I clarify? I am Grace O'Malley of Alkalurops, and my colleagues and I are here to hire mercs."

"Alkalurops," the Staff Sergeant echoed.

"You heard the man, Sergeant Godfrey," Sergeant Major growled. "He'll give you fifty more push-ups than you give him. Assume the position. And who told you tourists to stop and gawk? You will give the Staff Sergeant one push-up for every one he gives this potential employer." The kids groaned, but went back to bending and raising as Jobe and the Staff Sergeant did their guy thing. *God, I'm glad I wasn't born with one of those things between my legs,* Grace thought for the millionth time.

The Sergeant Major watched the proceedings, sweat darkening his tan uniform. Grace and Chato stood beside him, sweating as well. After the count reached three hundred, and two of the "tough" guys had collapsed on their faces, the Sergeant Major removed a com device from his belt. "Major Hanson, we have three potential clients at the recruit barracks. I thought you might want to deal with them. They're from Alkalurops."

4

Roughrider Base Camp, Galatea
Prefecture VIII, The Republic of the Sphere
26 May 3134; local summer

Major Loren J. Hanson was enjoying himself. He had a new promotion, a new staff job and responsibility for seeing that the forty-seven IndustrialMechs recently acquired by the regiment were properly modified. There were hints that he might get command of the new battalion being formed from them. Life was very good.

Then Topkick called and dropped a whole bushel of hot potatoes in his lap. No one else's lap. The Colonel seemed to be enjoying himself far more than L. J. thought senior officers should with their clothes on. "You *are* our leading expert on Alkalurops, Loren. Handle it."

"Yes, sir. Colonel, do we want a contract from them?"

"I'm not sure we could accept one. Your contract has an options clause on it. Client has two years to call it in. I don't see how we could accept any other contract involving that backwater for at least twenty more months."

"And I can make no reference to the existing contract. It has a gag clause covering the next twenty-five years, sir."

"So go find something else to talk about with her. I understand she's not unpleasant on the eyes."

L. J. saluted. "Yes, sir."

Halting his jeep at the recruit barracks, L. J. took in the scene. Sergeant Major Tanuso and two civilians stood in the sun. Someone had extended them the hospitality of the regiment in the form of large mugs of water. Staff Sergeant Godfrey and another civilian were doing push-ups, a bit slowly. When he heard "five hundred and fifty," he excused the sluggishness. Four recruits groveled in the dust, apparently overwhelmed by this display of athletic prowess.

"Atten-*hut!*" the Sergeant Major shouted on L. J.'s approach.

The recruits stumbled to their feet. The Staff Sergeant tried to do a smart conversion from his position to attention, but something in his gut didn't cooperate, and he ended half bent over, gripping his left side and trying to suppress a groan.

L. J. extended his hand to the woman. "I understand you are in the market for mercs. My colonel has asked me to introduce you to the Roughriders—the best force your money can buy. I'm Major Loren J. Hanson, at your service."

The woman, a few centimeters shorter than L. J., with the flaming red hair and creamy complexion that turned heads, accepted his handshake firmly. "I'm Grace O'Malley, mine owner, mayor of Falkirk and

representative of Alkalurops in negotiations for mercenaries to assist us in the defense of our planet."

Falkirk! Had he been trying to kill this woman a
couple of months ago? If so, she had returned the
compliment—very well, thank you. He forced his face
into a mask, showing nothing at this turn of events.
Topkick did raise an eyebrow. Godfrey made a face,
but in his condition, L. J. doubted anyone would
notice.

"If you and your associates will come with me, I'll
be glad to introduce you to what the Roughriders can
do for you. Sergeant Major, are you busy this
afternoon?"

"No, sir. Sergeant Godfrey can handle the recruit
situation."

Godfrey pulled himself up to full attention, struggled through a salute, and said, "Yes, sir," through
gritted teeth.

L. J. offered Grace the front passenger seat of his
jeep. The two unnamed men loaded their baggage in
the back. The backpack looked heavy for its size.
Were these people lugging around their wealth? He'd
never met hicks unwilling to trust a bank, but then,
Alkalurops had been an interesting assignment.

"It's getting on toward noon. Have you eaten?"
he asked.

"Ship's breakfast was a while back," Grace told
him.

"Why don't I take you for lunch at the Officers'
Club?" That seemed to go over fine with her and the
men in back.

"Sir, if you could just drop me off at HQ," Topkick
said, "you could pick me up after lunch."

"That would be fine, Sergeant Major."

L. J. dropped him off, waited until he was halfway
up the path outlined with white-painted rocks, then
said, "Oops, I should have mentioned something to
him. Just a moment."

A soft "Sergeant Major" got Tanuso to pause. "Print me out a cost sheet for a battalion. Add a fifty-percent surcharge, but don't let it show up on the sheet."

"Understood, sir. We don't want to encourage them."

"You got it, Sergeant Major."

As L. J. returned, the three cut short their conversation. "Isn't the sergeant allowed to eat with us?" Grace asked.

"The Officers' Club is open to me and my guests. Sergeant Major could be just as much of a guest as you will be. However, the regiment has a long tradition of officers dining with noncoms only under specific circumstances. Tradition is often what holds a regiment together. For Sergeant Major to share a meal with me today Just Is Not Done."

"I think I understand traditions," Grace said with an unreadable smile.

At the club, Grace asked him to order for them—none objected to T-bone steaks, baked potatoes and mixed vegetables. During the meal Grace talked of Galatea's hot weather and the ugliness of the war-ravaged land. Only when they were finished eating did she bring up her strong desire that Alkalurops avoid anything that might leave her planet similarly ravaged.

"Defense, yes, we need that. But we don't want to become a target like Galatea. Yet at the same time, we don't want to become a victim," Grace said, putting down her water glass. "In past wars, we defended ourselves. Today, defense seems to be a bit harder than it was for earlier generations."

L. J. studied the last of his steak. "Have you had some recent experience in defense?" For the next five minutes he listened as she gave him her view of the battle from the modified MiningMech that had opposed him. *A woman mine owner was giving me all that grief!* He kept that thought off his face as the Navajo, Chato Bluewater, described preparing the traps that caught his hovertank and damn near broke his *Koshi*'s leg. Maybe the Roughriders should pay more attention to combat engineers, he thought as he nodded to Chato. Then Grace explained what they had learned from the hovertank, which was not quite as disabled as he had been told.

"Yes," he said, nodding as Grace ended her story, "our sensors are calibrated to detect heat, metal concentrations and electronic activity kilometers ahead of our scouts. You can understand how much a professional military unit wants to avoid a trap."

"And how much a militia needs such ambushes if they are to have any chance of withstanding such attacks," Grace answered.

L. J. waved for the check, signed it over to the regiment's account and thought furiously. He still wasn't sure what kind of contract this woman wanted. Until he figured out what she meant by militia, a general introduction to what a professional merc unit brought to the battlefield seemed in order. With luck, he'd put enough fear of the Lord into this redheaded Fury that she'd fold her tent, give up any hope of fighting mercs, and meet the next batch of raiders with milk and cookies.

"Let me show you our 'Mech practice grounds. Even though only a select few command BattleMechs, we introduce all our infantry to them. You never can tell when you'll come across the occasional recruit with a natural knack for 'Mechs. Also, any infantry may be called up to close assault and capture disabled 'Mechs. We have mock-ups for assault practice, but they'll give you a feel for what you were facing. You don't know how lucky you were to have a mountain to—" L. J. bit off the "run away to," and chose a more professional "retrograde up." He had not seen this woman's temper and suspected it might be easier to dissuade her if he did not get her hackles up.

"We met some troops without our luck," Grace said as she settled into his jeep. The two men loaded them-

selves and their backpack into the rear. "Strange. The
raiders didn't stop to strip the bodies of personal
armor. I would think that they would," she said.
"What's your professional opinion?"

"I'm not trained as a raider, ma'am," he replied,
which was true. For the Alkalurops mission he'd had
to develop his own procedures. That was one of the
reasons he'd gotten the job. "None of us know anything about this kind of op," the Colonel had told
L. J. when he got the assignment. "Why don't you see
if you can figure it out."

L. J. chose his words carefully. Now was no time to
show too much knowledge of this raid. "From what
you say, I would guess it was thrown together at the
last moment. Used low-quality personnel"—Godfrey,
for example—"who were quite inexperienced with this
sort of thing. With the HPG down, there are many
reports of lawlessness. Pirates and bandits who were
small stuff in better times now try their hand at bigger
prizes. Planets with no professional force can't stop
them."

"Fortunately, they didn't have enough backup or
spare time to really strip us down," Grace muttered.
"What I can't figure out is how they killed the
Legate."

"I was wondering about that," L. J. risked. "You
didn't mention him in your battle critique. Why didn't
he fight?" L. J. had wondered about that when his
client's last report assured him that the Legate would
not interfere with the raid.

"Because he was bleeding out in bed," the large
black man, Jobe Kang, said, "his throat cut before
the raiders' DropShip touched down. Somebody on
Alkalurops was helping things along, killing him and
the Governor."

"Oh," L. J. said, and forced his face into neutral as
he drove them to the training field. His regiment had
not contracted for murder. All he had was a faceless

client's promise that the local government would not interfere with the raid. *Remind me not to do business with that man again,* L. J. said to himself. Killing a man in compliance with a contract entered into by his colonel was occasionally unavoidable when two BattleMechs met. Slitting a man's throat in bed— that was not something L. J. wanted to be associated with.

In the shade of the hangar, it was almost cool. "What 'Mech would you like to have a go at?" L. J. asked, pointing Grace at a dozen 'Mechs or mock-ups connected by supports and scaffolding.

"That short one," she said, pointing to a *Koshi* hulk. "If I wasn't fighting that one, I was fighting its sister."

"Very likely," L. J. said, taking her up two flights of stairs to the scaffolding that allowed access to the cockpits. "The *Koshi* is a light unit, good for scouting, and one of the less expensive to acquire or operate." There was a step down to the platform around its cockpit. "This unit is a hulk, so you're not feeling the heat one of these fusion power plants gives off. Your MiningMech uses a low-powered internal combustion engine, doesn't it?" The woman flinched at that observation.

"I never thought Pirate was low-powered, but is this for real?" she said, examining the painted wooden power readout. "What are these other things?"

L. J. knew a *Koshi* cockpit in the dark and blindfolded. "That power readout is a replica, but its values are real." He pointed out and named the targeting computer and the ammo supply gauge. Grace whistled in awe at the number of reloads. L. J. casually dismissed the sensor suit with, "These may not be what spotted you. The benefit of a combined-arms force is that we blend the strengths of 'Mechs, armor and infantry, using each for what it does best."

Grace swallowed hard, maybe more than a bit intimidated. "This monster was enough to keep me and another AgroMech running up the nearest hill. You train people to capture this thing. How could a single person do that?"

L. J. considered his options, and chose to apply the full power of the truth. "One person can't, but a team is another matter. See that hatch just above the knee?" Grace nodded. "It's locked and armored, but a close shot from a high-powered nine-millimeter slug can blast it open. Inside are the control wires for the lower legs. Yank them and the machine isn't going anywhere. Work your way up higher to that hatch on the back—the lower one. Blow it open and you can disconnect the controls to the missile launchers. Now he can't run and he can't shoot. Slap a sticky bomb on the back and give him a call on the emergency channel. If he doesn't pop the cockpit and come out, you blow the reactor and he's a very dead MechWarrior."

Grace shook her head. "Assuming his friends don't shoot you down while you're doing any of that."

L. J. chuckled. "That is the usual problem in an assault." While the redhead mulled that over, L. J. continued to overload her. "Would you like to refight your battle?" Few MechWarriors ever passed up a chance to go over a victory or a loss.

"I've heard you have simulators. Do you have one that could redo my battle?" Grace asked distractedly.

"Right this way." She was taking it hook, line and sinker.

He ushered her and her companions into the air-conditioned cool of the sim-lab. Inside, dozens of troopers were going about their business in the hushed tones usually reserved for a cathedral. L. J. waved at a line of gray boxes perched on stilts. Some were jerking about as if shaking drinks for a thirsty giant. "If you wanted to really refight your skirmish, we could strap you into those simulators. You'll feel everything you felt in the fight. Walk, jump, knock-down. All of it."

Grace shivered. "Did that once. Not hot to do it again."

"Everything?" Chato put in. "Heat from the reactor?"

"Of course," L. J. said. "Half the time I go by how hot my toes feel—hardly spare a glance at the systems temp." Turning back to the woman. "If you prefer, we can go over the battle on the holotable."

"That sounds better."

Most of the tables were occupied with 'Mech trainees reviewing their performance, or lack thereof. L. J. guided his guests to one that was free. "We do not have topo maps of Alkalurops in our training system." *But if you looked in my personal computer . . .* "Not exactly a place we expect to operate on."

"Use a flat plain with foothills rising off it," Grace said.

L. J. did, and a ghostly landscape appeared. She added a road with the familiar bend, then a couple of gullies running up the hill. Quickly she described his deployment. He ordered up the units she described and their ethereal images drove or marched across the map. Her own forces intrigued him. Two slightly modified AgroMechs to his left. Two probably over-armored MiningMechs to his right, and one Mining-Mech and an AgroMech with a hopped-up field burner in front of him. "We don't have computer images of these IndustrialMechs—certainly not ones with your irregular modifications," he told her. What he did not say was that his regiment's computer support contractor was busy remedying that deficiency and expected to make a small fortune if it could get that module to market first. He finished the deployment with a sprinkling of irregular infantry for her.

"Not a bad formation," he told her, meaning it. For an amateur it was a good start. "Then what happened?"

She described the crazy action on his right. L. J. was careful to do nothing she did not tell him, to add nothing to her battle critique. She got the tank's movements wrong; he went along until Chato corrected her. "So you tricked a tank driver into doing a nosedive into a gully just as his fire completely disrupted your left flank," L. J. noted.

"I guess so," Grace said, gnawing on her lower lip. "I was afraid the short 'Mech was going to chase after the miners on my left. That was when I tried to damage his leg and found out I really couldn't. Then things got bad when he noticed me," she said, shaking her head. Her eyes went vague as if focused on something far away and unpleasant. Not long past, either. And her dreams were probably lousy with this battle. Amateurs didn't know how to process the experience of battle. Too bad for her.

"Would you like to run the battle through the way it went, or maybe modify it? What if the tank had not been ditched?"

"No thank you, Major," Grace said. "I think you've shown me enough. While I might have had com links with all my people, still, they moved individually, and usually in retreat . . . or what did you call it? Retrograde."

"Correct."

"But the raiders moved as one, just the way their commander told them. Or would have, if Chato and Coyote had not thrown a wrench into their plan."

"Too true. Once your left broke, the tank would have swung around and pinched off the two center 'Mechs. Then the raiders would have had their pick of either of the other two pairs. Probably the ones on your left. I suspect those two would have just popped their cockpits and started running if they thought the raiders were after them."

"Right. McCallester and Brady are out of their depth organizing anything beyond a barroom brawl." Grace sighed.

"That is why mercs train recruits for a year. We want them to know in their sleep what to do when I issue an order. And they will do it, in their sleep or scared to death. This is also why, Ms. O'Malley, my colonel would be most unwilling to mix his Rough-riders with local militia. Our troops have to know they can trust the man on their right, the woman on their left. If we can't, we become no better than your showed-up-today militia or these raiders," he said, waving a hand dismissively at the effort that had won him his promotion.

"If we contracted to defend your planet, we would defend it. I doubt my colonel would accept a contract for less than one battalion plus a training cadre. That cadre would train your local troops, but they would train them our way—day and night for a year. I'm sorry, but we do not work with militias. We like to win, ma'am. Spread too thin, we'd be in the same mess you were in: waiting for someone stronger to come along and collect our gear."

The Sergeant Major appeared at his elbow, a piece of paper in one hand. L. J. glanced at it. Right. A battalion-sized task force: one company of 'Mechs, one of armor, two of infantry. Under the HQ company were platoon-sized elements of engineers, medical, supply, maintenance, communications and a section each of tube artillery and long-range missiles. There was a total cost for the battalion as well as individual prices for each unit.

"Very good, Sergeant Major. Ms. O'Malley, this is the unit I would suggest for defending a planet of your size from raiders. And the cost breakdown." He passed the paper to the redhead.

5

Roughrider Base Camp, Galatea
Prefecture VIII, The Republic of the Sphere
26 May 3134; local summer

Grace's thoughts spun like a rock cutter on stone it barely scarred. Pirates and bandits had sent the Falkirk militia reeling? This merc officer thought a bunch of thugs out for loot had kicked her butt, her and her folks who stood between their homes and a bunch of punks? *No! No way!*

Her enemy had turned into her trap without hesitation. They'd stormed up the hill after her miners and farmers, ignoring fire as only men trained for a year or more, as only men driven by a tradition that made them unhesitant in their obedience to orders. Grace had faced mercs all right. Damn good ones.

And now she was being presented with the cash price for such men. One glance at the paper and she almost dropped it. Behind her, Jobe whistled low. "Man of my men, mercs don't come cheap."

"Not at all cheap," Chato answered.

Grace had to move her finger slowly over the cost of the task force. Yes, there were that many zeros after the 32.

She focused on the cost of just one lance of Battle-Mechs like the one she'd fought and looked at today. The monthly rental for—No, she divided the cost by four and still got a figure way larger than her last year's profits!

"Is this some sort of joke?" she said, rounding on the Major. "There's no rational excuse for these prices. Or is this just an opening bid, because I'll tell you, mister, haggling is not something we waste time on back home."

"Neither do we," the Major said, so calm, so cool. He'd be like that under fire. "Those are the regimental rates."

"You'll fight what, one battle a year?"

"Yes, ma'am. You use your MiningMech every day. And we'll use our 'Mechs and tanks and infantry every day, sometimes every hour of every day. We train, day in and day out, because we never know when the day will come that we need that training. Do you think men and women advance on my order into fire just because I tell them to? No. They advance because I've ordered them to do it day after day. Every day is the same. Only one day, it's for real. So they do it by the numbers, just as if it were another training day. And that is why we win."

Left unsaid was, *And that is why you lost.*

He turned away, paused, then turned back and pointed his finger at her, sharp as any laser. "That is our price. You can come with me to talk to Accounts about posting bonds and other requirements of the Mercenary Review and Bonding Commission. If not, Sergeant Major will provide you a lift to the gate. If you want to think about it, come back any time. Have the guard at the gate call for Major L. J. Hanson, and I'll collect you. Have a good day," he said, then turned and marched for the exit.

Grace turned to face her associates, struggling to keep her chin from trembling. *Men never show emotions. Damned if I will.* She shook her head. Jobe pursed his lips for a moment, then shook his head, too. Chato turned to the Sergeant Major. "Where are you parked?" he asked, as calm as Grace had ever seen him.

"Outside. We should move along. People are waiting to use this table." The Sergeant Major escorted them out with what Grace was coming to expect as the usual merc efficiency. He deposited them at the gate in less than five minutes with a "Have a nice day" that was just as empty as his Major's.

"How do we get back to town?" Grace managed to get out as Jobe and Chato unloaded their gear.

"Don't know, ma'am," the Sergeant Major said. "Taxis don't come out this far. Bus comes by once a week, but you missed it."

"Don't your people ever leave?"

"We move in convoy on regimental transport when we travel on regimental business. When we grant a unit a pass, Transport sets up a shuttle van service."

"So we are on our own."

"We're still looking for recruits, ma'am," he said. He had the civility to not drive away until she turned her back on him.

"Heartless bunch of bastards," Jobe observed dryly.

"At their prices, they are rich, heartless bastards."

"I would not want to pay their medical bills," Chato said. "Did you notice the number of teachers in the computer center who were limping or missing an arm?"

"No, I was concentrating on that Hanson. On not letting him infuriate me," Grace said, picking up a duffel and checking the sun. It was still high. The road back to the main highway wavered in the heat. "We'd better see if we can catch a ride."

It took them an hour to get back to the main line, and Grace found herself regretting she'd left so much as a drop of water in her lunch goblet. Twice they were passed by Roughrider jeeps leaving the post. The hard-eyed women behind the wheels didn't afford them a glance as they whizzed by.

At the four-lane road there was plenty of traffic, but none of it slowed down for them. They started hiking toward town, looking for a bit of shade from the broiling sun. Low shrubs were all that had managed to grow out of the hard, cracked dirt.

"Might as well be concrete," Chato noted, scuffing the toe of his boot against the yellow hardpan beside the road. "When was this place attacked, a hundred years ago?"

"Space-based weapons burned the life out of this soil, down to the bedrock," Jobe said. "No way to treat a planet."

"I don't want Alkalurops looking like this five hundred years from now," Grace said. The others nodded.

The whine of a truck coming up behind them signaled that its brakes had begun to bleed air. "I do believe someone is stopping," Grace told her companions as the truck roared by, still slowing. It pulled off the road several hundred meters past them.

The driver leaned out the window. "Hurry up. I got a schedule to meet. You like it out here in this skillet?"

Despite the heat, they ran.

The truck was a big quattro-trailer. The cab was huge behind a rumbling motor that made Pirate's seem small. "You guys stow your gear in back and get comfortable on my bunk. Little lady, why don't you take this seat right next to me."

Grace took an immediate dislike to the big-bellied driver with his wandering eyes, but since the seat "right next to" him was almost two meters away, across the wide cab, it seemed safe. Chato and Jobe weren't that much farther away, and in the mood she was in, she almost hoped the guy would do something she could mash his skull for. *Not a good day,* she admitted to herself.

"There's water in the cooler back there," the driver said as he concentrated on getting his rig back in motion. "You folks look like you could use a couple of gallons. Must be hot out there." He laughed and jacked up the air-conditioning enough to make Grace shiver. "I could turn the AC off. Then you wouldn't need all those clothes, little missy."

"I'm quite comfortable," Grace assured him, pulling her thin sweater tighter around her.

"Just that some women, grateful for a ride in this out-of-the-way place, like to show a driver their appreciation."

"See how grateful I am in Galaport," Grace said, swallowing her first dozen replies. She didn't want the man to dump them out here; from the looks of all the options that had passed them, the milk of human kindness didn't run deep in this desert.

He leered at her as the rig put on more speed, forcing her deeper into her chair. "You might want to put on that seat belt, little lady. Wouldn't want you hurt if I have to swerve out of some idiot's way." He was belted in with five-point restraint.

Grace eyed the harness on her chair. It was the same. She'd seen vids where off-world people kidnapped strangers by locking them in a harness. "I'll take my chances on your good driving record."

That brought a hack of a laugh, and he regaled her with a list of near misses that would terrify a battle-hardened merc. So she swapped him tales from the mines. They spent the next hour one-upping each other. When signs of life started dotting the side of the road, the trucker asked where they were staying. "Don't have a place," Grace admitted.

"Well, I got to drop off these four loads. No reason why you and your fellows need sit around while I do. I know a decent place. Not on my route, mind you, but I can drop you off close."

Grace and the others accepted his offer and got out when he pulled up at a stoplight. "Three blocks thataway—Hillman's Last Stand. Can't miss it. Tell 'em to clean up a room for me."

"Will do," Grace said, and added to herself, *In my nightmares.*

Three blocks down, Hillman's Last Stand took up a block. Grace didn't much care for the looks of the couples entering. "I suspect they rent by the hour. Maybe the minute," Jobe said.

"Guys, why don't we look for someplace else farther down the road. Anyone opposed to the walk?" Neither was.

The Hilltop Refuge at least looked better. Cleaner, too, on the outside. Grace and her crew were the only ones checking in at the moment, but no pimps or streetwalkers appeared to be in evidence.

"We want two rooms," she told the desk clerk.

"Good, 'cause we don't rents singles to threesomes. We ain't that kind of place, if youse knows what I mean. Youse do wants the single, don't you?"

"Yes," Grace agreed. "Does it have a bath or a shower?"

"Shower. The water's metered. Pays for it by the liter."

Grace sighed. She started to produce Wilson's smart card, then reconsidered and found a free diamond rolling in her pocket. "Can I pay for the room with this?"

"No way." The clerk shook his head. " 'Stones or the road,' the boss tells me. The door's thataways."

"No problem," Grace said, producing the smart card.

The clerk ran it through, then frowned. "Ain't nobody's been usin' that card for a while."

"An old family heirloom, given to me by a trusted friend."

The clerk whistled. "Must trust youse a lots," he said as he passed her the bill to sign. "Two nights minimum stay. You wants to stay longer, we gots weekly rates."

"I'll tell you tomorrow," Grace said, signing.

"Don't get no rebates," he warned, handing her two key cards and pointing at the elevator.

An hour later, showered and feeling really clean for the first time since hearing raiders were in Allabad, Grace knocked on the men's door. Jobe opened it into a room no larger than her own. Brown on brown on brown decor helped to hide the dust, dirt, and rocks the cleaning people had missed. Grace had found dirty underwear in one of her drawers. "Anyone else hungry?"

Jobe stepped right out. Chato followed, the pack on his back. After wandering several blocks and passing up places that looked too greasy, too expensive or both, they settled on a place that promised DINNER LIKE MOM USED TO MAKE.

"Mom must have been trying to poison Dad," Jobe muttered as they left an hour later, half their dinners still on their plates, the other half indigestible in their guts. "My first wife is no cook, but even she treats a man's belly better than that."

The night was dark, and no moon was visible through the thick haze. They walked under streetlights that gave flickering light or none at all. Halfway back to the hotel, three men stepped from between parked trucks to bar their way. A half-dozen sauntered out of an alley that had appeared empty a moment before. Jobe wordlessly edged Grace back to the brick wall of a building.

Knives, clubs and chains showed in the solid front forming in front of Grace. She reached into a pocket and tapped her 'puter, but got only static where the Net should have been. Jammed. "Should have brought my walking stick," Chato said, shrugging off the pack and making ready to swing it. Jobe slid off his wide leather belt with its heavy copper buckle. Grace pulled her steel comb from her hip pocket, then inverted it so the sharp handle point was out.

"That's all you gots? This is gonna be fun." Someone laughed, then shouted, "Take 'em!"

The attackers came in one rush. Beside Grace, Jobe took a swipe at the closest with his belt, connecting enough to make the guy curse, then slammed him with a leather-clad fist on the return, but danced back to the wall to avoid a swinging chain.

Grace stepped into one oncoming thug and got his attention with her comb. He came up short in a hurry, falling back into the arms of a guy making ready to swing a nail-studded club. The two went down in a ball, but Grace was too busy deflecting a knife blade with her comb to take any advantage.

When she backpedaled to the wall, three guys were down in front of Chato. That heavy pack was doing a job. But now there were *ten* attackers in front of them. "Do it right this time, you guys, so I won't need to get no more," someone ordered.

The knife guy came at Grace, slow, crouching low. The club guy was using his weapon more to poke at Jobe. The one Grace had almost given a new belly button was back, only now he held a trash can lid ahead of him.

Six went for Chato.

He knocked two down, but the third, a big guy, got a hand on the pack and started a tug-of-war. Distracted, the Navajo missed the guy who hit him low, knocking him down. In a flash, two thugs were kicking him.

"Help Chato!" Grace shouted, taking a swipe at the arm of the guy with the trash can lid. He yelped and got in the way of the club guy, but the knife got a good slice of Grace's right arm.

She switched the comb to her left hand—not as

good but not bleeding—and realized there were even more attackers. Two of them held Jobe's arms while two more slugged him. Four were kicking Chato, while a fifth raised the pack high and made ready to slam it down on the Navajo's head.

The guy with the knife had a wicked twist to his lips where other people had smiles. "You and me, girlie, are going to have fun," he said, stepping in with two more right behind him.

Out of the night came a cry. "Spirits of Wind and Fire to me!"

"For Scotland and St. Andrew!" mingled with it.

Suddenly there was only the knife guy in front of Grace. "Huh," he said, turning around to check on the gang that was no longer there. Grace lunged, putting six inches of steel spike into his gut. She twisted it as he screamed, then pulled back as he dropped his knife to clutch at himself.

She turned to aid Jobe, but he was slamming together the two guys who had failed to notice that things had changed and were still holding tight to his arms. Their heads hit with the sound of ripe melons smashing, and Jobe turned with Grace to help Chato.

The Navajo was still down, but there were four others on the ground with him, one with a chest caved in by the pack. The big fellow holding the pack was doubled over, the fist of a white-haired man deep in his gut. The attacker went down as the pale man chopped expertly at his neck.

A man in a skirt was helping Chato up. No, that was a kilt, complete with sporran. What had they fallen into?

"Thank you, whoever you are," Grace said, offering her hand, then pulling it back when she realized it was covered with her own blood. "Sorry about that," she said.

"Only sorry we were not here soon enough to save you such bloodletting," the man said, hustling them around a corner and out of sight of the carnage. A bright liquor store sign cut the darkness, showing Grace the man's white eyebrows, white hair and pink eyes—an albino. "I am Benjork Lone Cat, and this is my associate, Danny O'Bannon, at your service."

"Aye, you kin say that again." The kilted man laughed around a brogue that would be thick even on Alkalurops.

"I don't know what would have happened if you had been a few seconds later in arriving," Jobe said, shouldering his pack.

"We would hae missed out on some good fun," Danny said.

"We had better look at your arm, ma'am," Benjork said.

"Grace. Grace O'Malley," Grace said as she offered her bleeding arm. The man produced a first-aid kit from a pouch in the back of his belt, cleaned her wound, and applied a bandage.

"Thank you very much, Mr. . . ." Grace struggled with his name.

"Most everyone not crazy calls him Ben," Danny provided.

"Crazy?" Jobe said.

"I was born a Nova Cat," the albino said, as if that explained everything.

"That's not as bad as the new ones prancing about, Spirit Cats, but he's still a bit daft, if you know my meaning," Danny said, also as if that explained everything.

Grace concluded further explanations would add nothing.

"Where are you headed?" Danny asked

"We took rooms at the Hilltop Refuge," Grace told them.

Danny snorted. "You have rooms at the Hilltop Recycler, you just got beat up two ways to Thursday, and you're going back there? That's good. That's very good. I don't know what you're lugging in that sack, man, but you can as well just start dropping little bits of it along the street here. You'll have about as much left tomorrow as you will if you go back there."

"What?" Grace said. "The truck driver who brought us back from the Roughrider post today suggested the Hillman's Last Stand. Should we have gone there?"

"They are run by the same gang," the albino said quietly. "With the HPG down, I imagine it is much harder for off-worlders to find out about conditions where they are going. Danny, cut them some slack."

"If I do, someone else will cut them their throats."

"So we should find other lodgings for tonight," Jobe said.

"If you want to be alive tomorrow," Danny answered.

"What would you suggest?" Grace asked.

"A less boisterous part of town," Ben said, "that benefits from offering the likes of Danny and me lodging in return for our walking their streets at night." He pointed in the opposite direction. Grace found her bandage a good fit, and the three found the advice equally good, so they let the albino lead the way.

"The gangs have about learned to stay off our turf. A pity—we hae to go elsewhere for sport or this nut will take off on one of his dream things," Danny said, ambling with them.

"Dream things?" Chato said.

"You mentioned you were at the Roughriders' camp. Were you looking for a job with them?" Ben said, changing the topic.

Grace thought a moment, then told their rescuers, "I'm a miner from Alkalurops. At the spaceport they mistook us for recruits and drove us out to their camp. We corrected that error, and a major showed us around. I want mercs to train our militia. He wanted a standard defense contract. We parted company."

"Your error would be self-evident if you thought it through," Ben said. "You mine every day. You learn to trust your machine, your instincts, your coworkers.

You know what you can depend on when matters take an unexpected turn. In battle you can depend on two things: that matters will always take unexpected turns and that you can depend only on the man or woman next to you who has been there, training day and night, for as long as you care to remember. A militia's a waste of air."

"That's what the Major said," Grace snapped. "But it's our home we're fighting for. Not cash, not plunder. Those are our neighbors and our livelihood. We will fight for them."

"Your eyes say you *have* fought, and recently. Was it with militia? Did it go well?" Ben asked.

"No," Grace said. "We didn't know how to fight. You can't expect us to know everything the first day on the job."

"And how many lived to see a second day on that job?"

Grace could feel her face getting as red as her hair. She struggled with anger, both at Ben for being so hardheaded when his point was made, and at herself and her people for being caught so unprepared. "No one expected the HPG to go down," she said, then turned to Danny and changed the subject herself. "You were formerly a Highlander?" She left the real question hanging.

"Aye, as you can see. No one expected the HPG to go down. A lot o' us mercenaries were on the beach."

"But now they're hiring anyone who walks off a DropShip. What unit hired you and him?" she said, nodding at Ben.

"She got us there, Ben, me good man. No one wants to see the front or back of the two of us. You have any problem employees in your mining business?"

Grace nodded. "A few."

"Well, you're looking at two great mercs that no one wants to rehire. Isn't she, Ben?"

"The Roughriders give you a cost proposal?" Ben asked.

Grace produced it, and they paused under a working light while he examined it. "On the high side, but for a fully supported independent command maybe not too high in today's busy market."

"Can you suggest anyone not busy?" Grace asked.

"Roughriders are plenty busy," Danny said. "Remember that gig they got on Nusakan, the one with the gag rule that required them to take their armored DropShip out of storage?"

"I remember it," Ben said.

"Nusakan was the planet that guy was from, what's-his-name, that was offering to defend us," Jobe said.

"Alfred Santorini," Grace provided.

"And those raiders sure had a DropShip," Jobe said.

Ben whirled on him. "I am a mercenary. I have my honor. You give me a contract to defend your planet, I will defend it with my life. You contract for me to attack your enemy, I will pursue that contract to forty percent casualties. I am a fighting man. I am not a thief. None of us are."

Grace put out an arm to Jobe, pushing him gently away from the albino, who now showed red in the poor lighting. "I don't think we need to pursue this further, Jobe."

"Yes, definitely. No offense intended," said the big man.

"But you're always saying, Ben, that the times are a-changing," Danny said, elbowing his buddy.

"Honor never changes," Ben spat back.

"Is this the place?" Chato said, pointing with his open hand to a sign proclaiming AUNTIE VIRGINIA'S PLACE, ROOMS CHEAP, though most of the neon letters were long dead.

"Tell Auntie we sent you," Danny said. "If I were you, I'd wait until there was plenty of daylight to go back to the Refuge for me kits."

"We will," Grace said. "Good night, and thanks again."

Auntie had a large room to rent to the three of them, and breakfast was included in the rate. The next morning over cereal and juice, Grace talked to Auntie's granddaughter, Niki. She had just gotten her driver's license, might be able to get the car for the day, and claimed to know where all the merc camps were.

"They get drunk or otherwise delayed, and miss the last ride back. It's either pay some townie or wait for an MP to collect them, and I'm a lot cheaper than a month's pay and restriction. I've been doing this for the last two years."

"I thought you just got your license," Jobe said.

"And?" the teenager said, batting long lashes.

"The mercs don't give you any problems?" Grace asked. Around here, subjects seemed to need regular changing. *Worse than a squalling baby,* she thought.

"My brother used to practice hand-to-hand on me before he went to the Twenty-first Centauri. No drunk merc's gonna give me any trouble."

"We need to pick up our gear at the Hilltop," Grace said.

"I'll go with you. I know the clerks; they live around here." That told Grace she'd slept in the right part of town.

At the Hilltop, Niki took Grace by the elbow and headed straight for the desk with Jobe and Chato right behind. "Timmy, I'll be collecting this lady's kit. Hers and the two guys with her."

"Whaddaya mean?" a freckled-faced kid Niki's age answered.

"They're staying with Auntie now. Give me their duffels."

"They paid for two nights."

"We're not asking for our money back," Jobe said. "We're asking for our kits."

Niki got right in Timmy's face. "You heard the man. Now give."

Sullenly, the kid produced the two duffels. They returned to the old four-door Niki was driving.

Chato frowned. "They'd already emptied our rooms."

"Probably rerented 'em when you didn't get back from supper," Niki said. "Happens a lot, I'm told."

"And the police?" Chato asked.

"If somebody decides to join one of the more fly-by-night merc outfits on a sudden whim, who's to keep track? As Ben likes to say, 'The times, they are a-changing.' "

"Speaking of change," Grace said, "we need to stop at the port to check on some cargo. Could you drive by there on the way out?"

"No problemo—I know the way like the back of Ma's hand," Niki said as she pulled into traffic. But the stop at the port turned into a major problemo. Grace presented her ID and Wilson's smart card and asked to have the proceeds of the cargo's sale added to it.

"No can do, lady. The cargo ain't sold yet because I don't have a Certificate of Ownership."

Grace gave the man her best mine owner frown and repeated, "Certificate of Ownership."

"Listen, lady, I don't make up the rules, and I didn't crash the HPG. With it down, I can't call hither and yon to verify who owns what. Somebody smarter than me came up with this Certificate of Ownership. You got one—no problems. You don't got one—I've got to wait until one comes back on some DropShip. Didn't nobody tell you?"

"No," Grace muttered and asked to see a sample certificate. The date on the form was only nine months old. Maybe the requirement had reached Alkalurops, maybe it hadn't. Anyway, no one had told Wilson, and his cargo didn't come with a certificate attached for Grace.

"So you won't sell the cargo without a certificate."

"Maybe I will. Maybe I won't. But the market's soft as a baby's heinie, and nothing's moving today."

"So how long until I can get some stones credited to me?"

"Three months. Could be a year. Depends on ship traffic."

When Grace got back to the car and settled in, she quickly brought the guys up to date on their new problem. "Santorini?" Chato asked.

"Maybe. Or maybe just new rules we didn't know about."

"My bet's on Santorini," Jobe said.

Grace sighed. "But we need money."

"You have anything else to sell?" Niki piped up.

Grace pulled a loose diamond from her pocket. "Some gems."

"Then you need a jeweler," the girl said. "And I know just the guy. You'll love him." Ten minutes later Grace was ushered into a small shop with solid steel shutters on its front windows.

"Abe Goldman, Grace and her off-world friends are staying at Auntie's," Niki said by way of introduction.

"Always glad to be of service to travelers," a small man with wisps of gray hair and long delicate fingers said, with a smile that might or might not have any value.

Grace pulled the diamond from her pocket. The man produced a jeweler's eyepiece and studied it. "Lovely, fine color, well cut. I wish you had brought this to me a few years ago," he said, handing it back to Grace.

"A few years ago?"

"The collapse of the HPG has not been kind to markets. With taxes up, fewer people are buying jewelry. When we jewelers could talk to one another, we might invest on one hard-hit planet and sell on another more prosperous. Now such investments are more a gamble. If you need the money, I could probably afford to buy a few fine diamonds such as these from you, but I could not give you anywhere near the price they deserve."

Grace reflected a moment. Was this just an opening gambit? Certainly the jeweler's observations were supported by recent events. She signaled to Jobe. He opened his pack and carefully held up a golden pendant to the light, letting the diamonds on it sparkle. Then he set it on the table before the jeweler. Next he produced a silver bracelet banded in turquoise. The old man's eyes grew wide, and his nostrils flared. If Abe had been forcing a poker face before, his control slipped as he reached almost reverently first for the silver item, then the gold. Each was examined in a silence broken only by sudden small intakes of breath.

"My word. You see these so rarely. The art of old Terra has been lost. What passes for it is all machine made. This is real," he said, glancing up at Jobe, then at Chato. "Hand-worked silver and turquoise, made the way the natives of North America did it. Gold and diamonds made the way only the native Africans worked them. You have kept to the ancient ways," he finished.

"Our grandmothers still teach their granddaughters," Chato said, "and the young bucks still listen to their uncles."

"You have more," Abe said, gesturing at the pack.

"Yes."

The old man frowned and gazed at the ceiling, his eyes lost elsewhere. Then he shook his head and handed back the pieces. "I could not afford to buy one-tenth of what you carry. Another day and I would have mortgaged my inventory—my soul—to make them mine. Now?" He shrugged. "Space on JumpShips is commandeered without warning. Shipments go missing in transit, and you do not find out about it for months. I could not accept the risk."

"Might others share it with you?" Grace asked.

"There are some, but few would value the treasure they held in their hands. I could arrange a meeting between you and three, maybe four of us. Still, I doubt we could afford to take half of what you carry."

Grace considered the situation for a long moment. If they kept carrying it around, sooner or later a big enough bunch of muggers would catch them, and a crazy Cat and a Highlander might not be around. "Would you please inventory our jewelry, Mr. Goldman? If it would not be too much trouble, we would like to leave it in your care. You can keep it safer than we can carrying it around, and it would help you to find a market for it."

"Yes, it would," the man agreed, and produced a scanner. As Jobe withdrew each item from the pack, the jeweler scanned it, made a picture, and estimated a value. Grace excused herself to the rest room, unstitched about half the diamonds in her clothing, and added them to the inventory.

When Chato produced the loose jade, turquoise and emeralds, the jeweler sighed. "Your gem cutters are exquisite in their fashioning. Why did these never come on the market before?"

"They are family possessions, passed down for generations. Now our lives depend upon them. Stones and minerals can easily be replaced. The life of a daughter or son cannot."

The jeweler nodded his agreement.

It was past noon when he handed each of them a certified copy of the inventory in his care. Niki had watched the business with wide eyes. Grace glanced at her two friends, got nods, and turned back to the jeweler. "We need to change the inventory slightly. Niki, would you like to pick something?"

"Would I, but my granny would whap me something fierce."

"Not if I tell her it's a gift."

"Well, she'd still whap me if I took one of those diamond ones. But that one," she said, pointing at a silver necklace with turquoise teardrops, "she might not mind that one."

The jeweler smiled softly. "She has chosen one of the most valuable pieces here."

"It is hers," Grace said, helping Niki put it on. "Now, Mr. Goldman, choose a gift for your wife."

The jeweler chuckled, then ran a hand through the few strands of gray on his head. "You have my appraisal. You know what I consider the most valuable items in your holdings," he said, and chose a lesser one. "My wife died several years ago. My daughter-in-law will appreciate the gift. Let this be the beginning of a long and profitable relationship."

Niki got them to the Twenty-first Centauri Lancers well after lunch. To nonprofessionals, the regiment appeared to be a fine one, several battalions strong. The Major who showed them around invited them to afternoon tea at 1500 hours and a live-fire demonstration afterward. But the regiment was not at all willing to take on a contract to teach militia how to defend their own. "No, not done—bad show all around." The task force the Major proposed was identical to the Roughriders', the Lancers' prices only a bit lower.

The Eridani Light Horse the next day were no more willing, though they were a bit cheaper. After hearing their moans about cost for two days running, Niki took them to the Ronin. Grace found out where the tall man with the long sword at the port belonged. The Ronin were operating on a tight budget, no frills at all. They even seemed to be rationing their words. Still, teaching a collection of part-time soldiers was beneath them. And their prices were not that much less than the rest.

Niki drove them back into Galaport. "You folks look like you could use a drink. Let me take you to a place I like."

"Aren't there any mercs that don't cost you the whole planet?" Grace asked no one in particular as Niki settled them into a corner of Just a Wee One. A girl in shorts and not much of a top, who didn't look much older than Niki, showed up immediately.

"What're you drinking?"

"Whiskey for me, Kelly," Niki said.

"Grape juice for her, Kelly," Grace said. "A dark ale for me if you have it on tap."

"My grandma—" Niki started.

"Isn't here," Grace finished.

"Nice try, twerp." The barmaid grinned at Niki, took a beer order from Jobe, a tea from Chato, and left.

Across the room, Grace spotted Danny O'Bannon about the same time he spotted her, and raised a mug in salute. Ben was across the booth from him, head resting against its stone back, eyes closed. Grace opened her mouth to shout something, but Chato rested a hand on her elbow.

"Do not disturb one whose spirit wanders," he whispered.

Grace closed her mouth and watched. The albino did not move the entire time she waited for her order. As the drinks arrived, the Scotsman silently worked his way out of his booth and ambled over to kneel beside Grace. "Not much company when he gets that way, but usually a lot of fun comes of it. I'm not a man to mind a bit of enforced solitude, but not if I can avoid it. How's your search coming for a bunch of schoolteachers?"

"Not well at all, at all," she said, finding her own brogue deepening around the man. "As you say, no real soldier wants to be nursemaid to a bunch of fumbling amateurs. Two, three hundred years ago, our great-granddams could fight their own battles. Is it that we're made of weaker stuff, or has the battlefield gotten to be a rougher place?"

"Much rougher place. I've heard retired sergeants mumbling tales of doing things in battle that would get your hind end waxed but good if you tried them with the weapons and kit even a second-rate batch of mercs take to war. It's just no place for the temp employee. You use many temps in your mines?"

"No, though I hear the corporation mines do. Doesn't help their safety record none," Jobe said.

"There you got it."

"Doesn't the fact we're standing between our homes and those killing bastards count for anything? We're fighting for friends, parents, husbands, wives . . . ?" Grace let the long list run down.

Now Ben was out of his booth and walking their way. "No one interested in taking your contract?" Ben said.

"No one," Grace answered.

"You want to fight for your hearths and homes," he said, as if still half in a dream. "Not mercs fulfilling a contract, but patriots standing between war's fire and their homes, land, loved ones. That is not something we have seen a lot of lately."

"Might count for somethin'," Danny said.

"It should," Grace said.

The ex–Nova Cat blinked and slowly glanced around the room as if seeing it for the first time in a long time. "It is not as if we would be passing up a grand contract, now, is it, laddie?"

"I joined the Highland Regiment 'cause they were lads who enjoyed a battle or two and a good scrap in between. But no part o' me is enjoying this police work we've been surviving on of late."

Ben nodded, looked around, spotted a long table and waved the group over to it. "Even you, short stuff," he said to Niki. They settled down at the table, looked at one another, found nothing to say and just sat, occasionally sipping their drinks.

Jobe shuffled his chair after a long five minutes. "What's supposed to be happening?"

Ben turned from staring at the door, put a finger to his lips, and said nothing.

Ten minutes later, by the clock above the bar, and the door opened. A tall woman wearing a tartan skirt, carrying herself ramrod straight, came in with a shorter, sandy-haired lad in plaid britches.

"Oh no, not Biddy and the boy wonder." Danny sighed and took a long pull on his drink.

"What are you drinking?" Ben called to them.

"It seems to be about lunchtime," the woman answered. "I thought I'd have a bite to eat. Sean, being of an age, was hungry, too. I didn't expect to see you up this early, Ben. Daniel, I didn't think anything could get you out of bed before three."

"Maybe you'd like to have me in your own?" Danny shot back.

"You would need a hospital bed first, you drunken Lowlander," the woman shot back, but she and the boy came to the table and sat beside Ben. "Who are your friends?"

"Their planet, Alkalurops, got tapped in a little smash-and-grab affair. They had some luck defending themselves and came looking for a mercenary unit that might contract for a detachment to teach their militia how to put up a better fight next time."

The woman snorted. "Nobody is that hard up. Any takers?"

"None," Grace said, tired of having people tell her she was dreaming to think a militia could stand a chance.

"Good luck to you and yours," the woman said, and waved to the barmaid. "Kelly, the usual for me and him."

The young man at her side leaned forward to make eye contact with Grace. "Y-You've set a h-h-hard task for yourself. I-I studied for five years b-b-before I could even s-start practicing in a BattleMech."

"I was driving a MiningMech before I was Niki's age," Grace said. "I've kept Pirate upright when half a hill was sliding out from underneath me."

"But what do you know of preparing a battlefield?" the woman shot back.

"We dug pits, fighting holes and sapper traps, and covered over a draw to capture a hovertank intact," Chato said.

Ben cracked a tiny smile. "Captured a hovertank. Is it working? Have you hooked a plow to it and put it to work?"

"Yes and no," Grace snapped. "One of Chato's boys got it working. He was studying the sensor suite when last we saw him. Might have copies of it by now."

"So the farmers can learn," the woman said, raising an arched eyebrow to Ben. He nodded.

"Someone say something about a tank?" Coming through the door was a small man in patched gray uniform pants and shirt, polished black boots and a hat. "Kelly, you got a brew and some more of that stew Victoria is so daintily eating?"

"On its way," Kelly said from behind the bar.

"What's this I hear of tanks?" the man repeated, taking a seat beside Danny. Before Grace could open her mouth, Ben quickly filled him in on Alkalurops in MechWarrior fashion.

The newcomer snorted. "One captured tank does not an army make."

"We know that," Grace said. "The raiders didn't get all our 'Mechs. We can strengthen armor. We were working on rockets and Gatling guns." That got raised eyebrows from the others, but the short man in gray shook his head.

"MechWarriors, MechWarriors, MechWarriors—that's all you hear. But let those big walkers try to tramp across the battlefield without tanks and infantry to cover their flanks, or take down a temporarily disabled 'Mech or tank and you fancy-steppers will be in a world of hurt. Give me some solid treads on the ground and I'll show you a thing or two."

"We have hovertrucks and all-terrain tread layers," Grace said. "We have 4x4s that can take some armor and guns. We have the start of an army. What we need is someone to show us what to do with it. How to use it. Won't anyone give us a fighting chance?" she ended, looking around the table.

No one met her eyes. But this time no one told her to forget her dream.

The short man extended a hand to Grace. "I'm

George Stillwell. I fight tanks. Would you mind showing me what this planet of yours looks like—the terrain? Is it good ground?"

Being a miner, Grace had a good chunk of the topog-
raphy around Falkirk in her 'puter. She set it to PROJECT,
and a good representation of the Gleann Mor Valley
appeared, running down the table. Victoria and the boy
moved their bowls aside and studied the map. "Raiders
came up from the south," she said, "the hovertank in
the lead, a short 'Mech that I think was a *Koshi* next,
then a taller one with small wings and lasers."

"Probably a *Spider*," Sean said. Others nodded.

"Mixed in with them were two armed buggies and
two hoverbikes. They went off to shoot up Falkirk,
here." Grace stopped there, letting the mercs examine
the situation.

"What was your defense force?" Ben said.

"Three modified MiningMechs and three modified
AgroMechs. MODs consisted of extra armor and
hunting rifles forged into Gatling guns, field burners
and rockets. Also fifty or so infantry with hunting rifles. A few had short-range rockets."

Victoria and Sean stood up, and came around to
the side with George and Danny to look at the terrain.
Sean started to say something, but Victoria talked
over him. "You set up your ambush at this bend in
the road. Probably split your 'Mech MODs two, two
and two. Same with your infantry." Victoria stooped
to look up the valley from about where Grace's Pirate
had stood.

"They spotted you way back there," she said, pointing to about the place Grace first spotted the raiders.
"He would have deployed against you, one of him
against two of you being very good odds. Did any of
you get out?"

"I got my entire command out with only a few
wounded," Grace said.

The mercs emitted low whistles. "What didn't you
tell me?" Victoria asked.

"She forgot to mention the work my diggers did," Chato said, and described his side of the battle.

"Surprises, surprises," the woman said.

"Coyote is a fine trickster."

"Ah, Ben, one after your heart." The albino said nothing. "Still; cannot be done," the woman said, returning to her place and the cooling stew. So did the boy.

"You got somethin' better on your dance card, darlin'?" Danny asked. Victoria said nothing.

"You the folks from Alkalurops?" a woman said from a table well across the room. Grace had noticed her come in by the back door and take a seat. Her hamburger was just arriving as Grace killed the display.

"Yes, we are," Grace admitted.

"I hear you want to hire a training detachment."

"Yes."

The woman, dark haired, with an olive complexion, took a bite of her burger. "Interesting set of tactical problems. Don't see the political forces behind them, though."

"You interested in taking the contract, Betsy?" Ben asked.

"A girl would have to be really crazy or really desperate to take that on. 'Course, I bet some of the kids volunteering for infantry duty might be cute. Let me know if you find anyone, honey. Gracie, isn't it?"

"Grace O'Malley," Grace shot back, feeling ready to throw in her cards and catch the next DropShip for home.

An old man sauntered into the bar, wiping his hands on a blue rag. He ordered a beer, finished with his rag, and when the stein arrived he turned to the full table, saluted them with the suds, then took a long pull. "Now, that's a collection of bad luck if ever I saw one. Back in the days when I had a real job, just the sight of all you hot jockeys would boil my blood."

Danny was out of his seat in a moment. He took

Grace by the hand and pulled her across the room. "Here's a guy you really need to meet. He's the only man I know who can take in three smashed-up 'Mechs and give you back four. Sven, I want you to meet a miner from Alkalurops, presently in the business of adding armor and guns to IndiMechs so they can stand up to BattleMechs."

"Glad to have known you," the man said, ignoring Grace's extended hand. "Let me know when the funeral's gonna be."

"Been in one fight and didn't need any funerals after," Grace said, tired of it all and ready to lose her temper for a full, redheaded run. "Don't plan on needing much from the preacher woman after the next fight, either. Got a guy named Mick who can fine-tune a 'Mech so well, I once took Pirate dancing, not wanting to get tired on my own feet."

"Your Mick that good with his gyros, huh?"

"Did just fine," Jobe tossed in. "Danced better than my number one wife."

"And don't you know, that when that eejit Brady got himself buried in a cave-in, Pirate pulled out three loaded dump cars with their full loads and what had fallen in on top of them. Three loads at once."

"So your Mick knows how to soup up an Industrial-Mech engine as well as make a good gyro," the mechanic said slowly.

"And get fifteen percent more from a myomer bundle than the book ever claimed," Grace said, adding to Mick's accomplishments.

"Hmm," was all the old man answered.

A woman in a red bodysuit that left nothing to the imagination came in the back door and joined Betsy. Kelly took her a salad she had already prepared and a drink.

"Syn, you're late. Missed out on a great discussion of how to get yourself killed helping hicks who don't want to be fleeced by the next raider coming through," said Betsy, her tablemate.

"There an empty slot in the raiders I can bid on?" the other woman asked.

"Thought you might want to help the farmers," Ben said.

"Me! You've obviously mistaken me for someone with time on her hands. I've got a hot date tonight. Poker. No limit."

"The guy's wife know about this date?" Betsy asked.

"What she don't know can't hurt my tight little butt."

"Well, if you're looking for something to do to make up for your wasted youth, you might check in at the port around midnight tonight. There's a DropShip headed for Alkalurops," Ben said.

"You going to be on it?" came from several mouths around the room, including Grace's. All she'd heard so far were nos. When had yes entered the conversation? Hell, she wasn't sure she wanted this bunch, anyway. There had to be better available than this crew of unemployed misfits. *Yeah, right.*

Ben shrugged. "I grow tired of doing the cops' job simply because they fail to do it themselves."

"You see something in that nap?" Danny asked.

"What I saw was my future. What *you* will live, you must see for yourselves," Ben said, standing up. "Sven, these good people tried to do what civilians are not expected to do. Their mechanics tried their best with tools never intended for such use. I think it is time that you and I spent some time in a junkyard. You know a place with what they might need?"

"Ally's Goods and Not So Good?" Sven said.

"I fear that Grace's financial limitations will require us to spend most of our time among the not so good."

"Can't think of a better place to be." Sven grinned, then downed his drink.

"You guys going shopping?" Grace said, nailing down proof that this was a serious, for-real deal. She glanced at Chato and Jobe. They were grinning from ear to ear. So was she.

"Yes. I hope your smart card has plenty of room on it. I suspect my good friend Sven and a few MechWarriors may have some ideas about how they want to customize their 'Mech MODs."

Grace tapped her 'puter. "What's Abe Goldman's number?" Niki rattled it off before the Net answered. Grace called him. "Mr. Goldman, some newfound friends would like to spend some of the money you haven't found for us for our gems and jewelry."

"Oh, dear," the man said. "This could be a problem. Where do they want to spend that money?"

"A place called Ally's Goods and Not So Good," she said.

"Ally Portencallens!"

"The selfsame gentleman we have in mind," Ben said.

"I will be there by the time you are," Abe promised. "I can't think of a better man I'd love to help cheat himself," he said, sounding very much like a man who had been offered a spare berth on the Olympic Haggling Squad.

6

Galaport, Galatea
Prefecture VIII, The Republic of the Sphere
29 May 3134; local summer

The yard of Ally's Goods stretched over an entire block—a big one. A towering hangar with several bays ended with a glass-enclosed showroom displaying two nearly new BattleMechs. In the lot around it stood several used models showing wear and tear, or even major battle damage. A dinged 'Mech with a newly painted arm was pretty clear evidence that one had recently been ripped off. Several IndustrialMech MODs were also on display.

Sven took them to a human-sized side door. "Got some folks interested in your yard out back," he told a mechanic working in a 'Mech's cockpit.

"You know where everything's at," the mechanic

shouted, waving them through. "You put most of it there."

"Out back" stretched wrecks as far as the eye could see.

"I've heard there's a nearly complete Mackie somewhere back there," Danny said. "You ever seen it, Sven?"

"Maybe I have, maybe I haven't—but it's not that antique we're after. Let's see how good you 'Mech sissies are at walking."

"Ah, such disrespect from the likes of grease monkeys," Danny responded.

"No 'Mech, no MechWarrior," Sven said, and took off at a pace Grace would not have expected from an old man. They walked down dirt paths with 'Mechs hulking over them on either side, some looking ready to walk out, others barely able to stand up. Many were already being parted out; right arms for assorted 'Mechs were piled next to a larger stack of left arms.

"I found what I want," Danny announced.

"And what might that be?" Victoria asked.

"Here's an *Atlas* with a kilt."

"A kilt?" The normally perfectly controlled woman almost missed her step. Grace turned to find Danny eyeing what looked like a complete, if greatly scarred, *Atlas* BattleMech. Towering over them, it offered shade against the sun, but Danny stood well back to get a good look at his heart's desire.

Grace studied the monster. "I don't see a skirt on that thing," she said, making sure to put a smile on her face.

"It's there, sorrowfully just painted on," the ex-Highlander said. Now Grace spotted a faded tartan among the rust marks and slashes from a line of slugs across the midriff.

"Now, I ask you, how could such a good 'Mech, with an obviously bloodthirsty pilot at its helm, ever end up in a place like this, I ask you," Danny said, shaking his head.

Victoria sighed. "The pilot, no doubt, had tastes and misjudgments similar to our friend's here, and paid the price for them. Mark the lesson, Sean: Intellect is nothing without discipline and control."

"And life is not worth the living if you let Biddy keep you on a leash, boy."

"Ms. Birdwell does know her battles and tactics, sir," Sean said, the first time Grace had heard anyone "sir" Danny O'Bannon. He ignored the honor and continued to gaze at the *Atlas* as the others followed Sven.

"What are we looking for?" Ben asked the mechanic.

"The lady here can't afford to buy the BattleMechs she needs, but she's got 'Mechs of her own. Well, what we're looking for are the tools to make the 'Mechs she's got into the BattleMechs she needs. Tools, me boy, tools will do it."

When they found a rusting collection of junk against the back fence, Sven grinned. "Now, there, young woman, are the tools that will turn your worker machines into BattleMechs."

To Grace it looked like a pile of junk metal that ought to be recycled. "I don't see anything," she said diplomatically.

"See that rolling sheet over there?" Sven pointed. Grace saw a large metal box. Beside it were two sets of rollers, one upside down in the dirt. "I bet you thought when your friend Mick welded a double thickness of StrongArm plate to your pet 'Mech that he'd doubled your protection?"

"He said he did," Grace said.

"Sorry to argue with a man who knows his motors," Sven said, "but one plus one does not equal two in the armor business. Two centimeters of plate laid on top of two centimeters of plate is not as strong as four. You need four, or even six centimeters all the way around to distribute the hit, to give you the strength. That pile of junk over there lets me make a solid six-centimeter plate with all the composite layers in the right place. We need that," he said, turning to walk up the back fence. "We'll also need that shaper to form the plate to your frame," he said, pointing at another contraption.

"How many autocannons you got on your planet?" Sven asked.

"I don't know of any," Grace admitted.

"I'm gonna need that and that to forge barrels and machine action," Sven said, pointing, a grin coming over his face like a kid let loose in a toy store. "We'll need to soup up the engines. Mick good at that?" Grace nodded. "I'll need that carbon extrusion plant over there," he pointed. "Adding all that weight to your IndiMechs means we'll be needing to reinforce the frames."

"Is there anything here for making rockets?" Grace asked.

Sven laughed. "You did homemade ones, right? They go corkscrewing off in all directions?" Grace nodded. "An autoclave is what you want. There's a beat-up one down the other end. You said you used a Gatling gun. Six barrels. How'd you hold 'em together?" Grace described steel bands to hold the barrels to a central core and carbon blocks to hold the barrels in place.

"Did it stay sighted in?"

"No. I had to fire a few slow rounds each time to work the gun into the target," Grace admitted.

"And I bet the raider just stood there while you did that," Sven said. He wasn't smiling now. Grace shook her head.

"That drill press," he said, pointing to a machine on its side, "will need work but it'll drill out face and butt plates that'll keep Gatling guns sighted in from now till doomsday."

Grace studied the man in front of her, walking through what seemed to her was junk and tossing off opportunities like sparks came off a mining drill. She'd come to Galatea thinking she needed MechWarriors. Thank God she'd found a warrior who knew how much she needed a mechanical genius.

"Thought I'd find you here," someone said, accompanied by a soft hum. Grace turned to see a huge belly with a man attached driving up in a small electric cart. Abe Goldman was right beside him, a large strongbox clutched in his lap. Mr. Belly must be Ally, the owner of the Not So Good stuff she wanted to buy.

"Hi, Abe," Grace shouted, then put on her best mayoral face and said, "And you must be the famous Mr. Portencallens."

"Ally," Belly said, extending a hand and a smile that had enough oil in to match half of Alkalurops' annual production. "I understand you're in the market for some 'Mechs. Why'd you let this old bum"—he waved at Sven—"bring you out here. The good stuff's in front or in my new showroom. Why swelter out here when we can go inside, stay cool, and buy the latest model?"

"I don't think I brought quite that much cash," Grace said with as much sorrow as she could dredge up for the occasion.

"We do have some fine used 'Mechs. Repair work guaranteed for eighteen thousand kilometers or their first major fight, whichever comes first." Ally's smile got even broader.

Grace wondered how the guarantee defined "major" and decided she really didn't need to know. She also noted the way Ally had deftly offered her the more expensive side of his business without denigrating the junk pile here. Tough bargaining ahead.

"What I was really checking out was your obsolete servicing jigs. Sven here thought they might have a few more hours in them. Not much, maybe just enough to make them worth shipping back to Alkalurops to see if they were what we needed."

"These are not obsolete," Ally said, and almost looked like he might come out of his cart. "We've expanded our service options for BattleMechs, things being what they are. I've already placed an order to expand my service bays so we can get back to meeting our customers' needs for IndustrialMech maintenance. In a couple of weeks—a month at most—we'll be cleaning up this, ah, stuff and putting it back under cover."

"Looks to me like it's been out here for quite a while," Grace said, kicking gently at the drill press where it lay in dried mud. "When was the last time it rained in Galaport?"

"Six months ago or more," Abe said under his breath.

"I'll have to get on my foreman. I had no idea he was treating the temporarily out-of-use equipment so poorly."

"Ahem," Abe said, opening the strongbox in his lap and retrieving one of the gaudier African works in gold and diamonds. Ally took it in with a glance, then betrayed himself by letting his eyes go back for a second look. As he reached out to finger the gold and jewels, his eyes widened even more.

"Hand-worked," Abe said. "Want to feel the heft of this necklace?"

"If you don't mind my looking at your bauble. I didn't know you handled costume jewelry," Ally said. There was a noticeable sag as his hands took in the full weight of it.

Jobe stepped forward. "I dug the diamonds from the earth. My nephew panned the gold. My first wife cut the diamonds, poured the molten gold into a unique mold of her design, and hammered the diamonds into place to finish it. You will not find a finer piece of gold jewelry within the human sphere."

"So you say, but I might want to have it appraised myself."

Abe produced his 'puter, snapped a picture of the glistening necklace, and asked, "Who do you want to do the second appraisal?"

"Let me see yours," Ally said, and whistled when Abe handed him a sheet of paper. "I should have my security man throw you off my lot. I don't let thieves in here."

"Pay a stone less and you're the thief."

And so started the haggling. It went on for hours as Sven and the MechWarriors dusted off items, prepared them for shipment and loaded them on a hauler. Ally ignored them, except to reject the drill press. "That's gonna be needed here real soon. Steal it from somebody else, Sven." Sven pouted, but grinned at Grace when Ally wasn't looking.

"Had to include something he could yank. No worry, if you can't find a spare press in Allabad, I'm sure I can steal one."

Abe had surrendered about half of their stash by the time the negotiators were exhausted. That was when Sven turned to Ally and said, "We will need a few items out of your used-parts bin." That took them inside as Sven dug through the back nooks of the parts room, bringing out three targeting computers, several targeting-acquisition systems, two very old but usable sets of electronic counter-measures gear, and a dusty tool box Sven said might be usable to upgrade Indi helmets to something close to modern neurohelmet levels.

Ally looked at the stack, eyed the rest of the jewelry, and called for coffee. Abe asked for a bathroom break. The two hagglers went their separate ways, with promises to resume momentarily. Ben ordered a flatbed truck to haul what they'd scrounged out to the port, and Grace bought tickets on the next ship out.

Abe came back, but Ally was nowhere in sight. "He must have a lot of daughters. His wife can't wear all that," Grace said.

"He has a lot of *mistresses*," Abe said. "His poor wife will be doing well to get a pair of earrings out of this."

"You didn't bring the Navajo jewelry?"

"It's silver; he'd dismiss it in a moment," Abe explained. "Do you have enough for tickets? Your group seems to have grown."

"I was about to ask you if you could help with that. I have some more diamonds I held back," Grace said.

"There are three of us who will take about half the silver and some of the less flashy gold pieces. Do you want me to return the rest to you?"

"Would you be willing to serve as our agent and sell items here?" Grace asked. "None of the mercs have asked about their pay, but I'm sure I'll need cash on Galatea for that."

"I will, gladly," Abe said, offering his hand. They shook. "Now, Ally is back, and I do not think I should have let him get away." They had two hours to make the DropShip when the bargaining ended. Abe offered his car. From just three, Grace's group had grown to include Ben and Danny, Victoria and Sean, and George and Sven.

"I would have liked a few more. The infantry slot is still open," Ben said as they dismounted at the cargo terminal.

"You have room for one more?" Betsy Ross asked, sauntering over from where she'd been leaning against the ARRIVALS sign. "I don't have anything going, and this place is getting boring."

"I doubt Alkalurops will be boring," Danny offered.

"Could be just garrison duty," Victoria said. "Long hours of tedium interrupted by explaining to civilians who don't know a thing about our work why they should pay us for doing nothing productive," she said, eyeing Grace.

"If it comes down to that, I could sure use you working my mines. I have three of them that I haven't been able to open for lack of 'Mechs." She smiled wickedly, and Danny groaned. "But we do have good whiskey up the Gleann Mor Valley."

"Maybe driving a MiningMech would be tolerable under those circumstances," the Highlander muttered.

Poor Sean looked ready to burst out crying. "I'd really like to face one b-battle in my life."

"You will, boy," Victoria promised.

LoaderMechs sent their cargo off to the *Good Sense to Stay Home III,* leaving Grace with a bigger bill than she'd been told. Taxes had not been mentioned when she'd asked the cost before. Abe presented his smart card to cover the balance.

As they turned to the passenger lounge, a car disgorged a red-suited figure. The click of heels came quickly, as did her perfume that managed to overpower the smell of ozone and diesel. "What have we here?" Betsy asked. "Date not so hot, Syn?"

"Date was plenty hot. He didn't tell me his wife was combat-trained. She showed up halfway through drinks and wanted to know who I was. I excused myself to the ladies' room while he explained. He was on the floor with her standing over him when I got out, so I decided maybe I could use a job off-planet for a while. Ben, you still have an opening?"

"Grace, can you spring for one more ticket?" Abe said.

The eleven of them boarded a mere five minutes before the ship locked down for launch.

"Colonel wants to see you," is not the best way for a Major to start his day. L. J. knew there were worse things, and a morning visit with the Colonel need not be viewed as a challenge. It could be an opportunity. Their last meeting had been to pin on his Major's insignia. The one before that ended with orders to develop operating procedures for a raiding strategy. "An old military practice," the Colonel assured him, "that though somewhat unused of late, is sanctioned by long years of use on ancient Terra." Had there been a smile behind that?

L. J. paused before knocking on the Colonel's office door to clear his mind of the thought that kept running through his head, like what had he been doing, working for a cold-blooded killer? Face set, L. J. knocked.

"Enter," he heard immediately.

Colonel Ludwig Hanson V sat squarely behind his desk, looking as determined as the portrait of their grandfather behind him. His commitment to their grandfather's glower often made it hard to figure out exactly what he intended. Beside him, Major Keith Thomas, the legal officer, stood at parade rest, imitating his own regimental ancestor's portrait hanging in the hall. His staff officer's paunch made the image harder to carry off. Cousin Amadeus Hanson, the regiment's Chief Accounts Manager, and committed civilian as his loud vest emphasized, lounged lazily in a chair across from the Colonel as L. J. reported.

Without preamble, the Colonel said, "You recall a few days ago when we talked about that potential client from Alkalurops that I mentioned an option clause in your earlier contract."

"Yes, sir," L. J. said, remaining at stiff attention.

"It seems your earlier client has contacted us about activating that option. Were you aware of a pair of murders that occurred around the time of your raid?"

"I believe the planetary Governor and Legate were murdered just before we landed."

"Yes," the Colonel said, turning to Major Thomas. "I asked our legal staff to examine our duty in such circumstances. Unfortunately, he finds no governing legal precedent. Amadeus assures me it has no impact on our contractual obligations."

"I wonder what a first-year-cadet Honor Court might say," L. J. risked. Legal and contractual finagling must have some honor.

The Colonel glowered at L. J. in step with the portrait behind him. "I had similar thoughts. Sadly, my duty to the regiment goes beyond what one dreams about in school. We have a contract, and our client has asked for the full six-month extension."

"Six months, sir? The raid took barely three months, even with that long drop interval," L. J. said, allowing a frown on his face for the Colonel to see.

"Yes, initially I found that interesting as well."

"Is it another raiding contract?"

"No, Loren. We just received the full contract language, and this time he wants you to seize and hold."

"The contract allows for that change of scope?"

Now cousin Amadeus had the good grace to fidget. "It seems that sections of the fine print are new language," the Colonel said with a scowl directed at the civilian.

"New language is popping up in all the contracts," Amadeus complained. " 'Conditions beyond the client's control,' 'rising emergencies,' 'acts of God,' no less. Until court rulings define this new language, we can't be sure what it means."

"Then take it to court and find out what it means," L. J. suggested, "what with two murders out there."

"This language is so vague as to allow any interpretation." Major Thomas gave Amadeus a glare with more wattage than most battlefield lasers. "I discussed these clauses with the legal staffs at several other regiments. They don't want us taking into court language so vague it clearly favors the client. Sorry, Loren, you just have to suck it up."

L. J. relaxed his stance and considered the situation. Whoever the client was, he was capable of cold-blooded murder. L. J. didn't much care for sharing a planet with him for six months. Then again, he had not met the client during the last contract. With luck, he wouldn't for the next six months. But the regiment owed him.

L. J. stiffened back to full attention. "I was given the last contract because it was something new. I take it that your giving me command of a seize-and-hold expresses the regiment's full confidence in my command ability." *There—swallow that, Colonel.*

The Colonel slowly stood, eyed L. J., then scowled at the other two present. "No, Major, your selection for this command reflects my confidence in no way. My accounts manager tells me that his fine print requires that the commander of the previous raid command this operation. My legal assistant is no help at all. He says I must accept the crap-for-language that this civilian reviewed and told me I could sign.

"Major, I am not happy with any of the three men in my office. You, at least, will be out of my sight for the next six months." He turned to Major Thomas and Amadeus. "You other two will be around to irritate me. But you can take my word on this to the bank with your final paycheck. If there is another snafu the likes of this, I will personally have the best lawyer on Galatea review both of your employment contracts and terminate them. Am I understood?"

Their affirmations came back machine-gun fast. Even Amadeus was on his lazy feet, in haste to get out of the room.

"Look on the bright side," Major Thomas said once they were outside.

"There's a bright side?" L. J. asked.

"You've got a second independent command."

"Yeah," Amadeus agreed, "if he doesn't get his throat slit."

7

Grace may have paid for the tickets, but the Mech-Warriors selected their own accommodations. Betsy and Syn tossed their duffels into one cabin, leaving Grace with Victoria. Ben and Chato took one room, Sven and George another. That left Danny and Jobe together with young Sean. "You can't bunk that lad with Danny," Victoria insisted, beginning Grace's in-depth education on the people she'd hired.

"It's either them or one of the other two cabins with guys," Grace said, not willing to share her room with the youngster.

"You don't think Sean and I are lovers," Victoria snapped. "He's young enough to be my son."

"Yes, he is," Grace said. "And you two are close enough to be mother and son," she said, leaving it at that.

"He's just a kid who deserves better than he's getting. And maybe I do act like a mother hen," the older woman said, taking a seat on the bunk across from Grace's. "I've met a lot of MechWarrior wannabes, but never anyone as determined as Sean. He'd make a great staff officer, but he wants to fight 'Mechs."

"Is he good in a 'Mech?" Grace asked.

Victoria settled on the bunk. "Poor kid almost tripped his 'Mech over its own feet the first time they put him in one. Got dizzy from the height and lost his lunch. He looked so pathetic as they dragged him from the cockpit. They wanted to wash him out despite his sim scores. He was in tears begging for another chance. I said I'd help—give him a hand."

The woman stared at the ceiling. "The Clans raise kids without them ever knowing their parents. That harshness is supposed to make the kids stronger. I wonder if it isn't harder on the parents. The race's survival for millions of years has depended on us women mothering the next generation to manhood."

Victoria turned her gaze on Grace. "You have children?"

"Not yet. I suppose in time."

"There won't be any time for me. So, yes, I've helped Sean as his own mother might have if she hadn't died. And we both ended up on the street just before all hell broke out with this HPG failure. Him because he was untried and stuttered, and me . . . Well, me because I'm me."

Which was another question entirely, to examine some other time. "Once the ship steadies on 1G, want to go for a run?"

"I'm in. And maybe I can rescue Sean from Danny's clutches for some solid physical training. If Sean's not careful, Danny will give him an education in all the wrong things."

An hour later Grace and Victoria went running. Ben was also out in gym shorts and a towel. *Good-looking man,* Grace allowed. George Stillwell joined them, and Grace showed them aft to a trail among the huge containers.

The second day's run was with Ben alone. The man set a fast pace, but not so quick that Grace couldn't ask about Victoria. "Paths do not always lead where they should," the albino said. "Victoria is a superb 'Mech handler. An expert eye for the right target at the essential moment. However, she is not one to socialize. Danny told me that she once attended a dinner and kept the same glass of scotch in her hand all evening—untouched. She does not drink, nor does she carouse. While she does not judge those who do, I know that Danny feels the hot breath of guilt every time he sees her. Their banter is light, but there is true steel at the heart of it. With things the way they were before the HPG went down, that was enough to put Victoria Birdwell on the outside looking in."

That answered, Grace went on to ask the questions her own study of 'Mech warfare on the trip to Galatea had left unanswered. Ben shared lunch with her, and the others quickly joined them.

As days and weeks went by, they answered Grace's questions, but raised two new ones for every one they answered. And those two raised four more questions that usually resulted in three more answers and the fourth being met with a shrug. But since that fourth could easily kill you, Grace usually pushed the matter until the warriors glanced around the table and admitted there was no answer to it. You accepted it as part of the job or left for other employment.

"Are there no situations in mining that will kill you in a flash and do not yield to any of the safety precautions you can imagine?" Ben said by way of conclusion.

Grace pursed her lips at that. Certainly hard-rock mining underground could go from fine to hell in a flash if you tapped into an unforeseen gas pocket or water sump. "Yes, there are some things you just accept," she admitted.

"And there are things we leave to luck. When your luck runs out, it is just gone."

"Of course, a good man will be running right along with it," Danny said with a laugh, as he raised an imaginary mug in salute.

Grace continued her education, even during runs. One day she tapped George for a jog. "Isn't maneuver warfare pretty cut-and-dried?" she asked. "I've read the book the Twenty-first Centauri wrote on maneuver warfare. It says where to put your tanks and your infantry—and the tactics look pretty hard to beat, either in attack or defense. What does that leave a commander like you to do?"

George chuckled as he jogged along. "Everything, my dear mayor. Everything." He paused to let that sink in, then went on. "If you write the book, everyone who pays good money to buy it must consider you the expert. Is that the way it is in mining?"

"Yes," Grace said, dodging around a large-diameter pipe.

"Well, if you read the book and I read the book, who wins when we both apply the book?"

Grace didn't see an answer to that question. "In mining, I apply the book's answer and the minerals flow," she said.

"But minerals don't have the nasty habit of shooting back."

Grace laughed. "Not the last time I got to do any mining."

"And they aren't likely to develop that tendency the next time, but my opposition does so rather regularly. I want to be where I can shoot at him before he can shoot at me. If he studiously applies the book answer, I know exactly where he'll be at any given time. If I don't follow the book, he won't know where I am. Easier to shoot at him and not get shot at."

"Assuming you are smarter than the book," Grace pointed out.

"Assuming my boss is willing to admit that there is such a thing as being smarter than the Twenty-first Centauri's book. That's why I'm working for you, if you were curious. The Kell Hounds like to win. The present CO can't conceive of a better way to win than by applying the book. So long as he goes up against idiots who haven't read the book—and there are a lot just now—he wins. Even if he fights someone who's read the book, he won't do worse than a tie, which most clients find okay. Is a tie okay by you?"

"That's what I got last time. Cost Alkalurops good people and good 'Mechs. Probably would have lost more if they'd had a bigger ship. Next time, I want to win."

"Glad to be working for you," George said, reaching across to shake her hand without missing a step in his jog.

The JumpShip *Off We Go* was done charging, so there was no delay getting to Alkalurops. A few days later Grace learned more than she wanted about Syn Bakai when she was called to the captain's cabin at two in the morning. While the MechWarrior sat off to one side, buffing her nails and wearing nothing but underwear that covered little and interfered with the view even less, the captain fixed Grace with a gimlet eye.

"I don't much care for passengers sleeping with my crew. It's bad for the morale of thems what get left out, though your woman here doesn't seem to have missed many. What I will not allow is a passenger dealing herself into the crew's poker game and concealing extra cards on her person. That is hazardous to a player's life. The Line takes a dim view on the odd passenger showing up suddenly dead. You paid for her ticket. You keep her out of my hair for the rest of this run."

Grace escorted Syn back to the room she shared with Betsy Ross. "You will stay in passenger country or I will have Ben and Victoria space you, you understand me?"

"Get a sense of humor, Mayor. Those swabbies were just having a little fun feeling me up."

"And finding cards," Grace said, holding up the four aces the captain had given her to back up his claims. Slowly Grace tore them in half and gave them to Syn. "I don't play poker, Syn. I can't bluff worth beans, but cross me—cause us trouble before you prove you're worth the effort—and I'll see you dead."

Syn said nothing more as she slipped into her cabin. Back in her own, Grace asked Victoria what unit Syn was from.

"Bannson's Raiders. If you want a guess from me, they're the likeliest group to have taken a raiding contract. If you've got a snarling enemy in front of you and a Bannson's Raider behind you, turn around, or at least keep one hand on your wallet."

"Syn should have fit right in."

"Too true. I understand she was too much even for them. But I once saw her in a tournament. She had her 'Mech dancing on a wall not twenty centimeters wide. You'll want her. Either to fight for you or to slit her throat, but you'll want her."

Only Betsy remained an enigma to Grace as they approached their landing on Alkalurops. No question that the woman knew her infantry tactics inside and out. Her grasp of large-formations tactics left Sean silent in his seat, taking notes, and George nodding quietly. What she knew about small-scale, special-ops-type jobs left Grace shaking her head. She'd followed the news from several planets along the border of House Davion that had suddenly changed governors over the last several years. Betsy tended to let drop a bit of this and some of that to the point that Grace was pretty sure the woman had been involved in some way. What was someone like that doing looking for a job? Grace considered asking the woman if she had big enemies that Grace should know about, but somehow the topic never came up. After Betsy showed them some hand-to-hand tricks that left Jobe shaking his head and rubbing his throat where she could have killed him, Grace made a mental note to stay on Betsy's good side.

They were on final approach when Ben called them all into the ship's lounge. "We took our leave of Galaport rather hastily. Not that spending an extra day there would have been worth it," Ben said once they settled in. "Normally, a mercenary unit clears its contract through the Mercenary Review and Bonding Commission. I do not think Grace could have paid the board's minimum fee after Ally took her for the ride Grace was hoping Ally would take instead." That got a laugh. "And we did get everything Sven could beg, steal, or borrow to keep us alive next fight. But Grace had nothing left over to post bond. As I recall, none of you even paused to ask our gracious host what the pay was. Now, I understand a miner can expect to earn about fifteen hundred a month, so I've got a contract here calling for us to be guaranteed the princely sum of three twenty-five."

The warriors looked at one another. Danny groaned as if for all of them. "Clerks get better pay. But since you put it that way, I guess I can get along on that."

"In return for this monetary consideration, we pledge our sacred honor to the defense of the people of Alkalurops," Ben finished. He produced a pen and signed the contract. One by one, the others signed below his name. That left plenty of space on it when he handed the paper to Grace.

She studied it for a moment. "Sacred honor is highly

valued where I come from," she said, then wrote below their names for a moment. "In return, I pledge all that I possess in guarantee of this contract," she said, and signed it. Chato took the pen from her and added his name as well.

"My first wife is going to tan my hide for this," Jobe said, but he reached for the pen and added his name.

Ben folded the paper. "Now we begin—warriors, miners, farmers—to see where our dreams will lead us."

Allabad, Alkalurops
5 August 3134

Grace called Angus Throckmorton from the spaceport and tasked him with renting a wareyard or machine shop. Jobe set to arranging transport for their gear. Most of the MechWarriors stayed with him, but Grace, Chato, Ben and Betsy hailed a cab and headed for the Guild Hall. A meeting was in session, which sounded much like the last one Grace attended. She spotted the little old woman who had been the first to give her an encouraging word and joined her at the tea cart.

"You're back so soon," the woman said.

"Stranger things have happened," Grace admitted. "What's under discussion?"

"Whether we should apportion votes in the Council of Elders based on the taxes paid to support our government," the woman said with a smile. "That will decide how the election goes for temporary Governor, you know."

"I didn't," Grace said. "We haven't elected a Governor?"

"Oh, heavens no, dear child. I don't think we've agreed on anything since you left. Your wanting to hire people to train our militia raised the issue of taxes immediately. We can't defend ourselves on the small income The Republic generates here. No, we need to raise money, and that is such a touchy subject."

"Yes, I know." Grace scowled, having just pledged her own land as guarantee for eight paychecks.

"Grace," Betsy cut in, "is there any chance we could get the floor for a few minutes? We really need to know what Alkalurops is willing to pony up for their own defense, and they need to know what you've hired."

"I was kind of hoping I could talk to a few people alone first. Folks around here take to ideas a little at a time. Hit them too hard and they can get a bit skittish."

"Grace, I heard you were due back," Garry McGuire said from the head of the table. "Are those some of the MechWarrior candidates you brought back for us to interview."

"Candidates?" Ben said with an arched eyebrow.

"These are both fully qualified MechWarriors," Grace said by way of introduction as she walked toward him. Again, no surprise, her table was now occupied by men who headed small suburban communities around Little London. The Council was whoever the Council said it was.

"This is Ben Lone Cat, once a Nova Cat, and this is Betsy Ross, an expert in infantry tactics. I hired them."

"You hired them?" Dev Coughlin, who still sat at Garry's right, jumped up. "You did not have permission to hire anyone when you left here."

Grace would have to put a stop to this right now. "Dev, I had authority to commit as much as ten percent of what profits were generated on Alkalurops last year. I also *had* to hire them. It takes almost six weeks to travel here, one-way. People do not come here for interviews. They come here for jobs."

Garry pulled on the sleeve of his crony, and Dev sat down. "I can see how you might have left with that impression," Garry began soothingly. "Why don't you give us a few minutes to talk to your, ah, associates. We do need help, and if you think these fine people can defend Alkalurops, we should hire them."

"Who will be defending whom?" Ben said to Grace.

"Just let them get comfortable," Grace said. Chairs were produced, but that caused a debate on where to set them. Finally, a space was cleared on the side at right angles to Garry and Dev.

"See the nice animals," Betsy said, her smile showing plenty of teeth. "Grace, assure them we haven't bitten anyone lately."

"And, dear Betsy, I thought you were about due for your rabies shot," Ben said, disproving Grace's conviction the man was incapable of humor—she hoped.

"Young lady," Garry said to Betsy, "I didn't catch what merc unit you were from."

The olive-skinned woman smiled at him. "I didn't say."

"How can we get references from them if we don't know them?"

Betsy laughed, a clear bell of an affair. Beside her, Ben muffled a chuckle, and Grace began to suspect today was not going to go as she planned. "Old man, I would not ask any of my former employers for references. I can't recall one that would admit to having employed me, and I can't think of one I would want to admit to being employed by."

"Every good employee carries references," Dev said.

"For jobs like maid or street sweeper," Betsy shot back. "But that's not what you want. You need someone who can kill a man five ways before his body hits the ground. You want a commander who can turn your town into a death trap for any 'Mech stupid enough to stalk your streets. People like that don't come with fine pedigrees and completed paperwork. We are few, and we are rarely remembered fondly."

"Turn our streets into death traps," came in a gasp from several mayors. "What would that involve?" Garry asked.

"A 'Mech with a long-range rocket or laser can pick off what it wants, be it a man or a building. Out on the battlefield, you have to work hard to get close to a 'Mech without it making you very dead. I understand that quite a few of your local Constabulary, hired, no doubt, with full paperwork, ended up quite dead when they took on 'Mechs across grassy fields. Grace told us she barely survived her first battle." Betsy stood, eyed the room, and walked around her chair. She continued, her body swaying gently on the balls of her feet.

"Grace survived because she had the luck of a few well-placed boulders—a few firing positions where the rolling hills rolled in her favor. With worse luck, she would be dead.

"If you want to kill 'Mechs, you hire 'Mechs. None being available, you train infantry in the fun sport of 'Mech hunting. It's a sport best done in towns, where you know the sewers and basements." She whirled to address the foot of the table. "I didn't see many power lines on the drive in. Are they underground?"

"Yes," a technician behind Garry answered. "The tornadoes and winds would whip them around all the time. We put them underground years ago."

"So you have tunnels under your streets filled with com cables and power cables," she said. Around the table a lot of mayors nodded.

"Good. We can pull the cables out and put explosives in. A 'Mech strolls by, we detonate the charge, and poof; no 'Mech."

"But what would we do for electricity?" objected several around the table. "That's our infrastructure. It cost money!"

"And you don't think defense should cost anything?"

"Your salaries, of course," Garry said, "but, but—"

"Grace, you might want to fill these folks in on your hiring efforts," Betsy said, but didn't sit down.

"I went to four merc units on Galatea. I got four cost estimates for a battalion-sized task force of 'Mechs, armor and infantry with support." Grace read off the prices of each offer. Around the table mouths fell open, while others whistled softly.

"But we could never pay that," Garry finally said. "We've never had to pay anything like that."

Betsy barked a harsh laugh. "In The Republic you didn't have to. One Knight shows up and everybody starts making nicey-nicey. Now your Legate's dead and no Knight's in sight. Folks, the HPG is dead, the night is full of hungry wolves, and you're bare-ass naked to a cold winter wind."

"Young lady, mind your language," Garry demanded.

"You want me to mind my language, but you've already had your first visit from wolves that didn't mind your gavel. Do you want to defend yourselves?" Betsy asked, slowly turning to let her eyes circle the room. "Or do you plan on throwing yourselves on the tender mercies of those who will rob, rape and kill you?"

"What we do, we will decide for ourselves," Garry snapped, hammering his gavel. Dev was on his feet and quickly recognized.

"Grace O'Malley, we sent you out to find someone to defend us, not maniacs who would turn our streets into bombs. We've spent generations building up our property. Nuts from off-planet can't just walk in here and tell us to turn it all into a wild shooting gallery. We won't make our planet into someplace not worth raiding by making it someplace not worth living."

"That's not what she said!" Grace shouted, jumping up.

"We all heard it," Dev shouted back as Garry whacked away with his gavel.

"Some places—maybe Allabad—might need to be

fought for inch by inch," Grace shouted, "but if we beat them back where they land, they'll never get to the rest of us."

"Right—never get to out-of-the-way places like Falkirk," Dev shot back.

"Would everyone quit shouting!" Garry screamed as he gave up on his gavel and joined in the verbal slugfest.

"That woman is crazy," Dev shouted. "Both of them!"

"Get out of here, Grace. It's clear you can't keep a civil tongue in your head," Garry ordered. Two men at what Grace still thought of as her table stood, strong arms out, threatening. Betsy gave them a hard look that froze them in their tracks.

"I suggest you two ladies take a break to regain your composure," Chato whispered. "I'll stay here."

"There's nothing more to say," Betsy said.

"No, you slapped them in the face with it fast," Ben said.

"You know a better way?"

"No," Ben said. "Not with the little amount of time these people have to decide their fate."

"Little time?" Grace said as Ben led them from the hall and signaled for a cab.

Betsy shook her head. "It's time for me to go my way and you to go yours." She turned to Grace. "There are too many questions about who is doing what here. Let me hunt down a few answers while Ben helps you get ready for what's coming as sure as grass grows." Before Grace could argue, Betsy was gone and Ben was helping Grace into a cab, whose driver demanded to know where she wanted to go.

Flustered, Grace called Angus. "I've leased a warehouse from an optimistic young mechanic who opened a major IndiMech repair facility just before so many of the local 'Mechs disappeared." He gave Grace an address in the district along the river, and she and Ben were there in ten minutes.

A large sheet-metal-and-pole building offered room to park four flatbed trucks and their loads. A fellow of maybe thirty extended a hand to Grace. "I appreciate the rental," he said. "I really like working with your man Sven. He knows his machines. He's got a few of mine humming like I've never heard them before."

Grace found Angus at Sven's elbow, the mechanic half under a drill press. Not far away, Sean was tweaking the programming of the control 'puter. Danny and George were prowling the building, examining other tools and figuring where to place their own. "I haven't managed to rent a 'Mech loader," Angus apologized. "All were lifted by the raiders, and we haven't got any replacements."

Grace glanced back at Ben. He didn't seem surprised or bothered by this slowdown. Angus' 'puter beeped, and he answered it. The old man's happy smile morphed to a frown, then his eyes grew round and his breath came fast. "It's my man at the port. There's a new JumpShip in-system!" he gasped.

"Commercial?" Grace asked.

"No, no . . ." Angus listened for a second longer. "It didn't use the main point. It jumped into the nearest La Grange point around Vesuvius. It'll be here in two weeks."

"Damn," Grace said, "that's got to be a raider. I need to get back to the Guild Hall."

"Use my car," Angus offered.

"We will gas the trucks and extend their leases," Ben said. "Then we will get them moving for Falkirk."

"You don't think the mayors will fight?" Grace asked.

"I have found that dreams offer guidance, not road maps. Still, I would not depend too much on your assembly."

Sven got to his feet. "I'd like to take some of this man's machines along with us if I could."

"You planning on shipping everything to Falkirk?"

the young owner asked, a catch in his voice. Grace nodded.

"I got a wife and kids, ma'am. Everybody says we got off easy last time. It didn't feel all that easy. One of my workers was in that attack on the spaceport. He left a widow and three kids. My Mara took them in. I don't want no one having to take in Mara and my daughters. You see?"

"I do," Grace said. "Sven, how much of his gear do you want?"

"All of it if we can get trucks to carry it."

"I know a guy with three trucks," the young man said. "I'll get them over here. Can folks around Falkirk put up three new families?"

"We'll make room," Grace said. "I know Mick will be dancing a jig at getting all these tools to play with."

"Then let's get moving, crew," Sven said.

Back at the Guild Hall, Grace found the news had preceded her. The council was already in an uproar; several chairs were empty. More small-town mayors left as Grace entered. "They ain't gonna do nothin'," one told Grace in passing. And nothing was what they did for the next hour. The big-town mayors rejected any fight that put their people in the middle of it.

Grace settled beside Chato and listened. As best she could tell, the debate centered on what kind of milk and cookies to offer the raiders. As more of the small-town mayors left, Grace stood to demand a vote on fighting. For ten minutes she stood, while Garry did his best not to notice her. Fuming, Grace stomped out. With luck, she and her MechWarriors might make the Gleann Mor Valley too tough a nut for the raiders to crack.

8

Falkirk, Alkalurops
Prefecture IX, The Republic of the Sphere
7 August 3134; local summer

Grace's caravan pulled into Falkirk after thirty-two
hours of straight driving. Grace put a sleeping four-
year-old aside and climbed down from a truck's cab.
She tried to get the kinks out of her back as she
crossed the dirt parking lot to Mick's main shop. The
morning was hot, but the scent of Scotch broom carried from the bushes along the verge of the road. It
smelled like home.

"This place stinks," Danny said as he dismounted
a truck.

Grace ignored that as Mick came out to see what
all the noise was. He took one look at seven flatbed
trucks loaded with machine tools and whistled.
"Gonna need more space."

"Mick, I want you to meet a friend I've made. Sven, come over here." The BattleMech mechanic stumbled over, rubbing sleep from his eyes and life back into his legs. The men eyed each other like two roosters, then went off to play "stump the genius" over the tool hoard. *That should keep them busy for the day,* Grace figured.

Jobe borrowed a jeep and raced for the Donga River Valley, "to see my second wife," he said. Chato's nephew was there, the hovertank fully operational and available to give Chato a ride home.

Grace filled in Wilson, Ho and Laird over lunch. She had to stop several times to let them absorb things. Wilson shook his head after she told him the *Dyev*'s cargo had not helped her cash problem. "This Santorini, he was on the *Dyev* and tried to have someone steal the diamonds. He probably queered the transfer of funds to you on Galatea. A real pain, huh?"

No one disagreed with that.

Grace finished with how the MechWarriors had signed for a pittance. "They deserve more, but that's what they agreed to."

"Not what one normally hears about mercs," Ho said, patting his round belly. "Do you trust them?"

"Yes," Grace said, with no hesitation. "Most are as straight up as you and me. True, they didn't fit in where they were and probably won't fit in here. But right now we need them. Syn, well, she's a case all her own. Don't let her in a card game, or let your wife see you with her," Grace advised. "Sven's a genius and knows it. I hope he and Mick get along because we need 'em both."

"Wasn't there another? Betsy?" Laird said.

"Betsy Ross. She stayed behind in Allabad to find answers. I sure hope she can."

"So we fight," Wilson said.

Grace took a deep breath. "That's the way I see it."

"Maybe the next raiders won't get this far," Ho said.

Laird agreed. "There are all those 'Mechs over at the big corporate mines. That would be the place to go next."

Wilson snorted. "If Santorini is behind this, he's already cut a deal with the corporations. We little guys are the ones that have to look out. And we'll have to do it alone."

"Then you think all this is no accident," Grace said.

"Anyone disagree?" Wilson asked. No one did. "I say we fight, but I think we'll be surprised at who we end up fighting."

The town meeting went long, but the people of Falkirk were for a fight if one came their way. When the hands went up for the vote, Grace checked the eyes. Many were looking around furtively. They were ready to fight, but no one looked forward to it.

The next day the Net reported that efforts to raise the DropShip got no reply. Talking heads offered thoughts, fears, hopes, doubt. No one really knew anything. Grace ignored the Net.

She had plenty to do. Jobe returned with two dozen 'Mechs from the entire Donga River Valley as well as trucks, and men in the trucks to form the infantry. Chato returned, too. More Navajos were crossing the mountains to join him every day. No one could tell another the path for his feet, but where a man like Chato led, many followed. They made superb engineers.

But with Betsy gone, who'd train the infantry? "No problem," Ben assured her. "It will be a while before there are any 'Mechs to train in. Danny, Victoria, Sean and I can organize an infantry school of some quality."

"Yeah, Biddy could show them how to march by a pub without stopping." Danny laughed at his own joke, but got serious when all three glared at him. "All right, I can show them how to march, too."

"You can't just order these men around," Grace said. "They have to know why you need them to do what you tell them."

"Sean will be perfect for that," Victoria said as the young man reddened. "He knows battles. He can show your militia where good men made the difference."

So that gave a purpose to the men and women who drove up from the valley and even from the plains, but that didn't put a roof over their heads. Grandpa had had a large family, but Grace had found his house rather spacious for just Mother and her. It absorbed the mercs. Wilson's bunkhouse took in the early-arrival volunteers, and other folks around town found room for the families who came with their would-be warriors. Tents in a wash above town where trees took the worst heat off the day handled others.

Constabulary Lieutenant Hicks brought in a dozen men, rigged a crane, and unloaded battle armor from a flatbed truck. Grace slapped him on the back. "You're looking a lot better than the last time I saw you."

The lieutenant flashed her a rueful smile. "You know, after that last raid, I was going to take up chicken farming, but the warehouse behind the shop had these boxes gathering dust for more years than I can remember. I figured I'd check on them as I left. Turns out we have twelve sets of Gnome battle armor. A note from the Legate five back told our commander to use these if he thought his men had time to master them. Guess my boss wanted us out giving tickets rather than learning 'em." He turned to Ben, stood to attention, and saluted. "Sir, can you train my men to use this gear?"

"With a glad heart," Ben said.

"There're a few other Constabulary posts finding stuff in their inventory that dead captains didn't want to mess with and the raiders missed. I'm just the first; there'll be more."

And there were. Of course, that meant more men

and families to feed. Mother and Auntie Maydell took charge, but still Grace wasn't left with time on her hands. Others saw to that. One afternoon Sven came out from Mick's shop. "I have something for you."

"Problem?" Grace asked. *Why would this man want to show me a problem? If he can't solve it, I sure can't.*

"We've been taking 'Mechs apart. We're about to put them back together. Thought you'd like to see what'll make your Pirate a real cutthroat." Grace followed Mick into the shade of the shop. It smelled of burnt plastic, hot metal and men's sweat—not a bad perfume to attract a mining woman.

Mick joined Sven, a proud grin on his face. "You gonna show the mayor what we can do." Thank God, St. Peter and St. Patrick the two fellows hit it off. Grace didn't want to think what would have happened if they had pulled at cross-purposes.

"Here's the chassis, stripped to the buff. I hope we're not offending a young lady's fine sensibilities." Mick grinned.

Grace made a show of looking around. "Don't see any ladies. Never met one in Falkirk. Just us hardworking miners with dirty fingernails," she said, waving a hand at them.

"I'm using that fine carbon filament Sven brought to wrap the legs, arms and thorax. It doesn't add much weight and should nearly double the load they can carry."

"The engines are a given," Sven said with a nod to the good word Mick had given him, "but your man here is a prince among motor men when it comes to jacking up the output. These engines will be putting out a good twenty percent above advertised horsepower. Thirty percent for short bursts."

"It's all in the injectors. What's making 'em fighting machines is the armor this old scoundrel lifted from some blind man," Mick said, pounding the other man on the shoulder.

"It's easy to get this old rig to spew out composite

armor," Sven said. "The new armor-repair kits work only on the Armstrong stuff they use for IndiMechs. This old press was made from an even older design, when IndiMechs were new. It remembers where it came from. We run the outer armor through. Aligned crystal steel is ACS whether it's for an IndustrialMech or BattleMech. That fine young man you recruited at Allabad was kind enough to donate the ceramic-fiber spinning mill he used to repair bumpers. It gives us everything we need for some serious ferro-fibrous armor."

"And I had plenty of artificial diamond monofilament," Mick chortled. "What do you think I use to retip all the drills you miners bring me to sharpen? The cubic boron nitride composite looked to be the show stopper, but Ho had a ton of the stuff. He uses it to insulate freezers. We have to melt it out of the honeycomb matrix, but it works fine."

"One run through the autoclave makes the outer skin. The next run makes the inner protective layer. A third run binds the two together. Not quite as solid as you get from the factories, but damn better than any other stuff." Sven finished, and both men grinned like a pair of well-fed cats.

"Great," Grace said, "but can the 'Mechs take the weight? Mick, didn't we about max out Pirate's gyros when we added that armor? Brady landing on his ass was funny, but his own gyros had as much to do with that as the rocket that just missed him."

The guys looked at each other. "We can't make bigger gyros," Sven said, as though he was admitting to not having the right screwdriver, "so we're doubling up on them. The raiders took all the 'Mechs around Allabad, but they didn't hit the spare parts all that bad. Mick got the word out, and we're due for a truckload of gyros that'll let us put two sets in every 'Mech."

"And the good part is, I got one hundred and twenty days to pay for them. With luck, we'll be converting these 'Mechs back to workers by the time the suppliers want their bill paid," Mick crowed.

"They're charging you!" Grace exploded.

Mick just shrugged. Grace had the feeling she'd taken the hook in bait and switch. "About those gyros . . ." she said.

The guys eyed each other. "Well, there's a reason there's only one set of gyros," Mick said. "You get two sets and they can argue with each other, end up working against each other. Anyway, in the spin-up checklist, we've added SYNCHRONIZE GYROS."

"And if you take a knock or a hard hit, the gyros can go out of sync, so you may have to resync them. Nothing we can do about that," Sven said, scuffing the toe of his boot on the floor.

"That's why we insist that only the smart ones operate the 'Mechs," Grace said, then took the guys off the hook. "Okay, we've got good armor, but I'd kind of like to do something nasty to the raiders. Throwing dirt clods isn't the fun it used to be when I was ten and trying to get even with the boys."

"Oh, you haven't heard," Sven said.

"No, she hasn't heard," Mick agreed.

"What haven't I heard?"

"We've got two things up our sleeves," Mick said. "Sven here brought in everything we need to make a nifty thirty-millimeter Gatling gun. Not as fancy as an autocannon, but something we can make here. Johnny Shepherd, our gunsmith, came up with a caseless shell that feeds real nice and lets us keep the machinery pretty simple."

"Caseless, no brass," Grace said, trying to think fast.

"Yeah, we don't got a lot of brass," Mick said.

Grace frowned. "But if you're using glue or something to hold the propellant together . . ."

"It kind of gums up the works," Sven agreed. "Gatlings are pretty forgiving, but we'll have to clean 'em good after a fight."

This whole lash-up was one compromise after another, but Mick was still grinning. "A painter drove in yesterday. Brought a whole load of paint with him."

"So now we can paint the 'Mechs?"

"Yes, but not with his stuff. His aluminum powders are going straight into the explosives mill," Sven said.

"I don't think the girl understands you," Mick said.

"Aluminum is great for sheeting," Sven said. "In a fine powder, it gives paint that silver look that lasts and lasts. But aluminum powder makes great rocket propellant, too. Mix it with the stuff coming out of the Kilkenny fertilizer plant, and we've got power for medium-range rockets. The painter knows a chemist with a magnesium supply. I think we'll have everything we need for shaped charges on our rockets. I know you look at every new joe who walks in as another mouth to feed, but some are bringing in the know-how we need to equip a damn fine army, ma'am."

Three days before the DropShip was due, Grace called a supper meeting at her home for her leadership crew. To the seven mercs, she added Wilson, Ho, Laird and Mick. Chato and Jobe saw to their own interests. The composition wasn't exactly representative, but at least there was no bickering over rules. They knew why they were here. With luck, they'd all agree on what they were going to do.

Done with one of Mother's great meals and ready to move to business, Grace turned to Wilson. "Did you bring them?"

"Signed, sealed and attested to. All registered at the courthouse," he said, handing Grace a folder.

Grace stood, and let her eyes rest on each of the six MechWarriors at her table. "All of you were kind enough to sign on to train us. To fight with us. I want to personally thank you for that." The muttering around the table told her it was nothing, just their job. Ben eyed her quietly.

"We, the people of Falkirk, want to thank you. We have a saying: 'Words are cheap. Land is forever.' So I'm not going to say a lot, just give these to you." She walked around the table, placing before each warrior a deed for six hundred and forty acres of prime foothill land. "If you want to farm, there's good bottom land and water on each of these. Wil, there is water, isn't there?"

"I checked each plot," Wilson said. "There's enough water there to support a good herd. If not, bring that deed back to me and I'll personally swap it for any square mile of land I have."

"There's also solid rock under the hills above your farmland. There's no way to tell, but most every hill around here has some valuable minerals in it. As for petrocarbons, you'll just have to take your chances with the rest of us."

Grace paused back at her chair. "I know you are warriors, and land may not mean the same to you that it does to me. But this is the best that I have to give you . . . this land that we stand on . . . and my thanks."

Ben stood as Grace took her chair. He glanced at his comrades, then spoke to the townspeople. "Times have been strange for us. We trained in the art of war, but lived in a time that did not demand greatness from us. When the fighting came, no one wanted us. I thank you, Grace, for giving us a chance to show our skills. And I thank you for giving us this land, the land of your ancestors. Now we stand with you, on land that is yours and ours. Thank you."

The others said thank you, though Grace doubted Danny was interested in land that lacked a pub. Probably none of them ever thought of more ground than the six-foot plot they would be buried in. Well, times were changing for all of them. *We'll see what tomorrow brings,* Grace thought, and cleared her throat.

"Getting down to business: Are we anywhere close to ready?" Around the table, heads shook slowly.

"They're good men and women," Danny said, "but they're good men and women who've spent less than two weeks learning how to soldier."

Ben leaned forward. "The Navajos have shown them how to dig, and Sean has told them why a shovel is the infantry's best friend. Most know to hold their first shot until it counts. Beyond that, I don't know. They don't know the men to their right or the women to their left nearly well enough. When the first one runs, the next one may run, too," he said. "How is our ammunition?"

Sven pursed his lips. "Not as bad as I feared. The chemist is a miracle worker. We'll have high-explosive antiarmor shells for the rocket grenades and tungsten penetrators for the thirty-millimeter guns. Any 'Mechs meet our infantry, they'll know we are there. Medium-range rockets for the 'Mechs and the gun trucks. One load, no more. I've got Gatlings enough to go around, thirty-millimeter for the 'Mech MODs, twenty-millimeter for the gun trucks. And don't shoot it all off the first time a blade of grass bends, you warrior types. There's not a lot more ammo where that comes from."

"So the raiders show up tomorrow, and we are not ready," Grace said in summation.

"You didn't really think it would be different," Syn said, lounging in her chair. The ex–Bannson's Raider wore a brightly colored wisp of cloth she'd bought from a Donga River merchant. Jobe eyed her as though he wanted to make her his third wife, or at least tonight's wife. The eyes she threw his way were full of yes.

There was a knock at the door, and Angus ducked his head in. "I thought I'd find you here. Have you been monitoring the Net?"

"Not since it quit saying anything helpful," Grace said.

"The inbound ship broke its silence. It wants all town mayors to meet the ship on landing. It rattled off a list of fifty. You were right there in the O's."

"Were Jobe and Chato included?"

The old lawyer paused for a second. "I don't think so."

"Why do I not feel offended at that?" Jobe said with a toothy smile. "Grace, you cannot go. This smells like a white man's plot to get all his enemies in one place and kill them."

"Jobe, you have to quit assuming everything is a white man's trick to get at everyone else. As young Sean can tell you, the English white man was using it on his Irish and Scottish cousins long before he knew there was anyone else to beat up."

"I'll take your word for it, Grace," Chato said, "but I agree with Jobe. This does not look like a place you want to be."

"She could wear battle armor," Sean said.

Grace shook her head. "That's not the image I want to project."

"I agree," Ben said. "Go gracefully or not at all."

"I am going. If the rest are greeting the raiders with drinks and munchies, I don't want to stand out like a grenade among the chicken wings," Grace said, smiling at her own joke. "Let's play it the raiders' way for now since we aren't ready to waltz into the spaceport and start the fight.

"Chato, Jobe, Ben, you're in charge while I'm gone. You call the meetings and see that everyone is happy by the end."

"Grace, I will not be able to. I go with you," Ben said.

"You aren't required to."

"That's exactly why I go. You need backup. It can come from an unexpected direction if I am with you."

"You're needed here."

"Now, didn't they tell us the first day in camp," Danny drawled, "that no man jack of us is irreplaceable. I say if the crazy Cat dreamer wants to go, we let him. I sure don't want him organizing a battle I'm in based on one of his wet dreams."

Ben's growl showed teeth, but Danny kept smiling.

"Well, if that's all settled," Syn said, standing in a way that backlit what she was wearing and showed all she wasn't, "I have places to go and things to do tonight."

"Me, too," Jobe said.

"I will pick both of you up in the morning," Angus said to Grace and Ben.

The drive to Allabad was both faster and slower than the trip up. Two weeks ago, they had driven straight through, but the heavily loaded trucks had kept them to a slow pace. Now they drove as fast as Wilson's new 4x4 could go on the gravel or heavily potholed roads, but called a halt at dark to spend the night at a small hostel.

Grace figured this was a good time to get to know Ben better, but she found him as strange a person as she'd ever met. For someone who had ten fingers and ten toes, the man was totally alien. Raised as part of a battle group from his earliest memories, she could not relate to his youth any more than he could understand her fond memories of learning her trade at her father's side. Her feelings surrounding the loss of her father left him silent.

In the end, they spent the trip studying the terrain they drove through, and ways to defend or attack across it.

Garry McGuire called Grace as they drove into Allabad; he wanted to talk to her. Angus offered his home to Grace, but slipped out to meet with friends before Garry showed up at five.

"The raiders are landing tomorrow, you know, at ten. Lots to do," Garry huffed.

"I hear you were elected Governor Pro Tem," Grace said.

"Yes, yes, unanimously," he said proudly. By the last twenty-seven members present, Grace had heard. "Now here is how I want things to go. We'll all line up in the terminal, all fifty of us. Strange—none of those who were so fast to show up at the Guild Hall are fighting to get into this meeting. Anyway, we line up, I tell our visitors they are welcome and the Constabulary has been dissolved and no one will shoot at them. You understand? No one will provoke them in the slightest."

Grace wanted to ask Garry what he'd do when the first merc grabbed his daughter, but she knew he had only boys. Another one of those great plans thought up by guys who didn't think about how the other half of the species lived. But Grace only nodded nicely. Now was no time to fight Garry.

If she was going to fight, he was way down her list.

Angus returned late and more than three sheets to the wind. As she helped him to bed, the old man mumbled what he thought was important. "They don't have any idea what to do, Gracie. They don't have any idea. The men are scared. Wives are terrified. Everyone who can is getting their families out—out anywhere. I told them about what you'd done at Falkirk. I told them to take three months' supplies. Some said they'd go. Others just don't know." He was mumbling, "Don't know," as he drifted off to sleep.

Done, Grace went to her room, wondering if she would die tomorrow. If Jobe was right, the raiders would machine-gun them to . . . what? Impress the locals. Get rid of opposition. From the sound of Garry, there wasn't any opposition. She could almost hear him going from door to door, telling everyone to just be quiet, to not cause trouble.

What would he say to the raped widow, if it came to that? On that thought, Grace changed into her nightdress and got in bed. Thirty minutes later she was no closer to sleep, then there was an annoying rattling at her window. She got up, unlatched it, and was about to slam it down solidly when a hand reached in.

"Took you long enough. You asleep?" Betsy Ross

whispered as she slipped in. Tight black pants, sweater, boots and hood made her nearly invisible.

A soft scratching on Grace's door was followed by Ben slipping in, also all in black, but unable to hide the whiteness of his hands, face, and feet.

"What have you found out, Betsy?" he asked the woman.

"Who killed the Governor and the Legate, for starters," Betsy whispered, as Grace struggled to catch every word. "Headmen got offed by a couple of ex-Constabulary boys. You know the type—dirty cops thrown off the force instead of being sent to do hard time. But the trail led off-planet. Don't know where, but I got a job as a maid at the townhouse Lenzo Computing Industries has kept for off-world salespeople the last couple of years. Lately it's been full of meetings. I've got a pretty solid org chart. Most are Industrial Trade Group. I know the players. What I don't know is what they're playing at. I'm not sure *they* do," she said, frowning.

Ben nodded. "You have done a good job, Betsy, at a hard task. Tomorrow we will find out which merc organization has the contract and what they intend to do. Unless you know already?"

"Nope. The off-planet crew is playing it very close. No one here knows what's coming; they're just getting ready for anything."

"Santorini works for Lenzo Computing," Grace pointed out.

"Yes," Betsy agreed. "He's a loose cannon there, full of talk about his contacts with Landgrave Jasek and the Stormhammers. Strange, you don't hear much about him from Jasek." Betsy smiled. "For what it's worth, I'm betting Santorini is deep into this—but what I'm willing to bet on and what I know are not the same."

Grace nodded at the ambiguity. She also noted the quality of information Betsy had just given, far more than she would have expected of an out-of-work merc-infantry type. *Who would know what was going on across three, four planets? Interesting.* Back to what mattered now. "Will you be at the port tomorrow?"

Betsy shrugged. "Never know where I'll be until I get there."

"Have you heard anything about what's going to happen at the port? Uh, some of us are—"

"Wondering if you need to bother buying a round-trip ticket?" Betsy finished for Grace. "No guarantee on this, but I'd buy the extra ticket. Worse comes to worst, your kids can inherit it."

"I don't have kids," Grace said.

"Don't blame me for your poor planning, honey. Now I've got to go. My break is sure to be over, and I've got floors to clean."

Grace turned to say something to Ben, but he was gone as silently as he had come. She closed the window, locked it, and went to bed. Tossing, Grace tried to assess what Betsy had let spill. She wondered if more than the people on Alkalurops were concerned with what happened on this planet. No answers came to any of her questions, but she fell asleep trying to make some up.

The port parking lot was mostly empty when Grace drove into it. She'd skipped breakfast. Even with Betsy's erstwhile promise, Grace's stomach was little interested in food. Others got out of cars and walked toward the terminal. No one hailed anyone. Alone, they walked in silence. In the terminal hall, no one worked the ticket booths. No one was visible at all. Grace took her place in a group of people growing in disorder around Garry. She found a metal trash can next to a pillar; it should provide cover.

The building shook with the sonic boom of a DropShip entering atmosphere. Several mayors made a hasty retreat to the rest rooms. All came back sheepishly by the time the weight of the DropShip settling into its berth made the terminal groan.

For five long minutes they waited. Then sounds began to come from the concourse that led to Drop Bay One. Grace could not make out the words, but she didn't need to. She'd heard orders being shouted at the merc camps. She'd heard feet moving in unison. Troops were disembarking, forming up. An engine gunned to life, and hoverbikes moved unseen. Deeper down, on the heavy-equipment level, she heard the unmistakable tread of BattleMechs. The building trembled as if a tornado was loose inside it.

The next order she did understand. "Forward, march."

The tread of a hundred fighters marching in step came up the concourse. Two hoverbikes came out first, their drivers eyeing the group as they circled them. The gunners kept their weapons pointed at the roof, but it was clear that the machine guns rode free on their pintles. A quick bend of the elbow, a twitch of the fingers was all it would take for them to turn deadly.

Running feet added to the noise level as several mayors broke for the rest rooms, some for the second time.

Now marching feet filled the terminal. Two platoons, two companies—Grace had no idea, but there were plenty of hard men and women in khaki with guns held at the ready. They moved as one as they marched into the hall. Behind them marched a small group. Grace didn't need to be told this was the command group—the Sergeant Major was there, towering like a rock.

Grace spotted him before she recognized the commander. "God damn you, you mercenary bastard," she breathed, and meant every word of it with a flaming anger that fit her red hair and would get her a long penance from the padre next time she was in town. "God damn you to hell," she said, "Major Loren J. Hanson."

9

Allabad, Alkalurops
Prefecture IX, The Republic of the Sphere
11 August 3134; local summer

L. J. enjoyed the rush. He loved the cadence, the movement of uniformed and armed troops through the military ballet that allowed large numbers to move from one place to another with efficiency and poise. He'd been told by civilians more than once that it was terrifying, but to L. J., it was a thing of beauty.

Then civilians galloped for the latrines. Did they really think he'd shoot them? "Battalion," he called, to be echoed immediately by "Company," from the company commanders. "Halt," he ordered.

The tromp of marching feet cut off like the sound of death itself. Well, maybe there was good reason for civilians to be scared. L. J. stepped forward. He spotted the fool who'd made himself Governor. L. J. didn't know who his client was, but he wouldn't give a handful of wet sand for this man's chances.

"Leaders of Alkalurops, now hear this. I am Major Loren J. Hanson of the Roughriders. I am under contract to conduct the seizure and occupation of your planet. There being no military opposition in evidence, I will consider your planet seized and advance immediately to occupation. Are there any objections?"

He eyed the collection of trembling civilians huddled before him. They seemed hard-pressed to stay on their feet, much less to resist the troops surrounding them. No, not all. That redhead way in the back—she was more mad than scared. She must be from a small town because he didn't have her picture. She did look familiar, though. . . .

"There being no objections, I am placing Alkalurops under martial law. Violation of any of the articles of this law can and will be punished accordingly, up to and including summary execution. Your 'puters have received a copy of the new laws. Read them. Obey them. Copies are also being posted on your global Net. Note that civil gatherings of more than ten people are now illegal. That means the gabfest at the Guild Hall is over. All civil appointments are now subject to the confirmation of my officers. For now, you mayors will continue to function and maintain civil order. Fail in that and you will be replaced and punished as seems appropriate." *Damn.* L. J. had read the riot act to drunk and disorderly troops, to troops on the verge of mutiny. He'd seen more life in the eyes of a two-week-dead dog. How could people call this living?

"If there are no further questions, you are dismissed."

The mob broke for the doors. In a moment his troops were alone in the echoing hall. Not quite. The sound of one woman walking toward him with the measured tread of a soldier drew his eyes to the redhead. *Lovely woman. Be a shame to kill her.*

"Redhead is Grace O'Malley, sir," Topkick said low behind him. "She tried to hire us a short while back on Galatea."

"I remember her now. Sergeant Major, dismiss the troops to guard duty or work details. Adjutant, see to quartering the troops. XO, oversee the unloading, please."

The woman approached as the Sergeant Major sent the troops to their duties.

"Should I thank you for not killing us, Major?" she said.

"Wasn't called for in my op orders, Grace," he said.

"Thank God and St. Patrick for small favors," she shot back. "So that was you in the little BattleMech I fought."

"I've never thought of a *Koshi* as little. Agile. Perfect for a long-range scout or a distant raid. What can I do for you? As you can probably surmise, I have a busy day ahead of me. And you need to get back to a small town up north, don't you? By the way, if you check Section Two of the new laws, being under arms is a capital crime if you aren't working for me."

Grace spread her hands, giving him a good view of a healthy, athletic body in a red dress that clung nicely. "I think it's pretty obvious I'm not armed. Or do you want to search me?"

"Your outfit has already convinced me that a beautiful and angry miner is unarmed."

She glared at him for a moment longer, then snapped, "You are a first-class bastard. Are you here to steal more 'Mechs?"

"I remind you that my lineage is fully documented, so the first comment is out of order. And no raiding this trip. We're taking over. I *will,* however, confiscate any 'Mechs that are modified for combat."

She showed red at her cheeks. Her anger made her chest heave, and the divide between her creamy white breasts was eye-catching. L. J. knew women whose company he enjoyed, but he had never let his attraction to a woman interfere with his mission. If he wasn't careful, this woman could be a first.

"If I may interrupt," the Sergeant Major said as he stopped at L. J.'s elbow.

"Yes, Sergeant Major."

"I believe the woman signed on a small group of mercenaries. Quite irregular, no papers filed with the Bonding Commission."

L. J. nodded. "Since they are not here to resist this landing, I will consider their contract failed and declare it null and void. Ms. O'Malley, please inform your former employees that they have forty-eight hours to present themselves unarmed to one of my officers and begin the process for their deportation. Is there anything about that you do not understand?"

"You've made yourself perfectly clear, but I don't think you are properly briefed on conditions here," the redhead said, a tiny smile dancing at the edge of her lips. L. J. concluded this woman was not someone he'd want to deal with on a daily basis.

"The men and women who accompanied me here have all filed for homesteads and are taking rather well to the farming life. You can check the Status Records at the Land Office."

"Farmers," Topkick spat.

"Have someone check out her story," L. J. said. "You have been informed of your obligations under martial law. You will not be informed twice, Ms. O'Malley."

"I wouldn't think of asking twice," she said, spun on her heel, and marched tall and straight for the door. L. J. enjoyed the view for two seconds, then turned his back on her and took on the balance of the day's duties.

Hours later L. J. sat in a comfortable chair in front of a crackling gas fire in his suite at the LCI Manor House. An olive-skinned maid by the name of Betty Rose had just served drinks and left. Now Eddie

Thomas, his adjutant, lounged lazily in an overstuffed chair next to the fire and gave his report. "Our client does provide fine quarters. All vehicles are housed in several nearby vacant warehouses, now surrounded by barbed wire and under guard. Our officers and staff are quartered in a good hotel across the street from here. Our troops occupy a college dorm three blocks from here that fits them nicely. Looks like good duty," the man said, always happy when his job was easy.

His XO, Arthur St. George, a wiry, hard-charger with distant family connections back to the old Colonel himself, nodded from his seat across from L. J. Captain Mallary Hardy, a short, severe woman who filled the Operations slot with her excess energy, activated the computer screen in the coffee table between them. "Our satellite, which the DropShip put into orbit on the way down, is working fine. No sign of any hostilities anywhere," she said.

"We move out tomorrow to the larger towns," she said. "I've set up platoon-sized task forces of 'Mechs, armor and infantry. The 'Mechs and armor should intimidate nicely. The infantry will provide the boots on the ground to keep the locals quiet and out of our hair. We are going to be a bit thin, Major."

"Looks like a great recruiting ground," Art said. "Be nice to take out a battalion and return with three or four, sir."

That *would* be nice. The old man hadn't given him a company of the BattleMech MODs he'd captured. Instead L. J. had a ragged collection, the leavings from the other battalions. But there were bound to be 'Mechs to confiscate, trucks to be taken over and armed. If he signed up eight, nine hundred recruits, he could triple his command. With demand for mercs growing, officers who grew their units would be noticed.

"Do it. Flag a sergeant from each platoon as recruiter. Put recruits immediately to work on guard duty. If these hicks are half as impressed as their mayors were, we ought to have kids standing in line to join up." That settled, they went on to supply. Always more details.

Grace breathed a sigh of relief when Ben came in right after she got back from the port. She started to brief him, but he cut her off. "It was on Net. Nice eye-catcher, that dress. Did the Major add anything during your private talk?"

"What, it wasn't carried live?"

"The Net had two feeds, one from the Governor's tie tack, the other from the battalion's com feed. Battalion cut the feed as you started up to talk to Major Hanson. Did you practice that sashay, or does it just come naturally?"

"Do all guys forget everything else when they look at a girl?" Grace shot back. "I thought you Nova Cats might be different, all controlled-like."

"We do not take vows of chastity, if that is what you mean," Ben said, with that hint of a smile that he sometimes allowed himself. "But did he say anything to you personally?"

"Yes. All mercs in my employ should report for off-planet processing immediately."

"I thought he might do that."

"I told him there were no mercs. All the folks who came back with me were homesteading. Had their land grants and all."

Now Ben did throw back his head and laugh, a nearly childlike thing that started in his belly and quickly worked its way up to his eyes. "Is that part of your dream?"

For a moment Grace wanted to take credit for whatever put the look of admiration in his eyes, but she couldn't lie. "No, it was what I told you: the greatest gift I could give you."

"I would love to share your dreams, Grace," Ben said in a way that made Grace warm where she didn't need to be. Then suddenly all business, he finished. "You truly have given us a great honor."

She sighed. *And as soon as honor is served, you will be gone.* "Did you meet Betsy this morning?"

"Her and a few people she trusts. We made plans for what she needs to find out, and how she might go about it."

"If we told Hanson his client is a cold-blooded murderer, could he cancel his contract then?"

Ben slowly shook his head. "Is it like this with all civilians? Do you cancel your contracts because someone says someone did something not nice?"

"Murder goes a bit beyond 'not nice.' But no, we don't break our contracts unless we have good cause."

"And we do not break contracts even for what you might think of as good cause. Grace, where a merc goes is death's land. No one that you would consider sane goes there. Why do you think your people ran so quickly? But that is where I live. That is my land. None of my kind will run from our duty to that land. Not for any reason. So long as we are paid, we do not run. Hanson is being paid. He will not run."

"Damn! Isn't there a court you can go to?"

"In the middle of a battle with laser fire all around and mines under your feet?" Ben laughed again. This time there was nothing childlike in it. It was cold, cynical, deadly.

"It's not easy to be a merc," Grace said.

"Yes and no. It is easy to do our jobs. All you need do is fear failure more than death. And no, it is not easy. It is hard, painfully dull work, interrupted occasionally by sudden, soul-searing terror. Now, come, we must get out of town before Hanson sends detachments across the countryside."

"He won't stay here?"

"He is ordered to hold this planet. He can't do that from Allabad. Tomorrow the roads will be filled with convoys making for all the major towns. Only when he has them patrolled will he begin to enjoy the boring part of his job.''

When Grace and Ben told Angus they were leaving, he thanked them for the offer of a drive up-country but passed on it. "This is my town. I don't know what an old lawyer can do, but I will do it when I see it." They made it back to Falkirk a few hours before sunset the next day, driving through without stopping, except for gas and food.

Victoria greeted them as they rolled in. "We saw the show," she said. "You looked good, Grace. Of course, the others looked like something a Scotsman might include in his haggis. Too bad Danny's not around to hear that one," she said, relishing her joke. "Danny is south of Kilkenny, setting up observation posts to warn if someone comes calling. Your Auntie Maydell also has her friends from down the valley looking out for them. But we need something of our own we can count on."

"Good. What are we doing for practice?" Ben said, looking at the sky.

"We've set Condition Zed for overhead security last evening when we spotted a new satellite. No drill, no battle suits in the open. No 'Mechs on parade. It's playing hell with training, but until we know for sure, it's just lecture and more lecture. That and taking care of the crops, digging a bit of metal the hard way. Anything that breaks a sweat."

"Very good. Now, Grace, where do we fight them?"

Grace had expected that question all through the drive. The merc thought in terms of stand-up fights, death's ground. It was time for Grace to let them in on how Alkalurops made a name for itself as somewhere you don't want to fight.

"Ben, Victoria, I've listened to Sean tell your stories. I was reading your history books even before I met you. But none of your stories are Alkalurops' story. Let's go down to Auntie Maydell's and give Old

Man Clannath a chance to sing you a few songs. Boy-wonder Hanson has no idea what he's walked into."

Major Hanson had a hard time making his daily report sound exciting. In two weeks he had occupied half of Alkalurops—the independent miners' half. His client had been specific about leaving the corporate west side alone. The map showed a nice circle around Allabad. The Roughriders held all major towns and significant trade routes. This place was as occupied as it was going to get.

Also, growing the battalion was succeeding beyond expectations. Each platoon leader wanted to be a company commander. Every platoon now had several recruit platoons attached to it. Most platoons had found an excuse to confiscate an IndiMech, some several. That gave L.J. a chance to reward some hardworking trooper with MechWarrior status. With the Constabulary walking a supervised and unarmed beat in town, their jeeps were now regimental property, being up-gunned and -armored to afford the armor boys promotions. Competition always got the best out of a command.

But it wasn't just raw recruits joining up. His Maintenance and Supply platoons were now battalions. Signals had only doubled, but recruiting there was picking up. People of this quality wouldn't take a year to shape up, either. He'd have a major task force to show for this trip, and in only six months! Life was good.

Of course, he also needed to show he could fight. There, things were not going well. Other than a few MERCS GO HOME signs smeared on walls, there was no opposition. Unless something came up soon, the Colonel would tag this mission a Sunday-school picnic. That wouldn't help anyone's career.

"Sir." Mallary stood at the door of his office.

"Yes," he answered his ops officer.

"A tank patrol's in a bit of a situation in Little London."

"They were attacked?"

"Not exactly, sir."

"Then what exactly?"

"They were set upon by little old ladies upset about how their tracks are tearing up the road and interrupting their grandkids' naps, sir."

"And why did a tank stop for this argument?"

"The sergeant says a little old lady with a cane was in the crosswalk, taking about a month to cross, so they stopped."

"This sergeant have a name?"

"Godfrey, sir."

L. J. wanted to laugh. If he had an armor problem, Godfrey would be attached to it. At the same time, he had to wonder why the lead-footed tanker had stopped. A Godfrey problem would likely involve him running the old lady down.

"Tell Godfrey to negotiate his way out of this. I don't want our tanks damaged or old ladies hurt. Tell him to get out of this mess or he'll be back with the infantry again."

Mallary smiled at that. "Yes, sir," she said, and turned to go.

"Mallary, any change in our client's arrival date?"

"No, sir. His ship just did a 1G midcourse flip. He's two weeks out."

"Any answer to our hails?"

"None, sir. 'Curiouser and curiouser.'"

"Lets us know how they felt down here while we ignored their signals on our approach."

"Yes, sir," Mallary agreed. "And makes me wonder why a client would want to do that to us, if I may say so, sir."

"You may say so to me, but let's keep this little problem under our hats, shall we?"

"Yes, sir," she said, and was gone.

Who was this client? He killed people who got in his way. Either didn't like talking to his contractors, or he loved a grand entrance more. Whatever he was, the regiment was under contract, and that was that. L. J. checked his situation board. A patrol was hung up, debating nap problems with grannies. Not exactly your normal attack—but then again, other than maybe being thrown up on by a baby, his men were at no risk.

Grace parked her rig behind the Beef and Brewery in Little London. The necessary work of keeping services going was done at the Town Hall, but nothing more. Important business was done in the back rooms of out-of-the-way places. As Grace got out, a man approached. "Nice of you to make my party," he said.

"Driving is so easy with the mercenaries directing traffic," she said as countersign.

"I'm Glen Harriman," the man said, offering a hand. "I'm kind of the acting mayor now that Garry's run off."

"What's the matter, the Governor's job no fun?"

"Let's say present conditions weren't quite what he expected when he maneuvered himself into the job. He's running scared."

Glen led Grace into the back of the restaurant, then took a hard left into a private room. Grace spotted a few mayors from close by, but most were young men and women, or gray-haired ladies. An unusual mix. Glen got Grace a mug of beer from kegs on a side table, seated her, then rapped his glass for attention. The room quieted. "How's security?" he asked.

A girl of maybe twelve ducked her head out the door, then waved a thumbs-up sign as she stood back up.

"Is she your security?" Grace asked.

Glen smiled. "She and a dozen kids her age. If any patrol comes near, we'll know. But none will. We know their schedule for tonight. Nothing like having half the patrol on your side to make sure you know where it is." He turned to the room. "So how's the Granny Gotcha Program going?

Several gray heads exchanged remarks, most along the lines of "You tell 'em," before they settled on one. She had her hair in a regulation bun, and the maroon dress with large yellow flowers reminded Grace of a dress her grandmother wore.

"We're doing quite well," the older woman said proudly. "We're catching at least one patrol a day in most towns. We concentrate on the off-worlders. You can call it womanly intuition, but I think some of those fellows are starting to get the proper attitude. I had two over for a good home-cooked dinner." Other women agreed, and applauded one who'd had four mercs for supper the night before.

"Anyway, we're putting a face on Alkalurops for these guys. Who's handling the gals?" she said, sitting down.

"We are." A young man stood. He had those disgustingly good looks the vids love. Grace steered clear of them; many lacked a work ethic, and she didn't want people thinking she hired men for their tight butts.

"We've got dates with most of the merc fems. They're hot, man." This last remark got him a swat from the lovely blonde beside him wearing a halter top and miniskirt. "Anyway, once we get one going out with us, it's easy to get her to bring along a few of her friends that want to party," he said, distancing himself from his girl as she really wound up to slug him. "You realize that our sacrifice to help the women mercs get to know us could leave us poor guys damaged for life."

"I'll show you damaged for life," the girl said.

"Mary Anne, leave something of him for Friday night. We have a major party at the Bubbles to You, and Alkalurops needs him."

"See, I told you, I'm just doing my patriotic duty."

"Yeah, but you don't have to enjoy it."

"So," Glen cut in, "as you can see, Grace, we're

doing what we can to make the mercs see us as people, not targets."

"And we'd like to know," the gray-haired woman said, "how you are doing raising an army."

Grace shook her head. "As I've told everyone, that is a misunderstanding. Yes, I hired several former mercenaries who were out of work. They have taken out homesteads and are now enjoying farming," Grace said, giving the official line.

"So we hear," Glen said, "and for now, that's fine by me. But in a week these mercs' client lands. After that, I don't know what'll happen. Granny here might need some armed backup. This civil not-quite-disobedience is kind of fun. But if things start to head south—well, you know what I mean."

Grace shook her head. "No, I don't know what you mean, and I'm not sure I want to know what you mean. Let me be perfectly clear. There is no army being raised, and there won't be anything of the sort . . ." Grace let the pause hang as the room fell into total silence. "Until and unless we need it. You get my drift?"

"Deep as any snow I ever floundered through," the gray-haired woman said with a chuckle. "I didn't hear nothing, and I know exactly what to tell my lady friends."

"I think a lot of us will be glad to hear that we aren't all that Alkalurops has going for her," the young boy said.

"You're serious about this? This isn't just another excuse for guys like Romie to play around?" the girl next to him asked.

"Lots of people are playing at this," Grace said. "And when the Roughriders' client lands, we'll find out what kind of game *he's* playing. Then we'll do what we have to do to close it down and send him and the mercs packing. Until then, play it cool. Put a face on Alkalurops for the off-worlders. And you girls—there's no reason why you can't take a merc to the party if your guy is taking one of their gals.''

"That sounds pretty fine to me," Mary Anne said.

"Hey, that's not what I had in mind."

"Well get used to it, Romie; it's what *I* have in mind."

"I think I'd better go talk to a few folks," Glen said, getting up from the table.

"Did I do something wrong?" Grace asked.

"No. I'm kind of surprised it didn't come out sooner. But now it's out, and I think I'd better talk a few kids through it."

"Enjoy your job," Grace told him.

"Oh, don't I just?" he said, sighing.

Grace stayed in her chair as others circulated by her. There were people to praise and fine points to help them work out. She spent some time with the Harper Street Irregulars, their name taken from a vid program the kids liked. They blushed and stammered when she told them they were doing well. "But be careful," she said, which got her accused of being just like their moms. She was late leaving the Beef and Brewery that night.

Glen needed a ride home and she provided it. "They're a good bunch," he told her.

"Have they had much trouble staying nonviolent?"

"A bit. A young hothead here, a boyfriend there. Not all the girls are toying with the mercs. A few have lost their hearts, or at least think they have."

"I'd hate to be young, fragile and in the middle of this."

"There's something else. This Hanson guy thinks he's won. Some of us think we ought to show him things aren't done yet—like just before his boss lands." Glen talked a few minutes about a small operation that would leave no merc dead, but their boss clearly on notice that things weren't finished. She liked it.

"Your mom must have told you the story from the

old wars about the Maid in the Mist?" Grace said when he was done.

He chuckled. "My grandma swore her grandma was the original Maid. 'Course, my other grandma made the same claim. Even my five-year-old mind was a bit skeptical. Still, they were fine, tough gals—just the type to pull it off."

"Think Mary Anne is up to being the next Maid in the Mist and sending Hanson a message?"

Glen laughed. "It would serve Romie right."

Grace slept at Glen's house, on the couch among toddler toys. It was a risk to him, but it beat her using a smart card that was probably flagged for any use. She got gas from Wilson's tank and always carried enough in spare cans to get her back to Falkirk. Being a leader of an underground revolt was not on her short list of fun things to accomplish during her life-time, but it seemed to be what she had to do this year.

A hungry baby woke her at five-thirty. Child and mother were back to sleep by six. Grace was on the road by six-fifteen.

Major Hanson frowned at the message. Alkalurops' "Leader" would land in two days and "required" him to have all significant town mayors present, as well as himself. Grace O'Malley had earned specific mention.

"Mallary, get this list distributed. Two days isn't a lot of time. Tell Grace O'Malley we'll provide her a high-speed transport if she can't make it otherwise."

"Anything else, sir?"

"Raise the alert status to Condition Three. There haven't been any problems, but now is no time to have any."

"I'll get the word out immediately," she said, then paused. "There's a kind of celebration tonight, they call it Oktoberfest, and there's going to be a big town party."

"This isn't October," L. J. said.

"Yes, sir, I noticed that, but it has to do with the

hops harvest up on the caprock. They come in in late summer, sir. At least that was what they told me."

" 'They?' " L. J. said, raising both eyebrows.

"Okay, Heinrich told me. His beer hall's brewed up triple stock, and if they don't have a party full of drinkers tonight . . . well, he won't be a happy little camper for us, Major."

"And he's made at least one merc a very happy camper, huh?"

"Personal business, sir. What I do on my own time is my business, right, sir? Colonel knows there's little enough of it."

"Maybe too much lately, since there's been damn few bad problems," L. J. snorted. "Okay, enjoy your party. Make sure your desk is as clean as it always is when you leave, and be back at it by 0800 tomorrow. How long is this party?"

"All weekend, sir."

"Lord, we'll get to know real quick what our new Leader thinks of this stuff," he said, dismissing her. *And if there is any God up there who gives a fig about mercs, let things keep going smoothly for another forty-eight hours.*

MechWarrior Brevet Sergeant Steve Torman, newly promoted, led his patrol. Eight years of putting in hours on night courses and every spare minute of sim time he could beg had paid off. His LoaderMech MOD wouldn't stand up to a *Jupiter,* but, by God, it could face down anything this stinking hot planet could field.

Not that the locals had put up any kind of a fight. Not when you led a patrol that included a Joust medium tank and three trucks from the Constabulary's impound lot. They were armed and armored and commanded by newly made corporals who'd only dreamed of getting a command when they landed.

So why was the lieutenant so hot for patrolling? Maybe the last 'Mech repair shop owner did have an

overstock of gyros he couldn't account for and three
units stripped down but not being worked on. So
what? Besides, patrolling wasn't bad with the local
kids waving and dancing along beside his 'Mech. The
world was fine.

"Ah, Sergeant," the motorcycle on point said on-
Net.

"Yes, Private." Technically he was a recruit, but
being one of the first to join, and bringing along his
own transport, he was already being treated as part
of the regiment.

"Sir, on hot summer afternoons like this, we cool
down at the swimming hole. It's up here about half
a mile."

"Sounds great by me," Sergeant Godfrey said from
his Joust tank. "I could use some cooling down right
about now."

Some might consider Sergeant Godfrey senior, his
being the highest nonbrevet rank. Steve started to say
they'd skip the swimming hole just to show who was
in charge, but the rumble of "I could sure use a swim"
and "Damn, it's hot" on-Net made it clear he'd have
a leadership challenge on his hands if he called for a
pass. Why not let them have some time to cool down?
He'd hit his last checkpoint on the nose. HQ wouldn't
mind if they were an hour late returning. They'd be
on their own time, and other patrols had taken to
eating supper at good—and free—restaurants on their
way back in.

"Let's go swimming, folks," he ordered.

He was just coming around a tree-lined bend when
he heard, "Oh crap, the girls got there first," from his
point cyclist.

Through the trees, Steve couldn't see the water.
What he could see was a rock and a beautiful blonde
doing a perfect swan dive off it—wearing nothing but
a smile.

"Is there a problem?" Steve said, loosening his harness.

"Sir, it's our folks' rule. Everybody skinny-dips—

like, who owns a suit on this planet? So if the boys get there first, the gals leave it to them. Gals got there first today."

Three girls, giggling and laughing, went off the rock feet-first, hand in hand. No question about the skinny-dipping part.

Steve popped the release on his cockpit. "Recruit, let me explain a thing to you. You're a merc. The Colonel makes our rules. You cross one and you'll be up on charges so fast your head'll be left behind with your ass. But if the Colonel didn't make it, we don't pay it no heed. Right, Sergeant Godfrey?"

"Right behind you," the armor man said, bailing out of his tank, stripping off his shirt, and loosening his boots.

"Recruits, you're on guard duty until some of us cool down and take your station. Understand?" Steve said, dismounting.

"Yes, sir," came with a hint of "Why'd I have to open my big mouth?" but the recruits stood by with their weapons.

The patrol's mercs made quick time through the bushes to the swimming hole and just as quickly were naked. Steve counted two dozen—plenty to go around. He hadn't seen an ugly girl on this planet; those in the water were drop-dead gorgeous.

None compared to the one who did another swan dive off the rock ledge. Steve was first in the water, splashing and running for where he expected her to surface. She came up, wiping water and maybe surprise from her eyes, then brushed back her hair.

Steve stood only knee deep, letting her have a good look at all he had to offer. "I am Steve Torman, and you are my date for tonight," he said, grinning.

She smiled at him, took a few strokes to get closer, then stood up, coming out of the water up to her thighs and offering him a view more spectacular than his wildest dreams.

"I am the Maid in the Mist, and you are my prisoner," she said, smiling back.

It took him a moment to disconnect the smile from the words. "Huh," he got out before the soft snick of rifle safeties clicking off drew his eyes to the bank. Seven recruits stood with weapons aimed at their maybe-not-comrades in the water.

"You heard my sister. You are prisoners of the Maid in the Mist. Get your arms up. What you do with whatever else is up is your business, but I'd be letting it down real fast."

Steve glanced around for Sergeant Godfrey. "Oh, shit," the man whispered. "L. J.'s gonna have my head *and* my ass."

Steve raised his hands as a whole lot of him deflated.

L. J. came in that morning to a clear desk, a clear board and nothing but routine matters to cover. Not a bad way to start the last day before the client or Leader or whatever he wanted to call himself showed up. Mallary came to his door as he was settling into his chair. She had two mugs of coffee, a service not usually offered by a captain in the mercs. Then again, she looked as though she could use the coffee. "Good beer?"

"Heinrich said it was the best—no hangover unless you really swam in the stuff."

"And you did the backstroke?"

"I did some swimming," she admitted as her clipboard beeped. L. J.'s board did the same thing. They glanced at their com units, and said "Oh, shit" in unison.

L. J. mashed down his com link's REPLY button. "Why wasn't this reported sooner?" he demanded.

He found himself eye-to-eye with the duty recruit at the Little London Com Center. She gulped and hit her own PANIC button—the real one that passed the

message straight through to the lieutenant commanding the occupation platoon.

"Sir, they did not report in before quitting time. We
had the watch set to keep an eye out for them, but
patrols have been stopping for dinner at some of the
high-end joints that offer them free meals. I don't
know if you are aware, but this weekend is a long one
in celebration of the hops harvest, sir."

"I know. Get to the stuff that matters."

"Well, the sergeant of the guard was a brevet, and
after a local recruit explained Oktoberfest is 'party
time' spelled long, the sergeant kind of relaxed how
much he was looking for them."

"And didn't inform you."

"No, sir."

"Even when you made your night rounds."

"I was kind of delayed in my night rounds, sir. The
Queen of the Hops kind of wanted me as her date,
sir."

L. J. rolled his eyes. Mallary frowned. Did they have
a King of the Hops? Was Heinrich . . . ?

"Get a patrol out to find that bunch. When you find
them, take their boots and let them walk back to post.
Then we'll talk punishment. Understood?"

"Yes, sir."

"Mallary, did Heinrich distract you from your
duty?"

"I don't know, sir. Maybe so, sir. But I think we
have worse problems than that, sir."

"Worse!" L. J. said as his board lit up, flashing red.

"Somebody sugared the fuel tanks at three—make
that four posts, sir. I'm alerting all occupation platoons
to check their fuel condition before firing up any vehicles. Sir, that may slow down Little London's search
for their wayward platoon."

"Better to drain the gas tanks than to carbon the
engines."

L. J. paced to the window. Outside, everything was
normal. *So this is how it happens. Lull us, seduce us,*

then hit us when we're fat, dumb, drunk and have our pants down. Damn!

If I had bodies. If I had hurt men, they know I'd hammer them. But this. Nothing! Damn! Damn! Damn!

10

Allabad, Alkalurops
Prefecture IX, The Republic of the Sphere
9 August 3134; local summer

Grace O'Malley was well back in the herd that met the new Leader at the spaceport. She'd wanted to be in the front line but had run head-on into a consensus that she be in the reserves—what they'd throw at the Leader and his mercs if things went bad.

Besides, the ones who sugared the gas and pulled off not one but two Maid in the Mist routines figured they'd earned their front seats. Actually, one Maid used a swimming pool outside Lothran, so it wasn't quite a Mist. Still, forty mercs missed roll call on the second day of Oktoberfest. In the past two days, the mercs had been too busy searching every rock, log and toad to party with their affectionate local friends.

Grace surveyed the mayors at this landing and noticed that most hadn't been here last time. Some were older, grayer heads, but many were younger and less averse to risk. The politicians were gone. Those who stood here knew their lives were on the line. Glen had picked Grace up that morning and sent her back to change out of her clingy red dress. "Something frumpy," he ordered. She wore a green affair with no waist, but doubted it would keep her alive if the new Leader wanted her dead.

The Roughrider Command Staff was there, with an honor guard. Grace hadn't known Alkalurops had a flag. The mercs stood well off to the right, out of the line of fire in case someone wanted to mow down the mayors. Unlike the mayors, they did not talk among themselves, but stood stiffly at what Grace had come to recognize as "parade rest." Knowing she shouldn't, Grace ambled over to where Hanson stood, face-forward and alone in front of his troops. It was wicked to talk to a man under those circumstances, but Ma always said Grace had no sense of grace in social situations.

"You enjoying our fine planet?" she asked.

"It stinks," Hanson said through unmoving teeth. "I understand we may get tornadoes soon. Maybe even a hurricane."

"Hurricanes are usually later in the year," Grace said. "You ought to study our planet more."

"I'm taking a quick course in its military history," the Major said. "Have you heard anything about made in the mist, or maybe the Maid in the Mist?"

"I thought you had intelligence specialists to find out things like that," Grace said.

"Intelligence tells me they've heard that phrase several times, but I can't seem to find it in the planet's history records on the Net."

So someone had thought ahead and taken that section down. "Maybe you should talk to our elderly, who remember the old songs or stories that never made it into the big Net."

"Or I might find something in backups if it was only recently taken down." He faced forward, but his eyes followed her.

"Might," Grace said as the sonic boom of the approaching DropShip shook the building. "I'd better get back to my place."

Now his head turned, and his eyes locked on hers. "Grace, I want my people back."

Grace knew she should ignore the demand. She didn't actually "know" about anything outside Falkirk. Still, Hanson couldn't be ignored. Grace leaned close to the Major's ear. "Your martial law says, 'Do not kill mercs.' You have not harmed my people. We have not harmed your people, and we will not harm them if the choice is left to us."

Grace turned and started walking back to her place. Glen stepped out of line as she went by. "What was that all about?"

"He doesn't want his people harmed."

"Of course we won't hurt his people. We're not crazy!"

"He doesn't know that!" Talk ended as the DropShip settled into its cradle and the terminal shivered. Grace hurried to her place among minor mayors doing their best to look harmless.

The sounds of a cooling lander were followed by loud noises, crashing sounds, shouts and curses. The mayors' quiet gave way to low chatter as they guessed about each loud noise. The occasion had all the suspense of Christmas with none of the joy. Still, talk relieved the tension. Grace glanced at the mercs; there were whispers among them.

Twenty black gun trucks roared out of Concourse A, with SPECIAL POLICE and a stylized vulture painted in red on them. Or maybe it was an eagle. The 4x4s circled the mayors and mercs, machine guns leveled, then came to a ragged halt. Four or five machine-pistol-armed men in black dismounted and leaned against the jeeps, leering at the mayors.

The unmistakable *clomp, clomp* of heavy BattleMechs shook the terminal. More gun trucks drove down the walkway of Concourse A. BattleMechs stomped beside them on the heavy-equipment road. As the trucks gunned in, one BattleMech stopped, took two steps and climbed onto the floor of the terminal. The ceiling was just high enough for the BattleMech as it began a slow, menacing tread toward the mayors.

"That's a seventy-five-ton *Ryoken II*!" a merc gasped.

"At ease in ranks," the Major whispered through drawn lips.

A few mayors took a step back. Beside them, others gently pulled them back into ranks. "Nobody runs," came from somewhere.

"We're all in this together," another whispered.

Grace gritted her teeth and examined the 'Mech closely. The cockpit was surrounded by missile launchers. Four autocannons all seemed aimed at her. The fists on the thing could smash her flat. Something behind the hands looked like meat cleavers. Mouth dry, Grace focused on keeping her feet in neutral. *I will not run. Everyone else can. I cannot.*

No one ran.

"Isn't that the Legate's *Ryoken*?" someone whispered.

"His wasn't painted red and black."

"Yeah, but that dent in the left cooler. Remember two years back when that trainee, what's-his-name, backed a truck into it?"

"Shut up," came back from Glen. Not as elegant as Hanson's "At ease," but effective at getting the civilians quiet. But if this was the Legate's 'Mech, how had it gotten off-planet? Was that why Santorini showed up when Grace had chased that poor steward? If she'd looked in the right place, would she have found a *Ryoken*? More evidence that Santorini had the blood of Alkalurops' two murdered planetary leaders on his hands.

Behind the *Ryoken* came a *Jupiter* and a *Legionnaire* in black and red. The terminal shook with each step they took. One mayor whispered, "This building wasn't made for those things. If they aren't careful, they'll bring the place down." But the 'Mechs spread out, distributed their weight, and the terminal shivered less. Other black-and-red BattleMechs and 'Mech MODs came down the heavy-equipment road but stayed on it, heading outside.

The *Ryoken* turned to face the mayors. It tried three times, like a new driver trying to parallel park a rig. There were snickers among the small-town mayors who spotted the problem.

Then the room grew silent. Even the gun truck drivers quit revving their engines.

The silence was broken only when the *Ryoken*'s cockpit opened to show Alfred Santorini in a jet-black uniform with silver piping. There was another long pause as he glowered down at them and they looked up at him. Grace froze her face in the blankest expression she'd worn since birth.

"People of Alkalurops," Santorini began. "You turned down my reasonable proposal to keep you safe from marauders and raiders. Now I've shown you how easy it is to pick off a planet like yours in these harsh times. Do not expect me to repeat my offer. I do not come to help you. This time I come as your conqueror." That brought a ragged cheer from the gun trucks.

Santorini leaned forward. "Here are my terms. Martial law will continue. Failure to comply with any and all of my legal regulations will result in summary execution." There was the slightest movement among the mercs. Their posted martial law covered some minor stuff. Would the rules of war allow them to shoot people for such infractions?

"Second, to support the security I now bring you, all sales will immediately include a thirty percent tax."

"What?" "That's outrageous!" "That'll mess up the economy," was whispered among the mayors.

"In order to provide an immediate source of operating funds for my administration, I am levying a twenty percent tax on all lands and buildings based upon their latest sales value. Such taxes will be paid within the week."

Grace started figuring what twenty percent of her mom's house and the mines would be—and if she had that much cash. Falkirk could go to a barter system to avoid money changing hands. Preoccupied as she was, she didn't miss the looks that passed around the gun truck drivers. So they were Santorini's tax collectors. None looked smart enough to count to ten.

"Some of you may be wondering if I have the will to hold on to what I have taken."

The autocannons on the *Ryoken* came to life.

In a blink, twelve mayors went down in a spray of lead that splattered blood, flesh and bone over the thirty meters behind where they'd stood. Grace touched a sting on her cheek, and her hand came away bloody. The woman next to Grace had a splinter of bone sticking out of her arm.

"Rest assured, good people, I will hold what I have taken. I have no patience for opposition. Do it my way, and we'll all survive these hard times. Annoy me, and you and your families will die. There are those on my staff who will make you welcome death—a long-delayed death."

Beside Grace, a young man stood as if in a trance. A shiver went through him. He uttered a low moan and took a step forward. Grace brought her heel down on his stationary foot, and he stumbled. People in front realized what was happening and fumbled for him. The man silently fought them for a moment, then dissolved into a hopeless rage of tears.

"Is that you, Grace O'Malley?" Santorini said, adjusting his seat and aiming the *Ryoken*'s cannons at her.

"Yes," she said, then added, "sir."

"No more chasing after windmills, is it?"

"It seemed like a good idea at the time," Grace said, backing down only so far. "Your way looks like a better idea just now."

"And for the foreseeable future, I assure you," Santorini said. He turned his head to the mercs but kept his guns aimed at Grace. "Hanson, you have done well. I consider Allabad and the major cities pacified. My special police will take over your quarters here. Redeploy your units."

"Yes, sir," the merc commander said.

"Now I think we understand one another. Obey me and you will live. Disobey me and you will die slowly. You may go now."

Grace turned her back, not sure if at any moment the *Ryoken* would splatter her across the terminal concrete. She walked for the exit, setting a pace neither suicide slow nor obviously hasty. Others followed her. Only after they were outside and the door closed did any mayor break ranks. Some ran. Others fell to their knees and vomited. More sat as their shaking legs could support them no more.

Grace searched the crowd for people she knew. "Where's Glen? Where's the new mayor of Lothran?" No one knew until a man, covered on one side with a thick spray of blood, looked up from where he had been emptying his stomach.

"They're gone. They were standing next to me, and then they were gone." Grace nodded—those two had pulled off the Maid in the Mist drill. She glanced around and found that about half the towns that had sugared the motor pool would need new mayors. A coincidence? Grace doubted that. The DropShip might not have been talking to Alkalurops, but someone down here had been keeping them up on what was happening. Hanson? Maybe. She spotted the mercs leaving by a different door. Hanson glanced her way, made eye contact, then broke it quickly.

Grace stood, wondering how she'd get back to town now that Glen wasn't there to drive. "How do I tell his wife? His kids?" she murmured. Suddenly, getting back to town seemed a minor problem.

"Major Hanson, sir," Arthur St. George, the XO, said with a nervous laugh, "any rumors you might have heard that I wanted your job. Believe me, they are exaggerated."

"Stow it," L. J. shot back through clenched teeth.

The rest of the walk to the command van was quiet, and at the cadence L. J. set. He waited until they were moving, Topkick driving, before he let another word out.

"In case any of you missed that, our client just splattered the mayors from the two towns with the missing patrols and about half of the mayors from towns where our vehicles were sabotaged. That is either an amazing coincidence or evidence that our client has sources on this planet reporting to him." He eyed each of his subordinates. Each met his stare. "We will assume the source is civilian. However, I am feeling less and less trust for anyone from this stinking hole."

Does that include a redhead?

"Our client wants us out of town, and wants our quarters for his . . . associates." L. J. would not call them either police or a force. Maybe against helpless civilians they'd be dangerous.

"Adjutant, see that all our troops, equipment, supplies and anything else with letterhead, a property number or anything that could be traced to us is on a truck out of here before sunset."

"Everything?" Eddie squeaked at the workload.

"Everything. We will not leave behind so much as a scrap of paper that could be dropped at a crime scene to connect us to it. You understand me?"

"I think so, sir."

"XO, drop your sense of humor in the next trash can. Our troops will need all the steadying we can give them. That leaves no room for jokes. I want you to . . ." L. J. called up a map of the area around

Allabad. The capital, Little London, Lothran, Banya and two others were taken. He looked for a good place to center his command. If trouble came from anywhere? There was Falkirk, way up that lovely valley. If he centered his troops on that threat axis . . .

"Art, get to Dublin Town. Call ahead and tell the lieutenant to prepare to receive the command and support company."

"And a big chunk of three battalions?" the XO asked.

That brought L. J. up short. Taking three battalions back to where he'd led out one had sounded great. But the vehicles with sugared fuel tanks had been under guard, and someone had to lead those patrols into whatever black hole they disappeared into.

"Eddie, message to all detached commands. Effective immediately all local enlistments are canceled."

"Sir?"

"You heard me. This planet isn't nearly as pacified as it's tried to look. And with a client running this place like his private madhouse, it's going to be a lot less pacified this time next week. Anyone remember reading the histories of mercs used as covering force for power-crazy clients?"

Nobody had.

"Not likely to be posted in a Regimental Hall of Honors." The van was approaching his HQ . . . his former HQ. "All right, boys and girls. We are about to face leadership challenges the likes of which you never dreamed. And that's just among our own. What the locals throw at us will match nothing you've ever studied. 'O Lord, for what we are about to receive, make us truly thankful,' " he recited, an ancient soldiers' prayer.

11

Allabad, Alkalurops
Prefecture IX, The Republic of the Sphere
9 August 3134; local summer

Dazed with shock, Grace talked with the mayors and Guild Masters in Allabad. They reached a consensus: they would keep their heads down and see how things developed before doing anything. Grace hoped that Betsy would contact her that night, but there was no knock at the window and Ben was emphatic that they not hunt for her.

"You could not find her if she did not want finding, and she would not like the attention you would bring as you failed."

So Grace kept talking to people. Angus was outraged. "Killing those mayors was cold-blooded murder. Mark my words, we are in a land without laws. And *this* lawyer does not want to live in such a land."

The next morning the coroner's office called. "You wouldn't be headed north by way of Little London, would you?"

"I guess I could," Grace said.

"I have Glen Harriman's body—what I can piece together of it. Could you take him home or do I just ship him?"

"I'll take Glen back to his wife."

Wilson's new 4x4 served well as a hearse, but the stop was more than just a good deed. Little London was mad. When Grace brought their mayor's casket to his widow, she walked into an impassioned argument over which street poles to hang the captured mercs from. That they would hang was already settled. Ben reddened and was opening his mouth when Grace stepped in.

"Did any of these mercs kill anyone?"

"Well, no."

"Have any of the mercs done anything since they arrived in Little London that made you want to kill them?"

"No, but—"

"No buts. Glen led you. He kept this place safe and the mercs decent to you. The son of a bitch who killed him is back there in Allabad, not here. What kind of songs do you think they'll sing about the Maid in the Mist if we string them up?"

"But what do we do with them? There's a story going round that the mercs are pulling out and those Black and Reds will take over Little London. We can't hold the mercs here."

"Send them to Falkirk. We'll keep them locked up tight."

So Ben drove a small van north with ten prisoners, and Grace made a quick detour to Lothran to collect ten more. She was back at Falkirk and eating breakfast after her first good night's sleep in a week when Chato and Jobe knocked on her door.

"Have you heard the latest news?" Jobe asked.

"I *was* enjoying a quiet cup of coffee and figuring how to pay my taxes," Grace said, pointing at her 'puter and its sad proof that owning a mine conferred no income unless it was worked.

Chato turned on the kitchen vid as Jobe poured coffee. A familiar business reporter was talking to Robert Carey, eldest son and scion of one of the first families to settle on Alkalurops. "I had my tax money in hand," he said, waving cash. "But as the tax collector pulled up, another guy jogged up and made an offer to buy my family's home, mines, ranch—everything. It was a good offer, but I can't sell out my family. This land is ours. So as he's leaving, he gives his offer to the tax man, and that's the bill I get. Not what my inheritance was taxed at but this new price, ten times higher. I can't pay that."

"So what now?" the reporter asked.

"I have twenty-four hours to come up with the money or get off the land. But I can't sell! Not with a thirty percent sales tax! I couldn't raise the money even if I tried."

"So you'll be moving?"

"Over my dead body," Robert said, glaring at the camera.

"So there you have it from Robert Carey's own mouth. And he's not alone in facing this—not at all," the camera panned down the mansions of Landers Row, where the wealthy families of Alkalurops kept their town residences. "Every owner here can tell you the same story. One did agree to sell," the reporter said. "But the offer was withdrawn and passed to the tax collector anyway. This is Clyde Hinman. I'll be here tomorrow morning, live, when the twenty-four hours expire."

"That was a rerun of yesterday's story," Chato said.

"What happens this morning?" Grace asked.

"You'd have to be on Landers Row to know. Seems

the reporter didn't show for work this morning. He shot himself last night. Suicide, the Special Police reported."

"What does the coroner's office say?"

"Body was sent for cremation immediately. Seems the Special Police can do that," Jobe said.

Grace went to the sink and slowly washed her coffee cup—a ritual her father did many times as he thought about things that needed hard thinking. "Santorini doesn't just want LCI to move its headquarters here. He wants to own most of the planet when LCI arrives," she said slowly.

"The better to profit from the sales of land to LCI's boss men and hangers-on," Jobe said. "Isn't that how a lot of old wealthy got started?"

"I'll remind you, Jobe, Irish and Scots had plenty of experience on the receiving end—and with Black and Tans, who seem to be wearing Black and Red hereabout."

Chato eyed the vid. "How far will Santorini's grasp reach—both in places like Allabad and out to places like Falkirk?"

"If we worry only about our own backyard," Grace said, "there will be few to help us when the Black and Reds knock on our door. If we're going to do something, we need to do it together." Grace put down her coffee cup. "Let's get Ben and the mercs."

Ben was deep in calisthenics, leading both his mercs and the militia who would be fighting with them. That included a young woman from Kilkenny who had taken over Pirate since she'd had more time to practice than Grace.

Grace waited until Ben came out of his exercise-induced trance. He and the other six quickly joined the three mayors, other MOD warriors keeping a respectful distance but not leaving, either. Grace filled them in on the extortion under way and the cost to the reporter who covered it.

"What are the networks saying about this?" Ben asked.

"Most have switched to old romance vids, no guns."

"Smart cookies, didn't need that message twice," Syn said.

"Are the Roughriders in on this?" Grace asked.

"No," Ben said with finality. "That is why Santorini moved them out of the major towns. No, he is rooting his tyranny where the money is. The Roughriders will be detailed to keep people like us from molesting Santorini's own while they fleece the sheep. I do not remember the last time a merc ended up with this mission. It is not something we like to think about."

"So what do we do now?" Grace asked.

Ben turned to his warriors. "We train harder. Now we know the face of our enemy. We know the evil he nurtures in his heart. We know why we must fight. And when we fight, we must win."

The students left quickly, quietly, with purpose in their steps and anger stiffening their backs. *Good,* Grace thought. *You're going to need all that, and a hell of a lot of skill if you're to survive a battle with the Roughriders and live to fight our real enemy, the Black and Reds.*

"Any word from Betsy?" Grace whispered.

"You will be the first to know when there is," Ben said.

"I'd sure like to know what Santorini's up to," Grace said.

"You think he knows what he's doing?" Syn said, laughing and shrugging her shoulders. How she kept her boobs inside that low-cut bodysuit was a clear violation of the law of gravity.

"You don't think he knows?" Grace said.

"Probably can't tell from minute to minute," Syn said, walking off. "Maybe I could help him make up his mind."

"I would not let that woman help any man make up his mind unless I knew how her mind was set," Grace said, eyes following Syn. Then she turned to Ben. "I want to talk to Hanson. He needs to make up *his* mind. Maybe, if we talk, we can settle part of this mess before it goes horribly bad."

"Grace, that is the miner in you talking. You look to the bottom line of your profit and loss and think you can agree to most anything that is mutually profitable."

"It's always worked before."

"But now you are talking to a Roughrider under contract. His primary concern has little to do with profit and everything to do with honorably fulfilling that contract."

"How do you honorably fulfill a contract to a tyrant?"

"That is a problem I imagine Hanson is sweating out right about now," Ben said with a thin smile.

L. J. hated sitting in tribunals. If a merc broke the law, terminate his contract and let the local police handle the rest. But today he sat in a tribunal with his XO fidgeting uncomfortably, and Mallary's face a mask. The prisoner was a mess: both eyes were blackened, a broken nose had been taped by the surgeon, and his arms above the handcuffs showed the yellow and blue of further beatings. Two female MPs stood at parade rest at the prisoner's elbows.

"Branson Quantrail, be glad your squadmates interrupted you," L. J. growled, "or I'd be forming the battalion for a rogue's parade, and before sunset today you'd have taken fifty lashes and swung by the neck until you were dead. Do you understand me, mister?" The man had raised his eyes when L. J. named him. Now he was squinting at the floor again.

"Yes, sir," he slurred from a badly cut and bruised mouth.

"If you had molested that civilian—'penetration, no matter how slight,'" L. J. quoted from the regs, "I would not have the option to let you live. If what you are about to face can be called living." Quantrail's not-quite-so-drunken squadmates had found him, pants down to his knees, knife at the throat of a terrified young woman, and had the presence of mind to pull Corporal Quantrail off the girl. She had fled screaming but, upon a request from the regiment, had presented herself for examination. Luckily for Quantrail, she was still a virgin.

L. J. turned to the adjutant, who flipped on the recorder for the verdict. "I find you guilty of attempted rape and sentence you to ninety days in the stockade on bread and water, forfeiture of all pay and allowances, and reduction in pay to recruit. You will present yourself for one hour of punishment parade with a one hundred and fifty pound pack at 0600, 1200 and 1900 hours each day. You will spend one hour double-timing around the post accompanied by an MP with a walking stick." That should guarantee all hands got a good look at him once, maybe twice a day. The women MPs were known for their liberal application of the walking stick if the punishment pace slowed. Quantrail would end his enlistment a reminder to all that Roughriders stood for more than mob rule.

"Upon the completion of your ninety-day sentence, you will be discharged immediately and locally. So you can talk this over with the girl and her family using whatever they bring to the 'little talk.' Guards, get this sack of shit out of my sight." The MPs, easily as tall and muscled as their prisoner, hustled him off. That was one man in a world of hurt.

Problem was, this entire battalion was in just as bad a hurt and getting in deeper every second. L. J. turned to his adjutant. "Eddie, see that all hands are read the following order: 'You are mercenaries, heirs to a proud tradition. As mercenaries, you live under and live by the rules of war. There is no place in those rules for misbehavior. What belongs to the civilians of this planet is theirs. If you drink it, you pay for it. If you break it, you pay for it. If it is not offered in free exchange to you, you do not take it unless authorized by your commanding officer. The regiment will not long remember what we do here, but the regiment will never forget if we return without our honor.' " L. J. turned to the Sergeant Major. "Did I miss anything?"

"That about covers it, sir."

"Captain, see that this is read to all personnel at morning formation. Inform the officers that if I have to flog a trooper, his officer will be strung up right beside him, taking lash for lash, fifty in all, and wishing I would hang him, too." L. J. slowly took in his staff. These were tough orders, but their situation would allow nothing less. No one questioned him.

"That will be done, Major," Eddie said.

"Very good." L. J. glanced around the room, now vacant except for his XO, ops, adjutant and Topkick. "We have problems. I want ideas—ideas far beyond any book written."

"I don't think the regiment has ever been a tyrant's enforcer," Arthur St. George said.

"XO, we are not a tyrant's enforcer," L. J. shot back. "His damned Special Police are doing the enforcing just fine for him. We are stuck out here, keeping the locals from doing what any enraged citizenry would do—throw the bums out. It is not the same thing, and I don't want our troops to even think it is the same thing. We can't let our troops see their hands covered with the same sewage Santorini's swimming in. If they do, we lose all discipline. And without that, ladies and gentlemen, we're no better than civilians."

The staff looked at one another for a long minute, absorbed all he'd said, examined what he saw for the battalion and their own careers. None much appreciated the view.

Topkick responded first. "Usual answer for problems like these, sir, is to keep the troops busy. Make sure they're too bushed to get in trouble."

"Most of them are working twelve-hour watches already," Eddie put in. "After we terminated the locals, just guarding the compounds is taking most of our troops' time."

"Keep them away from the locals," Art said as if reading a textbook's checklist. He shook his head. "Hardly need to do that. Since the Oktoberfest, the locals are damn standoffish, right, Mallary?" The ops officer scowled but nodded her agreement.

"Not a lot of patrolling going on," L. J. said, leafing through his 'puter reports. "What are the locals up to?"

"Don't know, sir," Mallary answered. "I don't know what anyone is up to. The Net's only playing old vids, no local news. I can't ask our client to report who his bully boys are thumping. The battalion is deaf, dumb and blind, sir."

"A great way to get massacred," Art said before L. J. could.

L. J. glanced at a map of his command, scattered over twelve towns. Once that wide deployment had given him control over the ground he walked, and recruiting fields with which to grow his battalion. Now security was eating his lunch, leaving him few troops for patrols outside his own perimeter fence.

"Mallary, if you were to concentrate the battalion down from the scatter-hell we're in right now, what would you abandon? Where would you center our force?"

She tapped her hand computer, and a map filled the table. "The new mining claims centered on New York and New Pittsburgh are not under our client's control. I would ignore them as sources of trouble."

"So would I," L. J. said.

"That leaves this area," she said, indicating a large expanse centered on Dublin Town. "Allabad is south of us, but there's not a lot south of it. Too hot I hear."

"This whole planet is too hot," Eddie moaned.

"Little London, Lothran and Banya are south of us. But I suspect you knew that when you picked your new headquarters," she said with a pleased smile at spotting what her boss was up to.

"Due north is the Gleann Mor Valley—lovely, I'm

told, this time of year with Scotch broom, thistle, and heather in bloom. Explain why a lot of 'Mechs have taken to walking its hills."

That surprised the other staff but not L. J. "When did they start their perambulating about in the open?"

"Two days ago. Our awe-inspiring client confiscated all that expensive housing that morning. Gray 'Mechs started drilling in full view that afternoon."

"Think our fearless Leader got the intended message?"

"If he did, it didn't keep him next day from confiscating what was valuable in the other four towns his toads took over. Nobody'll accuse him of being the compassionate, caring type," Mallary said.

"Not me, anyway. What kind of 'Mech force is up north?"

"I counted thirty-nine gray 'Mech MODs, several dozen gray gun trucks led by a hovertank, sir, and lots of infantry. And there's a surprise, sir—a dozen or more battle suits."

"Surprises, surprises," L. J. said. "Firepower?"

"Only a guess, sir. Our satellite's not the best. At full power, it's doing well to make out the battle suits. What they're carrying is anybody's guess."

"Can't be too bad," Art said. "The only BattleMech this planet had a year ago was the Legate's 'Mech, and our Leader is running around in that for kicks."

"Captain, how do you get minerals out of rock?"

Art stiffened. "I don't know, sir."

"Well, there are a hell of a lot of miners out there who do. And there are a hell of a lot of people on this planet getting madder by the minute at the man we are contracted to fight for. Don't you think you ought to know a bit more about what they can throw at you before you're fighting them?"

L. J. knew you didn't reprimand an officer in public. He knew it, but damn it felt good to let someone feel the temper he spent his days keeping on tight rein.

"Miners use explosives," Mallary said in her best schoolteacher voice. "Their 'Mechs carry superhardened drills and rock cutters. Hand to hand, an unmodified MiningMech can be a hazard to any BattleMech we have. If they're modified to project the explosives miners have in inventory, we could be facing a major force."

"You got that right in one," L. J. said.

His 'puter chimed "Incoming call," but the screen stayed blank. "I'd like to get together with you, talk about old times," a woman's voice said. He recognized it as Grace's. "The hills we climbed, the fun we had jumping around," she finished.

L. J. frowned. "Or staying one jump ahead of each other."

"Your memories are different from mine. If you can make it, meet me on Main Street, Dublin Town. Say, in an hour."

"You in a hurry?" L. J. wondered if a trap was already set.

"Time flies when you don't know what's coming next."

"What comes next could be a bullet in my back if I walk down Main Street just now." Mallary nodded at that.

"I didn't know mercs were so interested in dying in bed."

That was not encouraging. But L. J. had almost asked Grace for a meeting when they'd met at the port. They did need to talk. "I'll see you," L. J. said, cut the connection, and nodded at the Sergeant Major. "Draw a jeep. You're driving."

"Weapons load?" Topkick asked.

"Sidearms." Most thought them short-ranged, but L. J. had seen the Sergeant Major drill a man-sized target at very long range.

"Be careful, sir," Mallary said as L. J. went out the door. Coming from her, it sounded sincere.

Main Street in Dublin Town wound along MacGillion's Brook, which in summer was a muddy trickle.

L. J. had Topkick drop him off at the courthouse at the foot of the street. "Sir, that road winds a bit. I won't have a line of sight on you for half of it," the Sergeant Major said as he braked to a halt.

"We all take our risks," L. J. said, dismounting the jeep, checking his 9-millimeter sidearm, and settling it loose in the holster.

The walk up Main Street was long. The buildings were adobe, washed in pastels that took some getting used to but matched the flowers growing in boxes under every window. A low bluff to the west offered protection against the prevailing winds. The people he saw smiled and waved at each other and became cold as three-day dead when they saw him. A young man and an old lady looked ready to give him a piece of their minds, but others with them talked them away. He was five long blocks from the courthouse when he spotted a certain redhead seated on a stone bench beside the brook. She was feeding a goose and its goslings. "Mind if I join you?" he asked.

"It's a free country . . . or was," Grace said, and flashed him a sad smile that made him want to fight to the death for Alkalurops' freedom. "And your Sergeant Major won't have any trouble keeping you in sight," she finished.

"You'll have to excuse him. He's the nervous type," L. J. said, taking a seat. Grace offered him half her corn, and he took it. "I'd prefer to have my forty mercs back."

"Only twenty were really yours, and I'd gladly have you march all that's yours into your DropShip. Lot of sadness in life, isn't there? For now, they're safe in my personal custody."

"In Falkirk where the gray 'Mech MODs drill?"

"Actually, not there, but I'm glad you noticed our little demonstration. Ben told me you should know that what you saw was only one echelon. There's more," she told him. All sincerity.

"Or there might not be," L. J. said. "Part of the

fog of what I won't call war. You know you're in a deadly game."

She looked away. "Last night a couple in Allabad were walking home from supper. Black and Reds stopped them. Beat the man to a pulp and gang-raped the woman." She watched him from the corner of her eye as she threw a few kernels to the goose.

"I'm sorry," L. J. said.

"Two days ago people started getting offers from the Black and Reds to buy their businesses, their homes, for maybe a penny on the stone of what they're worth."

"I thought they were jacking up the prices?"

"That's the tax scam your client used to scoop up most of the big wealth here. No, this is little scum grabbing crumbs. Their offer is one you can't refuse. Some did and got hauled off to jail. The lucky ones got beaten. Others 'died trying to escape.'" Grace paused, then tossed all the corn to the geese. That set off a racket as they fought for it.

"Angus Throckmorton has been a friend of my family since my grandpa ran the mine. He's a lawyer," she said softly, gazing into some middle distance that might be less painful than where she spoke from. "Angus believed in the law and lived by it. Like lunch with your sergeant, there are Some Things That Aren't Done. He wrote up a request for habeas corpus and went to court. Black and Reds stopped him at the door, demanded to know why he was there. When he told them, they beat him. Beat him and kicked him down the courthouse steps."

Grace faced L. J. He met her eyes and tried not to show a caring his contract did not allow him to act on. "When I was a kid and bored while Da and Angus were in court, I counted those steps. Forty-nine. They kicked him down forty-nine steps and left him. An old lady took him to the hospital. He died there today."

"I'm sorry," L. J. said, hearing how hollow his words were. "I hadn't heard."

She shook her head. "No surprise. There's not a lot making the news these days. But there are other ways of spreading the word. I could send you copies of what I get."

"I don't think my client would be happy about that."

"And we know what happens when your client isn't happy. Loren, your client is a bloody murderer. Does your Colonel know what's going on here?"

"I doubt it. However, he signed the contract, and it will be in force for another four months." The duration of his contract was classified. Still, he gave it. Maybe the clash could be held off until he *could* march his mercs back aboard ship.

"In four months there won't be a planet left," Grace said. "Ben warned me that we'd reach this point—me wanting you to leave, you held here by your honor."

"Honor is all a merc really has."

"But you're backing up a thief and cold-blooded murderer!"

"If a client can't count on a merc to fulfill his contract, what do I have to sell?"

She stood, sending the geese scattering. The sunlight lit her hair afire. L. J. doubted he'd ever meet a more beautiful woman. He tried to measure the strange currents millions of years of evolution had woven into him that made this woman so attract him. She desperately needed his help, and that drew him to her. But there was also a power about her that challenged him to match hers with his own. Seductive stuff. But he commanded a battalion of mercs, and evolution was small stuff against the honor of the regiment.

"When next we meet, we will be enemies on the battlefield," Grace told him formally.

"We've been there before," he pointed out.

"Yes, but this time, only one of us will survive the fight." There was an absoluteness in her words that brooked no argument.

"Whatever the outcome, it will be a loss for both of us."

"You could be right," she said, and turned away from him.

L. J. scanned the street. No sniper. An old woman selling flowers shook her head at him. He walked for the square, but Topkick met him halfway. "From your face, I'd say the talk didn't go all that well," the Sergeant Major said as L. J. settled in the jeep.

"Now it starts, Sergeant Major. Send the word out to the NCOs through your private channels that the gloves will be coming off the locals in the next couple of days. Forget the candy ass and the white gloves. From here forward, it gets real."

"Kind of figured it that way, sir. Don't worry, Major, the battalion's solid. The Colonel will be proud of us."

"Didn't doubt the battalion was solid, Sergeant Major. Just wish we stood with a more solid cause at our side."

The Sergeant Major had no answer for that. They drove back to the post in silence.

12

Allabad, Alkalurops
Prefecture IX, The Republic of the Sphere
16 August 3134; local summer

L. J. did not like being out of the local news loop—
not the way things were going down the tubes. His
time in Allabad had been short and sterile, leaving
him no contacts he could trust. There had been a
chambermaid with raven hair and olive skin who
worked at the LCI Manor House. She could drop a
ton of interesting local tidbits in the time she took to
change linens.

L. J. found her Net address and sent off a chatty
note about how his present hotel had a definite lack
of staff and he might be looking for a maid. He ended
with a "How are things going for you?" which he
hoped might get her talking.

The next morning, things began to get interesting.

L. J. was enjoying his second cup of coffee when his 'puter beeped in four-part harmony with Mallary's, Art's and Eddie's. L. J. slapped his first and found himself looking at Lieutenant Brajinski, presently occupying Kerry, a small town between Allabad and Little London. "Sir, four of our MechWarriors woke up this morning to find daggers in their pillows and notes saying 'MechWarriors, go home while you still can.'"

The dagger the lieutenant waved looked more like a restaurant steak knife, but "dagger" certainly sounded more dramatic. L. J. raised an eyebrow to his staff. "You're billeted in a former hotel?" Eddie said, checking his 'puter for the answer.

"Yes, sir."

"Still using the hotel's support staff?" L. J. asked.

"Yes, sir. They've been very grateful for the work, sir. No problem at all. Frees our troops from—" The young lieutenant trailed off. "I see your point, sir. I will let them go."

"And see if those knives are similar to those in any local eateries," Mallary said.

"If I locate the people who did this?" the lieutenant asked.

"Let me know what you've found out," L. J. said firmly. "Take no action until I order it. Understood?"

"Yes, sir. Clearly, sir." The screen went blank.

"So it starts," L. J. said to his team. "Raise the alert level, XO. Mallary, have your intelligence staff try to get me some solid analysis on what's going on here. Since the news went all nice and fluffy I don't know shit about what's happening."

"I'll try, sir, but we aren't getting much hard data."

"Those knives looked pretty hard to me."

"Yes, sir," Mallary said, standing. "I'll get on it."

"Eddie, start looking into concentrating the battalion."

"Sir," St. George said, "if I may point out, that would make us an even easier target and make it even harder to track what's going on outside our line of sight."

"Good points all, Art, but there's more firepower at Falkirk than I have here. If they start moving, how much of the battalion will they overrun before we know it?"

"We've got the satellite feed, sir."

"They know about it. They only show it what they want it to see. If they move their 'Mech MODs from one barn to the next south, will we know they're here before they start shooting up Dublin Town? Damn the shoestring budget," L. J. snapped. They'd deployed without a single air spy vehicle. It was as if the guy funding this mess had no idea what a good team needed. Well, it wasn't as if Santorini knew a lot about what he was getting into.

Or did he?

If Santorini got in trouble, would a lot of Stormhammer or House Steiner stuff come running? It wouldn't be the first time in history that a small troop of soldiers were set up to fail so the bigger guns could gallop to the rescue.

"XO, Adjutant, you have your orders. It looks to be a busy morning. Let's turn to."

At his desk was a chatty note from Betty, the maid. She rambled on about how the place had changed since he left. "Some of the new guys seem to think a maid is there to help them get the sheets dirty as well as change them," answered one of his questions. "Cook says she can't buy good fresh fruit, vegetables and meat. The farmers' market just doesn't have anything like it used to." This told L. J. to look out for trouble around the food supply. Betty was also hunting for a new place to eat. Her old standby had changed hands and was now owned by an off-worlder. The cook had mouthed off to the new owner and been fired. "The new cook can't boil water." So Grace was right that junior scum were taking their own chunks and making a bad situation worse.

L. J. had not liked the looks of the Black and Reds the moment he'd seen them. The 'Mechs marched like trainees. The guys in the gun trucks looked like the thugs a real police force would put away for a very long time. What prison bottom had Santorini dragged to get a collection of gutter scrapings like these?

Betty finished her note saying she'd gotten a raise that doubled her pay, putting her ahead of the rising prices, and she probably wasn't looking to change jobs. L. J. printed the note for Mallary and her intelligence crew just as she appeared at his door.

"We've had our first attack, sir, outside Banya."

"Any casualties?"

"None, sir. Some bunch of locals planted a mine for a hovertank patrol. They guessed low on the amount of pressure one of those things puts out, and the mine blew before the tank got there. Real goobers, sir."

"Even goobers can learn, Captain."

"Think it was by that group up north? The Falkirk group?"

"Not likely. They have a hovertank, and the 'Mechs working with them would never make a beginner's mistake like that."

"How'd they get a hovertank, if I may ask?"

L. J. started to say, "Ask Sergeant Godfrey," but that moron was among the missing. "I've got this letter from someone I trust in Allabad," he said, handing Betty's note to Mallary. "Synopsize this so no one can recognize where it came from and get it out to our occupation platoons. Tell the lieutenants this supports the rise in alert status."

"I'll do that, sir," Mallary said.

"Then let's—" he started, but his com was buzzing and blinking a red light. His client. L. J. positioned himself behind his desk and tapped the com. "Yes, Mr. Santorini."

"I understand someone tried to bomb one of my tanks today," he said with what some might mistake for a smile of glee.

"An amateurish effort," L. J. said dismissively.

"You are launching a punitive action."

"I am taking appropriate action."

"And what do you consider appropriate for the attempted murder of my troops in their sleep last night?"

"We are investigating to determine what action to take."

His client frowned. "I would already have people hanging from lampposts. I see your Colonel sent me someone who has trouble making a decision."

L. J. nodded noncommittally and said nothing.

"I am having trouble and require a military operation," he said, as if uttering the magic words that would instantaneously turn a valley red with fire, blood and smoke.

"What trouble, sir?" L. J. said, trying to sound concerned.

"Farmers are withholding produce from market. I require you to conduct a sweep of land around Allabad and bring the farmers and their produce trucks in at gunpoint. If they resist, kill the first few. The rest will follow."

L. J. gave Betsy another mark for quality intel. "That'd be quite an operation, sir." About equal to killing the goose that laid the golden egg, but L. J. didn't say that. "Unfortunately, it is not covered by our contract."

"Not covered!"

"Our contract is to seize and hold this planet. We seized it rather faster than expected and held it for the month while you were in transit. You relieved us from holding the area around Allabad and other cities. You will have to use your own police to do that, sir."

L. J. considered suggesting he lower the tax rate on food sold at the market since it was pretty clear food was making it through back channels to other food providers. If the man couldn't figure out why meat was not on his own table, L. J. certainly wouldn't be the one to paint him a picture. Messengers for guys like Santorini tended to get killed for carrying what otherwise looked like useful bits of information.

It didn't matter. His com went dead immediately. "I don't think our Leader is happy," he told Mallary.

"Then he'll be even less happy when he finds out what I just did while you were on the phone."

"Which was?"

"A patrol inside Lothran was attacked by boys throwing rocks. I told the patrol to withdraw."

"Good order for today. Eddie, get in here, we're redeploying the battalion," he shouted. "One company here in Dublin Town and the others here, here and here," he said, tapping small towns in an arc between Dublin and the mouth of the Gleann Mor Valley.

"That our threat axis?" Mallary asked.

"It's the only real threat we face." Eddie ducked his head in L. J.'s office and listened to the new deployment. "Again, I want to remove everything with the regiment's stamp, seal or brand on it. Leave nothing behind."

"And you want it all done yesterday. I understand, sir."

"No." L. J. smiled. "I don't think you do, Captain. You see, while a unit is redeploying, it loses some of its ability to react to new orders. Its commander might even have to tell his client he was temporarily unable to perform a requested mission, if you take my meaning, Captain."

"Moving could be considered a reason to temporarily not do some things that you might not want to do," Eddie said.

"No, no, no," L. J. said as if to a particularly slow child. "The regiment is always ready to execute its orders. That is our tradition. It's just that in a redeployment, it might have to complete one order before doing another. And since we must be very meticulous about this move . . ."

"Yes, sir. Understood, sir. The battalion will always be ready for orders, sir, and I am about to set a new record for redeployment—just not one I'll mention on my next résumé."

"I think we misunderstand each other perfectly," L. J. said.

"Major," Mallary said once Eddie was gone, "in your next command, if you need an ops officer, I sure hope you'll skip my name."

"Mallary, my friend, unless we're careful, all of our names will be entered on the rolls of the regiment with a little note to 'pick this one last.' "

Grace had a new intelligence source, thanks to a couple of Jobe's boys. They had rigged a search on the Net—not the public side that was about as exciting as cold potatoes, but the personal side with its notes and letters. It painted an ugly picture.

The Black and Reds were spreading out from their five main towns, demanding that farmers sell them produce, crops and meat at a discount to cover the cost of taxes. That amounted to near confiscation, but since it was at gunpoint, objections were limited to notes and mail among farmers.

The Black and Reds were still buying homes, businesses, farms—anything they wanted. Those who resisted didn't go to jail; now they just died right there in front of their families. Sales resistance dropped to nil even as the mail got hotter and hotter. At least the people who were bought out were allowed to live in their homes and run their businesses. The thugs had a big appetite but didn't seem to know what to do with what they stole.

Unfortunately, they knew what to do with women.

Alkalurops had never made a cult of a girl's virginity, but here girls decided. Grace could still hear Ma's instructions. "When you make up your mind, I know I won't be able to stop you, but don't let a boy be making up your mind for you. You decide. You call the shots."

Now Black and Reds were calling the shots.

In Lothran the new rules ended in a shoot-out between a family and the Black and Reds. The boys
couldn't stop the police squad that took their sister,
but they knew the town and how to use their gopher
rifles. From first reports, it looked as if the boys were
winning, almost a dozen Black and Reds down and
screaming for medics. Then the 'Mechs stomped in.

The boys were dead, their father and mother as
well. The sister was found with her throat slit. To keep
Lothran from thinking about doing this twice, the
'Mechs shot up and trampled the eight blocks where
the shoot-out took place.

Not all of it, though. The Black and Reds had
bought up a house here, a business there. They stood
among the rubble.

Alkalurops was a powder keg, waiting for the spark.

Two days later the spark came.

A gun truck of Black and Reds was out making
sure farmers got their produce to the now
government-owned packing plants. They must have
been getting plenty careless. They didn't fire a shot
when a farmer and his two sons nailed them with their
AgroMechs. The farmer shredded the Black and Reds.
Shredded them down to blood and scraps.

Now the farmer was running north with his sons,
their wives and children, trying to make it to the
Gleann Mor Valley. Grace hoped they would. She
hoped and she feared.

If they made it, the war would surely start.

L. J. found a note on his 'puter that morning from
Betty. He enjoyed her chatty rundown on life in the
big city. The woman couldn't seem to shake her small-
town amazement at what went on. "But the B and R
types have sure put a lid on the nightlife—not that a
maid has much free time at night, but it's gotten so a
girl can't walk the streets. Mr. Santorini gave me a
pass that he says will make anybody who stops me let

me go. Mr. Santorini is such a nice man." Betty had to be the only person on the planet who thought so.

The cook had plenty of food, but Betty said the meats were the absolute worst she'd ever seen. Why was L. J. not surprised?

"I hear the B and R are recruiting at the local jails." That confirmed L. J.'s own suspicion. "A B and R field marshal confiscated a gaggle of 'Mechs from all kinds of places and ordered a couple of the local 'Mech service and repair centers to come up with a plan to hang lasers on them. The repair guys tried telling him the dinky engines on a worker 'Mech can't power a laser, but he just got mad, pulled out his knife, and shouted threats. They got real agreeable and said they'd have a plan for him in three months. He said six weeks and that was that."

L. J. doubted those mechanics were half as good as the ones the redhead had up in her valley. He also wondered how many of them were heading there. Hang a laser on an internal-combustion-powered 'Mech?! Maybe a laser pointer for a really big briefing. So the Leader was increasing his troops and his 'Mechs. Well, he'd need all the help he could get, because in three months L. J. and his battalion were out of here. L. J. printed the note and took it down to Intelligence. Mallary was away, which gave L. J. an excuse to talk to the Chief Warrant Officer, who really ran Intelligence. A mustang, he'd risen through the ranks. It was said he could smell bad intel. L. J. needed that nose.

"You got another one of those letters for us," Chief Mohamot said, smiling eagerly.

"The same. She still won't take my job offer," L. J. said, handing over the note.

The Chief read it quickly. "Can't blame her for holding on to the job she has if it comes with perks like a get-out-of-rape-free card from our client," he said, then his eyes got wide. "How'd she get privy to table talk about 'Mech MODs?"

"Good question. She knows the cook well. Maybe she pulled temp duty as a server."

"Possible, sir, but I wonder if this isn't too good to be true."

"You don't think Betty's authentic?"

"Sir, I have to doubt everything I know about Betty because I know so little about her. I don't know where she comes from. I don't know who she likes, hates, has a bone to pick with. She's a clean slate that gets written on, that I don't know how to interpret. That's what you pay me for, sir."

The room suddenly got darker. L. J. glanced around, looking for the reason, when he realized that every monitor in the room had gone blank. "Net seems to be down," Chief said. "I'll give Network Disservices a holler."

"Network Services," someone shouted from down the hall, "is not responsible for what you are not seeing on your screens. The Net ain't down, it's gone. Gone on this whole stinking planet!"

The Chief stood. "I guess it starts now, sir."

L. J. held his next staff meeting on the parade ground in front of his HQ. It was the best place to be until Network Services got a backup local Net online. It gave him a good view of his command as it went, like a kicked-over hornet's nest, from ThreatCon Three to Four-plus. To an uninformed observer such as Santorini, it might look like frantic action going nowhere, but L. J. knew what every one of his men and women were doing, and provided the supervision that got them over the few rough spots.

For example, the Chief paraded his Intelligence staff in full combat gear in less than ten minutes. "You got any assignment for us? We got no data to mine, sir."

"You have your backup databases on this pesthole?"

"Everything on Alkalurops is right here." The Chief

patted a small bulge in his battle gear. So did those behind him.

"Hold here. When we see how bad it is, I'll let you know."

"We got a cycle coming up the road," someone bellowed from the front gate. "Appears unarmed. One man, no large packs."

"Tell the guard to stop him, search him, and send him in here on foot," L. J. told an Intelligence guy and sent him off in the ancient role of a runner. Two minutes later he returned with a small short-haired woman in shorts, sandals and a halter top.

"After the pat-down your guards gave me, I feel we ought to at least be engaged," she growled. "I mean, where would I hide anything in this getup?"

"I apologize for their thoroughness. Our Net has been cut, and we are still trying to figure out what's happening."

"That's why the mayor, my husband, sent me here," the woman said, spreading her feet, resting hands on hips, and taking on the gravity of a formal representative. "Our Net's down, too. We don't know why, but we want you to know we didn't do it. We suspect it had something to do with what happened down south."

L. J. frowned. "What happened down south?"

"You don't know?"

"Would you please tell me." L. J. knew that the woman might soon be certified as his enemy. She had to know, too.

"Won't do us any good if you only get his side of the story." She quickly told him what the farmer and his boys had done. "Pretty much rendered them down to liquid fertilizer fit for, say, ten acres. Some started a bit on the fat side," she finished.

"Thank you," L. J. said. So it *had* started. "Specialist, escort this young woman from the post. She entered under a flag of truce. She leaves under regimental protection, understood?"

"Sir. This way, ma'am."

"Eddie!" L. J. shouted.

"The move was started before the blackout. I've got the detachments coming up on backup shortwave radio. What are your orders, sir?"

Eddie Thomas had a tendency to coast on his family name. Then there were days like today when you realized being a merc *was* in the blood. "Have all forces commence immediate road movement. Use extreme caution. All units fall back on Dublin Town. Avoid city centers. Cross country if necessary."

"I'll get that out immediately, sir."

"We have one chance," L. J. said as Eddie double-timed off.

"What's that, sir?" Mallary asked.

"The local opposition didn't know what those damn farmers were going to do any more than we did."

"I'm not sure the farmers knew what they were doing before they did it," the Chief said. "Taking an autoscythe to unarmored people," he finished with a slight shiver.

L. J.'s 'puter beeped and flashed red. He held it up. "I was under the impression the Net was down."

"It is down when I want it down. There's no reason for me to provide it to my enemies. When I want it up, it will be up." Santorini's voice came back at him, cold and dry and maybe a bit brittle and scared. "Are you aware, Major, of the disorder?"

"No, sir," L. J. said, unwilling to admit he'd been talking with what now had to be considered the enemy.

"A dozen farmers attacked a Special Police patrol today. Unprovoked. Totally uncalled-for. They lured them into the farm country with a cry for help, then attacked them from hiding. They are now fleeing north, toward those troublemakers at Falkirk. I want them stopped. I want the lot of them hanging from the nearest pole, along with anyone who helps them." Santorini was shouting now. L. J. held his 'puter at arm's length. Everyone around him heard the orders.

"Sir," L. J. said softly, holding the 'puter closer only when the man fell silent, "I am not in a position to immediately comply with your orders."

L. J. got the 'puter back at arm's length just as Santorini shouted, "And why not?!"

"Based on the worsening conditions, I began a concentration of my battalion so I would be in a position to immediately respond if you were to issue future orders. At the moment my platoons are scattered and in transit."

"You are again telling me you will not follow my orders!"

"I am informing you that I cannot at this time launch the operation you request. The situation is in flux at the moment, and the opposition's action is temporally inside our decision cycle, sir," L. J. said, recording his reply for the competency hearing he was sure to face.

"Then I will do it with my own Special Police. If it is not beyond your competency, Major, please inform me when your command is once again able to function in accordance with the contractual commitments signed by your regimental commander."

L. J.'s 'puter clicked off, and his access to the Net vanished with his client's call.

Art whistled. "Better get my dress uniform pressed."

"Better get your head on straight or you won't be alive to wear it," L. J. snapped. "All of you. Forget peacetime drill, forget the candy-assed garrison shit. This is no sim. The worst that can happen to you is not an umpire bawling you out. Now you can end up very dead. Understood? Now it's real!"

Art and Mallary looked on the pale side. So did a lot of the troops standing close at hand. The Sergeant Major and the Chief exchanged a look, let tight hints of smiles cross their lips, then turned to him, came to attention with a soft snap, and saluted. "Yes, sir," they said.

There are moments that a commander will treasure forever.

Assuming they live the week out.

"Sergeant Major, Chief, see that the word gets to the troops here in camp. Mallary, get that word out to the troops in transit. This is no longer a Sunday picnic."

"Sir," and those with orders were gone. L. J. looked at Art. "So, XO, how fast can we concentrate the battalion and move it to the mouth of the Gleann Mor Valley?"

Art pulled a map from a case he wore at his side. "Always knew there was a reason why I kept paper maps around." He unfolded the right map and they stooped in the sun to study it.

Betsy Ross dusted the books in Alfred Santorini's library, which also served as his office. The books were old-fashioned, bound in leather. She had never seen him actually open one. She'd heard that the books had belonged to the Legate. The man probably hadn't been killed for his library, but lately people had died for less.

Bad times. So Betsy wore makeup that splotched her skin, thick black-rimmed glasses, and a frumpy gray dress with no waistline. Today the loose clothes that hid her figure from leering eyes also covered a comprehensive electronic suite.

She dusted as Santorini screamed at the poor Major. Loren Hanson had drawn a hell of a mission. Reports placed him as smart and a comer. He might survive Santorini. Slamming his hand down on the com link, Santorini stormed out of the room, leaving his workstation on. He'd done that before but never after turning off the entire network. Suddenly, Betsy had access to everything Santorini had, no competition to share it with.

Betsy continued dusting as she slipped her right hand inside her dress and began keying her 'puter to action. A quick glance showed that Santorini's computer presented the same screen to the world even as Betsy's computer hijacked its processing. Betsy's ugly glasses now showed her both books to dust, and file after file of coded and encrypted data. Quickly her spy system ducked inside files, hunting for keywords. Any that matched her interest were dumped to the storage that hung between her shoulder blades.

As she dusted, she viewed the files that produced strong hits. Some files by their very nature told her a lot. She wasn't surprised to find two sets of books, one for Lenzo Computing and one that seemed to match more with what she knew was going on. She was surprised to find a third set and a fourth. That was something Ben and Grace might want to see.

She was examining the fourth set when Santorini stomped back in, one of his more nasty minions following. "None of them—not one of those farmers gets out alive."

"They're heading for that damn valley," Field Marshal Pillow said, his short frame resplendent in a silver-encrusted uniform.

"Get them before they get there."

"Might have some trouble with the locals along the way. They might not want to tell me what they know."

"Hang 'em. Hang 'em upside down with their—" What followed was a plan for mutilating the dead— no, the dying—that exceeded anything Betsy had ever heard of, and she considered herself very well read in her specialty. She dusted and dug out more files. That fourth spreadsheet had to have some documentation around it. Just having a "What if I don't have to pay my mercenaries?" spreadsheet did not constitute a conspiracy to violate a contract. But how could Santorini avoid paying his bills? What would he do with the mercs he wasn't paying? Somewhere there had to be a letter, an e-note.

She'd dusted all there was to dust—or at least all

she'd risk dusting with Santorini around. She gritted her teeth and slid the ladder out. Climbing it would let her dust the high shelves. It would also show her legs—something cosmetics and frumpy dresses couldn't hide. Still searching Santorini's files, she climbed, dusted, rolled herself along, dusted, searched files, tried to ignore the horrors spoken below her, dusted, searched.

Cackling, the Black and Red ushered himself out. Betsy found the memo that explained the last spreadsheet and swallowed a low whistle at Santorini's audacity. Ready to leave, she started down the ladder only to find Santorini's cold eyes on her.

"You have very nice legs," he said.

"Thank you, Mr. Santorini."

"Call me Alfred," he said, coming to steady the ladder and running a cold hand up her leg well past the hem.

"I—I couldn't do that," she said, feigning growing terror as she calculated the situation. Given the right circumstances and distractions, she could twist out of her dress and her search suite in one easy motion that would leave Santorini none the wiser. She managed to get down the ladder with her dress still on. That offered her more options. Hiding coyly behind the feather duster, she let him see her undo her top button, then whirled away to put distance between them. She didn't think he actually killed his sex partners. Most departing staff left in a hurry, but only three had not come back for their last paycheck.

Betsy could live with those odds if that was what it took to stay alive long enough to give Grace the answers to all her questions.

Grace tried to look as confident as Ben did standing beside her. Around the table, now covered with the best map they had of the valley and the high plains beyond, stood the new commanders. Months ago most had been farmers or miners or store owners. Now they led the army on which the future of Alkalurops hung. *God, St. Patrick and St. Michael help us all.*

"Sean and I will lead twelve of our 'Mechs, the armed hovertrucks and all the infantry we can cram in them down the west foothills along this road." Ben tapped the tiny town of Nazareth, just south of where the Galty Range petered out. "Once here, my force will strike into the badlands and make contact with the running farmers. I assume they will be racing up side roads as fast as their trucks and 'Mechs can go. If I make contact, I will lead them into the valley, give them a guide and set up Blocking Force West." The others around the table nodded.

"Victoria, you get the center. Take most of what we have, advance up the valley on the main road to here." He pointed at Amarillo, the largest town anywhere in the valley, "Organize your defenses in front of Amarillo and dig in."

He nodded at Chato. "The Navajos will help anyone still unclear that a shovel is the infantry's second-best friend after his rifle or rocket. The only good road into the valley runs through Amarillo. They will hit it first. As soon as I get back in touch with you on our right, we can look at me nibbling their left. If I'm engaged, we will modify our plans."

"I just love the smell of freshly baked plans in the morning," Danny said with a fraudulent sigh.

"Which leaves the rest to me," Syn said, crinkling her nose at the map. "Who's all mine?"

"I'm with you," Jobe said, "and the Donga River crew."

Grace knew Ben wanted that crew. The west side put them closer to their homes, but Jobe and Syn's affair was too hot to ignore. "Just remember to keep your ass in your 'Mech when it matters," Grace said, "or someone may shoot it off you."

"Nobody's done it yet," Syn said in a sultry voice.

"There is always a first time," Ben pointed out.

"That was a long time ago. Who else do I get?"

Ben turned to Danny. "You go with the eastern detachment if Victoria does not want you."

The woman sniffed at the man as she might at a rat six days dead. "I'll need him," she said.

"Wilson, you back up to the east side," Grace said, putting at least one levelheaded adult with that team.

"I'll pick up more ranch hands as we move down the valley," he said, fingering the map. "This edge of the valley is rough. You need to know it or you lose a lot of cows up these draws. If I get some rangers right off these spreads, we can tickle those mercs where they aren't expecting."

"You do that," Ben said, imitating Grace ordering people to do what they wanted to do. A chuckle ran around the table.

"Is Amarillo where we m-make our stand?" Sean asked.

"No," Grace said, stepping closer to the map and taking full command. "We're trained, but nowhere near good enough to survive a stand-up fight with the Roughriders. No, we'll fight a series of short skirmishes, causing what casualties we can, then fall back before they can cut us up. Fight, fall back, fight, fall back, that's the best we can hope to do at first.

"However, as we gain confidence and experience, we'll fight longer and fall back shorter. Here—"she slammed her fist down on Falkirk—"here is where we make our stand."

"Our last stand," someone whispered.

"A patriot's stand," Grace shot back. "Ho will stay here. The women and bigger kids from up in the hills will take over Falkirk once we're gone. They've got a lot of digging to do. When we get back, you'll find their sweat and blisters have made this land ready for a fight."

Grace let her eyes travel around the table, taking each person in for a moment, then going to the next. "Battle-tested and true, here we will make a fight. A fight that no one will forget, so long as Alkalurops spins among the stars."

13

In and Around Nazareth, Alkalurops
Prefecture IX, The Republic of the Sphere
22 August 3134; local summer

Benjork Lone Cat led the 'Mechs and gun trucks of his task force south as quickly as he dared push trainees. Aware that the farmers were fleeing north, hounded by Black and Reds, the militia responded like pros. Only twenty hours later Benjork strode up the dusty, wide road into Nazareth. As Sean oversaw refueling the 'Mechs and rigs, Benjork dismounted and turned to the half-dozen men lounging in front of the town's one store.

Feet up on the porch rail, chairs pushed back, they tried to ignore the gray MilitiaMechs that loomed over their one-story town, but they nodded to Benjork as he introduced himself and asked if they had seen the hunted farmers.

"They ain't been here. May not make it if them Black and Reds have any say—not that I know nothing about this, you understand," said a man with boots of tooled leather.

"They will likely travel this road, *quiaff*?"

The men looked at one another, then shook their heads. "Nope," "Not likely," "Wouldn't do it if I was them," came back at him. He waited for silence to fall, then asked a new question.

"What road would you travel to Falkirk?"

"You come from there?" one asked.

"I fight with Grace O'Malley," Ben answered.

"We don't much want to fight with anybody," the one with the fancy boots said, letting his chair come down hard. "You see, them Special Police are hanging anybody they think might know anything about them farmers. They're stringing 'em up to signs, power poles, windmills, by God. Stringing them up like they had all the rope in the world."

"They string up a man, then go looking for his woman and kids," another man added.

"We don't need to know nothing about this fight. It's not ours, so you'd like to get your gas and get out of here," Fancy Boots said, standing and leading his cronies inside.

Benjork thanked them for their time and returned to his 'Mech. It was fueled, as were all the rigs. He offered Wilson's smart card to the young man who had watched them pump the gas.

"Your money's no good here," a voice came from behind Benjork. He turned. One of the men from the store was sauntering their way. "Ken, don't touch that card," he told the boy, who frowned but returned the card.

"Best we say that you took the gas at gunpoint. Hell, you got enough guns, don't you?"

"That is not our intention."

"But it's a story that will keep Ken there from dancing from his sign. The Black and Reds really want those farmers."

"I can well imagine. But if they are not this far—"

"They will be. Not by any road that sends 'em through towns where people can see 'em. Someone's bound to report 'em. No, they're traveling the back roads. I can think of a few I'd use."

"You would show me, *quiaff?*" Benjork reached for a map.

"White Hair, I don't know maps. Don't know the names of most of the roads I been driving since I was knee-high, but I'll take you there," he said, climbing into a dilapidated truck that might once have been red. "My Elly died last winter, and my kids are all moved away. If a guy like me can't do this, nobody can. So you follow me if you can keep up." And he gunned out of town in a cloud of dust and oil.

It took no orders to get the militia troops moving; they'd heard the man. Their eagerness as they piled into the gun trucks told him they believed every word. Benjork mounted up and led his team at a trot into the red truck's dust.

The old man raced with wild abandon over gravel roads and dirt tracks that were hardly more than wheel ruts. They passed ranches and homesteads, some looking more abandoned than lived in. The truck bounced over bumps and rocks Benjork feared might be too much for the hovertrucks.

After a while, the Lone Cat wondered if the truck was leading them on a wild chase after nightmares. Then the truck braked to a halt, sliding sideways as it did. The old man was out, gazing at a low butte not much taller than Benjork's 'Mech.

Benjork raised his 'Mech's arm to signal his battle team to a halt, then paced off the distance to where the butte ended in a ridge of eroding yellow dirt. With all the rolling terrain around Falkirk, Ben had had a periscope installed in his MiningMech MOD. Now he raised it.

In the next valley a battle raged.

The farmers had abandoned half a dozen trucks in front of a large outcropping of red rocks three kilometers away. They shot from its cover. Behind the rocks, one green and two yellow AgroMechs stood, stained with dust and rocket fragments. Their scythes spun slowly at the ready.

Black and Red infantry were strung out along a dry wash, half a klick to the left, riflemen and rocket launchers keeping up a desultory fire, giving Ben the feeling that this was the middle of a long and not all that successful battle.

In the broken ground between wash and red rocks, a burned-out Black and Red 'Mech MOD lay, still smoking. Its chest was blown in. Benjork guessed the farmers had explosives and knew how to use them. He thought for a moment on how a satchel charge might be delivered and shook his head. Desperate men did desperate things.

Two klicks behind the rifle line towered a dozen 'Mech MODs, some Black and Red, others still Agro green or Industrial gray. Most sported a single machine gun. One had a twenty-millimeter autocannon. Several showed recent damage. Well back from them and out of SRM range, a Black and Red *Black Hawk* squatted like a toad. It fired a pair of long-range lasers randomly, rarely hitting the rock pile.

Someone had a nice 'Mech they did not know how to use. Used properly, that *Black Hawk* could take out Benjork's entire troop. "To you, I will send my best," he whispered.

Then he studied the terrain. The wash twisted and turned as it made its way around the harder rock outcroppings of the eroded butte. A red-and-yellow streaked pinnacle shot up to his left. That should hide 'Mechs on an approach march. He activated his magscan and breathed a small sigh of relief. All that red in the rocks was iron. The magscan was hosed. Surprise was possible.

Benjork returned to his battle group, dismounted, and faced the old rancher. "I am grateful for your help. You have led me to my battle. You may go now. May you have blessed dreams for your service."

"I got a rifle in my pickup. Them farmers are just like me. Don't see how I can come this far and drive away," the man said. Returning to his rig, he pulled a scoped weapon from its scabbard with easy grace.

"You are welcome within our ranks," Benjork told him. Among his team, dust covers came off rocket launchers. Machine guns were lovingly checked. Maintenance crews climbed over the gray 'Mech MODs under the watchful eyes of their militia pilots, making last-minute checks on rocket launchers and Gatling guns. He had to remind himself that these were green recruits. Their purposeful strides and hard eyes would do any warrior proud who knew what he faced and ran to meet it.

With rifle fire and the occasional explosion to remind them of what lay ahead, Benjork called his 'Mechs and Lieutenant Hicks' drivers into a circle. In the red dust Benjork drew a map. "Over that hill are Black and Red infantry and 'Mech MODs. They are led by a *Black Hawk* that could destroy us all." He gave them a smile. "So we will ignore it and concentrate our fire on the 'Mech MODs. Hicks, that includes your gun trucks and infantry dismounts. Once I am sure you have the 'Mech MODs under control, Sean and Maud and I will redirect our fire to the *Black Hawk*. No battle is ever won by being strong everywhere. Today we will win by being strong against their 'Mech MODs first.

"But remember, the *Black Hawk*'s SRMs are Streaks. If he gets a lock on you, every missile will hit. Never stand still. Never take more than four or five steps without changing direction. You must zigzag if you are to live through today."

That got solemn nods from everyone.

"Remember that the four rockets you carry have no reloads. Use two of them on my command. The other two are yours to use sparingly. Take care with your thirty-millimeter Gatling gun. Mick and Johnny did their best with the guns and ammo, but do not forget that your caseless ammo will dirty up your guns. If you fire bursts that are too long, the gun will overheat and jam. Wait too long between bursts, and your gun may gum up and jam. Once you start shooting, keep shooting."

There were resigned smiles at that reminder.

Benjork turned to Sean. Maud stood at his elbow, she of the flashing brown hair and dancing freckles. Maud claimed she'd been driving 'Mechs since she was a child, whenever her pappy would let her. After watching her run the obstacle course Benjork had designed, he would not gainsay her. The MechWarrior remembered now how often Sean and Maud were elbow to elbow and tasted both joy and sorrow as he gave his orders.

"Sean, you and Maud stay close to me. As soon as the 'Mech MODs are suppressed, we hit the *Black Hawk*. If the *Black Hawk* attacks aggressively, I may order us to attack it immediately. Are there any questions?" There were none.

"Maintain radio silence until I break it. Hicks, give me ten minutes to get in place. Know that this is how the battle will start. How it ends, only the true dreamer can tell," he said.

The militia pilots and gun crews went to their posts. Benjork, Sean and Maud grouped at the head of the 'Mech MODs line. Lieutenant Hicks stood in the lead gun truck, eyeing his watch, waiting patiently for the moment to lead the gun trucks forward. The old rancher stood behind him, fondling his rifle, lips moving in prayer.

Gravel crunched under Benjork's 'Mech as it crossed the dry wash, headed south. He kept an eye on the ridge that separated them from the sound of battle. Sometimes it rose higher, other times it dipped. It never dropped low enough to reveal the 'Mechs he led. He found a rough gully just past where he needed one and led the three lances of 'Mech MODs through its rock-strewn bed.

Most rocks crumbled under the footpads, but one 'Mech came to grief when a rock rolled out from under it; even double gyros could not keep it upright. The following 'Mechs stood in place as that pilot struggled back up, leaning on a bent mining drill. As the 'Mech continued on down the path, it limped visibly.

Benjork nodded with understanding. As a cub he had been warned it was not always the enemy who made battle plans unravel. He signaled Sean ahead but paused, cockpit open, until the damaged 'Mech limped up. The youngster opened his cockpit and raised his visor, face set for a dressing-down. Benjork gave him the small smile he allowed for special occasions. "You will fight last in line," he said, and the MechWarrior winced. "Not because you stumbled. Any of us—even I—could have been given that fate. No, your mining drill is broken. You should not fight in a melee. Stand back and use your rockets and Gatling. You are one of the best with them. Use them well."

"I will, sir," came quickly as Benjork closed his cockpit and made his way to the front of his command.

They were now beyond the ridge, but a shallow fold in this land of scrub brush and yellow dust hid them from the Special Police. Benjork used his periscope to check out the battle. His team was where he wanted it—behind the 'Mech line, almost even with the *Black Hawk* and to its right.

The Lone Cat halted his troop and checked the time. He had three minutes to wait, to let his hot engines cool. He whispered a prayer that Sven and Mick and Johnny had done good work and might enjoy dreams that would tell them much.

The weapons' fire increased. Periscope up, Benjork saw change. The riflemen had spread out, up and down the dry creek and were now moving forward on their bellies from bush to bush, rock to rock, closing with the sharpshooters. The Black and Red 'Mech MODs now stepped off the distance to the dry wash.

Not the *Black Hawk,* though. It stayed well back. Shooting its lasers more frequently, it slashed streaks in the rocks or started fires in the brush. That must encourage the poor creeping infantry. Now they crawled through hot, blackened ash where concealment once had been. Time to end this.

Benjork broke radio silence with a firm, "Hicks, attack. Repeat, attack. Militia 'Mechs, charge! Charge and zigzag!"

Beside him, the militia pilots slammed their throttles forward, and green and gray 'Mechs charged into battle. Benjork charged with them, covering the hardpacked ground to the top of the rise with long distance-eating strides. As he topped the rise, the battle came into full view.

On his far right, Lieutenant Hicks led the charge of the gun trucks down the wash, dust blowing, Gatlings roaring. The second gun truck loosed a rocket volley at the surprised 'Mech MODs. One rocket struck a glancing blow on the chest armor of an AgroMech. The shaped charge left a long slash. Paint smoking, the 'Mech backpedaled and the other Black and Red 'Mechs suddenly took notice of the new fighters on their battlefield.

A Special Police rifleman stood up to run. A farmer in the rocks drilled him before he took a step. Other riflemen returned the fire. Here and there a Police crawler began to crawl backward.

One enemy 'Mech MOD stumbled as all of them turned to face the gun trucks. The *Black Hawk* fired off two fast laser blasts. One sent Hicks' gun truck sliding sideways into the wall of the dry wash. It bounced over a large rock, went halfway up on its side, then slid down to right itself. The old rancher steadied his rifle and put a bullet into the cockpit of the *Black Hawk.* The round ricocheted off, but it was still a hit at that range.

The Black and Red 'Mech MODs struggled to change the front from the rock pile to the increasing number of gun trucks firing machine guns, rockets and antiarmor grenades at them.

"Hold your fire," Benjork told his 'Mech team as they trotted forward, apparently unnoticed. When the *Black Hawk* to his right continued stabbing out with his lasers at gun trucks, the MechWarrior chose to take a major risk.

"Militia 'Mechs: Halt in place, target two missiles on a Black and Red 'Mech MOD, and fire immediately. Then charge them for all you're worth." It had been Grace's suggestion that the first round be fired at the halt. The idea had sounded good then.

Now Benjork throttled to a halt with the rest. "Sean, Maud—with me. Target the *Black Hawk.*"

In a ragged line, eight charging 'Mech MODs came to a halt. Without further orders, rockets rippled out from them, taking the Black and Reds on their flank. Some rockets corkscrewed across the sun-drenched sky. Others slammed into enemy 'Mechs, shredding armor. One smashed into the magazine of an Agro-Mech's autocannon. The armor held out against the explosion, but bolts must have sheared. The magazine was knocked up against the 'Mech's cockpit, and its stream of fifty-millimeter bullets quit chasing a gun truck.

Benjork turned to face the *Black Hawk* as its driver became aware of the new threat on its flank. "Sean, Maud—fire two rockets," he ordered as he emptied his right rocket pack. Far out on the left, the limping 'Mech with the damaged drill also joined in the shooting, sending four rockets straight and true into the *Black Hawk*'s backside, and following them up with a series of short bursts from his thirty-millimeter Gatling gun.

The *Black Hawk* stumbled back as missiles hit him from the other three, shredding armor, but doing no major damage.

"Everyone get moving!" the Lone Cat shouted, slamming his 'Mech into five quick steps forward at a right angle. Sean and Maud jinked their own way as the *Black Hawk* salvoed off one of his four quad-packs at each of them. The missiles hit where the three of them had been, but the limping 'Mech hadn't moved fast enough. The militia pilot took a full salvo on his 'Mech's chest, knocking it flat on its back.

Benjork had no time to count his losses. He led his three remaining 'Mech MODs against the *Black Hawk,* forcing it back even as its laser flashed over them, heating them up. Missiles slashed rock, sent up plumes of dirt, and burned sagebrush around them. Still, they advanced and the *Black Hawk* backpedaled.

Off to their right, the eight other 'Mech MODs charged at the remaining eleven Black and Reds, trading thirty-millimeter tungsten slugs as they moved. One enemy 'Mech caught a group of dismounts before they could disperse, cutting them down in one bloody clump. A second Black and Red sent a burst of machine-gun fire slashing into a gun truck, gutting it and throwing its crew to the ground like rag dolls.

But the Militia 'Mechs were hammering the Special Police, too, sending them stumbling back. With the *Black Hawk* otherwise occupied, the 'Mech MODs clumped up, leaderless. A pair of rockets took a damaged 'Mech at short range, slashing off its arm with a machine gun and setting fire to its ammo. The 'Mech burned, sending black smoke up in gusts. Another Black and Red fell, its knee smashed by thirty-millimeter shells.

Now the gun trucks rained grenades and cannon fire on the backpedaling mob. A gray Militia 'Mech closed with a Black and Red, bringing its mining drill to bear on its enemy's chest. The Special Police pilot had no stomach for that, and popped his canopy immediately, hands up.

Allowing himself a tight grin, Benjork concentrated on the *Black Hawk.*

It didn't seem to care much for what it saw. Firing off another full volley, it turned in place and shot into the air. Even as Benjork yanked his 'Mech into a left turn to throw off the missiles, he followed the *Black Hawk*'s jump, trying to lead it with short bursts.

Behind him came more stuttering fire followed by, "Damn!" in a high-pitched voice. "My bloody gun's jammed up on me."

"Try sh-short jerks on the trigger, Maud," Sean said.

"I'm trying, I'm trying."

"Get all the power you can get out of your engines," Benjork ordered. "We've got to catch that *Black Hawk.* He can still snipe at us—pick us off one by one if we leave him alive."

"I'm f-following you," Sean said.

"Me, too," Maud said. "I just can't shoot anymore."

Ahead of them, the *Black Hawk* landed hard on its right leg. Maybe there was a rock. Maybe their fire did something. It fell but caught itself by its big left claw, then took off running again. Something must have happened in the landing, though. Benjork's infra-red now showed more heat radiating from the reactor area than armor and cooling should have allowed. "Did you split a seam?" he asked his pursued enemy as he snapped out bursts of thirty-millimeter slugs at the *Black Hawk.*

The Black and Red twisted as he ran, sending a spray of SRMs that did not come close to any of his pursuers.

Benjork kept the feet of his 'Mech in long strides that ate up the distance. "You'll have to do better than that," he said, then suppressed a cringe as a stream of thirty-millimeter shells stitched the ground close ahead of him.

"I've got my cannon working," Maud rejoiced.

"So I noticed," the MechWarrior answered.

"I'm sorry," came in a much smaller voice.

"Watch where you point that thing," Sean said.

"I'm watching, I'm watching," she said as a stream of shells arced ahead of them, missing to the left of the *Black Hawk*.

Ben put his engine in the red and focused his attention on the path ahead. He did not concentrate on any one place, but let his eyes guide his pedals without thought. Here he lengthened his stride to miss a rock, then shifted a bit to the right to avoid a patch of sagebrush. The friction of branches on his legs might slow him. A root might trip him. While one part of his mind targeted the *Black Hawk* for short bursts that chipped away at the rear armor, raising the unexplained heat plume a bit more, another part guided his feet.

The *Black Hawk* was faster than any 'Mech powered by an internal-combustion engine. No matter how much Mick might fine-tune fuel injectors and timing, fusion engines had the power of the sun at their beck and call. Still, whoever was driving that *Black Hawk* was little better than a civvy. Benjork trod the pedals that set the pace for his 'Mech as if they were a part of himself. The *Black Hawk* pulled ahead, but nowhere near as much as it should have.

Again, the *Black Hawk* took to the air. This time its driver leaned it forward, trying to get as much distance out of the jump as he could. An experienced MechWarrior never would have made that error. Even without the patter of thirty-millimeter tungsten slugs on his BattleMech, leaning into a jump was a bad idea. The *Black Hawk* landed, took two running steps to try to catch its balance, then—with its gyros screaming almost loud enough for Benjork to hear—fell flat on its face to spend the rest of its forward momentum in the dirt before it came up hard against one of the rocks that time and erosion had left dotting the plain.

For a moment the *Black Hawk* just lay there, venting heat from more places than it should have been. Then its driver pried it from the dirt with its huge claws, got its feet underneath it, and began again to run for the distant horizon.

Not averse to kicking a *surat* while it was down, Benjork squeezed off his last rockets as the *Black Hawk* struggled to its feet. The fleeing BattleMech ran right into them—and the two Sean had fired, then two more from Maud.

Reeling, it almost missed a step. Catching its balance resulted in a dance complicated by the rock it had hit going down and the shells all three gray 'Mechs sent its way.

As if maddened beyond reason, the *Black Hawk* fired off a full salvo that hit nothing but sky and dirt. Straightening itself in a hail of tungsten slugs, the BattleMech fired lasers and volley after volley of its missiles at its tormentors.

Benjork zigzagged, trying to throw off the *Black Hawk*'s targeting computer. He succeeded, but Maud took a full volley before the Black and Red turned to flight again.

Ben slammed his throttle forward, and his 'Mech began to eat up the dry ground with long strides. His Gatling gun renewed its staccato, sending chips of armor flying from the Black and Red's back. Sean followed, Gatling blazing. Even Maud stumbled forward, though at half-speed, her fire doing less damage as the *Black Hawk* lengthened the distance between them.

Benjork gave chase, footpads moving in long strides, Gatling striking sparks or chips off armor. He watched with grim satisfaction as the strange heat vent on the back of the *Black Hawk* grew. The fleeing BattleMech twisted as it ran, turning back its left arm with two SRM quads on it. The Lone Cat angled off to the right, forcing a deflection shot. Missiles set sage to burning, but nothing else.

Benjork concentrated on the hot spot. He aimed his Gatling gun, but modified the targeting computer's aim to match the correction he saw in his heart. Then he fired. A stream of thirty-millimeter tungsten slugs stitched a circle on the back of the *Black Hawk*. The infrared readout flared in Ben's cockpit.

Now the *Black Hawk*'s other arm with its missiles came around. Benjork sideslipped to the left. Eight missiles volleyed into the sand and sage as Ben's thirty-millimeter slugs again flaked armor off.

Twice more the *Black Hawk* tried to shoot while running. Twice more it only slowed him down. The process started again, with Benjork again edging outward to complicate the Black and Red's firing solution. This time the runner did not fire.

Suddenly the *Black Hawk* came to a hopping stop, twisted in place, and fired off a barrage of SRMs and lasers.

Benjork did not slow down but twisted his course hard right. The shooter tried to compensate, but the missiles only left a stuttering line of explosions behind the MiningMech MOD. All but one, which slashed into Ben's rock cutter, smashing it.

Again the *Black Hawk* turned in place to flee. Having centered his fire on the closest gray 'Mech, the fleeing pilot had left Sean free to close—and free to carefully aim his fire.

Now both Sean and Benjork concentrated their fire on the back of the *Black Hawk*. Again armor flew, only now in larger chunks, and the heat plume shot out white hot for a second.

But only for a second, because the next moment, the *Black Hawk* disappeared in a flash that made the blue sky seem shadowed.

"What happened?" Maud asked on-channel, hurrying forward.

"H-hellfire escaped and claimed its own," Sean said.

The flaming wreckage spat and smoked—its own little hell—as Benjork slowed to a pace that dropped his engine gauges out of the red. Turning, he began a cooling jog back to the other battle. Sean held back to assist Maud's limping 'Mech. They were good warriors. Benjork wished them whatever joy they could find during this time of sudden death, glory and grief.

As the wash came into view, it looked like Hicks had the situation well in hand. Ten Black and Red 'Mechs were surrounded by nine gray ones. The militia pilot had even managed to get his limping 'Mech in. Things had turned out better than the veteran had had any right to hope for.

"Sir, am I glad to see you," Hicks called on-channel. "We have a problem here that's beyond my pay grade."

"The situation, Lieutenant?"

"Sir, these civilians have seen a lot of their people killed. Most ran because the Special Police strung up people they loved."

"And they want revenge, *quiaff.*"

"In spades, sir. They want the captured Black and Reds hung from the arms of their 'Mechs, sir."

"They are our prisoners?"

"They surrendered to me, sir."

Benjork popped his canopy to cheers and awed stares at the damage. A few quick words with the survivors verified that any offer of assistance to the fugitives, or even to have been in a position to possibly help meant quick death. Some joined the flight because they had had enough of Santorini. Most joined because they had no other choice. Of the three AgroMechs at the rock, two were from people recently joined in the flight. Somewhere to the south were two burned-out AgroMechs holding what was left of a father and his oldest son.

"They're gonna hang. Hang 'em now," spat the widow with cold anger as Benjork approached.

"You hang convicted murderers on Alkalurops, *quiaff*?"

"Yes, sir," the young man at her elbow answered.

"These men are my prisoners," Benjork said, "taken under the rules of war. I cannot allow you to be judge, jury and executioner, ma'am."

"You think you're better then me—better than us," the woman said, her eyes cold slits.

"I am no better than you, ma'am. I just follow the laws laid down for me. If these men have violated those laws, they will be so charged, tried, and punished. It is not our place."

"Ma, there's been enough blood today. Let it go to a judge. Nothing's gonna bring Pa or Brother back," the young man said.

Finally the woman wept, leaned on her son, and turned away.

Benjork eyed the prisoners. "Who are they, Hicks?"

"A mixed bag, sir. Some punks from around here. Others who somehow managed to buy 'Mechs off-world and get Santorini to hire them. That *Black Hawk* you burned was the boss man of this crew. Field Marshal of Special Police by the name of Pillow."

"Field Marshal, quineg?"

"I swear it. Santorini is easy on promotions."

Benjork shook his head and changed the subject. "Where is our guide?"

"He lit out in his pickup. Said Nazareth needed to hear about this fast. I think I can follow our tracks back."

So the gun trucks led the withdrawal. One of the Black and Red trucks had a complete suite for hijacking 'Mechs, so ten poorly done 'Mech MODs crewed by the next-best militia pilots grouped themselves as a cover for the exhausted fugitives. Benjork led his 'Mechs as rear guard. If they met more Black and Reds, it would be a hard fight. Their rocket launchers were empty and the magazines of their Gatling guns were not that far from it.

Nazareth was empty except for their old guide. "Most folks lit out north as soon as you went through here the first time. Them that stayed left plenty fast when I told them what happened out by the old Harlingen place. I figured I'd hang around to catch anyone who missed out on getting the word."

They gassed the rigs, then headed north, the old rancher showing them a faster way. Benjork suspected they'd need it.

L. J. knew his client was mad; these days Santorini called only when he was screaming hot. It was also the only time the Net came up, so it was easy to respond when his 'puter blinked red and beeped. Santorini always seemed to pick the worst times to call.

L. J.'s last platoon was just motoring through the gate—dusty, bullet-holed and straggling. Scrawled in tall letters on each of its trucks was "Please ignore us. Save your ammo for the Black and Reds chasing us." L. J. really wanted to get that story. Instead he activated his 'puter and said, "Yes, Mr. Santorini. What can I do for you, sir?"

"Can you do anything for me?" came like a slap of cold iron.

"I am concentrating my battalion, sir. Several more platoons came in today. They were pretty beat up on the drive in, lots of sniping going on out there."

"A lot of lawlessness. If you'd apply the same procedures my Special Police do, you might have less trouble."

Or more, L. J. didn't say. "Sir, I am not a police force. I operate within the rules of war."

"Well, that damn woman up the Gleann Mor Valley is waging war against me. She has sent her troops to aid insurrection and to shoot down my police."

"Oh, is it that bad out there?" L. J. said, keeping a solid grip on his tone. The mayor's wife had made another trip out and given him their side of what took place outside a small town called Nazareth. The town had been burned to the ground by the Special Police, she reported. Fortunately, everyone had fled into the valley. *Damn, but that valley must be getting crowded.*

"You will move out as soon as you consider your battalion capable of offensive action. You will seal off the Gleann Mor Valley and conduct search-and-destroy through it. All arms, all commercial facilities capable of dual use, are to be destroyed. All people taking up arms against their lawful government will be turned over to the Special Police I assign to interrogating such prisoners, their wives and families. Understood?"

L. J. could almost hear the recording being made. Nothing in his military training applied to this. How do you keep your fighting honor when given orders for mass murder? *Guess the academy needs some new courses.* "I have recorded your orders, sir. I acknowledge them and will be ready to move out in two days, sir. Where will I rendezvous with your Special Police?"

"Amarillo."

"I assume they will be outside my chain of command."

"Of course. They are *my* Special Police."

L. J. wanted that clearly on the record. "Understood, sir."

"Good-bye then, Major."

"Good-bye, sir," L. J. said. He closed the com unit with a firm click, watched until the Net died, then turned to Mallary. "Now let's find out who came up with the idea of writing messages to the locals on the sides of that platoon's trucks."

14

Outside Amarillo, Alkalurops
Prefecture IX, The Republic of the Sphere
24 August 3134; local summer

Grace studied the sun-seared rolling land before her. As her mind switched from miner's to soldier's thoughts, she could almost hear a click. Beside her, Ben eyed the defenses thrown up ten klicks south of Amarillo where the main road made a series of hair-pin curves through a deep wash. A culvert covered a trickle of a river, but a gully-washer anywhere in the valley would have water pouring over the riverbed's five-meter-high banks. Regularly washed out, the road was mostly potholes this summer. Few folks were feeling motivated toward their civic duty to repair the road.

Chato's Navajos had taken a good three hundred riflemen from the south valley and shown them how to vanish. Even 'Mech MODs were either in cover, in fighting positions or hidden behind rocks. The command post was a small cattle shed, its roof falling in, lined with a double wall of sand bags. It smelled of heat and shade and cows.

"We have the main road blocked here," Grace said. "East and west of here, the riverbank is deep and nasty. Bliven's the only other good crossing," she said, pointing to a map and the town a hundred and fifty kilometers east. "Syn and Wilson are down there setting up ambushes. West is your territory, Ben."

"Any other defense in front of Amarillo?" the albino asked, his pink eyes squinting as he studied the potential battleground.

"None. Everything from here to town is too flat."

"So we give up the town when this falls, *quiaff*?"

"We'll have to. Most folks have already fled. Everyone's heard stories of the Black and Reds. Nobody wants to be here when they show up. 'Course there are always stragglers, but with luck they'll be too few for the mercs to notice."

Ben eyed the land for a long time. Below them a rickety, overloaded truck chugged through the potholes at the bottom of the wash, then began its slow climb out. Once at the top, it halted and a woman in a huge straw hat and shapeless dress struggled down from the packed flatbed. She shouted her thanks, then plodded toward the barn as the truck drove off, its people, bedding and boxes swaying. One of the passengers began to sing, and others joined in.

"Nice people, those," the woman said, setting down a box in the shade of the barn and sitting on it.

"Excuse me," Grace said. "We're kind of busy here. Don't you belong somewhere else?"

The woman lifted the sleeve of her sweat-drenched smock, sniffed, and made a face. "Three days on the road, and I think a barn's the only place that'll take me."

"Totally untrue," Ben said, turning to the woman

and actually smiling. "On you, mademoiselle, it is merely what other perfumes strive to be." Grace looked at her Lone Cat. Had he gone totally crazy? "Grace, do you not remember Betsy Ross?"

Grace looked closer at the woman under the straw hat. The interloper stood, made a formal curtsy, then hiked up her dress, giving a good eyeful, and rummaged around her waist for something. With a slight victory yell, she pulled out a flat block which, when unwrapped from a reeking cloth, turned out to be an unusually large 'puter.

"I have here the full download of Alfred Santorini's personal files. Brilliant of him to turn off the Net. Most of his security went down with it. Left his files wide open once I cracked his encryption. Here's everything you need to know about his little operation."

"What's the most important thing you found?" Grace asked.

"My old master always used to say, 'Follow the money,' so here's the money," Betsy said, and brought up a spreadsheet. "Or *here's* the money," she said, bringing up another. "Or it could be this or that," and two more screens filled with numbers, then flashed away. "I've been in a few ops that ran two sets of books, but four! Santorini's way twisted."

Betsy frowned for a moment, then shuddered. "By the way, we are killing this bastard, aren't we? 'Cause if you folks aren't, I'll do it myself. He dies. Slow and very dead."

"As far as I'm concerned," Grace said, "that's the plan. You have the proof in your 'puter that says we should kill him."

"There and a few other places," Betsy said, started to rub at her hip, then stopped herself. "Just so long as we're agreed that bastard dies, I'm in this with you all the way."

"What do you make of those spreadsheets?" Ben said.

"I'm sure an accountant will find all sorts of funny

money in them, but taken as a whole, they point in too many directions. This one," she said, bringing one up, "is what you'd expect him to send to his boss at Lenzo Computing. Nice, easy-to-swallow numbers for not a lot of activity."

She flipped to a new screen. "This one has a lot more in it. For example, he lists his acquired properties. Seems that all the property that got into tax arrears was sold at auction. A very private auction. He bought it for not even pennies on the C-bill. Even that was covered by a loan he wrote himself on the Allabad Mechanics and Agriculture Bank. He's gonna make a killing when Lenzo Computing moves here.

"But then there's this one," she said, frowning at the screen. "I think it's for if he gets in trouble and has to call for help, say Landgrave Jasek Kelswa-Steiner and his Stormhammers. Here he sells a lot of stuff at a discount."

"And the fourth?" Ben said.

"A whole lot more interesting. Note the bottom line," Betsy said, pointing at a blank space on the sheet. "There is none. Everything gets converted to cash-producing holdings. And there's another change. The mercs go from the cost side of the sheet to the asset side. All their property's there, but no costs."

"Troopers have to be paid," Ben said. "No avoiding that!"

"He thinks he can. Santorini sends a lot of e-notes to the Roughriders' adjutant. This one didn't get sent. He wrote it the day things started to go bad, so maybe he was saving it. He asks the adjutant to take on a cook from Santorini's staff."

"The mercs are that hard up for staff?" Grace asked.

"The Major was trying to hire my maid services."

Grace scowled. Hanson hadn't come across to her as the kind who couldn't keep his hands off the help. Betsy shook her head. "What I really think he wanted was info from Allabad. Anyway, I turned down the

job offer in a chatty letter that told him stuff that
would have cost him a pile of stones if he was paying
my usual fee. He came right back with another nice,
friendly note, and we kept up the chat, me feeding
him intel before he asked for it. But why would Santorini send a cook?"

"He knifed the Governor and Legate," Grace
pointed out.

"And if he declared the mission accomplished and
called for a victory dinner, there might be few survivors if his cook had orders to poison them," Betsy
said as if she were practiced at that.

"That wouldn't get every merc," Grace pointed out.

"No, but it would get so many that even his Black
and Reds could sweep up the leavings."

"The mercs would take bloody revenge," Ben
growled.

"Not if Santorini shot the cook and told everyone
he was one of the terrorists the mercs had been fighting," Betsy said slowly.

"A profit-and-loss sheet that turns the mercs' equipment into a source of annual income for Santorini
and that letter makes for pretty damning evidence,"
Grace said.

"Now all you have to do is tell that to Hanson.
Good luck," Betsy said.

A specialist manning the long-range radio in the
corner sat up, took the earphone off one ear, and
stood. "Grace, Ben: The mercs are pulling out of Dublin Town, heading this way."

"How long till they get here?" Betsy asked.

"Tomorrow," Grace said, looking back at her map
table.

"Uh, ma'am, a Black and Red column, battalion-
sized or larger, is skirting Lothran," the specialist
added.

"Looks like Santorini has everything headed north,"
Ben said.

Grace tapped Dublin Town on the map. "The mercs are coming out. I'd have expected them to wait until early morning, but this will put them here around noon tomorrow or, if they push all night, just after first light."

"Count on them pushing," Ben said.

"It's the Black and Reds that are the question. They can take the road to Amarillo through Dublin Town, following the mercs, or go due north until the road forks just short of Nazareth and heads east along the Colorado River to Amarillo." Grace shook her head. "This doesn't fit together for me."

Betsy traced the road lines with her long fingers. "Santorini would never put his Special Police under the mercs. He knows Hanson won't string up civilians."

"A separate approach march would keep them out of each other's hair for a while," Ben said. With one hand he traced the route between Dublin Town and Amarillo. With the other, he covered the dogleg route between Lothran and Amarillo.

"Could the Black and Reds try a push into the valley along the west side?" Betsy asked.

"Not after our fight at Nazareth," Ben said. "I am not saying they all are bad. But the ones sent out so far have not demonstrated much skill against armed resistance."

"Santorini has some good MechWarriors he picked up drunk or deep in gambling debts," Betsy said. "The head of his shock troops was a captain in a 'Mech unit—don't remember the name. He got off-planet one jump ahead of a firing squad for rape. I think he's found his calling with Santorini," Betsy said, this time massaging her left breast.

Grace started to say something, then swallowed it. Betsy would talk about what happened to her in Allabad when she wanted to and not before. *We'll get all those bastards,* Grace promised herself.

"I have an idea," Ben said.

"You haven't been dreaming while I've been standing here," Betsy snapped.

"Only about you, my fine, raven-haired beauty."

"Nova Cats don't take a vow of chastity, do they?"

"I certainly didn't," the albino said.

"So this isn't just a waste of air. Good, keep it up. The girl likes it. Somebody show me where I can get a bath. I have a sudden need to be clean."

As Betsy left with a guide, Grace leaned across the table. "Now can I talk to Hanson. Tell him what I know. Certainly he can break a contract with a client who isn't going to pay him. A client who is planning to kill him and his mercs at the victory party."

"That is certainly good cause to break a contract. However, Grace, you cannot talk to him just now."

"And why not?"

"You are his enemy. He is now under orders to attack you. He cannot talk to you, and he will not talk to you until your conversation consists only of you negotiating your surrender."

"You're crazy!"

"No, Grace. We are at war. We fight now. When one of us is prepared to surrender, we talk about surrender—and maybe contracts. But first, we must do something about those Black and Reds. It will be much easier to arrange things with Hanson if the Black and Reds are not turned loose in Amarillo."

"But that would mean a sortie outside the valley. Won't Hanson have us bottled up pretty well in the next day or so?"

"Yes, but what if you hold here stubbornly? Put up more of a fight, and, say, Syn and Wilson fold quickly and fall back. Hanson knows how to fight. He will reinforce success."

"And if his right is successful, where will he pull reinforcements from to send there?" Grace asked.

"That, my commander, is what we help him decide."

Grace eyed the map. She pulled up a chair and studied it from her vantage point, then moved the chair around to study it from Hanson's side. While she sat, Ben moved a few pieces of paper and wood around the map.

Santorini was running with his plan. Should she change hers? "Ben, I see what you're up to. Now, what if Wilson and Syn . . ."

"How bad is it?" Major Hanson asked Captain Graf, CO of C Company and Hanson's point on the drive for Amarillo.

"Not good, sir. Your best view is from the upstairs porch of this old house." The house was deserted but undisturbed. L. J. followed the captain out a window and stood on the porch roof. The land had looked flat from his command van. Now he saw what he'd missed. The land was rolling, and ahead was a slight but significant rise. The two lead platoons of C Company were deployed to either side of the road. A Joust tank had rolled out of its treads on the road. The infantry had gone to ground.

"What happened, Captain?"

"A mine damaged the tank, sir. There're so many potholes it's impossible to tell which are just potholes and which have mines under them. I ordered my sappers forward to clean the road, but they came under very accurate sniper fire, which I couldn't locate. I deployed my infantry. Snipers dropped four including a lieutenant and a sergeant, and I still can't identify where the fire's coming from. When they dropped a second sapper, I quit, sir."

"How far is it to that deep gully on the map?" That was where L. J. had expected resistance.

"Almost two kilometers, sir."

"So somewhere in those two klicks are a couple of guys with rifles. Can't your sensors find them?"

"No, sir. We've got the magscan gear up, but it's gone crazy. The dirt around here is red—rich in iron—

and somebody spread a lot of tacks out there." The captain pulled a small carpet tack from his pocket. "Between the iron in the dirt and these damn things, my sensors say there're a thousand rifles out there. Do we have enough artillery to flatten a half-klick around the road for the next two klicks, sir?"

L. J. scanned the ground. Rocks, brush, a few trees—mostly dead—more rocks, and more brush. "No; we're light on artillery this contract," he said as Captain Fisk of B Company joined them on the roof. "C, form to the right of that road. B, form a line to the left. Let's see just how far out those snipers go."

L. J. remembered his own recent experience with Grace's resistance. "Watch for woven mats—the grass around here matches the dirt. Get the infantry moving. Put them in the lead to check for holes. Have 'Mechs and tanks cover them."

"Yes, sir," came back at him. Grace O'Malley was a terrorist and too damn smart for either of their good—her and the six MechWarriors she'd hired. "Get your teams out. Find their flank. Let's get behind them, come up their asses and put them down. We've got to secure this road."

An hour later a hundred men, plus tanks, gun trucks and eight 'Mechs had beat the bushes. A small rise that seemed the source of their trouble had gone quiet as a church when they reached it. Now the next ridge over put fire on them.

Casualties came in dribs and drabs, but they kept coming. Men whose ceramic armor had shattered under a hit were sent to the rear to draw new armor. L. J. checked with Supply; there wasn't a lot more armor to issue.

A sniper was finally flushed and brought in. "We dug him out of a hole under some brush," the sergeant told his commander.

"Yes I was, under that brush and unarmed. They told me to bust my firing pin when you guys got close, so I busted it and I was unarmed and you guys treated me right nice," the fellow in jeans and a plaid shirt said without taking a breath.

"How many of you are there?" L. J. asked.

"They told me you'd ask that, and they told me I didn't need to know so I honestly don't know. But there's a lot of us, and we're out there with our water jugs and our rifles, and if I was the first one you got, there's a lot more of us still there."

L. J. got in the guy's face. "How many are out there?"

The guy bent his head back. "I told you, they didn't tell me and I don't know."

"What were you, a platoon? A company?" L. J. roared. The man looked back as if L. J. was speaking some strange language. The guard took the prisoner away and Mallary stepped forward.

"Sir, if what he said is right, they're behind us as well as in front of us. We've got a mess on our hands. I just got a report from A Company outside Bliven. They met resistance where they expected it and brushed it aside. They are advancing unopposed into the Gleann Mor Valley."

L. J. followed her to the map table on the porch below. In the shade with a cold glass of water, it was pleasant. Strange, the refrigerator was still running. "Where's D Company?"

"Sir. They haven't gone far since they broke away from our route three hours back. Seems the locals have been out digging the potholes deeper. With water in them, trucks and 'Mechs don't know if it's just your garden-variety hole or a bottomless pit. Makes for slow going."

"Company A report anything like that?"

"No, sir. I get the feeling the defense kind of fell apart on our right."

"And the gang to our left is the bunch that swallowed a pretty good slug of Black and Reds," L. J. muttered. Two good roads came out of Bliven that a flanking company could use to hit Amarillo. He faced an opposed crossing here, as would D on his left. *Why fight for more crossings when he already had one?*

"Order B and C Companies to fall back. Have B Company get on the road to Bliven. Tell D to have a platoon task force set up a roadblock on good ground and the rest fall back on us."

"Yes, sir," Mallary said, and went to execute her orders.

L. J. studied the map. *Grace, you're good, but I'm better. You've put together an army in damn fast time, but I brought an army trained and equipped to this fight. "Training will tell,"* he thought, quoting his uncle. He frowned. On his left somewhere was a mess of Black and Reds. They'd be road-marching across the front of whatever was holding the west entrance to this valley. So far the enemy had dug in and fought where they stood or run as they had at Bliven. True, the west group had gone out to find the fugitives. The satellite had caught the end of that battle. The Black and Reds had been taken by surprise on their flank. One amateur fighting another, and the Special Police had shown they weren't all that special.

Should he have that platoon from D Company search forward to make contact with the Black and Reds? L. J. weighed the problem and found that he had a solid basis for assuming the B and Rs could hold their own, and that if he extended his platoon he risked his flank. No, the Special Police should be able to handle any problem that came their way.

L. J. turned back to the situation on his right. That would make or break his attack.

Outside Bliven, Alkalurops
25 August 3134

Captain Yonni Brassenbird, commander of A Company, realized he might have misled Hanson a bit as he heard the new orders come over the static of the long-range radio. He hadn't actually forced a crossing of the river up ahead. What he had done was flush out six snipers and *they* had fled in their pickups for the river. Minor difference.

Yonni urged his first platoon forward—a task force with two tanks and two squads of infantry mounted in Giggins armored personnel carriers. "Keep those trucks under fire, but don't hit them. If they got the need to flee, let 'em go, and anyone they talk to."

That was Major Hanson's idea. If a bunch ran, encourage them. Send enough fire their way so they don't forget why they're pedal to the metal. Prisoners were to be passed through to the Black and Reds. Yonni didn't need that blood on his conscience.

First Platoon reached the last bluff this side of the river. Yonni halted them on overwatch and ordered Second Platoon to pass through. Second had two hovertanks well suited for the riverbed. Its infantry were in trucks. They dismounted and began the river crossing on foot. Third and Fourth Platoons, 'Mech-infantry task forces, would come up on each flank, provide cover fire, and be ready to exploit forward. The 'Mechs should have no trouble climbing down the riverbank and crossing a river barely two centimeters deep.

Yonni led his headquarters section forward in his newly assigned *Legionnaire*. This big 'Mech was one of the best in the battalion, and Yonni intended to show he knew how to lead from the front. Chasing a running bunch of civilians wouldn't be much of a test, but the Major expected this push wouldn't stop until they took Falkirk. Yonni intended his *Legionnaire* to be the first Roughrider into that burg.

Leaving his command van with First Platoon, Yonni joined Second Platoon as it made its way gingerly down the riverbank. There were plenty of paths worn by the local cows, but only the bridge offered an easy crossing. One squad of infantry moved across it under desultory and inaccurate long-range rifle fire.

"Bridge is rigged for demolition. We're yanking wires," the corporal leading that squad reported.

Well away from the bridge, the hovertanks sped down the bank, bouncing right and left as they nosed over. A Condor landed hard on its bow at the bottom and ended up stalled sideways. Yonni took his *Legionnaire* down a cow path, then patrolled back and forth in front of the stalled tank. Stopped dead, the tank was a perfect target for a antitank rocket, but all the hostiles got off were a few rifle shots.

"We got a tank stopped dead on our front and a *Legionnaire* just prancing back and forth," Syn Bakai reported on radio.

"Hold your fire," Wilson reminded her. He could spot her 'Mech MOD, as well as Jobe's, under cover behind an iron grain elevator. "I'm coming up. Remember the plan."

Syn snorted. "You won't let me forget it."

Wilson's son gunned the jeep forward. Two pickups passed them, headed north out of Bliven. The good old boys in the back waved, rifles in hand. They'd done their jobs. Wilson shook his head. Sometimes herding dumb cows was easier than getting 'Mech pilots to do what they were told.

There was no cover the last hundred meters to the elevator. They took some fire, but nothing came close. Yep, there was nothing wrong with Syn's eyes. A hovertank and a huge 'Mech with one nasty-looking rotary autocannon marched back and forth in front of a parked hovertank. Across the gulch came the sound of a starter grinding. That would be the dead tank.

A Navajo trotted out from the elevator's office, grinning. "We've got everything in place," he said, climbing in the back of the jeep. "Those mercs are going to love dancing with Coyote."

Wilson pointed for his son to park at the foot of Syn's MiningMech MOD, and reached for the large wrench he kept under his seat for just such occasions. Shouldn't be long now.

The stalled motor caught, and the tank got under way slowly. "I think we bent a blade," the driver reported. Infantry were halfway across the trickle that the locals called a river. Yonni waded in behind them. Here and there, rocks created eddies in the water. He avoided the potential deep spots behind them as consciously as he negotiated the questionable footing of the rocks.

Suddenly, on his left, two gray 'Mech MODs stepped out from behind a tall metal building. They fired missiles, as well as a long stream of slugs. He snapped off a quick burst of fifty-millimeter rounds and sidestepped right, positioning himself at an angle that would complicate their firing solution. He adjusted his pace to avoid a rock as he tried to sight in on the lead 'Mech for an aimed burst.

Then he felt his left footpad sink into the muddy water. He bent his right knee quickly, taking the pressure off his 'Mech's hips and hardly felt the explosion that sent water geysering up around his left leg. He pulled that leg up as a spray of enemy fire splashed a line of mud and water to his right. His footpad dangled uselessly.

"Damn."

Yonni tried to fire off a burst even as he set his left leg down gingerly. Standing on one leg and shooting was not something 'Mechs did. Gyros screamed, and he jammed down his damaged leg to keep his 'Mech from toppling over.

To his right, infantry fire reached out for the gray 'Mechs from the perimeter on the north side of the bridge. That squad had cut all visible demolition wires. A Demon medium tank from First Platoon slowly nosed onto the bridge, its turret rotating to take the hostile 'Mechs under fire.

Then all hell broke loose.

An explosion shattered the middle bridge span, sending chunks of deck and girders skyward. Then charges sheared off the two spans on either side of the middle one. Two final explosions dropped the last spans, intact, so they now led down to the dry riverbed at totally unusable thirty-degree angles.

"What did I tell you?" the Navajo crowed, tossing the remote detonator on the seat of the jeep. "They got the 'Mech. I got the bridge. Perfect!"

To Wilson's right, Syn's and Jobe's 'Mechs each took a step forward. They were supposed to be backing out. He was out of his jeep in a second, wrench in hand. Behind him, his son shouted, "Get back! Get back!" into the jeep's mike. "Remember the plan."

Wilson caught up with Syn's back leg and rapped it, then rapped it again. "Back up," he shouted in case she had her outside mike on. "We retreat now. Remember."

"You are no fun," came from the 'Mech's outside speaker.

Wilson hammered the leg again.

The tank that hadn't made it onto the bridge sent a large-caliber shell their way, reminding Wilson just how exposed he was.

"Maybe we should back up," came Jobe's voice from the jeep's speakers. "If they clobber this grain elevator, things could get real bad."

One 'Mech backed up. The second one joined it. Wilson ran to his jeep, and his son gunned out to the left, away from the 'Mechs who retreated into Bliven, snapping off short bursts at anyone who sent fire their way.

For a long moment Yonni watched the expanding clouds of explosives. Around him, everyone did the same. Here and there a man, 'Mech or tank maneuvered to dodge a falling chunk of debris.

Then the Demon tank that hadn't been blown up with the bridge expressed its opinion by snapping off a laser shot at the gray 'Mechs. They started backing up, firing back at anyone who fired at them. When they passed out of sight behind the multistoried buildings that must represent Bliven's main street, the riverbank grew silent.

"Uh, sir, you probably can't see it," the XO reported from the vantage point of the van on the south bluff, "but there are about a dozen pickup trucks beating it for the hills fast."

"Can you put fire on them?"

"Wait one," the XO said, and was back well before the full minute was up. "No, sir, First Platoon's tanks are out of position, and the 'Mechs were either heading down the riverbank or for the bridge. The land over there is full of folds, and we can't get any good shots as they duck in and out of 'em."

"So what else is new?" Yonni said, biting back worse comments he didn't want on the radio. "I'm all right. 'Mech's only slightly damaged. Call Battalion for the repair truck and try not to say what it's for." The cheap client had budgeted the companies for only one maintenance van each. That wouldn't help his *Legionnaire*. "Also advise Battalion that we will need a bridging unit here, five spans' worth."

"Yes, sir."

Thirty minutes later, First Platoon was across the river. Third was following them, and the HQ van waded to a stop beside Yonni. Climbing down his 'Mech to join the XO on the roof of the van he asked, "What's the situation?"

"B Company should be here in two hours. I've assigned Fourth Platoon to guard the ford until they get here. We are ready to exploit forward."

"Did the major have any luck in front of Amarillo?"

"Doesn't appear so, sir. Snipers made the advance tough sledding. We have the only troops across, sir."

"So let's get busy exploiting," Yonni ordered.

Outside Amarillo, Alkalurops
25 August 3134

"They are exploiting forward, sir," the XO said.

"Now they are," L. J. pointed out.

"That's what they said, sir." Art worked his jaw. If he wasn't careful, he'd need caps before he made Major. The Colonel did not like paying high dental bills and did not trust worriers. L. J. made sure his jaw was loose.

"Art, why don't you take your *Arbalest* and get yourself over to A Company—make sure its reports are accurate when they're made, not an hour later. And find out what their casualties are. They've made two requests for the repair rig, but I still don't have any damage report."

"Yes, sir," Art said, a big grin taking over his face. Getting free of the HQ in his BattleMech was great. Commanding the battalion's spearhead wouldn't look half bad on his next contract's résumé.

L. J. turned back to his map table. So Grace's right had turned out to be a bit tougher to crack than had first appeared. Still it was cracked, and as best as L. J. could tell, even the 'Mechs were just shooting and bugging out. If the opposition had any maneuverability, Grace should have counterattacked at that river crossing. Hell, if there was anything really in front of him, it should have attacked him when they saw one company head east, and before the other company got in from the west.

So, Grace, all I have to do is peel you. Wonder what that creamy white skin will look like when I have you down to the buff? L. J. glanced at the west side of his map. The Black and Reds still hadn't made contact

with his lone platoon covering his left flank. L. J.
frowned. They were overdue. As much as he really
didn't want them, by later this afternoon he would
have to go hunting for them.

Along the Colorado River, Alkalurops
25 August 3134

Jonathan Fetterman, Field Marshal of Special Police, wondered what the holdup was this time. Santorini, er, the Leader had told him it would be easy to
get three hundred Special Police up to Amarillo and
start cleaning out that nest of dumb-ass farmers who
didn't have the smarts to see which way the wind was
blowing. "Send me a lot of pics of full lamp poles,"
Santorini had told Fetterman before sending him off.

Well, moving a bunch of commandeered trucks and
sixteen 'Mechs in various states of conversion was no
picnic—no, sir, it wasn't. Fetterman scowled at the
Atlas under him. Buying it on time had really impressed Santorini back on Nusakan. He'd made him
a Field Marshal in a snap, or rather in a snap after Jon
had helped another dozen guys buy up every available
'Mech. Like him, they bought on time, mortgaging
stuff they really didn't own and wouldn't need if things
turned out as well as they looked here. Jon grinned,
remembering that he'd already tossed his payment
book in the trash can. Let old man Benton try to
repossess a Field Marshal's 'Mech on Alkalurops
when he's sitting at the right hand of the Leader. Fetterman enjoyed a laugh, which got his whole body
moving. He'd forgotten his hands were on the joy-
sticks. His laugh got the laser-equipped arm of his
'Mech moving. In the truck ahead of him, people
pointed and acted as if they were really scared.

He'd never gotten that reaction selling siding on
Nusakan. He could have used a bit of that fear-
mongering when he was foreclosing on scumbags who

didn't pay, claiming it was his fault for selling bad siding. It had cost him a fortune to keep judges around who believed in enforcing contracts.

"Field Marshal Fetterman, are you having problems with your 'Mech, sir?" Colonel Brisko called over the radio.

"No, I am not, Colonel. What I am is hot in here with the sun beating down. Do we have to travel in the heat of the day? Isn't it time for a break yet?"

"No, sir, we're due in Amarillo before sunset. Between potholes and breakdowns, we have to keep moving when we can. This is why I suggested you not wear your uniform, sir. Having it between you and your cooling vest is heating you up, sir."

"Hasn't anyone told you that clothes make the man? I am not going to show up in Amarillo half-naked. What's holding us up?"

"Sir, the lead truck has a flat. It's off to the side now, being fixed. Had to assign a new lead truck."

"Well, tell them to hurry up."

"I will, sir. Remember what I told you about moving those arms." Brisko started into what Fetterman knew would be another lecture on how to shoot the damn thing.

"I remember how to work it, Brisko. You just keep the trucks moving," Fetterman snapped. After all, he was the Field Marshal. Three months ago Brisko had been a cashiered merc who couldn't handle his whiskey. *I pulled you out of a homeless shelter. If it wasn't for me, you'd still be singing hymns for your supper.*

Fetterman glanced down at his cockpit. Damn, the yellow tabs he'd stuck on things so he could remember what was what and how to work it had come off. He reached down to collect them off the floor and found he'd accidentally bent his 'Mech at the waist almost to the ground and dumped the tabs in a heap on the controls. He'd get them straight later. There was a manual he kept meaning to read. Maybe tonight. Well, not tonight if the hotel had three hotties like last night's.

Fetterman concentrated on walking. Brisko was right. If you worked the pedals just right, you could miss most of the potholes.

Benjork Lone Cat wondered what he had done to deserve such a fate. The trap was laid, and then the lead truck went lame and limped to the side of the road. Now the convoy was moving again, apparently none the wiser, but six men were standing around that truck while three struggled to change the tire. Already they had all pissed. They had drunk water. Some were now passing around a bottle. How long before even blind men spotted that they were in the very epicenter of a trap?

Through the crack of the door, the MechWarrior eyed the terrain, which had decreed where to spring the trap. Here water cut a narrow passage through a tight canyon, less than a hundred meters wide, with walls of aged and worn rock almost ten meters high. All morning, troops had labored with pickaxes and shovels to dig rifle pits close to the road. Behind two parked dump trucks in a road-maintenance yard, a metal garage gave cover to a dozen gray 'Mech MODs not sixty meters from the road.

A blind cub should have spotted the danger here and sent a foot patrol to scout ahead. But the Black and Reds were truly blinded by their confidence that it was their destiny to kill, not to be killed. They drove into the trap with only a slight delay, as they argued who would take point and who would absorb any mines on the road ahead. Now the trucks full of infantry filed by. Coming soon would be the 'Mechs. A huge *Atlas* led them, or at least stumbled in the first position. That one would be almost comical if he didn't have at his fingertips the power to smash every machine that stood behind the Lone Cat.

But it was the *Spider* following the *Atlas* that caused fear. The pilot of that one knew what he was doing. While those ahead and behind him moved with a tipsy jerkiness, that one walked smoothly, even through the inevitable potholes. Ben turned to Sean and Maud, who were beside him. "That *Spider* is the one we must kill."

"Looks a whole lot easier than the *Black Hawk* we took down," Maud said.

"Th-three 'Mech MODs against one real B-BattleMech driven by a trained MechWarrior will be j-just about even odds," Sean told her. Usually, the boy agreed with whatever the girl said. Now Sean looked past her to the enemy. "It can j-jump. It has two lasers and a cooling system that lets it jump, f-fire, and run when others might be overheated and locked up. With an average warrior, it would take the th-three of us to bring it to ground. If th-that man is good, it will be b-bad for us, Maud."

"Aw, it'll be fun dancing with someone who knows how," the girl shot back. "Those guys out Harlingen way were pussycats."

"Close up," Benjork ordered. He tightened his harness and made sure all his cooling lines were free. The lightweight neurohelmet had shifted, so he repositioned it. He set his Gatling gun spinning slowly and punched his mike.

"Lieutenant Hicks, flares on my count. Three, two, one, fire. 'Mechs advance," he ordered.

Rather than charge out the garage door, the strike team had rigged the thin metal walls with charges. They blew out, dropping metal sheets on the ground. The 'Mechs stepped over the pole frame and in two seconds, twelve 'Mech MODs stood ready for battle, facing other 'Mechs that were still concentrating on following their leader.

Then the daisy chain explosions went off.

Dynamite charges set under the road blew up in a running explosion that quickly flew from the front of the line to the rear. The leading *Atlas* was just past the first explosion. Benjork doubted the charges were strong enough to knock that huge thing down, anyway. It swayed, but remained on its legs.

The *Spider* driver showed his worth. Knocked sideways, he hit his jump jets and shot into the air. Working his wings, he stabilized himself in midflight and even got off a slashing shot. Benjork gave the *Spider* a burst of thirty-millimeter tungsten slugs as it set down in the stream. Even with surprise, water, rocks and incoming fire, the *Spider* made a good landing.

Farther down the line, the explosive charges did their best to convert Black and Red 'Mechs into pretzels. Those that survived the initial experience came under fire from the gray 'Mechs from Falkirk. The Black and Reds that could, fired as they backpedaled into the river. Nearly half could do nothing more than pop their canopies and throw up their hands.

Trucks with their loads of potential hangmen came under fire from rocket grenades and machine guns. A good chunk of the men stood up in the trucks, hands in the air. Others grabbed at the mounted machine guns or tumbled over the truck sides, pulling back the arming levers on their automatic rifles. They died quickly. In the ditches on either side, men and women fired from the concealment of their fighting pits, taking down those who wanted to fight, usually missing those who did not.

The *Spider* clearly fell into the fighting category. He raced upstream, back the way he'd come, his laser raking the back of the fighting holes, killing men and women as they killed those around the trucks.

"Get him!" the Lone Cat shouted, sending bursts after the *Spider* and leading Sean and Maud in chase. Behind them, militia infantry began peeling drivers out of damaged Black and Red 'Mechs. Four men in Gnome battle armor began an assault on the still befuddled *Atlas*.

In a shower of white water, the *Spider* jumped for

the top of the stream bank. He landed well, twisted around, and fired twin lasers. He missed Benjork, but there was a short scream on the radio before it cut off.

Ignoring everything but the fleeing *Spider*, the MechWarrior put his engine in the red, raced for the wall, chose a fallen stone for his launch pad, and threw himself at the top of the riverbank. Here it wasn't quite ten meters high, and he landed just below the lip. Firing two rockets to keep the *Spider* busy, Ben used his repaired rock cutter to slowly pull himself up the rest of the way. Not pausing to regain his balance, he threw himself after the *Spider,* converting the near fall into speed.

Behind him, Sean's voice was intense. "I'm coming. Quick, s-somebody give me a hand up."

Benjork left Sean to others. The *Spider* was just disappearing over a small rise. Following, he upped his periscope for a quick check before crossing that rise.

The *Spider* was trotting backward, both arms up, lasers aimed back at the exact spot where he had crossed the hill.

Benjork sent his 'Mech ten long paces past that point, then pedaled it into a turn. Using his periscope—this time for targeting—he lobbed his last two missiles over the hill. The *Spider* staggered sideways, firing his lasers at nothing. Benjork trotted his 'Mech across the rise, sending stream after stream of heavy tungsten slugs at him. The *Spider*'s right winglet took hits—possibly the right rocket outlet as well.

"No more flying, rocket boy," Benjork growled.

The *Spider* backpedaled, bringing his lasers around to aim at his tormentor. Then a burst of thirty-millimeter fire from the right grabbed the *Spider*'s attention as it shattered his left laser.

"G-got you that time!" came from Sean on radio. "How do you like that, you bloody hangman?" He loosed two missiles that sent the *Spider* hopping sideways to escape them. The *Spider* regained its balance and fired its remaining laser at Sean.

That left Benjork free to carefully aim his Gatling gun at the *Spider*'s side. Rounds slammed into the BattleMech, spalling off its armor. The *Spider* tried to sidestep out of the line of fire, but Ben followed him, holding him, pinning the *Spider* and hammering it with shot.

So the *Spider* hit his jump jets.

Maybe he didn't know how damaged his wing and rocket outlet were. Maybe he forgot. It didn't matter. The *Spider* shot up, arcing to the left as soon as it left the ground. The pilot tried to correct, but the damaged wing drove the *Spider* to the left as misdirected plasma from a split rocket motor burned through the bottom of the 'Mech.

The flight ended in a pair of wild uncontrolled loops. Then the *Spider* buried itself in a surprisingly small hole only a hundred meters from where it had taken off.

"Let that be a lesson to you, Sean. Never trust one of those jumpers," Benjork told the young MechWarrior and anyone listening on the radio as he turned to the young man's gray 'Mech.

The 'Mech stood deathly still, a red-hot hole in its chest sending up wisps of smoke.

"Sean!" Benjork shouted, and put his engine in the red as he raced for the 'Mech standing frozen in place, as if even a soft breeze might be more than it could handle.

He slammed to a halt in front of the 'Mech. Now he could see that a laser had cut through it, straight as a diamond drill. He peered into the armorglass hood as it slowly fogged over with sweat and blood. Sean's lips moved. Over the radio Benjork heard a weak, "W-we got him." Then the gray 'Mech that had meant so much to the young man whose regiment would not entrust one to him, toppled over.

As a Nova Cat, Benjork had learned that the universe is a fickle place. He did not expect material things to reflect what other people call rationality. He knew that karma rules us all whether we be rock and water or flesh and blood. Nova Cats do not weep for what must be.

Benjork Lone Cat knew all of these things—not as a man might know it in his head, but as only a dreamer can know it in the deepest essence of his being.

So now he walked apart from the others who gathered around their fallen comrade, murmuring about how sad it was that the young girl had died, too. Distant from all others who mourned, Benjork opened his cockpit and let the spurious dampness that some might mistake for tears flow from his eyes and be swallowed down by the thirsty red dirt of Alkalurops.

When the dampness was gone, the Lone Cat lifted his right arm to the universe. He shook it, his threat to the very stars. "Know you who watch, you who send dreams. I will stand with Grace and all her kin. This land beneath my feet is my land, the land of my dream. And neither hell nor demons may take it while I breathe."

15

Kilkenny, Alkalurops
Prefecture IX, The Republic of the Sphere
28 August 3134; local summer

Damn near getting killed while leading a losing fight
had to be the worst day of Grace O'Malley's life. Or
so she'd thought. Now she knew she'd thought wrong.
Leading a losing battle while safely in the rear,
chained to maps, was a whole lot worse.

Worse still, it left her time to think she just might
be winning.

Grace looked out over Kilkenny from the Congregational Church steeple. For a moment she let the
wind blow in her face and blow the cobwebs from her
brain. She didn't feel any better.

The plan seemed to be working. Hanson was leading his hard-charging mercs right down her throat. In
the Gleann Mor Valley, people shot and fell back.

Chato said the ground around Falkirk was ready for the coming fight.

But did the fight have to be there?

Day after day refugees streamed past Grace. Did she want her friends in Falkirk reduced to that? She eyed a pile of reports held down against the wind by a thirty-millimeter shell. They said the mercs were paying for every klick they advanced. Tanks lost treads to mines. Hovertank fans were bent. Infantry used up their fantastic armor, which deflected sniper shots from their hearts, and now advanced much more cautiously. BattleMechs were a whole lot more careful where they put their feet. It didn't take long to fix a busted footpad, but every bent foot meant another 'Mech awaiting repair rather than charging forward.

Grace rested her eyes on the west and its just visible hills. Ben was out there, racing for Kilkenny with someone he said she had to talk to. Someone Betsy and Hanson would really want to talk to. Grace was new to this fighting thing. But new as she was, she knew that you planned the fight and fought the plan. Being a miner, she knew plenty of folks who'd paid dearly for not following their plans.

Despite it all, Grace slowly walked around her map. Done, she called Victoria to climb the steeple stairs and go over the map with her. Grace had a new plan to talk through.

L. J. scowled at the map in front of him. With the Net down and his client unwilling to bring it up for a "minor" thing like the decisive battle for Gleann Mor Valley and maybe this whole stinking planet, L. J. was reduced to pushing pieces of paper around a paper map and hoping the real fighting men and machines were somewhere near where his map table showed them to be.

Once upon a time, say three hundred years back, this planet had a Global Positioning System. But the satellites had worn out, and no one had replaced them.

So now Roughriders had to read geodetic ground markers to find out where they were, and report their location over the radio. Even his artillery was reduced to line of sight unless he wanted to waste what little ammo he had. *God! And I've wanted to command a battalion since I was a kid!*

L. J. worried his lower lip as he studied his western flank. He'd finally ordered the platoon guarding his left to advance and make contact with the missing Black and Reds. They'd found them . . . or what was left of them.

The good news was that the opposition was running. They'd left anything they couldn't grab, even some of their dead. The bad news was what he'd learned from the damaged 'Mechs left behind. Their armor was good. Their SRMs, from the damage done, were very good. L. J. rubbed his chin. Why had they taken off? He'd only sent a platoon. They could have smashed it. But when the platoon happened on the ambush, the enemy was long gone, not even dust on the horizon of this usually dusty planet.

No, Grace's troops had found something they considered important enough to make them abandon their own dead. L. J. shook his head. Whoever had taken out the Black and Reds could have charged straight for Allabad. Threaten Allabad, and Santorini would have been screaming for the Roughriders to protect his delicate hide.

L. J. flipped through the file he had of the mercs Grace had signed up. Woman, woman, woman . . . Hold it. He'd seen that woman before. That was Betty Rose, the maid he'd tried to hire! *Betsy Ross, huh? Wonder what her real name is.* He glanced down the file on her. Too damn short. He didn't need Intelligence to tell him this was a false résumé.

He shuffled the file again. Boy: tank driver . . . No tanks so far. "What have we here?" he said. "Benjork Lone Cat. Bet you'd enjoy taking Field Marshal Fetterman's thugs down." L. J. froze. He checked the platoon's report. Yep, there it was. The big, hulking *Atlas* was missing. "Not something I want to meet, not with just my little *Koshi*." But if they captured the Field Marshal, they captured the *Atlas*.

Damn; what I'd give for some decent pictures of my left flank. L. J. shook his head. Fighting with no bandwidth was like fighting in one of those ancient wars with the first tanks or knights on horses. "I don't know shit," he whispered.

The satellite had just made a pass over the valley. The Chief and the Network Services team had cobbled together a way to take very low-resolution pictures off the overhead coverage. He studied what he had. A major enemy force moving fast up the west road. That road led straight to Falkirk. It also met with a side road that could take you to Kilkenny. That town had a fertilizer plant turning out rockets. If he kept the pressure up, he could be there by late tomorrow. The valley narrowed there. He'd strung his forces across two thirds of the valley for most of the push from Amarillo. Kilkenny looked like a place to concentrate. "Mallary, do you have a moment?" he called.

"Be there in a minute," she said, then arrived sooner. "Casualty reports, sir."

"Bad?"

"No. Not if we had the spare parts to fix what's broken."

"Deaths?" L. J. asked, suspecting he knew the answer.

"Not a one again today, sir. Two more 'Mechs lost their footpads. Two more tanks are hung up waiting for spare treads. We've got three types of tracks on our rigs, sir, and six types of fans. We've grounded one of each and are parting them out to keep the others running."

"But no deaths. Grace has managed to inflict, what, twenty percent casualties and still not kill anyone?"

Mallary provided the exact level of his reduced strength. "Twenty-three percent, sir."

"She's trimming us, but not making anyone mad."

"Maybe the civilian doesn't have a taste for the jugular."

L. J. shook his head. "No, I've fought that woman. She'd have gladly killed me when I was chasing her up that hill. And she has to have people who've lost loved ones to the damn B and Rs."

"They kill Black and Reds, sir. Come out looking for them."

"But never came out looking for us. They fight us, careful not to hurt anyone, then run. Give up ground." L. J. tapped the map. "They run out of ground at Falkirk."

"So," he said, making a decision. "Let's concentrate the battalion at Kilkenny. We can blow that plant and get used to fighting together before we hit Falkirk."

Mallary eyed the map of the town, measuring the distance between the four scattered companies, and nodded. "We can be there by late tomorrow. Assuming this Grace you're always talking about doesn't decide it's time to fight more and run less."

"Issue the orders."

"You are changing the orders," Ben said as soon as Grace showed him her map laid out in the church steeple.

"I think this is a better plan," Grace said. Victoria didn't offer an opinion.

"But you have attritioned him only fifteen, twenty percent."

"We think we're over the twenty percent mark," Grace said, feeling like a schoolgirl who'd done the wrong homework and now had to convince the teacher it was a better idea than the original assignment.

Ben eyed the map table, unblinking, for a long moment. "You assume he will concentrate here," he said, putting a finger on Kilkenny.

"Yes."

"And if he does not?"

"We go back to Plan A."

"Order, counterorder, disorder," Ben said.

"That's what I told her when she first showed it to me," Victoria said.

"And Grace answered you how?" Ben asked his fellow MechWarrior. Grace answered instead.

"He knows we have to fight at Falkirk. He's watched us fall back from every other roadblock. He'll expect us to fall back at Kilkenny. We can use that expectation against him."

"So this is the dream that drives you," Ben said.

Grace took a deep breath. "Yes, this is the dream that drives me."

"I will have to tell Danny that we go into battle obedient to your dream. He said he was afraid of mine. We shall see how confident he is in yours."

Grace just shrugged.

"Well," Ben said, looking up from the map. "I have a man downstairs you must meet. He strode into battle commanding an *Atlas*. Powerful machine. Could have—should have—slaughtered our ambush all by itself."

"Why didn't he?" Victoria asked.

"This Field Marshal of Special Police thought that listening to one lecture by a MechWarrior would tell him all he needed to know to drive a BattleMech. He left yellow sticky notes on the switches he had to activate when he spun up his 'Mech in the morning."

"Sticky notes?" Grace said, having a very hard time believing it. "I tried them once to keep track of this or that on a busy day. I'd post them up on the inside of Pirate's cockpit. The pounding and vibrations around made them fall off."

"They fell off his board, too. He had all his switches in all the wrong places. He couldn't have hurt a flea except by stepping on it, and he got so confused when we attacked him that he was moving his hands instead of his feet."

Grace barely suppressed a laugh as she followed

Ben down the stairs from the steeple map room. In the vestibule, Lieutenant Hicks stood with his sergeant. Between them was a small man with sweat pouring off his bald head.

Betsy Ross was just coming through the side door. She took one look at the man and actually growled. The man saw her and stumbled back as far as the chain between his handcuffs and the sergeant would let him.

"We meet again," Betsy said, advancing on the Field Marshal. She didn't sound pleased to see him.

"Down, girl," Ben said, putting out an arm to restrain her. "I want him to tell Grace what he did with his loan payment book. The one for the *Atlas* we now own." Ben eyed the man, then Betsy. "Then, if Grace doesn't have any further use for him, you can have him."

"Please," the former maid said to Grace. "This scum has nothing of interest to you."

"Yes I do. I do," the man begged. "I told him, and he said you'd want to hear this," he said, nodding to Ben then pleaded with Grace. "Let me talk."

"Talk," Grace ordered.

"Yes," Betsy said, pulling a knife from the lieutenant's belt and playing it lightly across the captive's face. "Talk."

L. J. climbed the steps to the steeple of the Congregational Church. As promised, it gave him the best view of Kilkenny and its environs. To the southeast several large grain elevators blocked his view, but his main interest was to the north.

To his surprise, he found a table and chair already there. Mallary was right behind him, leading the Chief and the specialist who nursed the jury-rigged long-range radio. The radio operator hooked a wire to both of the bells as the Chief spread a map over the table.

"Fits. Think someone had a map up here yesterday?" he said.

"I never said Grace was dumb," L. J. muttered as he glanced down. In front of the church stood his command van. Two maintenance types were going over it, his *Koshi* and Mallary's *Arbalest*. The two 'Mechs were fast and together provided a balanced force. At the moment they were the main protection the advance headquarters company had.

The Chief put weighted markers on the map—the wind up here was strong, hot and dusty. "C Company moved through town as ordered and set up a perimeter at the dry riverbed about three klicks north of town."

"They're taking fire, sir," the radio operator reported. "Nothing they can't handle. Mostly rifle shit."

"Repeat only what you're told, Specialist," the Chief said.

"That's what he said, Chief."

"Then clean up Captain Graf's language for him."

"Yes, sir."

"D Company should be pulling into town about now, sir," the Chief said. "We'll have them dismount and police the place, burn the fertilizer plant, and serve as our reserve."

L. J. looked down the main road he'd just come up and saw a line of tanks and trucks with 'Mechs along their flanks. "Pass the word to Captain Chang. Tonight he's our reserve, but first he has to clean this place out."

"Yes, sir," the radio operator said, and passed along his orders.

L. J. was looking to the east, so he missed the incoming missile until it exploded close enough to make him duck to the floor. Silly reaction when you're twenty meters in the air.

He turned to see a second missile arcing in from the west. It fell short—or at least it impacted a block short of the church. Another one was already in the air and aimed more to the south. It exploded just ahead of C Company's lead gun truck.

"Give me the radio," L. J. said, and took the phone from the specialist. "Chang, you there?"

"Still here, sir," came with a dry laugh.

"Slight change in plans. Hook a hard left and go see what's happening on the west side of town. I've got a low hill blocking my view, but there's another rocket heading in. Be advised, we don't know what the west flank has, but somebody on our left took out the Black and Reds."

"I'll give them the regiment's thanks, sir. But if they've only faced that crap, they don't know what a real fight is."

"Knock 'em down, dust 'em off, and bring 'em in," L. J. said, even as the column that was C Company did a left wheel, spread out, and took off. Two more rockets and the fire died away. That could be all that the west had to offer. Then again, L. J. would wait to see what Chang reported.

"Where are A and B?" L. J. asked.

"A is just pulling into town on River Road, sir," Chief reported. "B's a bit behind them. It was held up by an ambush earlier today. Captain St. George left them to clean it up, and pushed on with A."

L. J. nodded. Art knew he wanted the battalion here, so he was making sure at least one of his two companies was.

It didn't take binoculars to spot A Company. Their 'Mechs strode into town from the southeast, walking past the grain elevator. A missile came in from a hill to the east, lazy and slow. If the battalion had had any area antimissile defense, shooting this one down would have been duck soup.

But Santorini hadn't funded them for that.

"It's going to miss," Mallary said. L. J. nodded. The missile was well short of the road. If anything, it was going to hit the grain elevator. Huge complex, must be a block long.

Something niggled at the back of his brain. Grain silos. They exploded if people weren't careful about the dust in them. "Oh my God. Everyone down!" L. J. shouted, and pushed Mallary to the floor just as the elevator blew with a force that probably exceeded anything the planet had seen. He landed atop Mallary as the steeple tried to launch itself into orbit. Failing that, it swayed back and forth beneath them.

When the swinging slowed, L. J. rolled off Mallary. He tried to get up, but either his legs were still shaking or the tower was. It took him a moment to work his way up to his knees. "You okay?" he asked Mallary.

She took his offered hand. "Wasn't quite what I'd fantasized, but for a first time, you weren't too bad." She managed a grin as she got to her knees.

"It was good for me, too," he told her, risking putting his weight on a broken railing to pull himself up. Mallary put her hand on the table leg in front of her, then thought differently and took his offered hand to stand up.

The operator had grabbed for his radio when L. J. shouted the warning. He was still holding on to it, but the table had been upended, and the left side had come down hard on his groin.

The Chief pulled the table away, then knelt down. "You okay?"

"I'm fine, sir," the man said, but there was blood on his lips. "Hurts a bit."

"We need a medic up here," L. J. shouted to his command van.

"On her way," a sergeant shouted as a blonde with a first-aid box raced into the church. She was beside the radio operator a minute later.

"A few steps will need watching on the way down," was her only comment about the trip up. She took over caring for the radio operator as L. J. gently removed the equipment from his bloodstained hands. Mallary righted the table, and the Chief again spread out the map.

L. J. checked the radio, found it still on A's allotted command frequency and called Art. "XO, you there?"

"Yes, but I'll never enjoy the smell of a bakery again," he said. "We've got wheat and corn burying half the company. We've got hovertanks on their backs like turtles. We're digging troops out as fast as we can." From the sound of heavy breathing, Art was doing that while talking. "Is anything else headed our way?"

"I'm up a church steeple in the center of town. I can't see past the smoke in your sector."

"Fourth Platoon, get an observation post on the other side of that damn river," came as a distant shout over the radio. "I'll get back to you as soon as I know anything. We're kind of busy, sir."

"Stay busy. The Aid Station is still en route. I'll have them join you as soon as possible," L. J. said. Then he called the company support column under the Adjutant.

"Eddie, A Company is bleeding from an explosion."

"We saw the cloud. For a second I wondered if there was a Blakist around here throwing atomics."

"No, just more dual use of civilian stuff," L.J. growled. "They need your medics and supplies, and I need the artillery. Someone's shooting at us with long-range stuff sighted on preselected targets."

"They haven't done that before."

"First time for everything."

"We'll put on all the speed this road will allow."

"See you soon," L. J. said, and switched frequencies. D Company was flashing. "Hanson."

"Chang here, sir. They've got quite a demonstration going on the west side. I make it a dozen 'Mechs on the next ridge. They've got infantry. Some I can see. A whole lot I can't. Gun trucks with machine guns and grenade launchers. I'd say they're at battalion strength at least. I'm digging in to defend, sir, but if they start spreading out, they can overreach both my flanks."

L. J. stared off to the west trying to see what at least one ridge hid from him. Could these guys maneuver? If Chang hit them, would they fire and fall back? Maybe trip over themselves? Hell, Chang was only outnumbered three to one; he should be able to take a bunch of green civilians.

L. J. started to click the radio, then remembered this might be the group that had at least one attack, maybe two under their belts. Sure, they'd only chewed up Black and Reds, but they'd taken fire and still chewed them up.

"Chang, probe 'em. See if you can make them do something. Charge. Retreat. Something."

"I'll get back to you, sir. What was that big bang?"

"A Company is up to its ears in popcorn," L. J. said.

"Okay, sir. Excuse me for asking. I was just curious," said the man, who didn't believe the answer he got and wasn't going to push his CO. L. J. didn't have time to set the record straight. C Company was flashing. He changed frequencies.

"Sir, there are an awful lot of bad guys on my front. Right now they're not doing much more than looking at us look at them, but 'Mechs keep walking over a ridge and walking back. There could be four of them, there could be forty."

"How are they armed?"

"Damned if I know, sir. We haven't exchanged fire yet, but those look like large-caliber multibarrel machine guns and something that gives off an IR signature."

"They had one of them in Falkirk when I fought them. Field burner or something."

"It's the 'something' that I worry about. What was that racket back in town, sir?"

"Grain elevator exploded. Buried A Company in hot corn."

"Grain elevators do tend to explode if you don't treat them with respect."

"A missile hit didn't meet with this one's idea of respect. D is on your left facing a battalion-sized force.

I've got Chang probing it. You up to probing the force on your front?"

"No reason why not. We've got them where we want them and outnumbered one to three. I'll do a bit of tapping, see if they run like they've been doing."

L. J. wouldn't bet on that, but a commander did not share negative comments with his subordinates. "Go for it."

George Stillwell grinned to himself. The Roughriders were coming out. He would have made the same mistake. No company of mercs could back down from a battalion-strength bunch of rabble. Problem was, the Falkirk militia weren't rabble—not after what George and the other MechWarriors had put them through.

Standing in the front seat of a gun truck, he signaled to the rest of his platoon. "Follow me." He could have had the Condor tank they'd captured, but he'd always argued that it wasn't the fancy toys, but the guts of the guys behind the guns that mattered—not that all of the folks behind the guns following him were guys. It made for an interesting team.

His gun truck bounced over brush and rocks as it shot forward, three more swinging out in rough echelon as they zigged and zagged behind him. Gunners hung on to their 20mm Gatling guns attached to the roll bars on the enemy side of the trucks. Missileers steadied their single launchers on the same bar to the right. Stillwell pointed his driver at the far right of the troops advancing from Kilkenny. "Swing wide of that *Centurion*. It has several ways of ruining our day."

The driver did. The *Centurion* tracked them as they crossed right to left across its front, then burned sagebrush behind Stillwell's truck with its extended-range medium laser. It and a Demon medium tank adjusted their course to confront Stillwell's team. Infantry squads in Gnome and Cavalier battle armor spread out around them.

"Good deployment," Stillwell breathed. If he wasn't careful, they'd cut him off and up. "But I'm just here to do some raiding and scaring," he said, and reached for the mike. "Task Force George, see if we got their range."

Behind him, 20mm rounds reached out for the Roughrider team. Some hit, but only at extreme range. No damage.

"Hold your fire. Let's see if we can draw them off." He pointed for his driver, and the turn got wider. In the distance, the Roughriders began a careful pursuit. "Ah, so you fellows have heard about the way our moles dig." Stillwell grinned—he was driving a gun truck for the same reason.

Only after Stillwell's task force drew even with the Roughrider line did the enemy task force step up the pace of its pursuit. "You don't want me getting behind you now, do you?"

Now that the Roughrider task force was in slow but earnest pursuit, Stillwell pointed his driver to do a hard right, and he led the platoon in what must have looked like serious flight. The Roughriders, true to their name, put the hammer down and came hot after him.

Which didn't bother Stillwell at all as he topped a small rise and dropped out of sight. Hardly visible in the draw that ran through the shallow valley, eight jeeps sat ready, Gatling guns and rockets balanced on their roll bars. At the sight of him, infantry vanished into their fighting pits. Task Force George was now complete: three platoons of gun trucks, two of infantry.

The *Centurion* used its height to snap off some Gauss rounds and LRM volleys to send George's gun trucks seriously into random S-turns. George timed his next move to the arrival of the Roughrider task team at the crest of the hill.

"About-face!" he shouted, and his four gun trucks

did hard U-turns and gunned from cover. From trucks and hidden infantry, rockets reached out to slash into the Roughriders.

"Charge!" George yelled. Zigzagging, racing for all they were worth, guns blazing and rockets flying, the trucks advanced. Militia infantry fired off rocket after rocket, marking their fighting holes, but the Roughriders were hardly interested in them.

The Roughrider infantry took hits but held their line long enough to fire off a volley. Then they backed across the hill. Firing off lasers and short- and long-range missiles, the Roughrider's BattleMech and tank covered for the infantry withdrawal, but flying shards of armor showed they were paying a high price. Finally the *Centurion* backed up, firing even as its legs disappeared in defilade. Lastly, the tank roared out of the valley in reverse, firing all the time.

There was no question in Stillwell's mind that he would not lead his task force across that ridge into whatever trap the Roughriders were setting for him. Cheers from the troops were softened by the Loader-Mech behind Stillwell holding up a single rocket.

"This is my last, sir."

The gunner beside her laughed nervously as he dug two 20mm shells out of the box magazine attached to his Gatling gun. "I was about empty, too."

"Then let's get out of here before they know we bamboozled them," George said, joining in their laughter.

The wheeled trucks did a fast turn around the valley to collect their dismounts, and then Stillwell let them lead the way to the rear, his platoon going last. His final glimpse of the battlefield showed the Roughriders he'd fought regaining contact with the rest of their company as another team of gray gun trucks was just starting to circle their flank.

Ten klicks back, they drove into a resupply park under the happy management of Auntie Maydell from

Falkirk. She laughed as George described their little ambush, but shook her gray head at the empty ammo boxes. "We can't keep this up much longer."

An infantry girl pointed at the five-kilo satchel charges in the bottom of the truck. "We were ready to take them down with those if George here had let them get close."

Maydell and George exchanged glances. "Grace better figure out a way to end this or it's going to be a bloody balls-up," George said.

"Not my way of putting it," Maydell sniffed, "but I do think she'd better put a stop to this before it gets past us all."

L. J. flipped the radio switch. "Hanson here."

"Art here. There's something on the other side of that river. They put a lot of fire on the guys who tried to cross to set up an OP on that side. We don't have a listening post over there yet, but we're sure taking fire."

"Art, B Company is coming up behind you. I'll have them cross the river well out and swing behind your troublemakers. I'd like to pocket a few of these shooters for a change."

"I feel a strong urge to talk to them myself," Art said.

"How bad is it?"

"That explosion blew out the panels on the silo pretty hard. I got a Joust tank that had everything sheared off right down to the turret armor. Quarter-inch steel sheets can do a number on tires, tracks, you name it. Then that damn smoldering corn comes flowing at you like lava, and all you want to do is run but you can't. We've dug most of our troops out but I don't think I have a vehicle or 'Mech with a stone's worth of offensive power. My *Arbalest* had one laser sliced in two by flying metal, something's sticking out of my right rocket launcher and I have no lights at all on my left one. Never thought all this damage could come from just walking by a damn pile of food."

"We're learning to respect a whole lot of new stuff, Art. Let me know when you see B Company."

Chief and Mallary eyed the map. They had only two markers for enemy battalions; they promoted a COMPANY marker to BATTALION as L. J. dialed up B Company.

"Fisk, how long before you get up here?"

"I've got Kilkenny in sight, sir. Least I do if Kilkenny is the town with all the smoke."

"That's us. We have reports of battalion-sized forces of unknown quality on our left and front. Something blew up the granary on our right and is resisting any effort by us to probe it. I'm assuming another battalion. Until A Company can pull itself together, I need you to secure the right flank with a minimum force and serve as my reserve."

"Understood. We're nearly there, sir."

"Swing a platoon out to the other side of that river and see if you can cut off a few hostiles. I'd love to have a heart-to-heart talk with a couple of them."

"I'll do my best, sir."

The medic hollered for a wire-cage stretcher so she could get the radio operator down. Two troopers carried one up, along with several coils of rope. Once the wounded man was safely strapped in, they lowered him down the outside of the still-swaying steeple.

"That man's earned his wound medal," the Chief said as the radioman kept silent even when the wind twisted the stretcher around and hung him facedown, fifteen meters in the air.

"A lot of people are," L. J. said as he glanced to the east, where smoke still filled the sky. It was getting late; there was less than an hour of daylight left. L. J. would not send his troops on a night pursuit across ground previously held by this enemy—not with their proclivity for turning holes in the ground into busted 'Mechs and hurt troopers.

Graf and Chang reported in. Both C and D Companies had engaged hostiles on their front who withdrew

in good order, only to have more show up on their
flanks and threaten their rears. Nobody was breaking.
Nobody was running. L. J. called off the attacks. Graf
and Chang began a retrograde of their own as the sun
sank toward the mountains to the west.

It was no better on his right, either. Fisk did swing
out a platoon, but the hostiles seemed to be expecting
that. The platoon came under immediate fire. A large
chunk of A Company was now in the field hospital
set up just this side of the burning granary. With A
dismounted, L. J. wasn't in a position to pull back
even if he wanted to.

He headed downstairs with Mallary. It was time to
do a walkaround of his battalion. Let the troops see
the skipper, and let the skipper see firsthand the mess
he'd gotten them into. He had just powered up his
Koshi when the command van's undercarriage collapsed in a shower of slugs.

Grace sat in Pirate as she had since noon, when the
first reports started coming in of Roughriders approaching Kilkenny. Her 'Mech almost touched the
ceiling of Flaherty's Dance Emporium. How Ben had
gotten the big *Atlas* to damn near sit under its not-
tall-enough roof was something she did not want to
know. A half-dozen 'Mechs MODs stood waiting
along the dance floor, like some gargantuan line
dance. At the back end of the hall, infantry held in
place the section of wall they'd blown out to get the
'Mechs in. At the other end of the hall, Betsy and
more infantry made ready to blow another hole. Two
blocks away stood the steeple Grace had used to plan
this new battle.

Betsy reported that Hanson was up in the steeple
now. May St. Peter, St. Patrick and St. Michael keep
him from using it as well as Grace hoped she had.
Reports from lookouts scattered around town and
brought by messengers through the sewers said that
the fighting outside Kilkenny was not going the

Roughriders' way. Except for that, Grace was deaf, dumb and blind.

Atop his *Atlas,* Ben stirred from his nap. "It is time," he called to Grace.

"Time to move out," she called to the other 'Mechs. The room hummed with electronics and began to fill with smoke as engines coughed to life. Grace made sure her neurohelmet was in place, then checked her cooling vest. She followed the new checklist, but her two gyros stuttered and did not sync. She let them spin for a minute, then shut them down and restarted them. This time they synced. "Watch them," the gal who'd had Pirate told Grace. "If you take a hard step or knock into a building, the gyros go crazy. I've gotten to where I can restart them real fast."

Grace was probably nowhere near as fast, but this was her fight and Grace would fight it herself. She tapped her radio. "Form two lances. Back four go out the back way and support us as planned. You two behind me, follow Ben. Understood?" They answered in the affirmative. Grace crossed herself. "Let's go."

There was a soft explosion as Betsy blew out the east wall of Flaherty's place. Beside her, two guards kept a short balding man on a tight chain. Betsy gave the 'Mechs a jaunty thumbs-up as they strode forth into what Grace hoped would be the decisive battle for Alkalurops.

Two blocks away a command van stood just outside the Congregational Church. Troopers in Roughrider tan looked up in surprise. Grace gave the van a short burst, but thirty-millimeter tungsten penetrators do not just flatten tires and blow out a radiator. The undercarriage of the command van was shredded. Behind the van a familiar-looking *Koshi* and an *Arbalest* got moving just as Ben sent an SRM volley at the two.

Grace quickly moved to the left side of the street, Ben began to lumber down the center, and the other two 'Mechs took the right. The Roughrider 'Mechs

backed up, zigzagging in a random fashion to complicate the big *Atlas'* firing solutions. Ben squeezed off
SRM volleys at random intervals, but only one struck
a glancing blow to the *Koshi*.

The *Koshi* returned fire, sending rockets at the
Atlas. One miss bounced Grace off the building beside
her, and her gyros lost sync. Stalled, she managed to
restart the pair and get moving just before the *Arbalest* burned the place she'd been standing with a
laser burst.

Grace fired a short burst, sending sparks and shards
of armor flying from both 'Mechs, to tell Ben she was
still in the fight. The Roughriders concentrated on the
Atlas as they backed up, failing to notice the four
'Mech MODs behind them until a barrage of rockets
exploded around them. The *Arbalest* spun even as it
danced right. Grace had a good guess what messages
were flying between those two. If she was going to
keep them from jumping out of this, she had to act
now.

She mashed her LOUDSPEAKER button. "This is
Grace O'Malley, Alkalurops Defense Forces Commanding Officer," echoed off the walls of the two
story buildings around them. "I wish to talk to Major
Loren Hanson of the Roughriders."

"This is Major Hanson," blared back at her. "I am
not prepared to discuss my surrender with you."

"That's fine, because I wish to discuss *my*
surrender."

"*Your* surrender?"

"Yes."

"Is this some kind of trick?"

"I am a miner, Major, not a murderer. I wish to
end this killing. If the only way I can is to discuss my
surrender, that is what I will do. Haven't I earned the
right to talk surrender terms?"

"You have done that," he said as the cockpit of his
Koshi opened. "You could write a book on Fabian
tactics."

"Why write a book that others would just use against me?" Grace said as she opened Pirate's cockpit. "My infantry leader has some data files she thinks you might like to review."

"You mean my maid, Betty Rose?"

"A gal takes whatever job she can," came with a laugh from behind Grace. Betsy was advancing along the sidewalk, machine pistol in one hand, a large 'puter in the other. Behind her trailed two guards with a very reluctant Field Marshal.

"I recognize the guy behind you," the Major said.

"I thought you would," Betsy called up to him. "Want to come down here and ask him a few questions? I think you'll find him both entertaining and possibly lifesaving."

16

Allabad, Alkalurops
Prefecture IX, The Republic of the Sphere
2 September 3134; local late summer

Grace was hot, filthy and tightly chained. Not her idea of a good time, but Santorini had sent very specific instructions on how he wanted his prisoners decked out for his victory parade. Hanson had obeyed. Hanson had obeyed every order Santorini had issued since the collapse of the opposition.

That included pictures of Kilkenny's lampposts strung with corpses. Fortunately, Fetterman had old photos he had not sent Santorini, so the demand had been met without too much trouble.

Grace staggered in chains down Landers Row in Allabad, toward the Guild Hall, renamed the Leader's Chancellery. In the brick-paved plaza in front of the clock tower, Santorini waited in full uniform, more shining silver than black serge. Imperious, he sat atop his *Ryoken II,* cockpit open to the slight breeze. Some poor lackey had been hooked to the outside of the BattleMech, sixteen meters up, to hold a parasol lest the morning sun that had now cleared the canyon wall above Allabad beat down uncomfortably upon the Leader. The scene was like some ancient vid of rajahs and elephants and slaves.

Grace struggled to keep such thoughts from her face.

"Take a good look at what happens to anyone stupid enough to cross your Leader." Santorini's voice boomed from an oversized speaker mounted on the chest of the *Ryoken II.* Up and down Landers Row, other speakers blared the same. Not surprisingly, the Net was back up and carrying this spectacle. Grace was counting on that. "Look at what everyone can expect who gets in the way of the future of my worlds."

Worlds, now, Grace thought. *This guy really is on a trip.*

"You sure this was part of your dream?" Ben whispered from beside Grace. Jobe and Chato struggled along on her other side. Behind them, Victoria and Danny shuffled in step, heads defiantly high. It was probably the first time in their lives that those two Highlanders had been together on anything. Sven worried Grace. Pale as new snow, he stumbled along, helped by Betsy and George Stillwell. Grace had been willing to let Sven skip the prisoners' walk, but he'd insisted. It was Syn Bakai who refused to risk breaking a nail, so Hanson had reported her killed while attempting to escape. Her lovely body was lashed to one of the following tanks, per Santorini's orders. Grace hoped Syn had forgotten her sunblock and burned tomato red.

Then again, they might all soon be red—red with their own blood. Not all calculated risks paid off as calculated.

Hanson led the Roughriders from his *Koshi* twenty meters ahead of Grace. Mallary's and Art's *Arbalest*s stalked along, two steps behind him with Eddie at their elbow, keeping Ben's *Atlas* close. The crowds lining the sidewalks were deathly silent. Children stood close to their parents. Grace had remarked at all the Black and Reds standing guard along the side of the road. Ben whispered that they weren't there to keep the crowd from the victory parade, but rather to make sure that people didn't slip away. Santorini wanted everyone to see his triumph.

So did Grace, but for a different reason.

Grace kept her eyes down, a properly dejected and defeated foe, but from under her eyelashes she studied the force arrayed around Santorini. His most dangerous BattleMechs were the *Legionnaire* to his left and *Jupiter* to his right. There were a smattering of *Centurion*s and *Catapult*s in the next rank around the big three. But over half of that dozen were 'Mech MODs formed in a square with an open front to the road. Behind them, in none too straight a line, were two dozen Mech MODs with nothing like the conversion package Sven and Mick had put together. Grace figured Santorini must have every Black and Red 'Mech on the planet here. Behind that, machine gun–armed jeeps and civilian trucks formed a line. *I wanted all the bad apples in one place,* Grace reminded herself. *Well, I've got them. Now all I have to do is survive them.*

As Hanson strode by his client's viewing point, Santorini treated them to the horrible thing that passed for his smile.

That brought Grace even with the Leader. She shot him a look of pure hate. The loudspeakers caught his cackle of a laugh as he pointed her out to his two subordinates. One of them—Grace thought it was the *Jupiter* driver on the right—said, "I'd shoot her where she stands for that look."

Santorini put his hand over the mike in front of

him, but Grace still heard. "But that would take away the impact of a trial and formal execution," said the other one.

"What more can we get?" the *Jupiter* driver shot back. "We've got the biggest crowd this hick town's gonna give us. We've got cameras taking this live around the whole planet."

"Good point," Santorini said, taking his hand off the mike. "Hanson, stop the parade a moment."

The mercs came to a halt in perfect one-two cadence. At Hanson's order, all faced left. Grace shrugged. She hadn't really expected a nice formal court hearing. So much for Plan A. Unlike some people, she did have a Plan B. She turned to face Santorini as the rest of her command group shuffled themselves into a line beside her.

"You have committed high treason against your Leader. Do you have anything to say for yourselves?"

Grace stepped forward. "We made a mistake," she shouted up at the *Ryoken II*.

"I can't hear you," Santorini said. Obviously delighted, he waved her forward with one hand as he jacked up the gain on his mike with the other. Grace took another five steps forward, the others trailing behind her by a step or two.

"We made a mistake," she repeated as Santorini pointed the mike in her direction. Her voice reverberated around the plaza. Behind her, the crowd shuffled unhappily.

"Of course it was a mistake to betray your Leader," he boomed, the mike back in his face. "I promise unlimited prosperity to the people who support me. I will make Alkalurops a mighty capital that will stand side by side with Terra, New Avalon, Atreus, Luthien and Tharkad. Why would you oppose me?"

This was where it got tricky. Grace took a few more steps toward the *Ryoken II* and raised her hands—not exactly pleading, but if Santorini took it that way, let him. "I mistook your generous offer for a landgrab."

The guy in the *Jupiter* scowled at "landgrab" and turned to Santorini, but the Leader had been titillated by the raised hands and "generous offer." "So now you realize your Leader is a generous man, and that following me will make the citizens of Alkalurops into a powerful people."

"You have certainly shown us what fear is, O Leader," Grace said, hoping the last tag would mislead Santorini. Behind her, the crowd was now murmuring. Beside her, Ben covered one hand while the other worked the key into the lock of his handcuffs. Grace edged forward, holding Santorini's attention.

"Just look at the power I brought you," Santorini said with a wave to the BattleMechs and 'Mech MODs around him. The guy in the *Jupiter* eyed the crowd and adjusted his neurohelmet. The man in the *Legionnaire* lolled at ease in his black-and-silver uniform. He made a thumbs-up sign to Santorini, and the Leader preened. "Those who considered Alkalurops a backwater will learn to fear us. I have the BattleMechs. I will lead you. We will rule the stars." Grace took tiny steps forward. Like snails, she and hers moved closer to Santorini. The right fist of the *Jupiter* edged up, its two autocannons not yet aimed at anyone, but clearly that one did not like the way things were developing and was taking preventive measures of his own.

"We should have recognized you for what you were," Grace shouted. "But you came to us as a minor businessman just looking for a place for someone greater to put a headquarters. We couldn't see your ruthlessness, your drive for power and your determination to trample in the dust anyone who opposed you."

A long spiel, but Santorini was lapping it up, even rewarding Grace with that sham he used for a smile. Hatred roared from every fiber of her being. She swallowed it, told him what he wanted to hear, and edged forward.

"I'm glad you've finally realized the error of your

ways. Fighting me is hopeless. I knew you'd see that," Santorini said, his confidence unshaken. "It was only a matter of time. What surprises me is that you folded so easily. I thought you had more backbone. Or is it you, Hanson? Is there a ruthless streak in you that you've kept well hidden? You and your men must dine with me tonight. The conversation will be very interesting."

"Thank you, sir," L. J.'s voice came across thin but undistorted. The Net was fully up—even the Roughriders' radios were on it.

Santorini leaned forward, but his *Ryoken*'s gyros made no complaint. He's locked it down, Grace realized. That BattleMech is little more than a statue. She noted the extra options that gave her as she listened carefully.

"I notice you have worked your way closer to me. Good. It will give me a better view. Hadrian, you've been dying to use that autocannon. Blow them away," he ordered.

The *Jupiter* pilot grinned. No surprise there.

"Now!" Grace shouted.

Across the Net came, "Forward, Roughriders!"

Everything happened at once. Behind Grace, the prisoners pulled glass bottles of clear liquid from under their clothes. With a short hop and skip that took them right out of their chains, Jobe, Chato, MechWarriors and mechanic lofted their bottles in high arcs to smash on Santorini's *Ryoken II*.

Among the Roughriders, MechWarriors brought lasers, missiles and miniguns to bear on the *Jupiter*. Tank turrets rotated, and shells, missiles and lasers slashed at it.

But Hadrian was ready if Santorini was not. Neurohelmet already on, he slammed his BattleMech into reverse, hopped it into a turn even as he sealed his cockpit, and urged his *Jupiter* off at a run, all thought of playing his autocannon over Grace and the other prisoners forgotten.

The *Jupiter* left Santorini behind, pounding on his controls, trying to close his cockpit. Bottles splattered gas over the 'Mech's front. One shattered in the cockpit, spraying shards of glass that cut Santorini's face and interrupted his frustrated pounding. *Doesn't the eejit know any of his controls?* Grace asked herself even as she took her own step forward to lob a thermite bomb. Betsy had one, too. They arced up last. One hit the 'Mech's chest, igniting the gas with a whoosh. The other glanced off the descending cockpit hood. It spat fire even as it tumbled into the cockpit. Santorini's scream was cut off as the cockpit sealed. A moment later the explosion inside blew the cockpit hood out. There were more screams, muted by the roar of the flames.

"Enjoy that, you bastard," Betsy shouted at the fire. "You deserve worse. Don't anybody shoot at him."

Grace was more worried about people shooting her. She'd hit the ground after hurling her bomb, wanting to get as much out of the line of fire of lasers and missiles and slugs as the cobblestone pavement allowed. She made a grab for Betsy to pull her down, but the woman knocked Grace's hand away.

Ben had a better idea. He swung a leg out, sweeping Betsy's legs out from under her. She showed her gratitude by diving on Ben, fists swinging. Anyone but Ben would have been in for a thrashing, but the Lone Cat parried blow after blow, laughing like some kind of maniac as the roar of rockets and cannon washed over them. Somehow Betsy came to see the humor. Her blows came more slowly and fell more softly until her own laughter joined Ben's.

"We killed the bastard!" Ben shouted.

"We killed the bastard," Betsy finally said. Looking up, she shivered. "And he is as dead as the very deadest."

He was dead, and the other Black and Reds were running. It was every man for himself among Alkalurops' late masters. The big *Jupiter* knocked over a

LoaderMech, stomped a gun truck, and ran, a hail of rockets following it. The black-and-silver-uniformed driver of the *Legionnaire* who had been at Santorini's left didn't react fast enough. Facing a Roughrider *Legionnaire,* its huge autocannon already rotating and leveled at the other's open cockpit, the pilot's hands went up. His "I surrender" came in a small voice.

There was at least one for the hangman.

"Damn, all these lovely BattleMechs just standing around for the taking," Danny said. "But I know which one's gonna work for me." He bounced to his feet and headed for a gray 'Mech MOD among the Roughriders' victory trophies. He went up the ladder fast, giving Grace an answer to what Scots wore under their kilts. The driver popped the canopy and handed Danny the MechWarrior's own neurohelmet. Only when Danny was ready to plug in did the driver unplug his own helmet. The 'Mech MOD swayed for a second as control passed from driver to MechWarrior, then steadied. Danny settled into the control couch as the driver dropped down the ladder. Behind Grace, Ben was doing the same, replacing Eddie in the Lone Cat's giant *Atlas.*

Still lying on the ground, Grace called up, "Good luck," as the hatch on the *Atlas* sealed. Eddie hit the ground and trotted over to her, fixing a radio to his belt. "Here's a radio for you," he said. "You're Roughrider A-8."

Grace settled the headset in place as she snapped the radio to her waistband. "This is Grace O'Malley," she said. Damned if she'd use a Roughrider call sign. "Loren, you available?" She turned to take in the scene around her.

Heavy weapons were silent now. Merc infantry trotted from their carriers to take control of the town and stalled BattleMechs and MODs that didn't make it out in the first crush. For a second, Grace watched the *Ryoken II* burn. When the flaming lump of what had once been a ruthless madman collapsed below the lid of the cockpit, she turned to see Ben and Danny trotting off in their 'Mechs. Hanson's *Koshi* stood in place with his two other command staff BattleMechs, towering over her, while providing cover and protection to her little sacrifice team.

Then it hit Grace, like fresh air when she popped Pirate's cockpit after a long, hot day—*I'm not going to die today.* She'd walked into Allabad, fully prepared to die if that could start the battle that would free her people. *I'm not dead. Santorini is—horribly.* She craned her neck to look up at Hanson's *Koshi* and keyed her mike on the Roughriders' command channel, a mere mortal standing before giants. "Why is everyone running?"

"Because there's an under-protected DropShip parked at the spaceport," Hanson said dryly. "Listen, Grace, this contract has been a big enough disaster without me having to tell the Colonel that I let a bunch of bozos run off with our armored DropShip."

"Leave me some of my MODs and your infantry," Grace said. "I'll police this mess and send patrols after the runners."

"And I'll secure the port," Hanson said.

"Danny and I will lend Grace a hand," Ben said over the command channel, "chasing 'Mechs running amok in Allabad."

With few orders and no debate, they organized themselves. Hanson led his mercs across the Alhambra River and out of town. Ben led Danny into town. Betsy led the infantry as they assaulted BattleMechs and MODs, and disarmed gun trucks that had smashed into buildings, 'Mechs or each other. Everyone had a task.

Benjork Lone Cat stalked the *Jupiter*. The one who fought in that BattleMech had power and the will to use it. That one had to die before he slaughtered innocents in his flight. Already, Ben had seen evidence of his prey's desperation. In its haste to escape, the *Jupi-*

ter had salvoed both fifteen-LRM pods to punch a gaping hole in a three-story building across the street from the Guild Hall. People were pulling crumpled bodies from the wreckage as he and Danny raced past.

Benjork followed the *Jupiter* by the gashes taken out of buildings as it swung around tight corners, but the panicked flight ended after just a few blocks. Then he caught glimpses of the *Jupiter* by the two or three meters it towered over the two-story buildings of Alla-bad. But central Allabad was mainly three- and four-story buildings, and that was where Hadrian quickly headed.

That took him away from the spaceport. *What dream paths does this one follow?*

"I found the *Jupiter*," came over the emergency guard channel in a thick brogue.

"Where, Danny?"

"Two blocks ahead of you, three closer to the canyon wall. Ben, he has hostages."

That did not slow down the Lone Cat, though it did drive his thoughts like a cold wind across a barren tundra. Hadrian had not fled to the spaceport. No, he went looking for his own ticket off-planet. Cold. Very cold.

"Freeze. Both of you," came in a tense voice on the guard channel as Benjork turned a last corner and found himself a long three blocks from the *Jupiter*. It towered over a pickup with a man at the wheel, a woman on the seat closest to the *Jupiter* and two small children between them.

A block closer, Danny's gray 'Mech masked the *Atlas'* line of fire. "Back up," Benjork ordered. "Give the *Jupiter* space."

"Yeah, give the madman the space he wants. You do that, and while you do, think about why you were dumb enough to chase me."

"We protect these people," Danny said as he backed away.

"Protect them? These people were fine," Hadrian

shouted, jostling the truck with the *Jupiter*'s huge fist. "Just fine before you made me take them for my ticket out. Now, don't you do nothing that will make me hurt them. See how you've scared that cute little girl? Woman, make her shut up."

The mother tried to soothe her daughter as the man held his baby son closer. This would neither take long nor end well. Nothing that combined a desperate, high-strung man and children could last long.

Benjork stretched out his 'Mech's right arm as Danny came close. The Highlander stopped as they touched. Good man.

"Mr. Hadrian, you can't get out of here," Danny said.

"You dumb-ass, I'm not Mr. Hadrian. I'm Mr. Hadrian Heckie to you," the *Jupiter* pilot spat while the Lone Cat measured the distance between them. Here, the yellow rock of the canyon wall kept the wind away. The *Jupiter* was a huge target, but Benjork was interested only in the cockpit.

"Then what, Mr. Heckie, do you want us to do for you?" Danny went on with dogged kindness in his voice.

"I want out of here. You will take me to the spaceport and put me on the next DropShip out of here and I want you to wave real nice as it takes off with me. You hear?"

The Lone Cat checked all his targeting readouts. They said he had the *Jupiter*'s cockpit dialed in to the last possible decimal place. He closed his eyes, slowed his breathing, and looked at the target without the errors that machines and eyes bring. For a long moment he meditated on what he would do, then opened his eyes and made a fine adjustment with his joystick.

"You know we can't make any agreement like that with you," Danny said. "Only Grace O'Malley can decide that."

"Then let me talk to her or one of these noisy brats is gonna find out what kind of a lullaby a *Jupiter*'s clamps sing."

"Yes, sir," Danny said.

The Lone Cat applied pressure, and Danny leaned his 'Mech MOD to the right, unmasking Benjork's Dragon's Fire Gauss rifle.

The slug made even the hundred-ton *Atlas* sway as it slammed down the magnetic rails. What it did to the *Jupiter* made even Benjork blanch. The Gauss bullet blasted into the BattleMech, ripping off the cockpit and splattering its superheated wreckage around the hole the slug drilled in the canyon wall. So fast was the destruction that the threatening fist had no time to flinch, much less mash the pickup beneath it.

For a long moment, the *Jupiter* just stood there.

Then the pickup driver dared to crane his head out the open window. He took in the smoldering hole that had been the cockpit above him and slammed the door open. Holding the toddler, he yanked his wife and daughter free. Hand in hand, they ran.

"You did that perfectly, my wild Highland friend," Benjork told Danny as they paced off the distance to his target. "You kept him occupied while I took aim."

"Didn't see my thirty-millimeter slugs doing much good. Would've just sent ricochets and fragments all over the place," Danny said.

"Right, Danny. I had the only weapon good against the *Jupiter*. When I was ready, you unmasked it. We are a good team—Lone Cat and Kilted warrior." The two shared a laugh, then examined the wreckage. Most of the huge machine showed only the minor damage of its flight, but the cockpit would need complete replacement. Small fires were dying down in the space that had once held a man, controls and armor. Mick and Sven would probably have it working again in a month.

"Well, that was fun," Danny half laughed. "Think there are any more like that around?"

"Let's go see."

They circled back toward the Guild Hall. The walk was informative. Here and there, a burned-out 'Mech

MOD or overturned gun truck showed where Black and Reds had been cornered. Other 'Mechs were abandoned and uniforms shed. More often than not, less than a block beyond such efforts to abandon the past, a body lay pummeled and pulped. "The streets may seem empty, but the walls have eyes, and have seen much that demands vengeance."

Danny snorted at Benjork's wisdom. "If you ask me, those damn Black and Reds aren't getting anything they don't deserve."

Benjork had seen no signs of Grace during the chase, and a glance around the Guild Hall's plaza told him why. Except for the burned-out *Ryoken II*, all evidence of the occupation was gone. Now people stood in small clumps, pointing and gesturing as they rehashed the events of the day. Danny popped the cockpit and climbed down, shaking his head. "Not talk-talk stuff again."

Benjork joined him on the ground. "Remember, my hotheaded Highlander, this is what we fought for." Then the Lone Cat took a long look around and finished with, "You'll have to remind me why." They shared a laugh and went looking for Grace.

Grace cleaned up the plaza quickly. One fallen Black and Red 'Mech MOD driver, intent on resisting to the end but not knowing what he was doing, fired both of his shoulder-mounted SRMs into the pavement beneath him. That didn't leave a lot of that 'Mech to clean up, or a lot of fight in the others. Hanson's infantry, with a bit of guidance from Betsy and a few choice words from the Sergeant Major, cleaned up the bent 'Mechs and smashed trucks. Those that could be walked or driven away were. Commercial wreckers handled the rest.

Then Grace discovered the true evil of Santorini.

He had created a special atrocity just for her: All the mayors had been summoned to Allabad for his grand performance, and now they wanted to reestablish the council. They had come full circle, back to the very point she had argued so eloquently five months ago.

Grace wanted to run. Jobe suggested that 'Mechs be used to chase the mayors out of town. Chato checked inside the Guild Hall and declared it ready, though in need of redecorating. A large throne dominated the hall. Jobe and several others grabbed axes and hacked at the throne until others demanded a turn. It became great entertainment. Chato found where the tables were stored and got others to set them up in one large square. No head, no foot, just one large square table. "I would make it round if I could but—" He shrugged softly.

"So what do we do now?" Grace asked.

"Govern ourselves, I suppose," Chato said.

People slowly filled the great room. Different people this time; younger, older, unfamiliar faces—almost none that Grace recalled from earlier meetings. Many of the mayors Grace had met with during the war were also absent, their bodies maybe still dangling from a signpost or streetlamp. The meaning of eminence, the price of leadership had changed under the pressure of blood and fire.

Just as Ben and Danny walked into the hall, the young woman from Kilkenny who'd succeeded Gordon Frazier as mayor handed Grace the gavel. "Shouldn't we get started?" she said.

Grace hammered the meeting to order, her mind awhirl as she hunted for what to say. The room fell silent as stragglers found chairs. It was the silence that spoke to Grace.

"People have died to give us the privilege of sitting at this table. Let us pause for a minute to remember those who welcomed a gory bed rather than accept chains and slavery."

Grace had never heard the Guild Hall so quiet. The minute stretched far beyond sixty seconds. Here and there a choked sob or softly called name broke the silence as loved ones were remembered by those who had paid in full for their right to rule themselves.

Beside her, Chato uttered an "Amen" that made its way like a wave around the room. That left Grace still searching to pluck a first order of business from a mind so full yet so empty that she could think of nothing to say.

Beside her, Chato's eyes slowly swept the room. "Months ago I rose from among you to place in nomination the name of Grace O'Malley for Governor of Alkalurops until such time as The Republic may affirm or change that appointment. I do so again."

Heads nodded as Jobe got to his feet. "I think I was the one who nominated her, Chato, but I will stand as second for your motion. Are there any other names to put forward?"

The hall remained silent, and it dawned on Grace that if she didn't do something, she would end up Governor. She turned to the Navajo. "Chato, a moment ago you said it was time for us to get back to governing ourselves. Now you stand to nominate a Governor that Terra may or may not accept."

Under her gaze, he sat. She turned to the assembled. "Look at what we have done. Look at what we did without Knights, without any help from Terra, without any help from The Republic.

"Alkalurops takes care of itself. Our grandparents said it before us, and we just showed what we can do. I thank Ben and Danny and all the MechWarriors who helped us, but in the end, it was us. Us using our brains, our hands, our guts and our blood."

Slowly, in silence, she looked at every citizen seated at the table, taking her own poll. Heads nodded, some softly, others with pure enthusiasm. No one stood up in the silence to argue with her.

"The Republic of the Sphere didn't help us when we needed it. I'll be damned if I'm going to see our militia drafted into their regiments and shipped off to help this faction or that pull their nuts out of the fire.

Alkalurops takes care of its own—and only its own."
Now people were on their feet, clapping, cheering,
stomping, yelling. A wilder demonstration of support
Grace had never seen. She let it run, even as she let
the tears run down her cheeks. Chato hugged her,
then Jobe joined in. Danny rushed up and gathered
all of them in one huge embrace.

Even Ben, the reserved former Nova Cat, came to
rest a hand on Grace's shoulder. Into her ear he whispered, "For years my dream led me away from everything I knew, but never did it show me my destination.
When I first saw you, something told me I might finally know what that was. Now I see that your dream
and mine are the same. I hope there is room alongside
you for this dangerous Cat."

"You've never been a danger to me or mine,"
Grace assured him.

Grace let the roar for Alkalurops run long, then
gaveled the room to silence. "All for Alkalurops
standing alone, ruled by its traditional assembly, raise
your hands."

Hands shot up around the table, joined by a roar
of "Aye!"

A long minute later Grace again gaveled for calm.
"That looks pretty unanimous, but I'll ask. Any
nays?"

A single hand rose. Grace recognized the gray head
that had first supported her in that long-ago assembly.
So she had survived it all.

"I'm sorry, Grace," the woman said into the quiet
hall. "I simply can't let you get elected unanimously.
Might give you a swelled head."

"I will remember that," Grace said, thinking the
matter settled, but the old lady stood.

"One question, Grace. Are we in rebellion against
The Republic of the Sphere? If they come, do we fight
them the way we should have fought Santorini?"

"Good question," came from several places around
the table.

"No," Grace quickly answered. "St. Mary and St. Patrick know there's enough blood being shed around human space. I am not raising a flag of rebellion. What I *am* raising is Alkalurops' ancient flag. When The Republic comes, we'll talk to them. We'll negotiate with them. But we don't take orders. Alkalurops takes care of itself, and The Republic had better be able to show how it can help us do a better job of that. Unless they can, thank you very much, but they can ride back out on the DropShip they rode in on."

That got another round of cheers.

Grace only had to make a few raps with the gavel to get silence the next time. "But taking care of ourselves means we'll need to defend ourselves. For that, we need more full-time troops than Lieutenant Hicks and the other gallant members of our Constabulary. Our militia will also need a commander. For that position, I offer you a man who has fought at my side with no questions, no qualms and never a lack of courage. I give you Benjork Lone Cat."

Grace did not even try to gavel the room to silence for a long five minutes. Ben called all of the surviving MechWarriors forward. Old Sven and George Stillwell accepted the crowd's thanks with a nod and a wave. Betsy gave Ben a kiss, and Victoria even suffered Danny to put an arm around her shoulder. Syn sashayed forward. Sadly for Grace, she showed no ill effects from her ride in the victory parade draped over the hood of a truck.

But saddest of all was that Sean could not be resurrected to celebrate what he and so many others had died for.

Grace gave Ben a hug, ignoring the dampness around his eyes that some might mistake for tears. She knew that one raised in the stern discipline of the Nova Cats would never let himself be ruled by emotions.

When Ben waved the room to silence, the people around the table complied. "As a young man, I was given a dream of Clan and Sphere coming together. Not just to share space, but to break down the walls that we let separate each of us. You do not need to know the Clans very well to know that such a dream is anathema for many. I took the name Lone Cat when I finally walked away from my Clan. I am a Lone Cat no more. You are my people. Together we need fear no stranger."

Once more the room erupted. Grace knew there was work to do. She'd examined the files Betsy had taken from Santorini's computer—as much as time had allowed. He'd gotten help in his crime from off-planet but also from on-planet. Grace needed to have a long talk with the Industrial Trade Group. Some of their management were definitely out of step with Alkalurops taking care of Alkalurops.

When quiet finally came, Grace sighed. "There's work to be done. I need seven mayors to volunteer to work with the militia. They'll need to be from towns with big service and repair shops. Maybe some iron mines and carbon fabrication shops, too."

And they got down to the business of running a planet.

Two days later Grace sat at a table in the spaceport bar. Thick armored windows showed acres of concrete leading to the DropShip landing pads above the blast pits. A metal bulge showed where the Roughriders' DropShip was making final preparations for launch. At her table sat Ben and Danny, there to see Betsy and Syn off.

The sound of military footsteps brought Grace away from the goings-on out on the field. Loren Hanson came through the bar door, saw her, gave her an informal salute, and marched for their table. "Mind if I join you?" met with no objections, and he settled comfortably in place.

"You've been hard to find," Grace said.

"I've been busy loading out a battalion and drafting

a report that is bound to be hard reading. The Colonel won't be happy, but the files clearly show Santorini was out to kill us all. That dinner invite at the parade! I just hope his bond holds up better than his word or this entire operation is way in the red."

"You'll excuse me if I'm not too sympathetic," Grace said.

"I fully understand. It's my own fault for not wrangling a contract to help you when I had the chance." That brought a laugh from the table. "There is one thing. We've gotten back our captives. Private Godfrey sends his compliments. You know: the sergeant who had that push-up contest with one of your men."

"He's a private now?"

"And for a significant while, I suspect. I've got about a hundred recruits who'd like to sign on. Does this planet have any objections to us removing recruits from here at this time?"

Grace turned to Ben. He shook his head.

"I'll wish them well," Grace said, "even if, after one ride with your topkick, I think them foolish."

"To each his own poison," Ben said.

Hanson smiled and seemed in no hurry to leave. He started to talk twice, but thought better of it, then finally opened his mouth. "There are two blanks in my report. Betsy, maybe you can help me with both of them. Who was Santorini working for?"

"Everyone and no one," Betsy said easily. "If I were Lenzo Computing, I'd take a good hard look at my recruiting practices. They can't afford too many bum hires like Santorini. Word is that they really are in the market for a new headquarters, and he was assigned to their search. As to how much Landgrave Jasek and the Stormhammers were using him or he was using them, I don't think Jasek knew. House Steiner is an even vaguer question," she said with a shrug.

"By the time we killed Santorini, I think he was freelancing something awful. What he said was probably what he thought he was going to do." Betsy rolled eyes. "As to what he'd have done if he'd lived, I say nothing."

"You'll say nothing to whom?" Hanson shot across the table. "Who are *you* reporting to?"

Betsy laughed—a lovely sound with tinkling bells in it. "I was just your maid. And a nice guest you were—not like some. But they're dead and I'm alive, so I'm ahead on points."

"Let me see," said Danny. "Jasek is in revolt against both The Republic and his pappy on Skye. He's come out for House Steiner. Now, who wouldn't want a Steiner base this deep in The Republic? Certainly House Davion and MI6 would be interested. Interested enough to send a Rabid Fox to sniff around?" he asked, innocently as a babe.

"If I were one of those foxy types, I'd have to kill all of you for blowing my cover, but I could also be a Ghost Knight for The Republic, concerned about this fine planet of yours. But most likely I'm a poor girl that's pissed off too many bosses and spends too much of her life looking for her next job," Betsy said as she stood and curtsied.

"Are you as confused I am?" Grace said.

"Nothing she said was intended to inform," Ben agreed.

"Look at it this way," Betsy said, signaling Syn to abandon her drink. "If you let this line of talk die a natural death, you can go about your business. I can go about mine. And someday, when you least expect it, you may find me at your elbow offering a helping hand."

"Not an offer I'd pass up," Hanson said, "and speaking of passing, it's time for me to board."

"I'll follow you out," Betsy said. Steel blinds clanged shut over the bar's windows, signaling the arrival or departure of a DropShip. Syn left with L. J. and Betsy.

"So that's that?" Grace said, standing.

"*That* is not to be denigrated," Ben said. "We won our battle. This land is free. And we have an IOU from a woman of mystery. Not bad for a month's work."

"No," Grace said, "not bad."

MECHWARRIOR: DARK AGE®

A BATTLETECH® SERIES

R020